# Moon Shadow
# The Legend

JOE BARFIELD

**CreateSpace Publishing**

**Moon Shadow the Legend**



ISBN-13: 978- 978-1511792448

# DEDICATION

To the men who risked their lives in air combat and to those who survived their ordeals. And to what I believe to be the best propeller driven aircraft ever made, the North American P-51 Mustang. And to the memory of the nineteen-year-old pilot, John Magee, who lost his life in the Battle of Britain. He left us with these few words I shall never forget:

## High Flight

Oh, I have slipped the surly bonds of earth
And danced the skies on laughter-silvered wings;
Sunward I've climbed, and joined the tumbling mirth
Of sun-split clouds—and done a hundred things
You have not dreamed of—wheeled and soared and swung
High in the sunlit silence. Hov'ring there,
I've chased the shouting wind along, and flung
My eager craft through footless halls of air.
Up, up the long, delirious burning blue,
I've topped the windswept heights with easy grace
Where never lark, or even eagle flew.
And, while with silent, lifting mind I've trod
The high untrespassed sanctity of space,
Put out my hand, and touched the face of God.

For those who believe this story is impossible, forget not David and Goliath, the Trojan Horse and the heroic action of men throughout history who have conquered insurmountable odds.

Recall the words of one of the first and maybe greatest fighter pilots of all time:

"It is not the machine but the man who flies the machine." Captain Manfred von Richthofen, the legendary Red Baron

# MOON SHADOW THE LEGEND
## TABLE OF CONTENTS

# ACKNOWLEDGMENTS

To John Hadfield; the wild adventure began in Kansas City.
And let's not forget **"Thunder Bunny"**

"The technical aspect of Moon Shadow is well covered, making what the P-51 Mustang accomplishes even more believable. A wonderful and thrilling adventure."

**-Pat Moran**, the first American pilot to fly the Russian Mig 29 and Sukhoi 27

America will never be destroyed from the outside. If we falter and lose our freedoms, it will be because we destroyed ourselves. –Abraham Lincoln

From the beginning of time, every empire has collapsed. There have been no exceptions. — The Author

Tolerance is the last virtue of a dying society. – Aristotle

I predict a black day for the United States. -- Osama bin Laden

**SPECIAL THANKS TO:**

**"SR-71 Blackbird"**
Cover art by
John Bedke
http://www.laughingcatsstudio.com

**"David and Goliath"**
by
Dan Zoernig
.www.danzoernig.com

**"Blackbird Up and Away"**
Philip Alexander
www.rb-29.net (click on Art Gallery)

My editor, Karen Gordon.

To my son Beau, daughter Becky and wife Lucia I want to thank for the wonderful adventures that have led to so many novel ideas. To John Hadfield and the long drives from Kansas where the idea for Moon Shadow originated in 1987.

# INTRODUCTION

Before you hear the story of Moon Shadow you must first know what led to the demise and downfall of the most powerful country the world has ever known: the United States of America. Most will point to the broken promises and greed of the corrupt politicians, which compounded the fiscal irresponsibility of an already overwrought, debt-ridden country that literally collapsed from within. Like the bankruptcy of Mexico or Russia of the Twentieth century, so too became the United States of America early in the twenty-first century. No historian could have anticipated the invasion of the United States, yet historians will always point to the obvious sequence of events and smugly say, "History repeats itself."

The financial collapse may well have started under former President Kennedy, but the Savings and Loan debacle and the losses near a trillion dollars under former presidents Reagan and George H. W. Bush that made Americans "turn the other cheek" were a major part of the problem. At the turn of the century, terrorist activities, especially the 9/11 attacks on New York and Washington, D.C., created a financial burden for America, but that was nothing compared to the activities of accounting firms and corporate executives. These two groups devastated the American economy more than any war or terrorist attack could. Wall Street never fully recovered. Those who held power and financial control traded their honor and integrity for an obscene level of wealth that even the robber barons of the past could not have imagined. Where George's son put America full speed towards destruction, Obama crashed and sounded the death knell of America. While he touted the Affordable Health Care Act, known to most Americans as ObamaCare, it was anything but affordable and in reality nothing more than just another huge tax. Obama called it a healthcare good for all Americans but Congress quickly exempted themselves. After the Affordable Health Care Act passed, and in actions highly illegal, Obama took it upon himself to make changes in the law without approval from

Congress. He went on to exempt select unions and even individuals that donated to his election campaigns. While Madoff went to prison for his billion dollar Ponzi scheme, Congress did the same with trillions and a budget that gave trillions to banks and business under the guise a stimulation package while jobs were lost and welfare increased. Martha Stewart went to jail for insider trading while Pelosi made millions and even said she was exempt from insider trading. Pelosi had even said Obamacare needed to pass so they would have time to read the over ten thousand pages nobody in Congress understood. Obama declared America a Muslim country and even said, "If I had to choose between Christians and Muslims I must take the side of Muslims. Christians were branded traitors. When the government shutdown in 2013, Obama refused to compromise and even went as far as having veterans banded from war memorials and even arresting war veterans while he and Pelosi opened up one of the closed parks so they could celebrate with "illegal" aliens. After that he denied death benefits to veterans that had lost their lives defending America and Freedom. American freedom died under Obama's regime.

All of this helped bring down America but it was an obscure event in 1991 that started the downward spiral of America.

In a deadly shell game, the president and Congress blamed Middle Eastern countries for America's internal problems, focusing the spotlight of scrutiny away from the strings-attached political contributions from Corporate America and redirecting the peoples' attention toward the trumped-up menace "over there." Americans attacked and bombed in one war after another while the financial gluttony of top-level executives continued unabated, slithering under the radar of detection. Meanwhile, Congress became a parasite with the American people their host. But unlike a good parasite, Congress drained the life from its chosen host. These factors contributed to the eventual collapse of the United States of America, but they had nothing to do with the invasion and the Legend of Moon Shadow. Plans for the invasion began twenty-two years before during *Operation Desert Storm* in 1991. Not unlike a taco or a hamburger, *Operation Desert Storm* was sold to the American public as an operation to free the Kuwaiti people. The real objective was protection of American oil interests and extended American control over the Middle East. Part of the collateral damage to America's bombing was the obliteration of an unknown Syrian family on vacation in Baghdad. Only the father and his son survived, and with each ongoing breath their grief hardened into a feverish, single-minded desire for revenge—and that revenge became their only motivation to take the next breath.

This particular bombing raid began with inaccurate intelligence information stating that an underground bunker held the target, Iraqi dictator Saddam Hussein, who had attacked Kuwait, one of America's allies.

A simple, precise attack was planned to rid the world of his menace, and the resulting low-level mission was carried out with a deadly precision never before seen in history. Two F-15s streaked across the desert toward their target in Baghdad with Colonel Jonathan Bryce commanding the attack from one; Commander Robert Brookin Gex flew the other.

Other agendas were in play as the two fighter pilots carried out the mission for their country—agendas so wide and varied that historians would never know the truth. The only obvious fact was Iraq had attacked Kuwait, and the commander-in-chief of the United States of America, President George H. W. Bush, had sent forces to Saudi Arabia in the action dubbed *Operation Desert Storm*. The goal: to free Kuwait. Although seen as a hero, former President Bush had ignored Saddam Hussein when the Iraqi leader earlier had indicated he wanted to invade Kuwait. A presidential cabinet—appointed, not elected by the people—all bringing their own personal agendas to the table, suggested the president wait. Meanwhile, Bush had his own agenda, and at the top of the list was his own re-election. A successful war would all but guarantee him another four years in the White House. Forget that all of Iraq's weapons had been obtained from the United States when a previous American president equipped Iraq to defeat Iran (which had also been equipped with American weapons by another former president when the Shah had been in power). So, once again, the United States found itself in the foolish and dangerous position of fighting American weapons and losing American lives in wars against former allies that had turned against the United States.

But the powers in charge had yet another agenda. The real plan was to leave Saddam Hussein in power. He was not to be killed. Instead, Iraq and Saddam Hussein were to be the perennial scapegoat whenever popularity waned for future American presidents.

*Operation Desert Storm* was designed to show America's overwhelming might and that American forces had the ability to do anything they wanted to do, anywhere and anytime they chose to do it. The two pilots streaking toward Baghdad were a show of that power. But what the American people failed to see was that Hussein could have been removed at any time with the precision of brain surgery. More puzzling was that no one asked why the United States would go to the aid of a country full of millionaires when it had turned a blind eye to the literally millions of people who died in Cambodia at the hands of the Khmer Rouge. The answer was simple. The defense of Kuwait, with the wealthiest per capita population in the world, was forced by greed—for oil, money, control and power: the most potent agenda of all.

Bryce and Gex homed in on their target with the heart-felt belief they would soon rid the world of an evil dictator and free Kuwait. Their agenda was the most noble and foolish of all: they fought for honor and the love of their country. In reality, they were merely pawns in the game, putting on a deadly show for the world. Saddam Hussein was not in the fortified bunker buried 30 feet beneath the earth. It mattered little to the leaders who ordered the mission, those who never actually fought the wars, that the underground bunker was filled with women and children. Neither Gex nor Bryce knew what they were really about to do.

When the target came into view both men fired. Colonel Bryce missed but not Commander Gex. Born and raised in Louisiana, Gex was called the Rajun Cajun for his fighting in the air and the defense of his French name Gex. He made a point to let others know his name was pronounced "Jay." He would even use his fist to better help them understand. He never failed to get his point across. He came from a line of Frenchman who centuries before had been the best swordsmen in Europe. Respect for their ability the French had named a city after then on the border of France and Switzerland. Robert Gex's great-great grandfather, Jacques Gex, had migrated to America. Fighting was inbred in the Gex's and Robert was a natural in the air, as good with his aircraft as Jacques had been with a sword. Gex seldom missed his target. The video-monitored rockets ripped through the bunker before they exploded, and the thirty-four women and children hiding inside perished. News media around the world replayed the video on the hour, illustrating the accuracy and power of U.S. armed forces in cold, lethal detail. Soon, Iraqi camera crews responded with their own video showing the devastation from a different perspective. The bodies of dead women and children strewn about the area startled and appalled people around the world. In response, President Bush and his crew quickly explained that the incident was the fault of Saddam Hussein, who had used the women and children as pawns in a war he started. Clearly, this hideous mistake was not the fault of the benevolent Americans, but instead the responsibility of the tyrant and dictator Hussein. Over the next few weeks televisions on all continents replayed the murder. The world called it a tragedy. The American military swayed between first calling it justified and then an accident of war that could have been prevented had Saddam Hussein not invaded Kuwait. The incident was declared an item of *national security* so the names of the pilots were never revealed. The F-15 attack mission was soon forgotten as most of the world went on to focus on other matters.

For the families of the thirty-four women and children murdered in the bunker, their world ended that day.

However, it was the survivors of one family who would forever change history, helping to bring the mightiest country in the world to its knees

## Chapter 1
# DESERT SECRETS

The full moon rose majestically over the dark shimmering Mediterranean Sea, while waves pounded against the desert sands surrounding the dead city. More than twenty-three years had passed since the *Desert Storm* operation of 1991. Two more wars had completed the devastation. Previously a beacon to tourists from around the world, the burned and bombed buildings stood like skeletons: a grim reminder of an elegant past. The once proud Lebanese city was a testimony to the destructive might of the United States of America. The destruction had come about to make the world safe from aggression and to protect the Jewish country of Israel, bordering to the south. A *New World Order* had been created to protect freedom and humanity—and to prevent wars. Still, men killed each other for God and country. The Muslims had succumbed, but had not forgotten and now their rapid rise to power terrified the world. While the United States became divided the Muslim world had united and ironically received their financial support from the President of America.

Beneath the Moon's glow a silver, ghostly whirlwind twirled about the cool, dark, desert floor, filling with thousands of timeless moonstruck grains of sand that frolicked freely through the changing spiral. Slowly it crept across the desert, toward the empty decaying resort. Moon shadows guarded the dead city. Desert winds howled their delight.

This night the desert rats were not the only ones stirring. The decaying structures of once beautiful architectural masterpieces were now a gathering place for Iraqi and Lebanese terrorists carrying out missions of retaliation, death, and torture. Inside the shell of a past ornate and exquisitely decorated hotel where people had once gathered to celebrate and dance, a lone lantern sent shadows dancing against the scarred stone walls and dusty, rock-strewn floor. Three men came to do their truculent work, while their captive waited for a death that would be long in coming.

In a far corner of the room, a lantern rested on an old, broken table. A rusted and bent metal barrel served as a leg for the warped and peeling desk. The prisoner was tied firmly to a worn out feeble chair. Two of the men held their intended victim's arms firmly against the tabletop, while the third watched.

The third man seemed out of place, like a person wearing formal attire to a mud-wrestling match. Impeccably dressed in a pilot's uniform, not a button was out of position. Even in the dust of the old building, his black boots retained their shine. Clean shaven, with a square jaw and a straight nose set in light skin, and with hair perfectly groomed, few would have guessed him to be Syrian. Except for the cruel eyes, he might have gone unnoticed in America. His heavy cologne presented a stark match to the pungent odor of his two companions. Carefully, he laid a small, dark green, metallic box on the table. Next to this, he placed a long slender knife, razor sharp on both sides.

The captured man's right eye was swollen shut with dirt caked in the wound above. Blood oozed from his nose, running down his chin and dripping to the cut stone floor. The impact of each droplet raised a tiny cloud of dust. An open cut above his left eye flowed crimson, making him turn his head sideways, move his cheek, and squeeze his good eye shut to clear his vision. Occasionally, he spit red from his injured mouth. He wore the uniform of an Israeli fighter pilot. The blood-soaked, matted blond hair, straight nose, and one visible blue eye were not that unusual for an Israeli, but he was not. The American pilot, dressed in an Israeli uniform, watched while showing no emotion.

The Syrian leader spoke. "I am Rasht Sharafan. They call me Cobra. You have heard of me, yes?"

"No," lied the prisoner. He had heard of Cobra, Syria's best pilot, who received his nickname from his exploits with and against the agile F-14 Tomcat. In combat, the F-14 was always his first choice. It was rumored that just for the opportunity to shoot down American pilots, he had flown for Iraq in the War of 2003. When not flying he would commit terrorist acts, exploiting the enemy through torture and terror. Cobra approached these abuses with the same vigor and excitement as a normal person anticipated sex.

"You any relation to Mickey Mouse? No, that must be your operations here. You must be Goofy," said the American fighter pilot. He paused to spit blood on the floor. Yes, he had heard of Cobra. Even during the second *Desert Storm*, or *Operation Iraqi Freedom* as it was called in 2003, his wing command specifically sought out the terrorist.

"Ahhh!" exclaimed Cobra with delight, when he finally recognized the elusive accent. His captive was American. Immediately he broke into English. "So you are an American! You did not look like an Israeli, but you speak their language well. So very few Americans come to our sacred lands except to steal our oil. Such a fine sense of humor—but it will not last long," he said, with a sly grin.

Sharafan took the knife from the table and slid his finger gently along the sharp edge, bringing his own blood. He smiled and licked it.

"Now you will tell me where the general's son is."

"Go to hell. Your men couldn't get me to talk; neither will you and your toys."

"No, no, you misunderstand me," Sharafan said, waving the knife almost apologetically. He pointed to his tool of torture and continued. "This is just the appetizer." Then he tapped the green metal container. "Inside here is what I call my box of pain. With it you will surely talk."

"I'll die first."

"Oh, you will die," he said casually, "and you will also tell me all I want to know." With those words, he pointed to the American's right hand. The man holding the prisoner's arm spread the hand flat and held it tightly against the table.

"You can't do this, the Geneva—"

Before he finished, Sharafan slapped his hand over the man's mouth, preventing another word from escaping. His face reflected his anger and bitterness as he finished the words.

"Geneva Convention?" he uttered with contempt. He moved his face until he was almost nose-to-nose with his prisoner. "Don't preach rules of war to me." With each word Sharafan became angrier. "While we fight with sticks and stones, America and Israel use rockets, jets, and tanks. We fight with honor; you fight the coward's war." He smiled down on his victim. "We will triumph. You will lose. Mark my words, they are the truth." He intentionally turned toward his men and raised his voice, "Allahu Akbar!"

In unison the other two men almost screamed the words that meant God is great: "Allah Akbar!"

A wicked smile filled Sharafan's face. "I will give you the same Geneva Conference you gave the prisoners at Abu Ghraib." He smiled at each of his companions. "Maybe we should strip and violate him like the Americans did our captured friends?"

With those words the anger of Aziz and al-Majid reached emotional highs that threatened to become explosive and deadly actions. Aziz chanted, "Allahu Akbar."

Al-Majid hit the prisoner on the head and pulled out his machete. "Let us take his head and show it to all."

In an effort to restrain his companions, Sharafan held his hand up to stop them. "The machete is swift and holds too much compassion."

The two hesitated and listened to the words. Ready to take instant action with the large, heavy blade, al-Majid lowered his weapon. Sharafan released the prisoner's mouth and tapped the deadly knife in his hand. His comrades watched and responded with grim smiles of sadistic understanding.

Hours earlier the American prisoner, Beau Gex, had been flying a retaliatory mission against Syria. His fighter group was ordered to intercept a bus of kidnapped Israeli children, which also included a top Israeli general's son. The bus was spotted on a road just inside Lebanon. Beau's fighter group responded quickly, finding the bus and making every effort to impede its progress. Low on fuel, all the airplanes returned—except for the American's. Somehow he forced the kidnappers into a ditch.

He waited for the children to run from the bus, and then, using the guns of his aircraft, killed their pursuers. Like the Israelis, the Arabs were also alerted and dozens more of the Arab kidnappers had joined in the pursuit of the children. Soon Beau ran out of fuel, and in an effort to delay the children's capture he aimed his plane toward their attackers. At the last second, he ejected, letting his jet score a direct hit.

Somehow Beau managed to gather the eleven children, including General Mosat's son Beginn, and reached the city in which the terrorists now held him captive. A few buildings away the children hid quietly like good little soldiers. Beau had used himself as a decoy to save them, giving Beginn orders to escape in the safety of darkness. Even in the face of death, the full moon gave Beau reason to worry about the children's safety.

Pain shot through his right hand as Sharafan sliced the tip of the small finger to the bone. He jerked and let out with a stunned groan. Smiling, Cobra slid the razor sharp blade down, then beneath the fingernail of the digit, and with a quick twist of his hand, removed it effortlessly. Puffs of dust rose from the floor as blood dripped through a large crack in the wooden table. Cobra aligned the blade with the first joint, rocking the knife gently back and forth, careful not to cut the skin. Unexpectedly, he snapped the sharp steel through the joint. Beau cried out in pain and caught his breath in short gasps. The small finger was neatly severed at the first knuckle. Cobra took a rag and wiped the wicked blade clean.

The American was about to die and he knew it. Still he remained alert in the hopes he could find a means of escape, however unlikely it might be. He found solace in his impending death, knowing the children were in capable hands with Beginn. The boy would control the others and lead them to safety.

"Your death will please Allah and avenge the dead of Iraq and Afghanistan that were killed by your country in *Desert Storm* and *Enduring Freedom*."

"We should've nuked you bastards and made you Desert Glass!" Beau snapped. For a moment he remembered his father, Commander Robert Brookin Gex, who had fought in *Desert Storm* and how he had expressed hatred against President Bush for not pursuing Saddam Hussein and finishing the job. His father had not lived to see Saddam Hussein's demise when Bush's son became president.

"Where are the children?" Sharafan demanded.

Again Beau refused to answer. Thoughts from the past flashed through his mind. They were thoughts of happier days with his wife Becky and his son before their tragic bombing deaths in Rome the summer of 2008—a bombing that had been in retaliation for America's deadly *Operation Iraqi Freedom* offensive of 2003: deaths he felt he could have prevented. He regretted never having found their murderers. More than five years had passed since they died. Their deaths were the reason he resigned from the Navy and enlisted with the Israeli Air Force in 2009, hoping to extract a measure of revenge. *Operation Iraqi Freedom* of 2003, or *Shock and Awe* as Secretary of Defense Donald Rumsfeld had affectionately called it, wasn't his war; it was his country's war. It had been similar to that of *Desert Storm* of 1991 and *Enduring Freedom* of 2001, only this time the United States had gone in to protect Israel and remove Saddam Hussein permanently, while still trying to stop terrorism. The war and ensuing attacks had centered in and around Lebanon. President Bush—George W. Bush—had used the war as a way of building national pride during a period of growing unrest and financial collapse.

*Operation Iraqi Freedom* also put major American oil companies in control of Iraqi oil production. Their profits soared, although company accountants showed little of the profit. Internally, America was suffering. There had been more riots, bombings, and deaths in the United States than there were in *Operation Iraqi Freedom* and *Operation Clean Sweep* against Lebanon. Prolonged financial and domestic unrest ultimately led to a third party. The Tea Party was recognized during the 2012 election.

During *Operation Iraqi Freedom*, as an F-15 pilot, Beau Gex, brash and young at twenty-two years of age, he had fought with honor and without question of America's actions, but America's success had brought his loss. A *fatwa* had been issued to kill the pilots responsible for the massive carnage and deaths of innocent women and children in Lebanon. One *fatwa* was for Beau. His personal war started when America's ended and his family was murdered. He no longer trusted anyone, except his fellow pilots who fought along his side. No longer did he fight for honor. Instead he fought for revenge. He had many unanswered questions. Who set the bomb that killed helpless people, including his wife and child? What had his revenge accomplished? With his life about to end, he still had no answers.

Soon death would be his eternal companion. He was afraid; no he was concerned, not so much over his impending death, but of being alone. There would be no one to mourn him. The Israelis would list him as missing in action. The Palestinians would celebrate his death. His friends in America would know nothing of his passing. If only he could have died fighting in his jet and not tortured in some God-forsaken place half way around the world.

From birth his life had been one violent storm after another. It seemed he would die in a city destroyed, just like the one where he had been born. In July 1980, Beau's family had moved to a small rural area just north of Brownsville, Texas. A month later, Hurricane Allen devastated the community. On August 9th, the day Allen came ashore, Beau's mother, Beverly, struggled through labor for more than twenty-four hours before giving birth to her son, Beau. He and his family had survived that violence.

It would be different for him now.

He watched catatonically as Sharafan moved the knife farther along the same finger. His thoughts flashed to his three brothers. A vision of home, Texas, and friends filled his mind—his best friend, Ruben Alonzo. He wondered if Ruben would be mad because he had not written. He thought of the times they went on missions and the way Ruben would imitate Scotty the Flight Engineer on the old *Star Trek* television series. It saddened him to know he would not see his friend again. Of them all he would miss Ruben most.

Pain jerked him viciously back to the present. The same finger lost another portion to the second digit.

"Talk!" Cobra demanded. Then calmly he smirked and said, "You have many fingers."

Finding new strength and determination in the pain, Beau tried to respond calmly like nothing mattered. "For everyone there is a time to live and a time to die. This is my time."

For a moment Sharafan was surprised but he hid it well. "Yes, this is your time to die. You will suffer now."

Dreary eyes stared at Sharafan, "Sadness and and death have been my life." Beau managed to smile as he caught Sharafan's eyes with his. "You will be giving me relief in death. Finish it."

This had never happened before. No one had ever wanted to die but this American before him, strangely, looked forward to death. He knew he was about to kill the American but the misery of his victims added additional pleasure to his work. The question was how to do that? With sadistic pleasure, Cobra bent over the helpless American, eagerly anticipating the next finger. He paused and stared upon his prisoner.

"Before you die, tell me your name."

The pilot hesitated but it no longer seemed to matter. "Beau Gex," he mumbled.

"You! You are the American they call the Mongoose," he stated more than asked. But he already knew the answer to his question as it was greeted with an affirmative nod.

Cobra jerked at the impact of the words, as though he had been slapped in the face. He stumbled back.

"You!" His mind raced and words failed him for a moment. "You are the American they call the Mongoose," he stated more than asked. But he already knew the answer to his question as it was greeted with an affirmative nod.

The American! The man branded a traitor, mercenary, and coward in his own country while Israel praised him as a hero. The same man hunted as a terrorist and murderer by the Syrians and the Lebanese. The same one who had become an "Ace" during *Operation Iraqi Freedom* over the skies of Lebanon in 2003. Now he, Rasht Sharafan, had him. Beau Gex would be punished for those crimes. There was a *fatwa* on the head of this pilot, and the punishment was death.

So this was the American. Another time Sharafan had almost succeeded in killing him but had failed. For more than five years the American had fought with Israel.

"You fight for revenge? Your family died in a shop in Rome?"

Pulling his head up to see his interrogator, Gex wondered why the sudden interest. Moving close, Cobra looked his victim straight in the eye. It was the first time he had come face to face with the condemned man. This time Gex would not escape. "I want you to take two secrets to the grave with you," said Sharafan with cruel pleasure. A devilish smirk filled his face. He knew the secrets he held would do more damage to Gex than any physical pain he could inflict. Death itself would be easier to handle than the information about to be revealed.

"Which secret do I tell you first?" He paused for a few brief moments, and then his own sinister laugh filled the old room. "Soon I will be part of a massive invasion that will bring your country down," he said, pounding his chest with his fist.

"Liar! The United States has satellites. They will know," screamed Beau.

Cobra grinned sadistically when he saw the anguish. "I speak the truth and like I know, now you also know. Your country is weak-kneed like a newborn foal. And we, the Coalition, much like a cougar, are on the prowl. Nothing can be done. We lost in the Iraqi war of *Desert Storm* but we learned much." He laughed. "The war of 2003—your *Shock and Awe*—was only a test: a sacrifice so you could be tested. We gained the answers from

Iraq in *Desert Storm* and *Enduring Freedom*. Now we dig deeper holes to hide our equipment."

Again Sharafan laughed. "As for your satellites, we let them see what we want them to see. We have made a "Trojan Horse" and your country is accepting what they see with open arms. The United States of America is fat on itself. No one believes an invasion is possible. But it is. Secrecy worried us the most, but seven years after your *Desert Storm* we realized our dreams could be fulfilled. You remember what happened." The last words were more of a statement than a question.

With a wicked smile, Sharafan continued. "India tested the atom bomb. Five times they tested! The United States never knew. We understood then the United States was weakening both militarily and with their intelligence gathering. If India could keep the bomb testing hidden, then it would be no problem for those we trusted to keep the invasion a secret. We realized an invasion of the United States was possible so we put our plans into action.

"In 1999 we began assembling our personnel. The first test was New York and the Pentagon in 2001. We succeeded beyond all expectations. We were still worried about leaks when three years later one of your 'child prodigy computer hackers' broke into your secret Pentagon files. If not for the publicity, we would never have known.

"One of our experts immediately attached to this child's home computer via the Internet. Never was anything so easy. The young man had his system open to everyone. We downloaded everything he found only hours before the Pentagon arrived and disconnected the system. There was nothing of interest except one thing: a list of coded names. It took a year to break, but we found they were names of American operatives in all the Middle East countries.

"At first we planned to destroy them all when I hit upon an idea: Cry wolf. Since the United States had become the shepherd of the world, we would leak false information about the invasion to these operatives. Simultaneously, we leaked accurate information on things we were willing to sacrifice. The plan was perfect. Two years ago we leaked information about the invasion. Because other reports had turned out to be false, the operatives now were hesitant about releasing this news.

"And for the first time the United States took no action. At that point our plans were safe as proved by what happened last year. We had five actual leaks, and your country only checked out one. Only our intense preparation prevented our discovery. Now we are about to invade the United States.

"And it will be done with its own planes. All we had to do was act like we were against America's enemies, and they supplied us with all our military needs. We have bought nothing. America has given it all to us.

America will help complete its own defeat. We will succeed where the Japanese failed. We will not stop once we start!"

Surely an invasion was impossible, Beau thought. While in Israel's service he had learned of America's *Aurora Project*, a series of satellites with military laser capabilities operated from the International Space Station. Special military modules had been installed on the ISS to control the deadly lasers. When completed the lasers would be capable of pinpoint accuracy from over 2000 miles to prevent an invasion of any kind. A minimum of three satellites would always hover over the United States. From anywhere in orbit the ISS would be able to manipulate and fire the lasers. Rumors were the project was near completion. Developed with the station was an aircraft capable of flying directly into space—an actual space plane. Unlike the time consuming and expensive space shuttle, it could be alerted and deployed at a moment's notice.

Beau's body trembled at Cobra's words, but his knowledge assured him his captor was wrong. Yet why would he make such a brash statement? For some reason Sharafan's words made Beau more fearful than did his own imminent death.

"Our military will stop you."

The words brought a momentary chuckle from Sharafan, "Your president refused to protect your borders." He shrugged his shoulders, "We simply walked across unmolested. Your president put Muslim Brotherhood in critical legal and military positions."

"No."

"Yes." Sharafan grinned at the torment of his captor. "All he had to do was claim to be a Christian and then he could finish his work. Your president hates America. He removed more than two hundred of your finest military leaders. He lowered physical requirement for soldiers and even allows them to have beards and wear turbans. The best was when he granted asylum to terrorists allowing our Muslim brothers to enter America freely. They only wait for the invasion to begin." He laughed, "Didn't you ever wonder why your government bought more than a billion bullets for non-military personnel?" He waited for a response and when he saw it in his prisoners eyes he continued, "The Muslim Brotherhood waits with weapons and unlimited ammunition, which will be soon in coming."

"Impossible!" he screamed. "The space station and—" But the words were cut short when Cobra slapped his hand over Beau's mouth.

"And the *Aurora Project*," Sharafan finished. "Already preparations are being made. The space station and its lasers are a year from completion, but the invasion will take place long before it is finished. But time is not critical. Your president has stopped the space program" An unnerving laugh came from his lips. He continued. "In two months we will bring a complete and total financial collapse upon your country. There is nothing your country will be able to do. Within six months we will be able to defeat you with brooms and shovels." Sharafan snickered, "We would never have been able to it if not for the greed and the predictable actions of your last two presidents, especially Obama, and your Congress. Your presidents were unwittingly our best allies. When President Bush stood on that aircraft carrier, with the sign "Mission Accomplished" behind him and then told the world how his faith in God led America to victory, he did more to unite Islam than any man in history. Those wanting to fight America increased hundreds of thousands more than ever before. Then he and Obama gave away America's wealth just like we had planned. Obama accomplished more to destroy America than any president in history. With your country bankrupt under his polices it couldn't have been easier." Sharafan laughed, "And less than a year after he was elected for his second term he signed a treaty with the UN to take away all assault weapons and it is almost complete. Now, with defeat assured, the invasion will come when no one suspects: a day all Americans will be unprepared. And this time, like in New York, we will enlist the aid of your own airlines, and we will succeed. By Allah it will be a day that will bring your country to an end—forever!"

"No!" screamed Beau, struggling unsuccessfully to free himself.

"Yes!" said Cobra, delighted at his victim's anguish. "Now let me tell you the second secret." He paused to enjoy the moment as he watched Beau squirm. "You see—"

The quiet room abruptly radiated with brilliant lights from beyond the decaying structure. Outside the building a loud voice echoed through every corner of the room, beckoning for the release of the American.

"This is the Israeli Army." The voice came from beyond the walls. "You are surrounded. We have the children. Release the American, or you will die."

Beau knew they would let Cobra live if he were released. He wanted the terrorist dead. Swiftly, he screamed a warning to the men outside. "Forget me, kill him. You must kill—"

A hard blow to Beau's head rendered him unconscious.

* * *

When he regained his senses, he found himself in the back of an Israeli military truck. Blood-soaked gauze wrapped his throbbing right hand. On a bench to his side sat an Israeli officer. "Cobra? Where is he?" Beau asked.

The officer motioned him to rest. "Rasht Sharafan is the worst of terrorists. Unlike others, he will do whatever it takes to save himself. He cares not for the lives of anyone, except his own. He is the most dangerous of all."

"Why didn't you kill him?"

"Because you knew where Beginn was. We needed you to save the general's son."

"But you said you had the children."

The Israeli officer smiled. "We lied."

Beau managed a feeble smile as he propped himself up with the aid of the officer. He looked at the buildings and pointed at one. "Beginn and the children are there. In the basement."

The officer waved to his soldiers and pointed to the building, "Get the General's son and all the children."

"The invasion?" Beau asked.

The officer turned back to Beau and shook his head. His face reflected sadness. "We have heard but we know not of the details. The Mossad is working on the information. We have warned your country. They were our greatest supporter until Obama was elected. Still they will not listen. When someone cries wolf it is better to prepare for the wolf and hope he doesn't come. Your country believes all the wolves are gone," he said shaking his head sadly. "That will be their undoing." He locked eyes with Beau, "We think your president is involved."

"No."

The officer nodded.

"I must go home. I must warn them."

"They will not listen."

"Sharafan is doing something else. Do you know what it could be?" he asked.

The officer shook his head. "I know not of what you ask. There is nothing else we know that Sharafan has planned."

Caught up in his own thoughts, Beau wondered about the second secret. What could be worse than the invasion of the United States? The medic filled a syringe, and then slid the needle beneath the skin of the forearm, forcing Beau into a fitful sleep.

* * *

The old prop-driven DC-3 droned on, rocking back and forth, gaining and then losing altitude. Many passengers were frightened, while some appeared accustomed to the rough flights. One, a military officer, hovered near sleep. Preoccupied with his thoughts he gave little consideration to the rough ride. To him the old engines were soothing.

Two months had passed since the incident with Sharafan. Beau's hand had healed and arrangements were made for his return home. Problems with his return were temporarily circumvented with the help of his old commanding officer, Admiral Ted Garrett, and with the recommendation of a few select others. At Ted's insistence they had succeeded, partly on the interest, rather more the curiosity of President Obama, who was in a no-lose situation. He could either save an American or punish him as public outcry demanded. Neither mattered, only what was politically advantageous and at the time, Obama was more concerned with his amendment that had almost passed with the required two-thirds states. In a few more weeks the twenty-second amendment would be voided and Obama was almost assured of a third term. It seemed most Americans, those on welfare, still wanted him as president even with his reckless destruction of the Constitution of the United States. The people on handouts from the government exceeded those that worked to pay for those benefits. People were even being laid off because they didn't speak Spanish and the local joke in Texas was that you needed to dial two for English when contacting business because the messages were all in Spanish. Ted had informed Beau and he knew the problems and the risks.

Casually he toyed with the small gold ring hanging from a leather cord around his neck, and for a moment his thoughts returned to the friends he left behind in Israel. The general, whose son he had saved, had been most gracious, taking Beau into his home. The general's wife had given him the gold wedding band hanging from his neck, a gift of gratitude for saving her son. Inside the simple gold band were inscribed the Hebrew words, "Love Eternal."

In Israel he was a hero, but in the United States it would be different; there would be no welcome home. He was considered many things in the States but hero was not one of them, except to the ones he once led into combat.

Despite the consequences, he must return to warn his country. Would they listen to him? A man most considered a traitor and who had fought to defend another country? Others only thought of him as a coward who fled his own nation. In the Arab world he was still a murderer with a price on his head.

Admiral Theodore Garrett had arranged for a small group of military officers to interrogate Beau in Washington, D.C. From there he would be sent to the Naval Air Station in Corpus Christi, Texas, where he would be questioned again. He would be assigned to Admiral Garrett's command, where he would remain until a decision could be reached on his status with the military.

Beau was afraid they would not listen, but it mattered little now, because he would soon know whether they would or not. Still, he thought of Cobra's words about the airlines but mostly he wondered about the second secret.

Time to go home, time to return to Texas and a chance to see his brothers and his friends. But most of all it was a chance to see Moon Shadow.

## Chapter 2
# THE REUNION

The New Year's holiday activity filled Corpus Christi International Airport to overflowing capacity with little room to move and find passenger's destinations. People congregated in masses for business and pleasure. Everything was as it always had been. With dark sunglasses hiding his eyes, the lone soldier went unnoticed,; bumping shoulder with tourists he melted with the collage of people.

The airport speaker system broadcast information and warnings: "Remember any inappropriate remarks or jokes concerning security could result in your arrest." No one listened. All were too busy trying to catch their next flight or shuttles to take them home or away from the airport. Passengers dealt with the DHS groping and search.

The soldier continued his way slowly with the crowds, through a revolving door, and into the daylight. Outside he dropped his duffel bag to the warm concrete walk. Beau was finally home—late December and the weather was still hot and extremely humid, but not unusual for the Texas coastal town of Corpus Christi. In December the weather could be freezing one day and the next over eighty degrees.

Nothing had changed in his absence, yet it all seemed strange and unreal. A flight attendant, running late, pulled her bags on rollers as she raced for the doors to the terminal, while her sweet perfume left an enticing trail. Near the arrival curb, a man kissed a woman and hugged a small little boy goodbye. A police officer busily filled out a citation for an over-parked vehicle. Facing the building, two newspaper boys kneeled down to load their machines.

Beau made his way to the newsstand, placed two quarters in the machine, and pulled *The Corpus Christi Times* from the rack. He folded the newspaper and slid it under his arm. Everything was peaceful and calm. So was the eye of the hurricane, he thought. His hometown and his country were in the eye, and once it passed nothing but death and destruction would follow. Glancing at the headlines, his eyes caught the warning of his coming, but nothing of the dangers ahead. No one in the airport knew who he was or that he returned to warn his country before the eye passed: a warning he hoped would come before it was too late.

An elderly woman moved slowly to the newspaper machine for the latest news. Her arms were full with bags and she dropped them when she removed the newspaper. Deftly Beau bent over and scooped her bags from the ground.

"Here, let me help you with those," he said.

"Thank you, sonny." The words seemed to warble from her old throat. "Could ya bring them to the curb for me so's I can get a taxi?"

Beau glanced down into her thankful eyes and smiled. "Yes ma'am, no problem." He swung his duffel bag over his shoulder and followed her. The elderly lady glanced at the headlines as they made their way to where a taxi waited.

"Well I declare," she bellowed. "This here heathen scoundrel is coming back to our own town. That murderer! The Jews paid him to kill those poor people. And our country is letting him back in. It's just awful, don't you think?" She kept jabbing the bold type with her small, shriveled finger. The front-page story was about a returning American officer who had been an Israeli mercenary.

"Maybe what's written in the article isn't true. I think we should wait and see if he's as bad as the papers say," Beau countered. The taxi driver loaded the scuffed luggage into the trunk. "No. If it's in the newspapers, he has to be guilty," she testified.

"What would you say if I told you I was that man?" Beau asked.

The little lady shuffled closer to the soldier, reached up and removed his dark glasses, and peered into the deep blue eyes. After a moment she tilted her head and said, "If you are that man, then the newspapers are wrong. Sonny, your eyes are just too kindly and gentle for this little old lady to believe anything else." She shook her head. "Eyes tell everything, but they also tell me you carry much sorrow." A sparkle came from her own as she squeezed his huge hand. "Sonny, I've never been wrong about the eyes."

The taxi driver coughed and the two laughed. Beau waved goodbye as the taxi drove off, then he slid the dark glasses back into position. She never noticed the medal for valor hanging over the left pocket of his uniform. The Hebrew word for "Israel" was inscribed in the center. Beau glanced at the newspaper machine and the bold headlines protected behind glass, and sighed. So they knew he was back. He had hoped to keep it quiet, but it was not to be. Surely Sharafan had seen to that.

Beau held his right hand out, turned the palm toward him, and studied the small finger—or what had been his small finger—to admire Cobra's work. He made a fist and released it; there was no longer any pain. The bronze tan of his hand and the pinkish tone of the recently healed stub were in stark contrast. His thoughts were filled with Cobra, and he regretted the Syrian pilot still lived. If anyone had seen beneath those dark glasses and into the pair of hostile steel blue eyes, they would have cleared a wide path. The anger passed. After all, he was home.

The airliners had been extremely uncomfortable and the flight had been long. He stretched the stiffness from each leg and shrugged his shoulders. Stopping at a small magazine stand, he searched the countless rows of various snacks and candies until he found the item he wanted. He went to the counter and paid for a small Three Musketeers candy bar. All he had eaten in two days were soft drinks, peanuts, and stale doughnuts. As he walked away, he didn't eat the candy. Instead he placed it in his shirt pocket, smiled with the slightest bit of anticipation, and returned to the passenger pick-up area.

He didn't like the airlines. If he had a choice, he would have preferred the F-16 or F-15 fighter jet he was accustomed to flying. But then, no one had offered him a jet to fly home. In the Navy it had been the F-14 Tomcat, a two-seated jet with retractable wings and excellent firepower. During *Operation Iraqi Freedom*, he and Ruben had flown the F/A-18 Hornet, a single seated jet capable of performing at Mach-2. It had the turning capabilities of a circus biplane. Neither could match the raw power and speed of the F-16 Falcon or the F-15 Eagle he had flown for the Israeli Air Force—both single-seated fighter jets with guns, bombs, and rockets, the likes of which man had never seen in action until 1991's *Desert Storm.*

Those thoughts faded fast as he kept watch for his friend Ruben, who would be there to take him to the base. He pondered how he would tell him of the danger so near at hand. It still seemed hard to believe when everything around him appeared to be so normal. Even so, he was sure an invasion of the United States was in the very near future. How could America been destroyed from within? He had heard rumblings from Israeli officers but he still refused to believe. Even when his captor Sharafan told him the same unbelievable story it still seemed implausible but the evidence was adding up and it appeared Americans were turning a blind eye. As long as America could dole out money to the poor Obama and his hand chosen czars would control America the same way Castro, Chavez and so many incompetent leaders in history had done. Obama had created a utopia of chaos, murder and mayhem. Christian black Americans acted on impulse and resembled more the radical Muslim Brotherhood. Holder and Obama continued the systematic elimination of Americans as they became "judge, jury and executioner," while specifically connecting whites with guns, murder and racism, as they supplied radical the Muslim Brotherhood with unlimited weapons. America's leaders demanded all individual American's weapons going as far as taking toy guns from children. They ignored and tried to destroy the Constitution and the Bill of Rights. The news media joined in giving false information while putting the stigma of white as a precursor to any person of another race who killed a black American; even in self-defense. Obama was not a peace maker joining the races and worthy of the Nobel prize, but rather he had created racial tension and terror never seen in America. He had become the killer not only of Americans but also freedom and democracy. So unbelievable, so unreal, so close. An invasion was imminent and it was coming within America.

* * *

Seldom was Captain Ruben Alonzo late for a meeting or appointment, but today he had been delayed in picking up his best friend at the airport. Five years had passed since he had last seen Beau. Now it was Commander Gex, his former rank having been restored. At the time of his resignation, he had ranked above Lieutenant Commander Alonzo; now their roles were reversed. The fact his rank had been reinstated at all was nothing short of a miracle.

As he neared Corpus Christi International Airport, his thoughts wandered. It seemed like only yesterday they were high school rivals in Corpus Christi. Beau attended Ray High School, while Ruben went to King. The first two years, Ray defeated King in football—or more accurately, Beau defeated King. Ruben remembered never having seen anyone so quick and strong, and at the time he had hoped one of his teammates would break Beau's leg. The games were close but Beau was one of those players with the ability to do what it took to win. In their senior year, Ray and King were rated one-two in Texas.

Then three weeks into the 1998 season, the King team learned Beau Gex had dropped out of football unexpectedly. Ruben's team celebrated, defeated Ray High School, and went on to the championship. Later that same year, Ruben learned Beau's father, along with other military personnel, had been killed in a bombing incident in Spain, related to a revenge motivated *fatwa*. Beau had taken it upon himself to help his mother financially with his three brothers, and had foregone football in his senior year.

Less than a year later Ruben and Beau met again when Ruben decided to take flying lessons. He found a biplane and a young crop dusting instructor outside Corpus in the small cotton-producing town of Petronilla. The instructor was Beau, his old high school nemesis. Beau flew like he had played football: untouched by anyone. Ruben learned quite a bit in those two months. They became best friends and together they completed college, joined the Navy, and became fighter pilots.

They both joined with the high ideals of serving their country and the opportunity of an adventure that would make them astronauts and offer a chance to go to the Moon or even Mars. Only Beau had come close when he was able to test the SR-71 Blackbird and take it to its known limits at the time. Their first military action had been in Afghanistan shortly after the terrorist attack on New York and the Pentagon in 2001. It seemed like the United States military was invading some Middle Eastern country every year after those first terrorist attacks that took almost 3000 lives on American soil. Since then, the U.S. had responded to terrorist threats almost every year.

Ruben's wife, Maria Domingo, had introduced Beau to his beautiful wife-to-be, Rebecca Jo Collins. What a sweet and wonderful person. Those were the days, Ruben thought. As he entered the airport and neared the passenger area, he wondered about Beau's enlistment in the Israeli Air Force. Never had Ruben seen a man so in control of any situation. He would trust Beau with his life at any given moment. He could still see the magnetic smile and those mischievous eyes.

Ruben laughed to himself and remembered all the havoc the two of them created. At the surprising age of twenty-one, Beau was group leader of "Operation Liberty" in 2001 during the standoff between Taiwan and China. He was always available when one of his men was in trouble. There was never a problem he couldn't overcome. Then something happened, and one day it all ended.

The end began with *Operation Iraqi Freedom* and the almost unknown *Operation Clean Sweep* attack on Lebanon, Iraq, Morocco, Somalia, Libya, and Syria. Beau commanded a small group and Ruben was his wingman. Reporters described the attack as something glamorous. It was hell. Ruben knew he could confront the Devil himself if Beau was along, because he felt his friend could get them away safely—even from the Devil.

He laughed at his foolish thoughts and then grew serious again. All Middle Eastern countries threatened revenge and death to the pilots who had flown *Operation Iraqi Freedom* and had issued a *fatwa* of death against them. Over the next few years, four former pilots of *Operation Iraqi Freedom* were killed while overseas. Extreme groups claimed responsibility and pointed to the *fatwa*.

In 2007, when four American reporters were taken prisoner at the Israel-Lebanon border, the president activated troops to the ready and many were sent to the Middle East where they were stationed in Israel, Tajikistan, and Kyrgyzstan. Years earlier, former allies Kuwait and Saudi Arabia had refused American troops on their soil. Then came the April bombing. At first Middle East terrorists were suspected, only to find once again it was angry fellow Americans in retaliation for more of the governments iron-fisted ATF actions and IRS seizures.

All of this was on the same day as the Branch Davidian deaths in Waco, Texas. These things only added to the conflict and turmoil that had escalated in the United States.

The bombing occurred the same week a group of pilots and their families were granted a week's leave in Rome. Ruben, Lieutenant Commander Thomas Sullivan, and Lieutenant Jack Warren were unable to make arrangements for the trip to Rome. Only Beau, Lieutenant Jimmy Galloway, and their families made the weekend excursion. All were close friends and pilots during *Operation Iraqi Freedom.*

Beau had what many called a perfect marriage and a six-year-old son, Shawn, who was a miniature version of him. Beau's wife, Rebecca, was tall with long, soft blond hair. She had the most beautiful round brown eyes and an ability to smooth over the worst situations. To Rebecca, every day was new and wonderful. Her main desire was to make Beau and Shawn happy, which she did. Not only were she and Beau truly in love, but they were also the best of friends. They had it all, and who knew better than Ruben, because the four of them worked and played together. The trip to Cairo was the first time he could remember they had not been together.

Beau and Ruben would laugh and tease and were always up for a practical joke. All those things changed the day Beau's wife and son were murdered. The Galloway's and the Gex's were shopping in a Roman market when Rebecca found some jewelry she wanted. She had left her purse in the rental car, but Beau refused to let her return for it, instead going himself. He made a dash from the building to retrieve the purse and her money, leaving his wife, son, and the Galloway's behind. No sooner had Beau exited the building than an explosion tore the structure apart, hurtling him across the road, breaking his shoulder and wrist. Rebecca and Shawn died tragically at the hands of terrorists, along with Galloway and his wife in the brutal bombing.

A small Iraqi group claimed responsibility and said it was a *fatwa* in retaliation for *Operation Iraqi Freedom.* Immediately security increased for the remaining pilots of Desert Watch: Sullivan, Warren, Gex, and himself. Beau had almost died like his father had died in another *fatwa* in 1996.

But America was involved with terror of its own. Few had even heard of the tragedy, where it never made the front page of any major newspaper: just back-page filler as a possible gas explosion accident. The president and his wife were having problems of their own as the American economy was in the tank and added to that Cheney's old company Halliburton had taken the seven billion for work in Iraq, built a worthless billion dollar embassy that had not been used and left the country for Dubai. America love it or leave and Halliburton had left. Bush's popularity was down and he had to find a reason to attack someone if he intended to win the next election.

With the American bombing, on-going Israeli/Arab peace talks, and the delegate negotiations for the release of the two American prisoners, the president refused to take a stand. Most believed it was a gas pipeline accident and not the act of terrorists, even though they claimed responsibility. To wrongly accuse Arabs would only add to his already tattered image. The president ignored the issue. Besides, the president's popularity increased two percent, which seemed to please his aides and advisors. The Rome bombing, or accident as it was called, was ignored.

After the bombing, Ruben never saw Beau shed a tear. Only once did he hear him speak about it, when his friend uttered the chilling words, "I'm going to kill all those God damn bastards, even if I have to do it myself!"

Ruben remembered those words as he pulled into the airport, and he could barely withhold a chuckle. "I bet those guys paid dearly," he muttered to himself.

Beau had tried to get the commanders to retaliate against the terrorists. They refused, reasoning you can't bomb countries just because a few people get killed. But the dead weren't just a few people; they were his wife and son; they were his life. When they denied his request, Beau resigned in mid-2008 and immediately joined Israel's air force, requesting combat.

The media twisted the story and made the most of it. "High Ranking Officer Turns Mercenary," they said. The tabloids had a field day saying aliens took him around the world, while the Palestinians said he murdered children, and the Israelis decorated him for bravery. With more bombings, riots, and financial strife within the United States, and a new President who promised to bring "hope and change," Beau Gex was soon forgotten.

Ruben received only a half dozen letters. None divulged information as to Beau's activities. Only one thing he asked; it was always the same request: put flowers on Rebecca and Shawn's graves. Now Beau was back and the United States had mysteriously dropped charges against him. Ruben knew something was happening but what? As he swung along the passenger pick-up lane, he recognized Beau and pulled to a stop. He sounded the horn and then jumped from the Jeep to greet his old friend. He yelled, waved his arms, and moved toward Beau.

There was no mistaking him, even in the uniform and dark glasses. Beau dropped the duffel bag to the pavement and the two men clasped in what was more than friendship, for they were best friends. Together, they had lived with and cheated death

Beau held Ruben at arm's length. His friend was almost a head shorter, but what he lacked in stature, he more than made up for in spirit. "Boy, you're a sight for sore eyes. I'll be honest; I never thought I'd live to see ya again."

Ruben noted Beau's brown skin. "Hell, you're almost darker than me. At least you got time to soak up the rays while you were gone.

"Yep, I did do that."

"Makes a guy like me jealous." The pink finger on the right hand stood out from the tanned body. Ruben pointed and grinned, "Beau you gotta quit chewing your fingernails. That is beyond the quick."

Raising his hand Beau looked at the stub and managed a smile. "Nasty habit huh?"

"Is that what they guy did?" Ruben asked. With a nod of his head Beau confirmed Ruben's question. "What was his name, Abdul Walley Walley?"

This brought a small chuckle, "Sharafan."

"Nice guy."

"He's evil."

For a moment Beau reflected on Sharafan, but Ruben quickly pulled him back when he slapped his hands together and said, "Okay, let's get your bags and get outta here."

Beau took off his pilot's sunglasses and held up the duffel bag. "This is it my friend. Everything I own is in here." The lines around his eyes revealed age far beyond his years—a lifetime of experience and grief. "Say, how's Sunday?"

Sunday was the nickname Ruben's wife, Maria, had been unable to shake since high school. With the last name of Domingo, Ruben had made so much fun calling her Sunday, the name stuck. Now only a few close friends called her by her nickname. Beau was one of those people.

"She's fine."

"Y'all doing okay?"

"Yeah, sure, but the military doesn't give an off base allowance for living anymore. Obama tried to tighten the budget but it didn't help. Like you always used to say, 'tax and spend,' and it's only getting worse. We haven't been paid in three months. Men are quitting in droves. We don't really have a military any more. Hell, the country is so deep in debt we'll never make it out of this. For the first time we have double digit inflation."

"Well, that can be expected with government spending," Beau said. "We had double digit inflation in the eighties."

"No I mean double digit inflation like Mexico had in ninety-four and ninety-five. We have had double digit inflation each of the last two months." Ruben laughed. "You might say the dollar isn't worth a peso. The country is in a full depression and unemployment is over thirty percent."

"Damn, I didn't know," said Beau, shaking his head. "Don't you watch CNN?"

"Not really. When I do it just makes me mad." He sighed then continued. "Anyway, I was asking about you, Ruben! How is everything?"

"Oh . . . well . . . I bought an old van and with that allowance gone and taxes on the house up, it's hard to make it. Just glad I didn't buy one of those $50,000 new ones. Gas is over five bucks a gallon. Gonna sell the van next month—if I can."

Beau laughed. "And I thought things were bad under President Bush."

"So did I but things have definitely gotten worse. Poor old Obama couldn't even slow down what Bush started."

Although the numbers were shown as 1.5 trillion added to the debt each year it was actually more than two trillion in debt each year Obama was in office and also the reason Congress failed to pass a budget so they wouldn't be required to show actual numbers.

Shaking his head Ruben continued, "You know, I used to get real pissed off at you for bad mouthing every politician, but something you said still sticks in my mind: 'as long as we only have a Republican or a Democrat—we have no choice.' It really seems true now." Ruben chuckled, "What did you call them? Oh, yeah. A Republi-cant and a Demo-crap."

Beau laughed. "It always seemed to me politicians could claim victory even in defeat."

"True. The balanced budget Congress finally passed a couple of years ago just about ruined this country. With a new tax the government increased spending to cover all the entitlements. That wasn't enough. Then they decided to protect all Americans' 401-k by controlling them. They immediately borrowed against the savings and spent the money. Even with all of this Congress gave themselves a fifteen percent pay raise to cover inflation. And they made it retroactive. You know Obama is having the National Guard seize weapons from all gun owners. I don't see how they could do it; there's nothing left." Ruben sighed.

With a knowing shrug Beau said, "You would have thought Americans would have seen what was coming with the Social Security all spent. The tax was just another way to spend more money. They will spend and tax until it's too late. When President Bush increased the deficit to near eleven trillion it was already too late."

"I hate to sound cynical but I think it's already too late now. A few days ago the news reported that almost all of the taxes collected go to pay interest on the National Debt. We owe over twenty trillion and the interest just went over ten percent which means the interest on the debt exceeds the taxes collected. As far as America's financial health goes it's a flat liner. "

Beau laughed. "Ruben, you surprise me."

Ruben said, "There's more. Obama tried to blame it all on Bush but when he cut welfare you'd have thought Civil War had broken out in the United States." Ruben shook his head and sighed, "I'm afraid it's too late."

Beau nodded. "I heard there were a lot of riots."

"More than a lot."

"I never did find out what they were over. They weren't race riots?"

Ruben shook his head. "No. The unions, welfare. They aren't getting what they've been getting, and tax protest riots. Protests that got out of hand. Made those Los Angeles riots seem like a picnic. North, east, and west—seems no big cities were spared. Not too much in the south but even Houston had riots over welfare." Ruben snickered, "But they didn't last long here in Corpus. Miami is still in chaos. In fact, people don't travel much in southern Florida. The president had to send the military into places like Miami, Washington D.C., Detroit, Chicago, Boston, and Los Angeles and should have sent them into a half dozen others. They say it's safer to travel in Mexico than it is in Southern Florida or Los Angeles.

"Hell, and the bombings keep happening. There have been too many and even more discovered before they exploded. The threats of bombings have federal employees real skittish.

"The attacks were blamed on militia and other radical groups. Rumor had it the CIA knew about one bombing but didn't do anything so their previous muffed actions would seem more justified. The president attacked two militia outfits in retaliation: one in Louisiana and one in Wyoming. Each of those was worse than that old Waco fiasco. In Wyoming more than fifty of the ATF forces were killed. Some of the militia even managed to escape. Right after that, anti-militia groups sprang up and they started killing members of the militia on the street.

"But the real problem is a group that calls themselves the 'Minutemen.' They plan to free America from the terror of Congress and have demanded trials of treason against all members of Congress except for twenty-nine specified in their documents."

"Twenty-nine?"

"Yeah, the ones that voted against the bailout the last year of Bush. They exonerated Ron Paul from Texas but demand the trial and execution of all the other congressional leaders including the President and his czars."

"I did hear about Obama's czars."

"Let me tell you they are really out of control, including Pelosi and Reid."

Beau sighed, "You can guarantee Congress will protect themselves from that." Beau noticed when Ruben shook his head no. "What is it?"

Ruben took a deep breath, "About a month ago a Representative in Minnesota was hung on his front porch."

"My God. I didn't know."

"No one knows. They're trying to keep it quiet but most military personnel know what happened. They caught the guy. He was from Alabama. Seems the Congressman took away some jobs and moved them to Minnesota. That guy lost his job because of the Congressman. A sign was stuck to the Congressman's chest, with a knife. It read; 'This is for the treason committed against the United States of America.' Below that was scribbled, 'Hope and Change coming, 506 to go.'"

"What does five-o-six mean?"

"It means the members of Congress. Minus the twenty-nine the Minutemen like. They are telling us, 'One down five-hundred and six to go.'"

"I heard the country was in turmoil but I didn't know it was that bad."

Ruben turned to Beau, his face stern and troubled. "Soldiers are quitting in droves. The government has already taken away most of our benefits but at least they still pay the pilots. There is no reason to join and no reason to stay. At this rate it won't be long before we have no military. In fact we don't have much now. The military hates Obama and that son-of-a-bitch made sure we didn't get to vote in 2012."

"That's not good."

"Ex-cons can join the service and they're talking about letting prisoners join to shorten their time in prison. And those in the military are kicked out if they are a little overweight. Our numbers are dropping drastically."

"That's no good at all."

"You have no idea," said Ruben. "We need somebody to represent the people but no Democrats or Republicans. They're all liars."

I heard Pelosi, Reid and Boxer were behind a lot of the financial problems."

"Yeah and all the other czars. And Treasury Secretary Geithner said America should have infinity for our financial debts. He should be called the Bankruptcy Secretary. Yeah and I should too so I can spend Monopoly money on whatever I want. Every one of Obama's men are communists."

"That bad?"

Worse. They should take all of 'em and send them to Guantanamo as enemy combatants."

"What about Obama."

In a fit of anger Ruben wave his arms, "And him too." Ruben turned to Beau and smiled sadistically, "And I want to waterboard Obama first."

Beau snickered, "You swore an oath to protect them."

"No, I swore an oath to protect America from all foreign and—Domestic Invaders." Ruben calmed down, "We are in the throes of a total financial collapse. Obama is living proof God no longer favors America. He has destroyed America. We are at the end of times and he is the Anti-Christ."

"I hope that's all," mumbled Beau as his thoughts returned to Sharafan and the possibility of an invasion. The idea of only a financial collapse seemed almost pleasing, when compared to an invasion.

"What?" Ruben asked.

"Never mind, it was nothing."

Ruben sighed. "Hey, enough of that. Where to?"

"First thing I want is a hamburger, with real meat, real cheese, jalapenos, lettuce, and tomatoes: the works. I always said if I made it back, a hamburger would be the first thing I got. Until we find one, I wanta listen to some good ol' Rock 'n Roll."

"You got it," Ruben said, grabbing the duffel bag and throwing it in the back of the Jeep.

The two men climbed in, Ruben cranked the radio, and the pair began their hamburger odyssey. In short order they rustled up two of the biggest double meat, double cheese jalapeno burgers they could find at a nearby Whataburger. With their "Hamburger Mission" accomplished and the radio blaring, they headed to the Naval Air Station.

The fabric top of the Jeep flapped noisily in the wind. "It's sure good to have you back, just like old times. Hey, you still have those nightmares?" Ruben asked.

"Not as often. But it's the same one over and over. I'm with Becky and Shawn on Padre Island. There's no one else around. I'm calling for them to return so we can leave. They run toward me waving their arms and laughing. It . . . it's all in slow motion. Suddenly, terrorists hidden in the sand jump up and start shooting them with machine guns. I can't stop it. I'm helpless. Then I wake up," Beau said. Memory of the dream brought beads of cold sweat to his forehead.

For a moment they drove in silence. "I want you to know Sunday and I take flowers to the graves real regular," Ruben said slightly worried about his friend's reaction.

"I'm grateful Ruben; that means a lot to me. You know, I joined the Israeli Air Force just to avenge their deaths. I've been involved in most of their raids; God only knows how many people I've killed. Women, children—who knows. Who's right, Ruben? I sought my own hell and killed innocent people. Becky would be ashamed of me."

"Hell, Becky would never be ashamed of you," snapped Ruben.

Beau hesitated then continued. "Sometimes her death is like a dream. In the mornings just before I wake, I can feel her hair against my face, the warmth of her body against mine. I can still smell her sweetness. Then I see her face but when I reach out to touch her, I wake up. Always, I try to go back to sleep in the hopes I can bring her back—if just for a moment." Again silence. "She died because I left her. I should have died, not Becky."

"Beau, it's not your fault. I know it's tough but you couldn't have done anything." They drove for a while in silence; then Ruben spoke again. "You know, one of those smut magazines, the *Enquirer* or *Star*, said some aliens took you into outer space. What was it like up there?"

Slowly, the old familiar smile creased Beau's face. "The aliens? Yeah, I heard about it too. Actually they took me to Tahiti, and we spent a week on the beach." Both men started laughing.

"Hey, what are the Israeli women like?" But before Beau could answer, Ruben said, "Shit, Beau, ya haven't gone faggot on me, have ya?"

Beau laughed and slapped his old friend on the shoulder. "Ya could always bring me around." He sighed and continued. "They're not bad. Some of them are really beautiful. That is, if you can get used to hairy legs and underarms, and no deodorant."

"Oh, man! You gotta be shitin' me."

"Nope. Strange, when I think back to the women over the last few years, I never woke up with one I wanted to stay with. You know what I mean?"

"Yeah," Ruben lied, not having the faintest idea what Beau was talking about.

"I don't think you do. I'm not trying to say going to bed with a woman is the only way I can tell if I love her or not."

Ruben snickered. "Hell, ya gotta test drive a car before ya buy it."

"That's not the same thing. A woman's not a car or a piece of property. I know I love a woman when I wake up beside her and I want to pull her close to me and just hold her near. I always felt that way with Becky. No matter how she looked in the morning, she was always beautiful to me. Before I got out of bed, I'd kiss her on the neck and hold her close for a few minutes," Beau said with a sigh.

"Well, I'll agree with ya there," said Ruben sincerely. "Feel the same way about Sunday."

"It's never happened with anyone else. There were some I liked, but that was all," Beau mumbled.

"I hope ya didn't fall in love, 'cause Sunday wants ya to meet a doctor friend of hers."

"Is she tall? Does she have long blond hair?"

"Come on, they can't all be like Becky," Ruben said, instantly regretting he couldn't retract his words.

"I know." Beau sighed. "I'm sure if Sunday likes this doctor, then she'll be just fine. Did she tell her who I am? If she knows my background, she may not be too eager to meet me."

"Aw, I wouldn't worry about Krysti, she's a fine woman," said Ruben.

With a smile of interest Beau asked, "Is she tall?"

Ruben snickered. "I'm not telling, but I will tell you she is the physician for our team, and she has a son, Justin." As an afterthought, he added, "Oh yeah, Sunday told me Krysti's ex-husband abused her. She hates to be grabbed."

"Ya afraid I might beat her?" Beau asked with a laugh.

"Aw hell no, not you. You're about as gentle with women as anyone I've ever seen. Sometimes I think you're a big pushover."

"Well, thanks for the pointer. Oh, I almost forgot," Beau said as he searched for the small item in his shirt pocket. "Here."

Then he tossed the Three Musketeers bar toward Ruben who snatched it in midair. "Damn, you know I'm trying to stop eating these," he said as he tore at the wrapper with incredible skill, exposing the chocolate, which he bit into viciously. This was a ritual Beau had begun when they first started flying, and which continued through *Operation Iraqi Freedom*. Ruben always complained about his weight, so before every mission Beau would hang his friend's favorite candy bar in the cockpit. Ruben would complain—but he always ate it. Beau had not forgotten.

He grinned. "Yeah, I can tell, and it seems like ya got the same control." They both chuckled.

Again Ruben bit into the rapidly disappearing candy. With a full mouth he mumbled, "Well don't do it anymore. I'm eating this just for you."

"Say, how is Grandy?" Beau asked.

Ruben smiled as he thought about his Great-grandfather. "Grandy died a little more than a year ago."

"I'm sorry."

"No need to be. Still working the small farm the day he died. Ninety-five years old and active till the end," Ruben said, shaking his head with pride.

Beau knew Ruben loved the old man. Probably the only person he loved more was his wife, Sunday.

Grandy had been of Mexican descent but claimed heritage to the old Karankawa Indians. He still believed in the old ways and customs of the Texas Indian tribe, absorbed almost completely when Texas became a nation in 1836. But the old man held on to the customs and the legends of his past: legends passed down from Grandy's grandfather when Grandy was only a small boy. Legends and stories Grandy passed on to Ruben. Legends Ruben continued.

Beau placed his leg in the open door of the Jeep and turned to his friend. "Who's on the team? Sully, BJ? Ted didn't say but is he running the show?"

The Jeep rolled smoothly over the road leading to the Naval Air Station; a warm, sultry salt breeze from the Gulf of Mexico filled the air. Sand lined the road on both sides. A hundred yards to the left was the bay of Corpus Christi, and lagoons filled the area to the right where residential subdivisions were slowly taking over. Already they could see the Station.

Ruben confirmed Ted led the group. Their old friends, Commander Thomas "Sully" Sullivan and Lieutenant Commander Jack "BJ" Warren, who fought with them in *Operation Iraqi Freedom,* were also attached to the group. Along with them were seven other pilots: four Americans and three from a pilot exchange program developed between the United States and its Allies. The three were from Britain, Canada, and Australia.

Beau was the eleventh pilot on the team and was assigned to them until the protests of the Syrians were cleared. Only then would he be free to pursue his future or suffer the consequences of the military tribunal. "Any hotshots?" Beau asked.

"Well, there's a kid, Lieutenant Mark Fitzhenry; we call him Fitz. He's damn good. Maybe better'n you!" Ruben Chuckled.

"Good, I've been wanting to step down," Beau said, leaning back in the bucket seat.

"Quit my ass!" snapped Ruben.

"Think so, Ruben. I wanta go to West Texas with my brothers. I don't wanta fight any more," he said. "Besides, I'm getting too old for this shit."

"Too old." snapped Ruben incredulously. "You're only what . . . thirty-five and a half?"

Beau started to laugh uncontrollably. "Only you could say something like that."

In the distance loomed the gates to the Naval Air Station. As they neared them, Beau noticed crowds gathered at the entrance.

"What the hell is going on?"

In front of the gates were pickets protesting Beau's return—something he anticipated. And there were other protestors. A line had been drawn between them, and the road was the line. On one-side anti-abortionists held placards claiming murder, yelling taunts to the pro-choice across the road; a minister knelt in prayer with his right hand on top of a bible. Blacks patrolled both sides with signs demanding jobs, housing, and food.

A cluster of armed MPs stood their vigil prepared, should the present protests get out of hand. Some environmentalists held up signs saying, "Save the animals and our children. Stop drilling for oil." Four Hispanics held signs with the words, "Make Spanish the national language."

Beau pointed to the environmentalists and said, "Those posy-sniffers will never change—until they have no gas for their cars." Ruben nodded and then Beau pointed to the four Hispanics. "Are they serious?"

"Serious, hell. Where have you been?" Ruben immediately thought about his words. "Oh, yeah, I forgot. While you were out of the country a half dozen counties in Florida made Spanish the official language. Last year, El Paso did the same and Brownsville almost did too, but the referendum lost by a thin margin."

"Insanity."

"Yep," said Ruben.

Something was missing, "Ruben, the manger scene, the cross, Jesus?"

Ruben shook his head. “It’s against the law to have anything in reference to Jesus or Christianity on display on any federal or state property.”

“You’re kidding?”

“Wish I were.”

Something caught Beaus eye. Incredulous, Beau pointed, “What the hell is that?

Ruben followed the direction Beau glared and caught the two military personnel that had caught his attention. A group of soldiers clustered near the gate where two of the men had thick beards but it was the turbans they wore that stood out. Ruben shook his head, “You’ve been gone too long. Three years ago the President authorized beards and turbans for Muslims in the military.”

Shaking his head in disgust Beau mumbled, “What the hell has happened to America.”

Ruben grunted, “When you said hell you were real close to where America is now.”

“I expected problems with my arrival but why are the others here?”

“Some big-wig politicians are coming to our New Year’s party.” Ruben sighed. “They still want to give everything to the ones that do nothing. It’s the same thing. They want more from guys like you and me.”

“Maybe the country is in worse shape than I thought.” Near the gate they passed a man who at first appeared more like a derelict than a protestor. He held a sign plastered with the words, “No Housing. No Peace!”

“What’s that?” asked Beau as he pointed to the sign.

“A bunch of winos have demanded free housing. If not, they’ve refused to leave the downtown park. They threaten anyone who enters. The ACLU says it’s illegal to remove them.”

“You’re kidding?”

“Nope. ‘Fraid not.”

“I never understood people like that. If they worked real jobs half as hard as they protest, they wouldn’t have to demand housing; they could earn it.”

“I know but you can’t tell the politicians,” grumbled Ruben. “Same old shit. Nothing has changed since you left, except our government has just about broken us. Democrats and Republicans. Nothing changed until now.”

Beau sighed. “Outa sight, outa mind. If you don’t see or hear the problem, it doesn’t exist.”

“Yeah.”

“Hope it’s not too late.”

“It might be too late already,” Ruben said somberly.

When Beau heard his friend's words it caught him off guard. Ruben was the type of person who was always upbeat. They neared a large group chanting, "Death to the Murderer. Hang the Traitor." The mob had worked itself into a frenzy of anger. At the gate Ruben handed the guard their IDs. Just inside Ruben stopped.

Beau looked back at the mob. The scene reminded him of the Israeli-Palestinian confrontations he had seen. Nothing good came of those confrontations. Nothing good was going to come of this.

"Hey, let's have some fun," he said, smiling mischievously.

Beau rolled his eyes. "No, Ruben, don't do it."

"Aw, come on." He had already lifted himself from the Jeep and was walking back toward the gate. Reluctantly Beau followed. On the other side, Ruben approached a man who appeared to be leading the protestors. "Can I be of assistance?" Ruben offered.

"We're here to make sure the traitor doesn't return to Texas," roared the protestor. Instantly, the others chimed in with their leader.

"Don't tell anybody, but—," Ruben cast an apprehensive eye about, "we're on your side. We hope you get that son-of-a-bitch." Ruben nodded to Beau. "Right?"

"Absolutely," he agreed, nodding his head affirmatively.

"What are your names?" asked the protestor.

Without hesitation Ruben pointed to Beau. "This is Commander John Smith and I'm Captain Jim Jones."

"How can we recognize him?"

"Easy," Ruben said as he turned. "Commander, take off your glasses." Ruben pointed to Beau and continued. "The traitor you seek will be just like him. But pay close attention to his eyes. The guy you want just looks evil. You can't miss him." Beau slid the glasses back into position. The protestor shook Ruben's hand. "Thanks for the help, we appreciate it."

"Any time," said Ruben as he and Beau moved back within the safety of the gates. "If you need anything else just ask for Smith and Jones." As they returned to the Jeep, they failed to see four-redneck cowboys approach the four Hispanics carrying the Spanish language sign. One of the cowboys wore a shirt with a picture of an atomic bomb exploding and the words, *SAVE AMERICA, NUKE WASHINGTON D.C.* One cowboy had a picture of a gun on his shirt. The gun was smoking and it looked like there were bullet holes printed on the shirt, along with the words *TERM LIMITATION.* Gradually, two of the cowboys unfurled a sign of their own, while their two friends pulled down the one that read: Make Spanish the national language. The cowboys' sign read, "If you don't speak English, GO BACK TO MEXICO!" The two groups started to scuffle but the alert MPs hurriedly separated them.

Ruben and Beau saw none of this as they walked toward the Jeep. They heard more noise but failed to notice as they laughed uncontrollably, their sides aching before they reached their vehicle.

"God, I haven't laughed so hard since you and I got in trouble in Saudi," Beau said, straining to stop laughing. "Smith and Jones." Again Beau burst out in laughter.

"See, just like old times." Ruben started the Jeep and they were on their way again. "I have so much fun playing with those protestors. The politicians cater to their every whim. Any decision seems to be based on how many votes it would cost them, instead of the good it might or might not do for the people or the country."

"You're right, but you'll never make a rattlesnake safe by cutting off its rattler, so don't ever expect politicians to change," Beau said, still chuckling over the exchange with the protestors. "I had almost forgotten how good it feels to laugh." After he regained his composure, he continued the questions. "Who else is in the group?"

Ruben proceeded to tell him about Major Fred Deberg who was called Cozmo, since he seemed to be in another world always chasing women; Lieutenant Barry Pickett from Canada; a real Choctaw Indian, Lieutenant Dean Blackman; and Major Jonathan Kippurn Mulholland from Australia.

"Jonathan Kippurn Mulholland? What a name."

"Yeah, well, we just call him Kipp. He's a real riot to be around. Then there's a guy from England, Colonel Mike Marix. He's been dating the girl you're gonna meet tonight."

"Hey, I don't want to step on any feet."

"No way. Their relationship is up and down. She's sweet, he's a jerk, and now they're on a downer. Besides, he's one of those dedicated 'For the Crown' guys. He'll even tell you how good he is. It's just bullshit; he's an egotistical asshole. It's enough to make ya puke."

Beau let out a slow whistle at his friend's comments.

A sheepish grin came over Ruben's face. "Marix says he's some kind of royalty, I think a duke or lord or something. Well, I was pissed and the guys were bored, and Marix has this reddish hair, so I blurted out *Yeah, just call him The Red Baron.* Let me tell you, he was plenty mad but the guys just cracked up." Ruben chuckled. "The name's stuck like glue. In fact, it's become his call sign. He hates it. So if he makes you mad, just call him the Red Baron."

"You were always good at getting somebody stuck with a name."

"Yep, that's why they call you Mongoose," Ruben Said. "Hell, you drove that old black '63 Corvette since high school. When you taught me how to fly and we used to drag race in Robstown with your Corvette, I called you the Cobra killer. Mongoose just seemed like a natural when we entered the service."

"Wonder whatever happened to that old Vette? Auctioned off with everything else, I guess?" Beau said with a sigh, almost pleading for an answer.

The answer was something Ruben knew. "When you joined the Israeli Air Force, the government swarmed your place. I'm sorry, Beau, but they auctioned off everything. Back taxes or something. Ted got some of your personal things, like your pictures."

"Good, that helps." For a moment he thought about the group and remembered Ruben hadn't told him about all of the men. "Isn't there another pilot?"

"Oh, I almost forgot the guy from Philadelphia, Larry James. He seems okay but there's something about him. I don't know why but I just don't trust him," said Ruben, shrugging his shoulders.

Ruben turned into a curbed asphalt parking area surrounded with palm trees and azaleas. He brought the Jeep to an abrupt halt in front of a Quonset hut, where some of the men were quartered. Beau was genuinely surprised at Ruben's reaction to the two men, Marix and James, since Ruben liked everyone. Beau hoped he would not have problems with them. He knew it would be rough for him, especially if they knew who he was—and they would already know.

A kid, a Canadian, an Indian, a Yankee, an Englishman, a womanizer, an Aussie, his three friends—BJ, Sully and Ruben—and himself, the renegade. A most interesting group, Beau mused. At the front of the Jeep, Ruben snapped to attention and saluted Beau. "Welcome home, sir."

"Cut the shit," said Beau rolling his eyes and shaking his head. "Take me to Ted."

Ruben snap-turned on his heels, gave Beau a wide grin, and the two headed for the Officers' Quarters to find Admiral Ted Garrett, the man responsible for both the charges against Beau being dropped and for his reinstatement. Beau would have preferred not to be reinstated, opting instead for civilian life. The situation was sticky politically and it was the only way to succor his return.

Before they reached the office, Ruben turned to Beau and asked, "Do you really believe all that stuff about an invasion?"

As they continued toward their destination, Beau drew in a deep breath and said, "I'm afraid so."

"They couldn't do that," said Ruben.

Beau responded with a snicker. "Think about what we saw when we came in the gate. I see those protestors and I realize man is the same everywhere in the world: South Africa, Bosnia, Russia, Mexico, Somalia, Israel, and here." Beau shook his head. "In fact, just remember Bosnia. As soon as we pulled out, they started killing each other again and all for God or Allah. And now we fight among ourselves as fiercely as with our enemies. There are wonderful people on both sides of every conflict. It only takes a few hateful people to stir up others and ruin it for all of us."

Ruben quipped, "You mean like Democrats and Republicans."

"Yeah, like them." Beau managed a smile but his mind was still set on serious thoughts. "While I was in Israel, I met some great Israelis, but I also met some extremely nice Palestinians. There are many that truly want peace, but for the most part I have a hard time deciding which side is right. Although both sides talk of peace, both are determined to eliminate the other—not live with each other in peace! As long as both sides exist, there will be war; as long as men are alive, there will be conflict and war. And worse than that.

"Not until recently did I see the answer. It wasn't until years and years after Rabin's own people killed him that I knew the Israeli people were not chosen, as they believe. Now the Israelis fight and kill each other the way they used to fight the Arabs. Although I love the Israelis, I no longer see any difference between them and the Arabs. Both sides are wrong. When I was a kid my father cut a cartoon out of the newspaper. Remember Pogo?"

"Yeah, that possum and his buddy the alligator."

"I remember the possum, Pogo, talking to the alligator, Albert. They were looking for intruders when actually it was them all along. When they came to a river they looked down and saw a reflection of themselves. That was when Pogo said, *We has seen the enemy and they is us.*" Beau hesitated then continued, "Ruben, we are our own worst enemy."

"Aw, c'mon, Beau. Surely there is a way to have peace?"

Again Beau laughed. "The only way a man can live in peace is to live alone—and that is what I intend to do."

## Chapter 3
# THE AURORA PROJECT

The secretary told the men Admiral Garrett expected them, and she led them through the door and into his office. Ruben and Beau entered and immediately snapped to a salute. Admiral Garrett in a heated discussion on the phone, paced back and forth behind his desk.

"I don't give a damn. Call the MPs and have them get Colonel Marix away from the protestors. There are no Smith and Jones here. Get him inside, now!"

Ruben and Beau grinned at each other.

Beau gazed around the office. Nothing had changed. It was the same when he saw it the last time five years earlier. Pictures of planes the admiral had flown filled the walls. In glass displays were decorations and awards he had received. The old antique mahogany desk still wax-shined to a mirror reflection would never change. Only his plush chair showed signs of age. The ashtray was full, and on the desk to the right was a picture of Beau's parents. He knew Ted and his father had been best friends.

"Damn," muttered Garrett as he slammed the phone back on the receiver. Immediately his disposition changed when he saw Beau. "It's good to have you back. Excuse the call. Some protestors at the main gate have Colonel Marix's car surrounded. They think he's Beau. They claim a Smith and Jones described the man to them and Marix is the one. At least you two made it through. Smith and Jones . . . you'd think they could be more original." Garrett watched the two men closely for a sign that would indicate what he was sure to be the truth. He frowned. "You two didn't—?" He waved his hands in the air and shook his head, "Never mind, I don't want to know."

Ruben and Beau could hardly restrain themselves as they turned mischievous eyes on each other. "Excuse me, sir, may I be dismissed?" Ruben asked sheepishly.

"Go on, get out of here and leave us alone," said Garrett, dismissing Ruben with a wave of his hand. He touched the intercom button and bellowed to his secretary, "Send the sergeant major in."

"Yes, sir," came the quick response.

The admiral stood erect. "Beau, I want you to meet Master Sergeant Robert Schmitt. He is on loan from the Air Force and will be working with our little group. I'm sure you have heard of the *Aurora Project*?"

"Yes sir."

"There's something I haven't told you. A public showing of a manned space plane is scheduled for tomorrow at 1200 hours. It will bring years of preparation to a successful conclusion."

"Blackbird?" asked Beau. He was confident of the answer, knowing the SR-71 was probably the swiftest aircraft in the world and one of the few capable of reaching in excess of 150,000 feet. If he could only fly the Blackbird again.

Previously only Air Force officers were allowed to fly the Blackbird, but under Bush's New World Order the military was to mix. No longer would Naval Aircraft be restricted to aircraft carriers nor were Naval officers forbidden to fly the modified SR-71. This change gave Beau Gex and others an opportunity to test and fly the modified space plane. Although Beau was familiar with the aircraft, he had never flown the modified version.

But the presidential military changes did more than just allow Gex the opportunity to fly the Blackbird. Under Clinton there was no control and it continued under former President Bush's son. More Americans were killed by American soldiers' mistakes than any hostile nation during the Bush and Clinton terms. American jets bombed American ground troops; helicopters crashed into each other for no reason at all. Even foreign ships were not safe, as emphasized when the American submarine sunk a Japanese ship full of students. Military personnel on the ship blamed civilians for distracting them. But the changes had enabled Beau to learn the intricacies of the SR-71 Blackbird.

"Correct, but not the Blackbird as you know it," Garrett confirmed. "The pilot is having ear problems and can't fly. You are the only one qualified so you will run the test tomorrow. The top brass can't fly in another pilot. They are afraid it will delay the project, which is what they do not want. For the *Aurora Project* to be successful it can tolerate no delays. Besides, having someone who is not on the active list will give more credibility to the project."

"Yes sir." Beau could not have been happier. "The space shuttle?"

"Obsolete," said Garrett as the door to his office opened. "After the Challenger they were determined to develop a space plane. Now we have them."

Sergeant Major Robert Schmitt entered the room and Garrett introduced Beau. Schmitt was a slightly built man with a large jaw and narrow shoulders. Years of working as a mechanic had increased the size of his hands and forearms, giving one the impression of the cartoon character Popeye. All he needed was a pipe and a sailor's cap. Traces of grime could be detected beneath his fingernails. There was strength in his handshake and a sparkle in his eye.

Robert had been around since the Vietnam War and at one time attached to a squadron of flyers, including Beau's father and Ted. Robert was a master of all engines, although his true love was old prop driven aircraft. His contention was the jets were too sophisticated and had too many problems. "They shouldn't have ever made jets," he would say. Kids taught him the use of computers, which he continued to despise, but despite all his verbal abuse of them, he was excellent with the hated things.

"Nice to meet you sir," said Robert. "I knew your dad. A fine man. Call me Robby, everyone else does. Next thing you know kids will be rebuilding the jets and I'll be watching instead of gettin' my hands dirty. They shouldn't ever have—"

"That's enough Robby," interjected Garrett, before his old friend went off on one of his tirades.

"Yes Sir. Sorry Sir."

"Would you like to tell Commander Gex the nature of the mission?" Garrett ordered more than asked.

"Captain, the SR-71 has been modified and can fly directly into space. Modifications are complete so as to accommodate two people on a mission. There is room for a small amount of supplies and equipment. There are two-, four-, and eight-man versions completed that are similar to the SR-71 but are pure space planes. Your test tomorrow in a converted SR-71 will take you to 300,000 feet at Mach-8. At 150,000 feet the scramjets will take over."

"Wait a minute . . . Mach-8, 300,000 feet?" questioned Beau.

"Correct, the chine or front nose has been modified—"

Beau interrupted. "You lose stability at three-point-five. How do you expect to reach Mach-8 safely? The slightest input is greatly magnified at those speeds and will throw the Blackbird out of control."

"Not anymore! It will surpass Mach-8 and do it safely, with control and stability you would expect to find at Mach-1 or Mach-2. Past Mach-2 a computer system takes control, adjusting the guidance and control system of the SR-71. It controls the rudder, ailerons, and chine forcing a larger input from the pilot for a smaller aircraft response, thus allowing greater control at such high speeds."

"But 300,000 feet?" queried Beau.

"I understand you took it to 130,000. It was capable of more and could have surpassed 150,000. In fact, Sir, this is just a test. The Blackbird is capable of flying directly into space and attaining a speed of Mach-25."

"Mach-25!"

"And with a tenth of the effort and ten times the ease when you flew it at 130,000 feet," Robert added. "In fact, if you've ever flown the Blackbird you can easily fly the modified version with just a few simple verbal instructions before takeoff."

In 1990 the rumor was the SR-71, the fastest aircraft ever constructed, had been grounded, while in reality it was modified and converted into a manned transporter—a small manned version of the original space shuttle. The Pratt-Whitney engines were replaced with smaller, more efficient ramjet engines reaching Mach-5 or 3250 mph. Something new was added to the Blackbird. Fully developed scramjets were built into the modified version and would take it directly into space at a speed reaching Mach-25.

"Sir, may I add we had the technology before you were born. In 1960 the X-15 reached a speed in excess of 4500 mph and an altitude of over 350,000 feet. That's seventy miles high. At 150,000, the Blackbird's liquid hydrogen scramjets take over and you have more control now than ever before. We never needed the Shuttle. The bureaucratic tampering stalled the space plane."

"All right, all right," said Beau, holding his hands in the air. "What is the purpose of this mission, if I may ask?"

"Yes sir," said Robert. "Just a show for the news media before the real flight next week, when the Blackbird will rendezvous and dock with the space station, Starburst. We have twenty-five men and women working the station now. The purpose of the mission is to prove we can launch men into space at a moment's notice. We can save billions of dollars. The old space shuttle will be finished. The new Blackbird will be capable of docking with Starburst and retrieving or leaving men anytime, from any place in America. Soon the larger space planes will completely replace the SR-71. Another space plane is being built to carry a dozen men."

"How will the Blackbird maneuver in space?"

"Small hydrogen-peroxide rockets installed on the side. Much like the old shuttle."

"Thank you Robert, the information was very interesting," said Beau.

"That's all, you're dismissed," said Garrett. When Schmitt closed the door behind him Garrett added, "We have made leaps and bounds in space research in the last five years. When NASA turned to private enterprise, it changed everything and made the *Aurora Project* possible." Garrett laughed.

"You'll like Robby. He's the best man with a wrench. If it can be fixed, he can do it, and no one seems able to touch him when it comes to computers. After your test flight the Blackbird is to be flown to the Kingsville Naval Air Station. Next week it will fly a mission to Starburst. We need to show the media we can fly anywhere, anytime."

"Progress, I suppose," said Beau. He was just happy to have a chance to fly the SR-71 one more time. Modified or not, it was still the Blackbird.

Garrett came around the front of the large desk and stood directly in front of him. He shook his head then reached out and they hugged each other. He pulled away, looked around stepped over to his radio and turned it up the volume. He hesitated then turned back to Beau.

"Damn it, son, I thought those Arabs were gonna kill you for sure. I swear, you must have more lives than a cat." He walked to his favorite chair. Before he sat, he motioned for Beau to take a chair. "Sit down, let's talk." Garrett pulled a chair next to Beau and put a finger to his lips for Beau to be quiet.

Confused, Beau said in a hushed tone, "What's going on?"

"What we're gonna say now is off the record," Garrett half whispered. "Everything is being monitored. It's hard to trust anyone in the military. Do you understand?" Beau nodded and Garrett leaned closer to Beau, "To be a Christian in the military is treason. The President wants all of those that believe in America out. He is determined to destroy America and I won't accept that but there are only a few men like me that remain. He reminds me of Hitler and what happened in Germany. They've asked other questions and if you refuse to say you will kill Americans you are drummed out of the service."

Beau smiled, "You're still here."

Garrett chuckled, "When they asked me that question I lied. But never the les it may be too late now." The shock reflected in Beau's eyes was evident. Garrett smiled, "Not much we can do. Now about the mission."

Beau began to relax. Garrett leaned back in the chair and sighed. Pointing to the picture of his mother Beau said, "See you still have Mom's picture."

A loving smile filled the deeply furrowed face as Garrett reached for the photo, grasped it in both hands, and pulled it near. "Wouldn't be without it." The admiral clung to the picture, and was momentarily drawn to the past. He had almost married Beau's mother, Beverly, but instead his best friend, Bob Gex, had captured her heart. Bob and Beverly were a strange duo. Bea, as he called her, had Norwegian parents and Bob Gex was a French Cajun of Acadian descent.

Garrett peered over the top of the picture at Beau. He noticed the man next to him had inherited the best of both. Beau had grown up fast after his father was murdered in the 1996 *fatwa.* He helped raise his three brothers, but Ted was always there if the boys needed something. He took great pride in watching Beau progress to become one of the finest pilots he had ever seen.

"She was a wonderful woman," sighed Garrett, gently putting her picture back in its rightful place on his desk.

"Yeah, I know. I miss her. You loved her, didn't you?"

Something seemed to be in Garrett's eye as he made an effort to remove the imaginary irritant. "Loved the old girl a lot." He coughed and tried to regain his composure and his voice. "Listen, I had to pull a lot of strings to get you back and it wasn't easy. Some special groups still want to skin you and hang you up by your balls. The president wants to hear your story, but first he has a trip planned to Las Vegas again with the King from Saudi. I'm sure all he wants to use it for is a political toy. But you tell me, what is this about, some God-damn invasion?"

Beau placed both hands in front of his face to where the fingers and thumb of both hands were touching each other, with his chin resting on his thumbs. The small finger of his left hand waved helpless in the air unable to find its matching companion.

"That's right, Ted. They intend to invade and I'm afraid it will be soon."

The missing finger did not go unnoticed. "Did that happen during your capture?" asked Garrett, pointing to the injured digit.

Sitting back in the chair Beau admired the stub where his finger had once been. Then he told the full story of his capture and rescue. He told Ted all he knew of the Syrian General, Rasht Sharafan, the man they called Cobra.

"Unbelievable!"

"Ted, this guy Cobra is the worst kind of terrorist. Any other would have sacrificed his life for Allah and all that bullshit—but not him! He bargained my life for his escape."

"Lucky for you," said the admiral.

"They should've killed us both. He's too dangerous!"

The comment shocked Admiral Garrett. "Maybe there's a reason you lived."

"What? Predestination, God's will, or just plain bad luck? There was no reason. It just happened. I don't believe in fate. Now, thanks to you I've come to tell my story. I only hope it will help."

"Maybe you're here to save the country."

"Wake up, Ted. There are over 300 million people in the United States. I'm one person."

"We'll see," said Garrett.

"Besides, after what I saw at the front gate, I wonder if Americans will stay together during an invasion."

Garrett shook his head. "I don't know. I've noticed it getting worse for the last ten years. Abortion, guns, religion, sex, gays, racial conflicts—all of them have become fanatical and violent. Both sides! All seem determined to eliminate the other to install their beliefs. I've never seen so many factions as diverse and varied, yet so determined to eliminate the others."

Beau nodded. "I know. I saw it first hand at the gates. If I hadn't seen it, I wouldn't have believed it."

Garrett shook his head. "I'm ashamed of my country. I never thought I would say it but I'm ashamed. Just recently it came out that Bush and Obama used the IRS and ATF to monitor and control dissidents. Our country. Can you believe it?" Garrett mumbled when he said, "One was a Democrat and the other was a Republican. No wonder they lost this election. You can't just steal people's rights." He sighed and continued. "If there was a problem they would go after guns and get them on gun violations.

"After the terrorists took out those Twin Towers in New York, the laws were changing every month under Bush. You could get anyone for breaking a law. After all of those CEOs almost broke the major companies in this country, they tried everything but couldn't get them until they gave the IRS more power and started nailing their asses. Now the IRS did something cute. Called it *indexing*. At the end of the year they would add the cost of living to the Income Tax and presto, everyone would owe more taxes. Almost everyone would owe more taxes even if they should have gotten a refund. So anyone with a refund was cheating in the eyes of the IRS."

"But that's a retroactive tax. That's against the law."

Garrett nodded. "Yes, *ex post facto*. It's in the Constitution. But nobody did anything. And guess what? This cost of living *indexing* started with that good ol' womanizer Clinton."

"I didn't know that."

With a cynical laugh Garrett said, "And neither did anyone else. Or no one bothered to do anything about it. Anyway, it's too late. They billed everybody, charged everybody huge penalties and interest, and showed it on the budget as accounts receivable. The money just wasn't there."

"So the country is broke?"

"Flat broke! The military missed their last paycheck. To be honest Bush and Paulson destroyed the country when they gave away a trillion dollars to their wealthy friends in 2008. Welfare for the criminally wealthy. Who would have ever thought that would happen?"

"Sounds real bad."

"It gets worse. Under Obama the National Debt has gone from eleven trillion to twenty-trillion. The interest alone is almost more than the taxes collected." Garrett shook his head and to top it off a few months ago China, Japan and the Saudi's refused to buy any more bonds."

"I thought Japan was our ally?"

"They are but they were told that if they bought bonds they get no more oil." Garrett stared at Beau. "Those three countries owned about ten trillion of our debt."

"What is the government going to do?"

"God only knows, but they say it will be okay and not to worry, that this was just a clerical error that will be cleared up when Congress passes another appropriations bill. Rumor is even Congress is sweating this thing after seeing the real numbers. Something about the interest on the debt exceeds the taxes collected. Son, our country is broke."

Rising from his chair, Garrett motioned to Beau. "I hate to put you through this again after they grilled you in Washington but the civilian review board needs to ask you more questions about this invasion."

"A civilian review board?" Beau asked incredulously. "We need the military on this, not any damn civilians! What the hell do they—?"

Garrett grabbed Beau's shoulders. "Listen! Don't you think I know how you feel! I don't like it any better than you, but the military is watched closely. The Air Force has sent General Waddle. He and another officer will be present. They will listen."

Beau shook his head as he stood up to attend the meeting.

"You are assigned to me. Day after tomorrow you and Ruben will fly to Del Rio to demonstrate the new electronics on the F-18. The rest of us will leave early the same morning in a caravan of cars, go to San Antonio to pick up an arms expert, then rendezvous with the two of you for dinner."

"On New Year's Day?" Beau groaned.

"Orders."

Admiral Garrett looked long and hard at Beau and reflected on the radical changes politicians had brought about in the previous five years. Under Clinton there was a move not only to admit gays, but to unite all the armed forces under one department. The forces themselves dismissed this move. The new century brought two new presidents who instituted their new programs and accomplished what Clinton had started. Soon the military fell apart, when hard-liners chose to retire rather than stay in with the new changes. Some, like General Waddle and Admiral Garrett, saw a necessity to remain and keep the military strong with their presence.

Still, under the financial mismanagement of the nation and the over-taxing of its people, the United States Congress brought about a steady decline in the people's trust and the military strength. While both military expenditures and the American people's net income dropped under the heavy burden, the promises to stop terrorism failed to materialize, and the national deficit continued to increase. The United States was bankrupt and the American people were beginning to understand the harsh reality of the facts at hand. The politicians, both Democrats and Republicans, had coerced the people into believing the monstrous debt was fine, while they continued to glut themselves with personal gain and American tax dollars through their ever-increasing entitlements.

President Clinton's failure brought cheers from the Republicans, embarrassment to the Democrats, and the anger of the people. The election of 2000 brought President Bush. Democrats and Republicans still maintained power. Then in 2008 they jockeyed for position, power, and control of the world. The United States faltered and crumbled from within. Obama took over and America fell off a financial cliff. China watched and waited, hovering over Taiwan like a cat over a canary when the master was gone. But a giant has farther and harder to fall. The United States had not reached bottom yet. Then the United States ceased giving aid to Taiwan.

Garrett could see the decline and fall of the United States of America was inevitable, even without war! War would only hasten the end. He sighed as he walked toward the door of his office.

"The men don't know but the country is broke. Don't know how Congress will budget the military, much less finish Starburst. Cuts are coming. Obama intends to cut the military in half unless he can kill more Christians or help the Muslim Brotherhood. If what you say is true about an invasion, it could destroy the country. I never dreamed 2016 would be like this. Already the military is half the size we were in 2000. First double-digit inflation in eighty years, bombings, riots, nothing but chaos, and the country is broke. God only knows what 2017 will bring."

Beau smiled. "I remember watching an old movie, *2001, a Space Odyssey*. I guess 2017 will be an American Odyssey."

Hesitating at the door to his office, Garrett regained his thoughts. "Our future rests with the SR-71 and the laser space station Starburst, if what you say is true. If you are right about the invasion, the *Aurora Project* will provide safety for our country and every American in it. When it's completed next year, an invasion will be impossible."

"I hope we have that much time," Beau countered sadly.

* * *

Sitting in the center of the room, he faced a group of five people, more like a prisoner being interrogated than a man on a mission with vital information. Standing to each side of the five were Air Force generals, one of whom Beau recognized as General Waddle. The five-seated interrogators consisted of Robert Newby, a Baptist minister to the far left; a local businessman, Charles Copeland on the right; then next to him, Judge Paul Medina; and two Texas legislators: Leonard Washington and Sarah Lipton. The only other person present was a painter at the back wall.

The room was large and used for small parties and dances. A small stage with curtains was behind the table of five interrogators. The painter was adding another coat to the white windowless room. Lipton was obviously in charge of the group and was seated in the middle. Beau recognized her as a local politician who catered to minorities and had made good in state politics. In the last five years she had also become wealthy. For some reason Beau's present situation seemed more hopeless than when he was in the presence of the Cobra, Rasht Sharafan.

Lipton started the meeting. She rolled a finely sharpened pencil in her fingers, with an air of going through a wasted exercise before it had even started. She had advanced far as a politician in the state of Texas and as a representative in the House of Congress, and her actions against the CEOs of American business nearly ten years earlier had earned her great accolades from the news media and the people of Texas. She came down hard on some of the CEOs while taking money from those that were most influential.

The show was good while few knew the most powerful CEOs and Board of Directors filled her election coffers. No one noticed that she actually accomplished nothing against those she attacked. But she had given a good show and she'd been re-elected. Now she had great aspirations and intentions to become a United States Senator, and she intended to use this meeting to advance those goals.

Lipton asked, "Commander Gex, would you like anything before we get started?"

"No ma'am. We need to work fast I don't believe we have much time."

She smirked at the comment, glanced to her right then to her left, and smirked again. Medina shook his head, then Lipton said, "All right, Commander Gex, we need you to tell us the truth. Don't you really think this idea of an invasion is a little preposterous?"

"They said the same thing in New York over ten years ago."

Lipton snapped. "That was ten years ago. We are prepared today." Her eyes stabbed at Beau. "Wasn't this story created in order for you to come back to the United States so you could be reinstated in the service?"

"Personally, I don't give a damn about the military service anymore. When this exercise is done, I intend to resign. But I stand by my story on the invasion."

She rolled her eyes, watched the response of the rest of the panel, and snickered. "Then you admit this was just a ploy?"

Beau gritted his teeth. "Nothing of the kind. I have proof."

"What kind of proof?" she asked.

"This," Beau said, holding his hand up, revealing the missing finger.

Newby and Copeland smirked, while Sarah rolled her eyes again, and Medina actually laughed.

Washington appeared put out and almost angry. A show was very important for him. He had won a great battle against discrimination and taken more jobs for blacks. The black constituency believed in him and loved him. They had received many new jobs through his hard work. Few noticed that it was the most powerful white business executives that also filled his political coffers with his promise to leave them alone if they would occasionally throw him a bone and help in his campaign to be re-elected as a United States Representative.

Coincidentally he and Lipton lived in a very upscale neighborhood of Corpus Christi. In public Lipton and Washington appeared to be the best of friends and crusaders for the people. In reality, they hated each other.

"What does your hand have to do with an invasion of the United States?" Washington asked.

"The work of Rasht Sharafan. He made the mistake of telling me of the impending invasion. He bragged about it before he was to kill me."

"Strange, you appear fine to me," interrupted Judge Medina.

"You appear to be alive," added Washington sarcastically. A powerfully built black man, he had served four terms in Congress and was someone to be reckoned with. He controlled many in the political scene and his voice carried the same power in the interview. He continued his questions. "Your story must be fabricated because I have heard of Sharafan. If your story were true you would be dead. You have a very vivid imagination, Commander Gex. You expect us to fall for this story? You expect the military of the United States and the president you serve to believe this?"

Infuriated, Beau shot up from his chair, forcing it to slide across the floor. "I didn't join the Navy to serve the military or the political factions of this country! I joined to serve and protect the people and the county I love." Beau's words were packed with emotion and frustration.

Admiral Garrett collected the chair; he tried to calm Beau and get him seated.

The Reverend Newby addressed Beau. "Your theatrics won't impress us or the president when he reads the report."

Unable to regain control, Beau answered hastily, "The president be damned!"

"Commander, I suggest you control yourself or we will be forced to turn you over to the military until you can cooperate," said Judge Medina. A show was also important for Medina. He was the most influential Hispanic judge in Texas. Secretly he believed the Hispanics were below him and loathed their living standard, but his reactions to his own people in the past year had been noticed. He had even carried more white votes than Hispanic in the last election. It was very important for him to get the Hispanic votes back.

The time had become critical for Reverend Newby to assert himself. He had problems of his own and tried to involve himself in every aspect of the community. He was trying to collect as much money as he could for the church. A woman in the congregation who was with his child was demanding money. A lot of money: money he had already given her and which was missing from the church. Even the day before, the church's accountant had brought up many discrepancies with the books. Newby was afraid his church and wife would discover his indiscretions.

Calmly and showing no concern, the Baptist minister almost haughtily said, "There's peace in the world. We have created a New World Order. The terrorism is over."

"A New World Order based on our demands. Demands other countries are tired of," scoffed Beau. The comment brought a thin but unnoticed smile to General Waddle's face.

"There is no way we could be invaded. The satellites detail all foreign activities. We are too powerful," Lipton said, shaking her head.

"Don't you see? It's so simple. Our military is spread around the world. We probably don't have enough armed forces remaining to protect us in our own country. The satellites only tell you what an intelligent country wants you to know."

"Where are they going to come from, Mexico?" asked Judge Medina with a laugh.

"It seems logical. That and Cuba," Beau said in all honesty. The reaction brought a chorus of laughter from the five comprising the civilian review board. It also brought a nod of understanding from General Waddle who stood motionless, listening to all.

Copeland smiled smugly but not at the crucifixion of Beau Gex. His thoughts were on how he had used a new accounting method to take more than one billion dollars from a company he had just purchased. Contributions he had made to Lipton and Washington had assured him there would be no investigation after the public's outcry of foul. Both Lipton and Washington and even Medina had soothed over the angry populace, saying they had investigated the transaction thoroughly and had seen nothing improper about the purchase.

"The United States could not be invaded from Mexico or Cuba," Copeland said.

"We already have been. Think about it. We've never been able to stem the flow of illegal aliens or the drug traffickers. What makes you think we can stop a well-planned invasion?"

"A foreign country would lose if they invaded us," Lipton commented sarcastically. "Lose what?" snapped Beau. "They have nothing. They are broke and starving. The only thing they might lose is their life—a little sooner! Remember the Cubans coming over in rafts? They have everything to gain and we have everything to lose. Don't you see?"

Copeland spoke. "Commander we're too strong. You're worrying about nothing. Besides, we have the *Aurora Project*!"

"But the space station is not finished!"

"There is no way they can organize such a massive invasion before *Aurora* is complete," snapped Washington. "Our intelligence gathering is far superior to that of any country in the world. We would know if something like that was about to happen."

"Cobra was right. He said you wouldn't believe my story. He understood." Beau stared long and hard at the five sitting in judgment over him and sighed when he realized they had made their decision before the meeting started.

"You should be making atonement for the death you have dealt to innocent people," sneered Reverend Newby. "Think of your country and not yourself."

Beau's broad shoulders dropped. "My country is the only thing on my mind. The country I loved and went to war for. The country I trusted and believed in that forced me to turn to Israel. And the country I want to save, I have come home for. And now no one will listen."

"This is foolishness. When we have time, we will check your story," Lipton said with finality.

A ray of hope showed in Beau's eyes. "When? Now?"

"Not so fast. You already had us believing it was Christmas Day before you arrived. Are you going to pick another date each time your previous choice passes? We can't expect to be ready each time you cry wolf," said Judge Medina.

The words startled Beau as he remembered the Israeli soldier's comments. "I'd rather be ready for the wolf, and have him not show, than think it will not come and have the wolf eat my flock," he retorted, the anger in his voice evident.

Again Copeland interjected. "New Year's is day after tomorrow and the president will attend the Orange Bowl. We can approach him with your story after he returns from the game. Our reconnaissance is excellent. We've heard of nothing to indicate an invasion. You can rest assured of that."

Beau shook his head. "They said the same thing December 7th, 1941. You just don't see, do you?"

Angered with the talk, Washington interrupted. "Your story holds no water. With hostilities building between Israel and Egypt, I doubt these countries would be capable of planning anything so grand as an invasion of our country."

"What hostilities?"

"For a man with so much information you don't seem to be up on current events. This began a few weeks after President Obama was reelected, but we felt it had become critical in the last few weeks and demanded our immediate attention. Already our fleet is being sent to the area and should arrive day after tomorrow. The carriers will handle the situation," Washington noted.

"The carriers? How many are here in the states?"

The small group conferred, and then Washington addressed the question. "Two nuclear carriers remain here: one in San Diego and the other in New Orleans."

"That would leave us vulnerable. Could it be?" Beau half asked himself.

The words caught General Waddle's attention.

"Another wolf!" Lipton laughed, which brought a chuckle from two of the others.

Beau's mind raced with the new information as he tried to piece together Cobra's elusive puzzle. Unrest in the Middle East was commonplace, although he thought Israel and Egypt would be a convenient distraction. It was well known Iran's hatred for Israel and the Jews, and if you added in Libya, Egypt with their Muslim Brotherhood, it was a cauldron boiling over. Cobra's words returned. And the part about the airlines being of help? The logical direction for the invasion must surely come from the south. Was that the second secret?

"Anything unusual in South America, like aircraft build-ups, or new airport installations?" Beau asked.

"You needn't worry. Constant satellite surveillance has shown no military installations. Mexico has constructed two new airports, one near Baja and the other near the Gulf of Mexico. They have quite a few commercial airliners but nothing else. Factions against the Mexican government have caused some internal unrest, but nothing our two countries can't work out. Besides, we were advised it's under control," Lipton said.

Airliners! The word started Beau's mind spinning as he again recalled Cobra's words. "Are the airports operational?"

"No. Why do you ask?"

"With all the airliners at the two airports, why aren't they open for business?"

For a moment the room was silent. Then Copeland spoke. "This is ridiculous. There are some military aircraft at those installations, but they are old and Mexico is planning a New Year's celebration with them. We have good working relations with Mexico."

Beau snickered, "You mean like the Fast and Furious you gave to the Mexican drug cartels? You couldn't even track those weapons!"

General Waddle could hardly suppress a smile.

"Enough," Lipton barked as she tried to wave Beau's words away. "Your statements could hurt NAFTA and ruin decades of work for our business enterprises."

"Are you sure? Caesar thought he had a good working relationship with Brutus," said Beau. "Sir, with all due respect, I suggest you take all the satellite photographs and examine them to see if military aircraft are camouflaged."

General Waddle interrupted. "Excuse me, if you will." He moved to the end of the civilian review board, picked up his briefcase, placed it on the table, clicked both snaps, and reached inside. "I have recent photographs of those airports here. If you don't mind, I would like to let Commander Gex take a look. Maybe he can spot something we missed."

The control in his voice brought a positive response from Sarah Lipton and the others. A few moments later General Waddle found the photographs and handed them to Beau. All watched and waited while he scrutinized the photos. Even the painter at the back of the room stopped. Beau hesitated and glanced around, spying the non-military person who had stopped painting. The worker made him feel uneasy throughout the questioning.

At the far end of the room the Mexican laborer had worked diligently painting the wall during the entire questioning. As all eyes turned on him he started working again. Dressed in old coveralls and leather boots, he painted awkwardly. His brush dripped and his strokes were not smooth and even. The paint ran in spots along the wall.

"What's he doing here?" asked Beau, pointing to the painter.

"You have a problem with civilian workers?" Lipton asked. "There are no secrets in this meeting."

Copeland snickered. "That's why we use a civilian review board. Too many unnecessary secrets with the military. After all, what can a painter do?"

A few of the board members chuckled. So did Judge Medina. He stood. "Hey you, the painter," he said in clear English. No response came so Medina called again in Spanish.

This time the man turned around and faced the judge. "Si," he said and nodded his head. He had clean-cut features, a finely trimmed mustache set in a square jaw, and clear skin. The thin nose was offset in the center where it had once been broken. Yet the eyes were those of a man of knowledge and not of a common laborer.

"What is your name? Do you understand English?" asked Judge Medina. No response. The judge repeated the question in Spanish.

"Me llamo Juan. No hablo Ingles," said the painter with a shrug of his shoulders.

Again the judge spoke in Spanish telling the man to continue his work. "I wouldn't worry," he said directly to General Waddle. Confidently he added, "He obviously doesn't understand English."

Beau continued scanning the images of the photographs. Only a half dozen airliners rested near the many large hangars. All the doors were closed. Heavy equipment surrounded each hangar. The runways were filled with tire marks from a well-traveled airport. He shrugged his shoulders.

"I'm not sure. I don't think I see anything. Maybe if I could see a series of timed photos?"

"I see no reason for that. Surely if there were to be an invasion the size you describe, there would be many more formidable aircraft other than airliners," Copeland blurted.

Lipton waved her hands. "Enough. I believe we can conclude this meeting. Commander, we know a lot more now than we did at Pearl Harbor. Something on such a grand scale could not possibly escape our intelligence."

"What the hell do you expect? You think they intend to advertise in the newspaper?"

"That's all, Commander! We will check into your story when time permits. As to the matter of your resignation, we will not accept it until you conclude your present tour. You are dismissed."

Beau watched as the five stood and gathered their papers before they filed from the room. He sighed and shook his head. The five standing before him controlled the destiny of the United States. Beau looked at the two on each side of Lipton and for a moment saw the Four Horsemen of the Apocalypse: War, Death, Pestilence, and Famine. For the first time, as he peered at Sarah Lipton, he understood that the Four Horsemen always had a leader. Throughout time the "Four Horsemen of the Apocalypse" had been led. And usually a politician of some kind led them. The fifth Horseman was Greed! Greed left a trail for the other four to follow and devour in her wake!

As the *Five Horsemen* walked away, Beau knew men in history had stood in his position, warning their countries of impending doom, only to be ignored. Even the mighty Roman Empire had fallen to its own glut and expansion. Just as the Romans had spread their conquest to the known limits of their world, the United States did the same, deeming themselves the policemen of the world. In reality, they were spread so thin across every continent and ocean, they had exposed their backside. He knew it was only a matter of time before someone would deliver a punch to cripple the United States.

General Waddle slipped the photos in his briefcase and walked over to Beau. "You really believe it will happen, don't you?"

The two were eye-to-eye. "Not if, but when, Sir."

General Waddle nodded understanding. "Commander, I'll do what I can." They shook hands and the general addressed Garrett. "Take care of the boy. His story has merit and is at least worth checking. That is unofficial. Understand?" Both men confirmed with a nod. General Waddle added, "I'm leaving after your test flight tomorrow. I'll see what I can do." He and the other general turned and walked from the room.

Garrett slapped Beau hard on the shoulder. "You've done all you can do for now. We'll try later. Right now I want to introduce you to the rest of the group."

"Our leaders are relying too much on the *Aurora Project*," Beau mumbled. Outside the building, they continued discussing the meeting and planned their strategy to get the information to men in higher authority. As they crossed an open grassy area, three F-14 Tomcats and an old F-4 Phantom thundered in from the bay. Beau turned his eyes skyward, shading them with his hand while he watched.

The two men came to a decorative brick building. They found their way to the demonstration and entered the dark auditorium. Ruben stood on the stage talking. He pointed to a screen and addressed a gathering of pilots, explaining the activities of the advanced fighter lessons and what was expected of them in the flying classes of Red Flag and Fightertown U.S.A. The demonstration film was coming to an end.

"Air warfare has progressed tremendously since the First World War nearly one-hundred years ago where the Spade was introduced. The Second World War brought such aircraft as the P-40 Warhawk and the P-38 Lightning. The most advanced were the British Spitfire and the American P-51 Mustang. Even today, the Mustang holds the air speed record for a prop. The P-51 Mustang brought Germany to its knees. The F-86 Sabre jet's design was based on the Mustang." He tapped the screen. "Today, we have the most sophisticated and advanced methods to accomplish aerial combat: the F-14, F-16, and the F-18. The days of the P-51 Mustang are gone."

What Ruben failed to say was that for more than thirty years no advances had occurred in the design of any aircraft. The tape flickered and the film ended. Instantly, the lights came on. Ruben spread his legs and put his hands behind his back.

"Many of you may soon have the chance to fly such aircraft. Gentlemen, are there any questions?" He waited but there were none. "Dismissed."

Ruben grinned broadly when he saw Ted and Beau at the entrance. He motioned them to the side of the small stage where Garrett introduced

Beau to the other men in the group. In uniform it was hard to notice any of the differences Ruben mentioned. Only three were at the training session, while the others were busy with duties or on leave in town.

Admiral Garrett introduced Beau to Lieutenant Commander Mark "Fitz" Fitzhenry. Slightly under six feet, Fitzhenry at first appeared to Beau to be just a scrawny young kid, but the firmness of his handshake made those thoughts disappear. His face was so youthful, one could tell he almost never needed to shave. Fitz had a hungry, eager desire in his brown eyes. At twenty-four he was the youngest of the group. Flying a jet was his childhood dream. The kid from Tennessee had everything it took.

"Commander," said Fitzhenry as he released Beau's hand. "Heard a lot about you. I sure look forward to flying with you."

Beau nodded. "Lieutenant. I'm sure the opportunity to fly will soon present itself." Then he took the Aussie's hand.

"G'day Commander Gex. Major Jonathan Kippurn Mulholland," said Major Mulholland and then with a twinkle in his eyes added, "My mates just call me Kipp." The wrinkles around his eyes revealed his age but they also showed his strength and experience. For Beau, Kipp was a pleasant break from the norm.

"All right, Kipp," he said smiling slightly. Grey, frizzy hair protruding from beneath his cap indicated his relative age. Friendly and outgoing, Mulholland just didn't fit in as a pilot, but his credentials as an Australian flyer were outstanding. Otherwise, he would not be attached to such an elite group. Over forty, Mulholland was older than most active fighter pilots. His youth was found in his enthusiasm.

"Are ya as wild as they say?" Mulholland asked. "Hope so, mate. Could make it a crazy party."

"Don't believe all the stories you've heard."

Marix clicked to attention and extended his hand; he seemed to squeeze intentionally hard which Beau reciprocated in like fashion. Marix was a few inches taller, with striking features and thick red-brown hair, a stately nose and stabbing brown eyes.

"Colonel Michael Marix," he snapped with authority, still continuing the overly firm grip. "Commander Gex." The last words added were with what seemed a tone of sarcasm, yet he pronounced the name perfectly. Both men eyed each other as Marix studied Gex intently.

"Colonel," said Beau just as firmly. This was no time for conflict, nor a time to back down. Maybe Marix didn't like his reputation; maybe it was his way of asserting power. Soon he would be in West Texas with his brothers and their home, Big Rock, and none of this would matter. "Hey, we've got to cut out," said Ruben, stepping between the two men, intentionally breaking them apart. "Sully and BJ are waiting." He took Beau and Admiral Garrett outside, leaving the others behind. They found Commander

Thomas "Sully" Sullivan and Lieutenant Commander Jack "BJ" Warren waiting.

The black officer, Jack Warren, was the first Beau exchanged warm greetings with. Slightly taller than Beau, he was extremely muscular. Dressed in a white tank top, sandals, and rainbow-colored baggy shorts, he grinned as his shaved head glistened in the sun. Dark sunglasses shaded his eyes. When Ruben, Beau, and BJ first met at flight training school, Ruben had started calling him Black Jack. Eventually everyone started calling him BJ, but the name Black Jack stuck, becoming his call sign.

"BJ, you black sumbitch," mumbled Beau. "How are you?"

Speaking in the most eloquent Bostonian accent, something most did not expect from such a rugged man as Warren, he replied in mock seriousness, "It feels rather good to once again be in the fine company of such a notorious bandit as you."

Beau turned to greet his old high school friend, Sully. "Good 'ol Sully. Ya still look like you did in high school. You doing plastic surgery?" Beau hadn't seen Sully in five years and he hadn't changed a bit. They had all attacked Afghanistan and Iraq together: Sully, BJ, Ruben, Jimmy, and himself. Only Jimmy Galloway was missing from the original bunch.

"Hell no. It's my Italian blood," Sullivan beamed.

"How's Natasha?" Beau asked.

"The little wife is just fine," he said.

Sully had met Natasha on a trip to the Ukraine just after the China-Taiwan incident in 2003. "Little wife" was a joke as Natasha was taller than him, standing in at nearly five-feet eleven inches with long blond hair and velvet blue eyes. She was an excellent athlete and runner and was capable of outrunning half the men in the group.

"Beau," interrupted Ruben. "The gang is going to the Island. You going with us?" The Island was Padre Island, the eighty-eight mile-long barrier skirting the coast of Texas from Corpus Christi to Brownsville at the mouth of the Rio Grande River.

"I'd love to, but I need to get some wheels first," he said. The comment met with a chorus of laughter from all.

"What's so funny?" Beau asked.

"Come with me," said Garrett, a big smile plastered on his face. "I have something to show you."

Ted led Beau and his three friends across the parking area, near the bluff overlooking the bay. They continued along a path past rows of tall palm trees and around a concrete block building where they startled a dozen seagulls, sending them into flight squawking. The seagulls were not nearly as surprised as Beau. Before him, in all its glorious wonder, shining bright in its black enamel paint, was his old '63 Corvette.

"Damn," Beau gasped. "How'd ya find it?" He rubbed the glossy black car with loving wonder, peered through the window, and checked the interior.

"Didn't find it," said Garrett. "I bought it at that God-awful mess our government called an auction." He laughed. "Actually, I made a pretty good deal on it and it paid your back taxes."

"It looks terrific."

Garrett waved his hand in the direction of Beau's three friends. "The boys deserve the credit; they did all the work."

"Here, catch," said Ruben, as he threw Beau the keys. "We'll meet ya at Shanghai Pete's around 1800 hours. Don't be late. Krysti will be there."

"He hasn't met Krysti?" asked Warren. He turned to Beau. "She's a very nice woman."

Opening the door Beau slid behind the steering wheel, coming to rest in the old familiar seat. Then he put the key in the ignition. For a moment he squeezed the wood grain steering wheel slowly in his hands. He reached for the ignition and turned the key. The old car came to life instantly. The familiar rumble brought back pleasant memories. He watched the tachometer resting on the dashboard above the radio respond to the slightest movement of his foot.

Garrett extended his hand and said, "There are things I have to take care of. You enjoy the boys tonight and I'll see you in the morning."

"I don't know what to say."

"Forget it. Your eyes have said it all." Garrett chuckled and with those words he spun about and walked away. Beau closed the door and gazed at his old car.

Squatting, Ruben rested his arm in the window and asked, "You want to follow us?"

"No, I need to do something first."

"You remember where to go?"

"Are you kidding?" Beau laughed. "It's hard to miss that old rundown shack they call a restaurant."

"Still serves the best seafood and margaritas," said Ruben, admonishing his friend with his finger.

"I'll be there," Beau promised. He slipped the Corvette into gear and gently engaged the clutch. He had a mission, and it was one he had to do alone. The day was humid and hot, and the old Corvette had no air conditioning, but once again Beau enjoyed the thrill of driving his old car. The Corvette responded to his every command. He drove along the shoreline and his old boyhood haunting grounds. So much had changed and yet he could still remember it all. He passed the old Baptist church behind where, as a small boy, he had caught frogs, snakes, and tadpoles from the ditch they had called "Boy's Canyon."

The Corvette rumbled to a stop in front of a flower shop. After selecting a beautiful arrangement of daisies, he resumed the trip to his predetermined destination. He turned away from the shoreline and headed inland. After a few blocks, he found the familiar street, Santa Fe, leading to Seaside Memorial Park. The old cemetery had become much too familiar to him as a boy.

The curbless streets of the cemetery were lined with friendly palms and ligustrums. Beau pulled the Corvette to a gentle stop when he recognized the spot. He walked slowly to the graves of his mother and father, stopping but for a moment. A solid hedge of ligustrums lined the back of their plots.

An empty space lay to the left of his mother's marker. Next to it were two new stones marking graves he had never seen before, but he knew they were those of his wife and son. His throat tightened as he stood next to his son's grave. He moved slowly to the empty space bordering the grave of his wife on one side and his mother on the other, a space reserved for him. Taking his cap from his head, he knelt beside the marker and laid the flowers gently before the granite stone bearing the name "Rebecca Gex."

Invisible fingers closed on his throat as he tried to speak. "Becky . . . I miss you . . . I . . . I'm sorry I lied to you. I love you. God knows I love you." Tears rolled from his eyes and he wiped them with the back of his hand. "Becky, I hope you understand, you see I . . . I have to let you go. Becky, I have to pick up the pieces and go on with my life."

The words stopped. For a few minutes Beau was motionless as a cemetery statue; then he raised himself heavily from his knees. Slowly he backed from the grave. Still facing it, he stopped and the tightness released from his throat.

"Thank you, *Angel Eyes*. I love you!" he said, somewhat relieved at finally saying what he had been waiting to say over her grave for years. It had also been a long time since he had used the words *Angel Eyes*, his pet name for his wife.

The mental burden he carried for those five torturous years was suddenly gone. Relief. Freed from the torment he had forced on himself through the guilt of the lie he told Becky, letting her believe their son was still alive as she died. Still, he felt responsible for their death. That would never change.

Once again in the Corvette he headed toward his next destination, the Naval Air Station. The drive was the first time he had relaxed and felt at peace in nearly five years. Beau wanted to get out of his uniform before meeting his friends at Shanghai Pete's.

## Chapter 4
# SHANGHAI PETE'S

On his return to the base, Beau parked the Corvette and continued to the brown, flat roofed, two story brick building, found his assigned room, and changed. It felt good to be in jeans and a shirt again. At least there would be no fear of terrorists in the restaurant. As he prepared to leave, someone knocked on his door. He answered, mildly surprised to see Mike Marix. Beau responded with a cheerful grin and handshake, and invited him into the room.

"What brings you here, Marix? Shouldn't you be gettin' yourself ready to go to Shanghai Pete's?" Beau asked. He sat down on the bed and spread his arms to his side, resting his hands on the edge of the mattress.

"We need to get some things straight," Marix said menacingly. "I'm the leader of this group. My rank gives me that authority."

"That's true and it's fine with me. I have no intention of moving in or stepping on anyone's feet. You're the leader. Stay the leader. I won't interfere. Besides, I have no intention of being here for long."

"Good! I know your record. Seems you have a tendency to leave when you are needed most."

First he was taken back at the accusation Marix aimed at him and found it hard to believe the words. Then Beau became angry. Was Mike referring to his resignation or his family? He quickly brought his emotions under control, knowing he was soon leaving the military and a confrontation would serve no purpose at all.

The intention of forcing a reaction did not work as Mike had hoped. But it wasn't his love for Krysti pushing him to confront Beau. As a child in England, growing up in a royal family, he lacked for nothing. At an early age he had always sought out other children's toys, pushing until he possessed the prized object. Once he had acquired it, he would later discard the undesirable item; each always lost its appeal after he gained possession. The quest was more important than the prize.

Mike knew he could make short work of the man before him. After all, he was an expert in the martial arts. No reaction only confirmed his assessment that Beau was a coward.

"One more thing," he said, as he stood in the open door preparing to leave. "Stay away from Krysti. She belongs to me and I shall not permit her to associate with someone like you." Then he pointed at Beau and added, "Do you understand?"

The absurdity of the situation and the half threat immediately struck Beau as humorous. He stood and faced Mike raising his palms in the air, shrugged his shoulders as though surrendering, and laughed.

"Hey, anything you say. Right, Baron?"

As he finished the words, Mike's face turned red. He slammed the door and Beau could hear him stomping down the hall of the Officers' Quarters. Beau shook his head. "Ya lost control, Marix." Pulling a blue windbreaker from the closet, he wondered what the eventual outcome would be. He was sure they'd knock heads again; he only hoped he could avoid it if at all possible.

Again in his familiar Corvette, he cranked the engine to life. The gentle motion and low rumble of the exhaust as it rolled peacefully along the highway made the incident with Marix seem meaningless. Marix was jealous and surely in love with the woman, and maybe she was in love with him. Their situation wasn't important to him. After all, he was going to see his friends, and interfering with Marix was the furthest thing from his mind. Besides, in a few more weeks he would be in Big Bend with his brothers and the problems would be far away and forgotten. He hung his elbow out the window, his old car like a soothing tonic on his nerves. Nothing mattered, and again his thoughts filled with Ruben and the others.

Across the bridge on Padre Island he noticed the commercial construction and fancy condominiums lining the road. When he was small his family would go to the Island, pay a dollar, and camp in the dunes, staying the weekend and sometimes never seeing anyone. Now people walked the beaches twenty-four hours a day and large motels jutted their gaudy forms into the waters of the Gulf. Beau turned right and headed south on the beach.

Fifteen miles down, the Island ceased to have the huge hotels and condominiums. Wildlife flourished and few structures were evident. Sand dunes loomed large and created a natural barrier from the sea. All the commercialism in the world could not convert the quicksand area that lay beyond. In the past he and his brothers spent many a day in dune buggies far down the island—far from any other people.

On his right he spotted what appeared to be an old pirate vessel. It was Shanghai Pete's Bar and Restaurant. The only change, from the way he remembered it, were the new neon lights across the front of the old building. Once isolated and the only structure for miles, it was now surrounded with a souvenir shop to the left side and a surfboard rental shop to the right. Shanghai Pete's still remained. It was one of the only structures on the island to survive Hurricane Carla in sixty-one. On each side of the entrance was a cannon from some long-gone Spanish galleon that had gallantly sailed the coast of Texas centuries before.

Beau parked his car next to Ruben's van. Next to it was a large four-wheel drive truck, with an empty trailer attached. He recognized the outdated bright red '96 Ford. It belonged to his three brothers: Brook, Jack, and Danny. Before he entered Shanghai Pete's, he paused a moment and watched as night settled on the island. A brisk Gulf breeze brought in wave after wave, only to see each melt away on the beach. The sand dunes turned to gold as the disappearing rays of the sun settled down to rest for another night. The stars slowly chased away the sun, taking their rightful place in the darkening sky.

The old, partially rotted wood doors creaked on their rusty hinges when Beau entered the bar portion of Shanghai Pete's. He knew the others would be ordering dinner on the deck behind the bar. For a moment he watched the people. Beach bums, business people, sailors and pilots frequented the popular getaway on Padre Island. Three slovenly, dirty men had gained control at one end of the bar near where a long hall led to the restrooms and telephones. The end of the hall opened to a large room used to store supplies and drinks for the patrons. The other end of the bar led to the back and the dining area.

Near a drunken stupor, the three men were well on their way to completing the task as they bellowed for more. The apparent leader of the trio created the most noise. Mauro Haun was a big man and dwarfed Beau, not only in height, but also in size. He easily weighed over 300 pounds. The pants that sagged around his rear end exposed a large portion of his buttocks. His sleeveless shirt was torn and dirty. The long, black thinning hair was greasy, and the oily skin of his unshaven face glistened in the dim light. Bushy eyebrows partially obscured the bloodshot bulbous eyes.

Leaning his back on the bar, the big man scanned the area eager for some kind of excitement. The rotund belly hid the huge belt buckle. A barmaid passed too close to the three and paid the price as she was pinched on the rear.

"Hey girlie! You wanna spend night wit' ol' Haun?" roared the fat man to his own delight. Rapidly he gulped the remains of his drink, and then ordered another round for his two friends and a bottle of wine for himself.

Of the three, he was the cleanest and best dressed. When the wine arrived, Haun turned it straight up and chugged it like water.

Beau gave them only a casual glance and continued to where his friends waited patiently for his arrival. Momentarily he paused when he noticed a woman coming toward him. A small brunette, hair bouncing below her shoulders at every stride, approached the bar from the restaurant area, unaware of the three men in her path. In a direct line past Haun and his horde, Beau hesitated and waited.

Haun saw her coming and his eyes locked on his next victim. "Lookey what we got here."

The woman saw Haun, frowned, turned her head, and continued, never wavering from her path. The bear of a man caught her shoulder and spun her around to face him.

"Hey girlie! You wanna spend the night with 'ol Haun?" He demanded more than asked. He slipped his free hand behind her waist and pulled her close. She tried to push away the hand snaking around her body. "Hey Monroe, Lawrence, you want me to share with you?" Haun asked his two companions.

"Let go!" she said firmly, in a slight Latin accent, not indicating fear. As she spoke, she shoved her left hand into his face, which he caught with his right. His breath, heavy with cigarettes and wine, hit her full in the face, making her turn her head in disgust. Haun's eyes filled with impatient anticipation of his wanton pleasures. The same evil eyes suddenly filled with pain. A groan mixed with suffering and shock came from his lips. The arm behind her waist jerked away, and Haun released her.

When the small woman saw this, she also felt the gentle but firm pressure of another arm. She was ready to retaliate against the new intruder, but as she turned to meet this new antagonist, she found piercing blue eyes, a smile, and a wink. She stopped and decided to wait. He was definitely the lesser of two evils.

The vice-like grip remained on Haun's wrist as Beau pulled the auburn beauty behind him. "Sorry I'm late. Hey Haun, thanks for watching my girl. I can manage now," he said, releasing Haun's wrist and backing away from the surprised trio of drunks.

They walked a few feet away when Beau asked, "Are you okay?"

"I'm fine," she said, sticking her chin in the air and again the slight accent was evident. A reddish-brown, almost auburn red mane of natural bouncing curls surrounded the striking green eyes, which were accented with long dark eyelashes and set in a round olive complexion. The small mouth and thin lips were clenched tightly. She was well-proportioned and barely over five feet in height. Some curls fell across her face and she brushed them back. The beautiful auburn hair radiated a fiery personality that bolstered her independence.

Entranced with her beauty, Beau noted she was small and petite like Ruben's wife. If only Sunday could see her, he thought with a smile.

"What are you grinning about? I want you to know I can take care of myself," she said, sticking her straight slender nose up in the air.

"I could tell," Beau said and chuckled half aloud.

She dropped her head and looked away as she tried to regain her composure but failed to do so. "Stop," she said, touching his arm as she spoke. Trying to maintain a serious demeanor she said, "It's not funny." Then she too burst out laughing and squeezed his arm.

Momentarily he gained control. "Where were you headed?"

She pointed to the phones. "I was about to call my father to see if he and my son are back at the hotel."

Beau noticed the accent almost completely gone when the anger dissipated. "Well then, let's go call them," he said, moving her in the direction of the phone.

"You don't need to bother."

"It's really no problem. Are you with someone?"

"Yes, I'm with some of my friends in the back."

Beau was sorry to hear that. "Make your call and I'll walk you to them."

She started dialing the numbers, and then she turned to him. "You needn't wait."

"My friends have waited a long time; a few more minutes won't hurt."

Their conversation was interrupted when her father answered. Beau could tell when she was talking to her son, and heard her promise they would all spend the evening on the beach. All the while she talked, she surveyed Beau with her entrancing green eyes. Then she put the receiver back on the wall. On the return trip past the bar, they made a wide berth of Haun and his friends.

Almost sheepishly she asked, "Are you with anybody?"

"No. My friends want to introduce me to one of their friends. She's probably short and ugly," Beau said, turning red after he had finished. "No offense, I mean—"

"What? Ugly or short?" She interrupted with a wry grin that relieved his discomfort. "I guess you want someone that is tall with long legs and blond hair. Doesn't every man? I'm sure if I could grow a foot you'd be happier." Then she laughed at the situation in which Beau had placed himself.

"You are an exception. You're very pretty and your hair—it's . . . beautiful. No one could go wrong being with you," Beau said with all sincerity, feeling the sudden warmth creeping up his face as he stumbled over his words.

"Well thank you," she said. "Tonight I have a blind date. Nothing worse than a blind date. But I promised. He's probably never had kids and won't understand my situation."

"If he doesn't like kids you sure don't want to be around him," Beau added, a little saddened she was with a date.

"You must have kids."

"A son," Beau responded. He changed the subject. "What is your name?" he asked as they stepped through the doorway into the restaurant at the rear.

"Krystina Socorro."

Instantly Beau spotted Ruben and waved. "I see my friends."

"So do I," she said sadly. "Now to meet this pilot my friend keeps talking about."

"Pilot? Krystina, are you a doctor?" Beau asked, already guessing the answer.

"Yes, I am. You're not Beau?" she quizzed.

"Of course, Krystina—Krysti!" This time they both laughed and failed to notice their friends approaching.

Ruben scratched the back of his head. "Do you know each other?"

For a moment they composed themselves, looked at each other and answered simultaneously, "Yes." Again they started laughing. Sunday grabbed Beau about the neck and squeezed till he thought it might break. Everyone turned to watch as she and then Sully's wife, Natasha, stole kisses.

Beau said, "Hell Sunday, I think you're prettier than I remember."

She blushed and acted angry. "You shouldn't have stayed away so long. And I'm still mad you didn't write more."

Beau didn't answer; instead he just pointed to her round stomach. "Is that what I think it is?"

"Yes, I'm pregnant." She blushed. "Due in—"

Beau interrupted. "Ruben, why didn't you tell me?"

"Are you crazy Beau?" she snapped. "He was so excited about you coming back it was all he talked about when he found out. Now maybe we can get back to normal." Maria, or Sunday, as her close friends called her, was only four feet eleven and for her size she had always managed to keep trim, except for her present condition. She still cut her black hair short. High cheekbones, set in an olive complexion with a thin straight nose, only accentuated her round black eyes.

"Come on you two, let's go eat," begged Ruben. They walked to where the others waited. Ruben pulled a chair away from an unoccupied table and placed it at one end for Beau. To his right sat Krysti, next to her Sully, then Natasha and Deberg. On Beau's left was Ruben and beside him Sunday, then Fitz, Pickett and Kipp. At the end of the tables, facing Beau, Warren sipped on a margarita. Ruben introduced Beau to Pickett and Deberg.

This was the first time Beau had met the two men, and the reception from both was warm and friendly. Pickett had no accent and gave no indication of being from Canada. His eyes were the first thing Beau noticed. A vertical slit in his pupils gave him a strange appearance and yet cast the warmth of a pet cat.

"It's so good to have you back," said Natasha, with a slight Russian accent. She had worked as a model after coming to the United States and was slightly taller than her husband, Thomas. Her silky blond hair hung to the middle of her back, and she still looked like she could adorn the front page of any fashion magazine.

"I saw my brothers' truck outside. Where are they?" Beau asked.

Warren spoke. "They took the buggies down the beach. They had already eaten. Said they'd meet us later."

"They never were much for sitting around," Beau said, nodding his head. From the shadows at the other end of the restaurant a pair of angry eyes watched the group. Haun had followed Beau and was prepared to force him into a rematch but thought better when he observed the men at his table. Haun and his two comrades would wait for a better opportunity.

Ruben poked Beau. "Did you know you're being observed?"

Nonchalantly, Beau sipped his drink. "Yeah, ya ever see three more capable gentlemen?"

"You been causing more trouble?" asked Ruben. Both laughed.

Beau changed the direction of the conversation. "Where are the others?"

"Dean is staying at the barracks. James, and Marix will meet us on the beach in a few hours." Then he bent over to whisper in Beau's ear so no one else could hear. "Marix is not too happy about us introducing you to Krysti."

"I know. He came to my room."

"He what? Well, tough shit," Ruben snapped. Then he stood erect and lifted his almost empty margarita: "To the Red Baron." All the men laughed and raised their glasses.

Krysti was confused and leaned toward Beau. "Who is the Red Baron?"

"Uhhh . . ." Beau almost choked on his drink. "You see, all the pilots get a call sign when they fly. It's like a nickname. Marix is called the Red Baron."

Mulholland heard and held his glass high. "Aye, mate, that he is."

Everyone was listening closely now, as Beau tried to evade the issue. "Take me, for instance. They call me Mongoose. Hey, you guys sound off."

Sully stood. "Flipper." It was a name Ruben had coined for Sully when he flipped two T-38 trainers in less than a week. Both accidents had been during bad weather and were judged unavoidable. Still, he had been stuck with the name.

"Grey Ghost," said Mulholland, a name he had received for his curly, gray hair and his age, since he was older than the average fighter pilot.

"Catman," said Pickett pointing to his face. Slits instead of round pupils filled both eyes making them look more like cat eyes.

Warren chuckled. "Black Jack. That's why they call me BJ."

"Boink," said Deberg.

"Boink?" said Krysti.

Deberg rolled his eyes. "Bumped a plane during flight and kinda bent the nose on my craft." Fitzhenry shrugged his shoulders. "I don't have one."

"Don't worry," said Ruben. "We'll find one for you."

Beau faced Krysti. "You can count on it. Ruben picked mine, BJ's, and Sully's."

"And the Red Baron's," said Ruben again, bringing a roar of laughter.

"What's so funny?" Krysti asked.

"Marix doesn't like it," said Sullivan.

"I think it's cute," she said, and again the men chuckled.

Beau turned to her. "Don't tell him you think it's cute. He's probably sensitive over the name."

"Why are you called Mongoose?" she asked.

But Ruben answered. "When we raced his Corvette against those Shelby Cobras and beat them I would call him the Cobra killer. Well, one Saturday morning when I was watching cartoons—"

Now Beau interrupted. "You notice he said when he was watching cartoons."

They all laughed and Krysti said, "I think that's sweet."

Ruben shrugged his shoulders. "I was practicing for when I have a little boy." He continued. "Anyway, I saw a cartoon show about a little mongoose called Rikki-Tikki-Tavi and recorded it."

"Rudyard Kipling, you know," Sunday noted. "A classic."

"Anyway," said Ruben, "I had that cartoon of the mongoose painted on the side of Beau's plane in *Operation Iraqi Freedom*."

"Shoulda been *Operation Iraqi Liberation*," Sully said with a chuckle. "Then the letters could have stood for what that war was really about."

Warren laughed. "OIL."

Natasha interrupted. "President Bush had to free the people of Iraq."

"Maybe," said Ruben, and then he added, "but the people of Iraq would have been a lot safer if they had had an oil well in their backyards."

BJ snickered. "Al Gharib was not freedom; it was torture."

With a wicked grin Ruben added, "It wasn't torture, it was just new management."

"They were enemy combatants," snapped Pick.

Shaking his head, Beau said, "We were supposed to be above torture. The war didn't bring Iraq up to our country's lofty expectations but rather we came down to their level."

Anger flashed in her words as Natasha said, "Remember what they did to New York. President Bush was right in what he did against terrorism."

Warren chimed in. "Iraq didn't do New York. Bush declared war against terrorism. You don't declare war against a word."

Ruben quickly added, "Yeah, what about Iran and North Korea, Bush's axis of evil?"

Warren snickered, "Iran. We should have known nothing would happen to them. Halliburton was doing too much work for them."

A few chuckled; Natasha rolled her eyes and groaned. "Someone had to pay for the thousands of Americans that died in New York."

"Natasha is right," said Krysti.

"Iraq was revenge not justice," added Beau. "If Iraq was for New York then shouldn't we have been flying up and down America's interstate highway blowing away yellow Ryder trucks for what Timothy McVeigh did?"

Natasha frowned, while Warren and Sunday chuckled.

Ruben asked, "So who pays for the thousands of American lives lost in Iraq?"

Sully nodded. "Not who pays, but who made the money? We may have freed the people, but Halliburton, Rumsfeld, and Cheney really protected the oil wells. How long were we there before Halliburton got that big paycheck?"

"About two months," said Ruben. "And they were paid a half a billion."

"Halliburton was the best qualified," said Deberg.

"Seven billion for the no-bid work in Iraq? That's a lot of qualified. God knows how much they made away with," Warren noted.

"A seventy-five million dollar bonus for the good work," said Ruben. He chuckled and added, "You know a good deal like forty-five dollars for a case of cokes."

"A few bad apples don't make Halliburton evil," said Pickett defensively.

"With Halliburton the whole crate of apples was bad," said Warren shaking his head. Ruben and Beau smiled.

"I wonder how much they got from the Iraqi oil?" Sunday wondered more than asked.

"A small fortune," said Sully sadly. "Cheney wouldn't have sent Halliburton unless they were going to make a bundle."

"Hey mate, didn't Cheney run Halliburton?"

"Yes, that was Cheney," Krysti confirmed.

The curiosity was evident in Kipp's face. "I thought Halliburton was fined for accounting practices when Cheney was there."

Ruben laughed. "Bingo, you won the game, Kipp."

"Sure makes you wonder about the people we elect," said Beau.

"We elected?" snickered Ruben. "You mean big business elected." He rolled his eyes, "I think there were more chads in the election than just Florida."

"I think Bush was sincere," Natasha continued in the former president's behalf.

Warren nodded, "Bush got sucked in by his cronies."

Nodding, Kipp added, "It was said down under that the oil was the real reason."

"It's like they couldn't wait to try the new weapons we had developed," Ruben said.

"Yeah, and we were part of those that tested them," Sully added.

"I think Bush did a good job," said Krysti.

"So do I," Natasha added.

"Better than Gore," snickered Sunday.

"No kidding," said Ruben.

"Gore?" Then Kipp asked, "Didn't he invent the Internet?" They all broke out laughing. Warren was in serious thought about something.

"It really is sad," he said, his smile gone. "When we were in Iraq I saw a soldier on CNN all excited when he was interviewed. He said that this is what he had been training for all of his life, and he couldn't wait to use his training."

Beau took a deep breath and sighed. "Actually, we trained to be ready for war but with the hope we would never need to use it."

Ruben, Sully, and BJ nodded and Kipp said, "Aye, mate, that we do."

"Whether or not Bush did any good or not, you can't deny the fact that Rumsfeld, Cheney, and others in his cabinet, especially Karl Rove, had their own personal agendas," said Beau. "And the people weren't part of that agenda."

"Did Rove ever tell the truth?" Ruben said more than asked.

"He had to be that way for security," snapped Pickett.

"Security?" steamed Warren. "Tell that to Valerie Wilson."

"That was treason," said Ruben.

"Rove didn't commit treason," pushed Deberg.

"And there are WMD's in Iraq," quipped Sully.

"That wasn't President Bush's fault," said Natasha.

"He surrounded himself with greedy men that lied to accomplish what they wanted," said Beau. "I never understood how Rove made two war veterans like McCain and Kerry look stupid and appear like cowards after fighting for their country."

"The WMD and the Rove CIA thing with Wilson made the military lose confidence in Bush," said Sully.

"True, but what bothers me most was the men in his cabinet actually running this country, and we didn't vote for any of them," Beau noted.

"Yeah, and somewhere along the line money and oil were a big, big factor," Ruben added. Again many of them nodded.

Warren shook his head. "Rumsfeld scared me."

Krysti agreed. "He scared me a little too. He didn't seem to care about Iraq or our soldiers."

"He was not a man you would want to run a country," said Beau.

For a moment Natasha shook her head too. "It is important to trust the people running this country."

With a nod Krysti said, "I agree with Natasha."

"I know you're right, Honey," said Sully. "But they never do anything for us that will instill our trust."

"Ethics," said Ruben, smiling.

"Ethics?" Natasha asked.

Ruben continued, "Yeah, there were no ethics. The Republicans changed the ethics to accommodate their crooked friends; just look at Tom Delay."

Sully laughed. "Yeah, old Delay. Every time he did something unethical he just changed the ethics code."

"It would be nice to trust them but just look at the condition of our country now," Warren sighed.

"Goes double for me," chimed Ruben. "The CEOs of America did their share to create this situation."

Most were nodding in agreement to Ruben's words when Krysti flared up, which also brought out more of her accent. "I lost my retirement and my father was forced to go back to work. He'll never be able to retire now."

Resentment was reflected in Warren's words. "Tyco, Global Crossing, WorldCom, and Enron were what really killed my father."

Sunday added, "It did the same for my parents. My mother had been retired only a few months when they lost everything on their stocks. She had to go back to work and died a few months later. My father died not long after her. I know the stock fraud killed her."

Looking at Sunday, Beau said, "I remember the executives saying they knew nothing and Congress would pass fraud laws, but if it was fraud why weren't they prosecuted?"

"Simple," said Ruben. All eyes turned to him as he continued, "Why do you think Martha Stewart went to jail and the others didn't?" No one ventured a guess. "She didn't contribute to Bush's re-election campaign."

A few groaned and shook their heads, while Ruben's words brought a chuckle from Beau and Warren.

"Their accountants helped," said Beau.

"Yeah, Arthur and Anderson called it creative accounting, but fraud is the real word to describe it," said Ruben. "That was about the time I figured out how to buy stock."

"Hey mate, tell me. I never figured out how."

"Neither did I," said Sully. "Tell us."

With a smile and a wave of his hand Ruben said, "First of all, see if the company you want to buy stock in has a CEO. If they do then don't buy any stock in that company."

Warren shook his head. "Ruben, they all have CEOs."

Ruben beamed. "Bingo. That's the same thing I figured out."

Sully, Beau, and Sunday laughed. Even Natasha chuckled, while Krysti and Warren nodded sadly in agreement.

Sully said, "They were traitors. All the CEOs were traitors. They should have been tried for treason for what they did."

"I don't understand how so few actually went to jail," said Beau. "And those that did go didn't stay for long."

Shaking his head Warren said, "Check the re-election campaign funds of all the politicians. I'd bet that a lot of the money the CEOs stole was deposited into many a politician's re-election fund."

Ruben could barely hold back a laugh. "Do you know what CEO means?"

Again Natasha fell into his trap. "Of course, it means Chief Executive Officer."

"Not really," said Ruben. "While Bush was president it came to mean Chief Embezzlement Officer." Sully, BJ, and Beau broke out laughing, while most of the others chuckled at Ruben's words.

"I can see Webster's definition of CEOs in a hundred years," said Ruben. All heads turned to him, and when he had their attention he finished with a wave of his hand in the air as though he were reading something: "CEOs, a group of men that undermined the security and integrity of a country once called the United States of America." Sadly none of the people at the table had an argument to his statement.

"It's kinda sad," Beau almost mumbled. "If you had a picture of the CEOs of WorldCom, Tyco, Global Crossing, and Enron along with Osama bin Laden, it would be hard to pick out which one did the most damage to the United States."

"Whew," said Warren. "That's rough."

"That's not a very nice comparison," said Natasha.

Thinking about her father, Krysti said, "Maybe not."

"I don't know," said Ruben. "Sounded fair to me. I don't think I could choose."

Turning to his wife, Sully said, "I'm sorry Natasha, but mark my words—" His voice was filled with anger. "One day those CEOs and politicians will get what they deserve, and I want to be there to see it."

"Me too," said Warren.

Thoughts of war and death filled Beau's mind. "No. You don't want to see it."

"How did all this happen?" Sunday mumbled.

"Greed!" said Beau, with a touch of sadness in his voice.

Krysti nodded but Natasha shook her head. "This is still better than my Russia."

Eye to eye with Natasha, Beau asked, "What makes you think this country is immune to what happened in Russia?" For a moment Natasha was in deep thought.

Sunday said, "When did it start? Who did it?"

"Reagan and Bush and that Savings and Loan debacle," Ruben said with conviction.

"Carter," said Warren.

"Not Carter, he didn't know what he was doing," snickered Sully.

Beau nodded. "Yeah, he might have been the only honest president in the last fifty years."

Krysti almost laughed. "You don't like our presidents."

"Just say I lack a lot of confidence in their ability to run a country."

"Both Bushes hurt us," said Ruben. "With the Savings and Loan under the father and the spending, war, and dot com collapse under the son, they almost destroyed us."

"Bush helped the economy when he lowered taxes. Interest was never lower," said Pickett.

"Pickett is right," said Deberg.

"Now we're paying for it. Look at the interest and taxes," said Ruben.

Natasha added, "President Bush created thousands of jobs."

"And most of those jobs went to India," said Sully.

"Don't forget that just before Bush left office that unemployment was the highest since the great depression of Roosevelt," said Beau.

"That wasn't President Bush's fault," said Natasha.

"I think it's time for a little history," said Warren. "When Bush got out of office in 2008 our country had been around for 232 years. The National Debt was almost eleven trillion dollars. It took 220 years to create a debt of four trillion. It took both Bushes only twelve years to add seven trillion dollars to that debt."

Natasha and Sunday were shocked and their mouth's dropped open in disbelief, but Beau, Sully and Ruben shook their heads in disgust.

"That much, really?" asked Krysti.

Sadly Warren confirmed the question with a nod of his head.

Sully added, "Don't forget Bush's son, Neil, getting a small business loan for that wildcat well."

"A real good investment," Warren said with a frown.

"That's okay Neil and Marvin Bush made it back with the help of King George, when he got their companies cream puff contracts with Iraq and China," said Warren.

Natasha frowned at Warren and said, "That is not a nice thing to call our former President."

"That's disrespectful of a former president," said Pickett.

"Truth hurts," said Warren.

With a twinkle in his eyes Ruben added, "The haves and the have nots."

"Well don't forget Clinton. He really screwed the country," Sunday argued.

Ruben put his arm around his wife. "Not really, Sugar. Clinton was too busy screwing the interns to screw the country." Sunday smiled and pushed him, while most of the others chuckled or laughed out loud.

"At least Clinton had a surplus," said Pickett.

Ruben shook his head, "There never was a surplus under Clinton."

"Tricks with words," said Sully. He looked at Warren, "Isn't that right?"

Warren nodded, took a deep breath and said, "Here is an example of how we have a surplus. The government collects two and a half trillion dollars in taxes. Congress sets a budget at two-point-nine trillion but only spends two-point-seven trillion. They're excited and tell the American people we have a two-hundred billion surplus.

Confused, Natasha shook her head, "That's wrong it's a two-hundred billion deficit."

With a nod Warren said, "Absolutely correct. It is a deficit but they try to spend all of what they don't have to match the budget thus adding more to the National debt."

"I didn't know that," said Deburg.

"Most people don't," said Warren. "But I will say that under Clinton it did get down to a deficit of sixteen billion in one year."

Sully asked but the tone of his words revealed he already knew, "And under President Bush?"

Taking a deep breath Warren said, "About six hundred billion each of the eight years he served as president. And one point five his last year."

Sully gritted his teeth, "What about the ten trillion in five years under Obama and his czars."

Ruben quipped, "Sounds more like Enron."

"Precisely," said Warren. "Might have been different if Obama hadn't stopped our energy production and cut the military. The guy was racist."

Some of the men laughed and Ruben piqued, "That sounds strange coming from a black man."

Warren shook his head, "Obama destroyed everything Martin Luther King accomplished and turned his dream into a nightmare. A compassionate man? Not Obama. If someone had told me he was the Manchurian candidate from the Muslim Brotherhood. Now that was something I could understand."

Again Sully was quick to respond, "He gave weapons to Al Qaeda in Libya, Egypt and Syria. Weapons used to kill our soldiers in Afghanistan. Friends of mine."

Krysti shook her head and mumbled, "It's not safe for Christians or Americans over there anymore."

"Israel is on its own. Obama saw to that," said Sully.

"Shoulda known he was trouble for America when he called his men czars. It means emperor. I never felt good when he did that."

"Neither did I," said Sully. "The communist bastard."

Most chimed in with nods and mumbles of confirmation.

Taking a deep breath and letting it out Beau said, "I think it all started with Kennedy."

Sully nodded and Warren said, "You are very close. Hasn't been a surplus since 1960."

Krysti also nodded in understanding. She realized they were all right. Looking down in thought she said, "In a way it was all of them."

Finally Kipp spoke. "I think the lass has the answer."

"That means there are only two problems with our government," said Ruben.

"What's that?" Beau asked.

Ruben smiled at his friend. "Democrats and Republicans." A few smiled, Sully and Warren chuckled, and the others nodded in agreement.

Almost talking to himself Beau mumbled, "We were deceived by the Republicans. I voted conservative, Republican. I expected government to be in check but Bush spent a hundred times more money on other countries than on his own."

Natasha noted, "Bush did lower taxes."

"But took it all back the next few years with the war debt," Ruben blurted out.

"Every time he turned around he was giving hundreds of millions to any country that would smile at him," Said Sully.

"And his friends didn't even need to smile. Remember we said half a billion dollars were given to Halliburton only two months after that war started," BJ added.

"But we needed experts," Natasha argued.

Then Sully asked, "But what could they have done in two months that was worth a half billion?"

"You could ask Cheney," quipped Ruben, "but he would probably claim executive privilege and refuse to answer the questions."

Beau interjected, "Remember the Army Corp of Engineers? They're trained to do those things."

Still defending the war, Natasha continued to argue. "It was to protect Iraq's oil."

BJ smirked. "They did that. What has always bothered me is the way they didn't secure the nuclear sites. If they were so concerned about Weapons of Mass Destruction, then the nuclear sites would have been the first places to secure. They were never secured until the people stole everything from those sites."

Concerned, Beau said, "The only reason not to secure a nuclear site is if you already know there really are no weapons."

Ruben said, "They managed to secure all of Iraq's wells in the first few weeks." In deep thought he added, "That war was for oil. Plain and simple." Most nodded in agreement and mumbled their concerns and thoughts.

"He gave Iraq freedom and democracy. We fought for them," snapped Pickett.

"I thought we fought terror," said Beau.

"It's not working very well," said Ruben.

Warren looked at those sitting at the table and asked, "And tell me this; why don't Saudi Arabia, Pakistan and North Korea need a democracy?"

Pickett, Deberg and Natasha had no answer for Ruben.

"I knew we were in trouble when President Bush was holding hands with the Saudi Prince.

"That's a tradition there," said Deberg. "He was using diplomacy."

"Diplomacy?" Warren belched. "Then it was a first for him."

"If holding hands is a tradition so are fair trials in America," said Sully. "So what happened in Guantanamo?"

"Enemy combatants," said Deberg. "They got what they deserved."

Beau shook his head. "If you're right then we're in real trouble."

"Just a double standard," Ruben said to Deberg. "I'm good, you're bad, and you firmly believe the opposite."

Again Natasha came to the former president's defense. "Operation Iraqi Freedom was to prevent war and stop future wars."

BJ groaned. "Dictators use the same terms for what they want."

Sully nodded and frowned at his wife Natasha. "It's called an invasion, and that's what we did."

Slightly irked Natasha said, "Saddam Hussein needed to be removed."

"You're absolutely right Natasha," said Beau. "But there are other tyrants worse than he was, but we don't invade their countries. Do you know why?"

"No."

"Because they have no oil."

"How can you say that about President Bush?" said Pickett. "He's a good Christian."

"A Christian President who established a democracy based on Islam in Iraq. There will be no democracy or freedom under Islam. Bush failed," said Warren.

Natasha and Deberg nodded in unified agreement.

Beau took a deep breath and let it out. "And that just might be the reason for our problems in America now. We've alienated the Muslims. Bush made it a religious war whether he intended to or not. Only Muslims were attacked during his two terms. No one ever won a religious war."

Defensively, Natasha said, "I think you are all wrong."

Beau nodded. "Maybe, but what BJ said about the nuclear sites is true. The site wasn't secured until after it had been vandalized. This was not the action of a president who was compelled to go to war because of Weapons of Mass Destruction. For me it only goes to prove he wasn't concerned about any weapons. Natasha, look at the facts and then you decide for yourself."

While Natasha frowned hard, Ruben nodded and said, "New Orleans showed how weak we were. The lack of action destroyed American's confidence in our government."

Deberg snapped, "Give me a break. Hurricane Katrina was not President Bush's fault."

"No not the hurricane, "interjected Warren, "But Bush's inaction. Three days after Katrina struck New Orleans Bush was still on vacation. When he finally arranged a meeting with his inept cabinet, Condoleezza Rice was too busy shopping in New York."

Ruben added, "Don't forget the play she went to."

The anger reflected on his face, "Yes and the play. Two days after the hurricane people were dying from heat and dehydration. Our President was still on vacation."

Deberg said, "The mayor of New Orleans was to blame for the deaths.

Pickett nodded to Deberg and said, "And the governor of Louisiana."

Beau shook his head, "True, but remember Bush promised if there was a terrorist strike against the United States he would respond swiftly and immediately to save Americans." He paused to look at Pickett and Deberg, "Our President did neither. Remember, Katrina was just a storm. It wasn't even an act of terror. All he accomplished was to let the world see our weakness."

"President Bush did help in New Orleans," said Natasha.

"Too little, too late," said Warren. "Some of my friends died in that storm and they didn't drown."

Natasha snipped. "Everyone blames Bush because a Bush hating media and Democratic Party would rather see the whole world blow up than lose their power."

"Someone must monitor our leaders. Not all of them are innocent," said Krysti.

Warren shook his head. "Wait a minute, Natasha. You mean if I'm a Democrat and didn't like Bush the world is going to blow-up?"

"Then if you're a Christian you should be happy the world is going to blow-up," chuckled Ruben. All eyes turned to him. "That is called Armageddon or the end of days. Rejoice for the end is near."

"Ruben," said Sunday, giving him a serious little shove.

"I'm not kidding Ruben," said Natasha.

"Democrats are a major part of the problem," said Pickett.

"And the Republicans the other part of the problem," said Sully.

"Bush and Paulson gave away one and a half trillion to companies and Obama finished us off when he gave away more than eight trillion during his four years. All for their big company buddies," said Warren.

"Welfare for the wealthy may well have destroyed our country. You don't reward incompetence with billions of dollars," Beau sighed

With anger in his voice, Sully said, "They should have gone to jail."

Ruben snickered, "I don't know why we searched for enemy combatants when we had five hundred and thirty-five of them in Congress."

Beau nodded in agreement while Warren chuckled.

Sully smiled, "Yeah, let me water-board Cheney and Rove."

Beau groaned, "Obama was worse giving away trillions each year. What do we have now? How many are on welfare and non-producing?"

And angry they aren't getting more freebies," said Sully.

"More than half or all Americans capable of working are on some type of welfare," said Ruben.

Firmly Beau looked at the others as he said, "No country can survive when half the people don't work."

"And we're still giving billions in aid to those that hate us," groaned Sully.

"Back to school and Common Sense 101," laughed Ruben.

"Yeah, and Obama's records are still sealed," said Warren.

Sully added, "I had two friends with sealed records. One killed two girls and the robbed banks. I wonder what Obama did."

"I bet he flunked college," said Warren.

"I heard he got a loan as a foreign student and it was paid by the Saudi Prince," snickered Ruben.

"Whatever it was he has something to hide and it was illegal," said Sully.

Natasha frowned but Pickett and Deberg appeared rather perturbed at the conversation.

Ruben quickly changed the heated debate with a shrug and a laugh. "Well, the war did accomplish one thing."

"What was that?" Natasha asked.

Smiling Ruben said, "It pissed the world off at us, and they sure are enjoying their revenge now."

The conversation continued as the group bantered back and forth on political issues. Eventually they debated taxes, but almost all agreed that higher taxes under President Obama had failed to bring the National Debt down, and all wanted to know where fifteen trillion dollars had gone under Bush and Obama. The *Tax Cut of 2003* had lasted only a few years before the deficit spiraled out of control with the enormous added expenses of war and preventing terrorists from attacking. In 2008 Congress failed to bring about a reduction in the National Debt. Just more pork-barreling laws and more added to an unfixable debt. The economy and many broken promises didn't change anything for the forty-five million Americans on welfare elected Obama for a second term, but it didn't matter. It was too late. The American people, like most of the small group of friends discussing the problems, bore alarming anger toward politicians and taxes as a whole. Very few had faith in Obama. He had accomplished nothing but debt and the second term had started the same way, with him blaming Bush and the Republicans for his failure in his first term.

Eventually the talk at the table came around to the new Middle East crisis that never seemed to end, and the American troops again sent to police the situation. The Muslim Brotherhood was making advances beyond belief. The conversation finally turned into a cozy fire, marshmallows, and a night on Padre Island's beach. With unusually warm weather for December the small group had decided to spend the evening closer to the water. It would be the last opportunity, as a cold front was expected to move through later that night.

During the conversation, Beau learned Krysti would accompany them as the team doctor, and for the first time he didn't seem to mind he'd be with the team for the next few months. They ordered another round of margaritas and made plans for the evening. With the meal finished and the pitcher of drinks drained, they agreed to rendezvous farther down the beach. Beau happily volunteered to take Krysti, but first they would get her son, Justin.

From the shadows, Haun and his men watched their departure closely, seeking an opportunity for revenge.

Outside, the night air began to cool, but was still warm enough for them to spend a pleasant evening on the beach. The calm water of the gulf glistened in the brilliant moonlight. Ruben would find a spot, start a fire, and wait for the others to arrive. Only Deberg would not go as he had a priority female engagement.

"Wait, I left my purse near that telephone when I called my son," said Krysti. "I'll be just a second."

"No," said Beau remembering the three men still inside. "You wait here and I'll get the purse." Without waiting for an answer, Beau returned to where he first met her. He saw the three men, and aimed for the long and wide hall leading to the telephone. A savage grin lit Haun's face.

Beau was relieved when he found the purse next to the telephone. He retrieved it, but when he turned to leave he found Haun and his two friends, Monroe and Lawrence, blocking his path. The only way out was through the three men. Haun had no intention of letting him pass. He had decided to punish the man responsible for his embarrassment.

Drunk earlier, he had sobered immensely during the last few hours. He laughed when he confronted Beau, and slobbered as he spoke.

"You think you're pretty tough. Whatcha gonna do now, boy?" Lawrence and Monroe slid to each side of the wide hall.

"Doesn't look like you left me much of a choice," Beau said, a slight grin crossing his face. "Well Porky, what are you and your sidekicks gonna do? I'm in a hurry and the lady needs her purse."

Livid with anger, Haun pulled his knife and charged the defenseless figure before him. Beau instinctively spread his legs, bent his knees slightly, gently tossed the purse aside, and prepared for Haun's onslaught while he watched the other two from the corner of his eye. Deftly he caught the plunging knife hand and delivered a crippling blow to Haun's huge stomach. Simultaneously, he caught Lawrence with a foot to the groin and sent him stumbling back. Beau wrenched the knife hand up and behind Haun's back, forcing him to drop the blade harmlessly to the floor. With satisfaction, he twisted the brute's arm.

Ruben and Kipp arrived on the scene in time to see Beau in complete control of the situation. Mulholland started to help his friend, but Ruben restrained him. He then glanced casually about, found an open case of beer, grabbed the long neck of a full bottle, shrugged his shoulders in Kipp's direction, and continued watching.

Monroe hesitated, and then mounted his charge, but it was too late. Beau swung, his fist connected, momentarily staggering the man. Again

Beau turned his attention to Haun, bringing his knee up into his midsection, and then releasing his arm. As the brute fell to his knees, Beau brought his left fist down hard into the thick bulbous nose, breaking it. Spinning counter-clockwise, Beau caught Monroe in the chest with his left foot, knocking him against the wall. Unconscious, Monroe slid limply down to the floor.

Lawrence, partially recovered, started to move forward when a glass bottle shattered over his head. He tumbled to the floor unconscious. Ruben dropped the remaining neck of the bottle and dusted his hands. As they approached, Beau retrieved the purse from the corner and inspected it.

"Thought you might need some help," said Ruben. "Hey, did you hurt your hand?"

"Nope," said Beau casting an almost casual glance around the hall. "Sure hope I didn't mess up Krysti's bag. Hell of a thing to do, meet a girl and ruin her purse."

Alerted to the noise, the manager arrived on the scene with a double-barreled shotgun. "What the hell is going on?" he asked. Instantly Kipp and Ruben raised their hands, while Beau pointed to the three men lying on the floor.

"Sorry for the trouble," he said, reaching for the billfold in his back pocket. "I'm sure willing to pay for any damages."

The manager looked around the small storage area, saw Haun and his two men, and then lowered the rifle. "Goddamn that Haun. I swear he gets into more shit. Well, doesn't seem to be any damage except to those who deserved it. Just glad he didn't do it in the bar this time. Forget the money, but don't come back for a while 'cause ol' Haun carries a grudge. First time I seen anyone beat the shit out of him like this. He's gonna be real pissed."

"Thanks," Beau and Ruben chimed in.

The manager waved his hand. "Haun has had it coming for a long time. Now get the hell outta here."

As they made a hasty exit from Shanghai Pete's, Mulholland shook his head and said, "Mate, I wouldn't have believed it if I hadn't seen it. I thought you might need help. Guess I was wrong."

"You never can tell. Thanks anyway ," Beau said. "I was just lucky they didn't know how to fight. Come on, let's go."

"Just like old times," said Ruben.

Beau laughed. "It's beginning to feel like it. You know, I could use help sometimes."

"Aw, hell," snickered Ruben. "I knew you were okay."

They left the incapacitated trio behind in the secluded hallway. Even the manager returned to the bar, leaving the three alone.

Rising to his knees, Haun held his stomach with one hand and his face with the other, and groaned from the excruciating pain. His lips were cut and bleeding, his nose was broken and dripping blood. Monroe, leaning against the wall, made no movements. Lawrence lay in a fetal position clutching his groin and his head. Shards of glass protruded from his scalp.

Surveying the situation, Haun blinked his eyes in disbelief and anger. "One day we will meet again. The woman will pay for this. I swear it!" Then a sudden stab of pain forced him on his side.

* * *

Outside, the darkening skies cut the heat, but the early evening gulf breeze was still warm and muggy. Along the water's edge, two large sand crabs were locked in mortal combat over a morsel of food stolen from Shanghai Pete's.

Beau gave Krysti her purse. "I'm sorry for the trouble," she said.

He smiled, and gazing into the stirring green eyes said, "No trouble." Then he motioned to Ruben and the others. "Let's go."

Everyone moved to their cars. Beau escorted Krysti to his Corvette and helped her in. A few minutes later they were rolling down the beach. Beau fumbled with the knobs of the radio, still intrigued with Krysti's slight accent.

"Say, what are you?"

"What am I?" She was stunned for a moment, and then responded. "A woman?"

"I mean what nationality?"

The accent returned with a haughty retort. "I'm American!"

Now Beau fumbled with his words like he did the radio stations. "I'm sorry, it's just your accent is so intriguing. I just can't place it."

"And what are you, may I ask?"

Beau felt stupid. "Touché. I'm American."

Krysti laughed. "My father was born in El Paso but raised in Argentina. My mother is from Mexico. I was born in Monterey, raised in El Paso, went to Texas Tech, and finished my medical training in Houston at Baylor's College of Medicine. I'm probably more Texan than anything." Krysti flashed her exotic green eyes and giggled. "Again may I ask, what are you?"

Beau laughed. "Probably Texan just like you. My father was a French Cajun from Louisiana and my mother's parents came to America from Norway."

"Norwegian," Krysti said. "You are part Viking. I like that." She took over the chore of tuning in the radio and asked, "What kind of music do you like?"

Beau shrugged his shoulders. "Almost anything except hillbilly and absolutely no rap. I prefer the sixties."

"Do you like to dance?" she quizzed.

A slight smile creased his thin lips. "I'll get on the floor with the best of them, but I'm not much of a dancer. I think the words *foot stompin'* music is a good way to describe my style."

Krysti laughed as Beau reached over and pushed the button to his favorite radio station, instantly singing along with the tune.

"*Imagine there's no Heaven,*" he sang. "Ahhh, *Imagine.* Remember—?"

Krysti finished. "Yes, John Lennon. He's one of my favorites."

The revelation was a pleasant surprise Beau did not expect. "Mine too. Probably the best song he ever made."

When *Imagine* finished, Krysti turned to Beau. "No one ever said what Ruben's call sign is. What do you call him?"

Beau raised his eyebrows and aimed the Corvette toward the hotel where Krysti's son Justin waited. "I thought you knew. It's a name he got from his grandfather, Grandy. We call Ruben Moon Shadow."

## Chapter 5
# MOON SHADOW

The van sped down the beach along the water's edge. The farther Ruben and the others drove south, the fewer signs there were of people inhabiting the island. Sand dunes grew more numerous and much taller the farther they drove. Finally they reached a point along the beach that seemed completely isolated. Ruben slowed the van and came to a stop. He spied an opening in the towering dunes, bordered with two long large pieces of deformed and aged driftwood. A startled rabbit scurried for the safety of the tall sand dunes when Ruben pulled the van next to the driftwood and parallel to the water's edge, creating a windbreak.

While Mulholland, Sullivan, Picket and Warren searched for wood to make a fire, Ruben, Natasha and Sunday unloaded the van and arranged the chips, coolers, and snacks. After settling in, Sullivan and Warren strolled bare-footed to the surf's edge. Mulholland's search for firewood took him deep into the dunes. Situated comfortably on one of the logs near the van, Fitz separated hangers for the marshmallows. He took a beer from the rotating top of the Igloo cooler, popped the tab, and settled back.

A sand crab ran along the beach and across Warren's foot. "Shit," he cursed under his breath while shaking his leg. His silhouette moving in the moonlight appeared to be following the more animate shadow cast against the beach in the brilliance of the Moon.

Quietly, Mulholland crept among the maze of dunes and came silently upon an unsuspecting coyote. The animal, sensing something, twisted its neck around for a better view, only to see the man who had managed to slink within touching distance. A startled yelp escaped the terrified dog's throat and the hair along its spine stood on edge. At the same instant, it leapt straight into the air and was off like a rocket.

Mulholland could not restrain a laugh. He still had the old touch. He moved deeper into the dunes and heard the strange clatter of a rattlesnake.

A nearby nest showed signs of life, the warm weather rousing them from their winter's nap. He gave the nest a wide berth and returned to the beach. A breeze from the Gulf of Mexico slowly cooled the evening air.

Ruben and Henry spread heavy blankets before the fire and the small group nestled near the warmth of the leaping flames. Beau arrived as Sunday spread the last blanket. He also aligned the Corvette parallel to the beach, nose-to-nose with the van, which added to the windbreak. With a cooler and paper bag filled with chips, Beau, Krysti, and Justin plodded through the sand toward the fire.

Almost as tall as his mother, Justin was slightly over five feet and a normal twelve-year-old, full of energy and curiosity. Skinny like most active young children, he had shoulders already wide and the bones in his body were large and strong, waiting for his body to fill with muscles and coordination. With blond hair and blue eyes, he could easily have been mistaken for Beau's son. Justin already knew the men, having met them during the Christmas holidays. He went straight for Fitz, and took a pre-formed metal hanger. Stabbing two of the soft white marshmallows, he held them into the crackling flames.

"Justin, be careful of the fire," warned his mother.

"Okay, Mom," he said, without even a glance back to her. He shoved the metal shaft into the fire and when the fluffy white balls burst into flames, he ran from the heat and fell to his knees in front of Beau.

"Beau, look what I've got for you!" Justin exclaimed, offering him the smoking mass that bobbed about on the end of the long, straight hanger.

Beau pulled the sticky black mass off the end and popped it in his mouth. "Umm, good, Justin." The boy made another dash to the fire.

Beau turned to Krysti. "That's what I call a crispy critter."

Everyone chuckled and Krysti grabbed Beau's arm, giving him a playful squeeze. She turned her head slightly, her green eyes sparkling in the firelight.

"Justin really likes you. Quite an accomplishment since he doesn't take to very many men."

Beau heard, but he was lost momentarily in the seductive green eyes. How attractive she was, he thought, and he found himself wondering what she thought of him. Casually he dismissed the idea when he remembered Marix's words and his own past. He stared at the gold cross hanging from the gold chain about Krysti's neck. A tiny diamond was embedded in each of the ornate four points on the finely detailed cross.

Pointing with his finger, curiosity prompted him to say, "That's a pretty cross."

"Well thank you," Krysti said, fondling her necklace. "It was a gift from my dad when I was eighteen." She laughed. "I don't know how he put up with me. I know he lost most of his hair on my account."

"Why do you say that?"

"I gave him so much grief when I was in high school. I rode dirt bikes against his wishes. Two months from graduation I had a wreck near our home in El Paso. I was sure he was gonna kill me." She smiled affectionately at the thought of her father. "I got this from the wreck," she said, pointing to a tiny scar just to the right of her lower lip. "I also broke my arm.

"My father's a devout Catholic and like all Catholic fathers he doesn't believe girls should do those things. Anyway he showed up at the hospital and never said a thing about the accident. He just gave me a hug and handed me this cross and the necklace. He said if I wouldn't listen to him he hoped the cross might protect me." Then she turned the pendant around and held it toward Beau. "Would you like to read it?"

He took the cross in his hand, and the flames of the fire provided enough light for him to read the inscription: "With all my love."

"Your father must be a tolerant man."

"He is," she said. She released the cross and let out a sigh. "He always called me his Little Princess."

"Did you quit riding dirt bikes?"

Krysti laughed, touched the cross, and shook her head. "No."

Near the van, Sunday waved her hands trying to attract Krysti's attention but it was Beau who noticed. "Krysti, I think you're being paged."

"What?"

"Near the van."

Krysti spotted Sunday, lifted herself from the blanket and strolled over to her friend. When Krysti reached her, Sunday coyly asked, "Well, what do you think?"

"I love it. We don't have a beach in El Paso," she said.

"No. What do you think of Beau?"

"He's nice, but I just met him, Sunday. What do you want me to say, that I have fallen madly in love?"

"Well no, but Beau is special to me."

"I don't doubt that, but what about Michael; you know he wants to see me. I don't need a conflict between these two men. I already have a problem being the physician for this team; I surely don't need to get involved with one of them, much less two," Krysti snapped.

The absurdity of the question was now obvious even to Sunday. "Well, you know what I mean."

The last statement was lost on Krysti as she tried to evaluate her own emotions. Justin liked Beau more than she had ever seen him like anyone. Michael was the one she hoped Justin would like. Her son had tried but he just didn't take to him. Michael was a gentleman with a fine background. She liked Beau but she knew nothing about him. Then she remembered

Shanghai Pete's and how she felt with him. Strange, it was as though nothing could harm her when he was near. He gave her a sense of safety, security, something she didn't feel with Michael—a foolish thought she immediately dismissed.

Krysti noticed the dejected look in Sunday's eyes. "Well, I do feel comfortable with Beau and Justin likes him."

Instantly a frown filled Sunday's face. "Comfortable? That's terrible, so unemotional you—"

"Sunday!" groaned Krysti.

"Oh, okay," Sunday mumbled. "Comfortable, huh?"

The headlights of the car first alerted those around the fire, since the approaching vehicle could not be heard above the splashing surf. Larry James and Marix emerged from the shadows and into the light. Their only welcoming committee was Krysti who went to meet Mike. He put an arm around her and together the three neared the fire.

Beau suddenly felt a twinge of jealousy. He knew he had no right to feel as he did, but he was pleased when Krysti pulled away from Mike and walked straight to her former place beside him. She motioned Mike to sit on her other side. Beau passed off his apparent jealousy to the conflict between him and Marix.

Mike brought Larry James before Beau. "Commander Gex, this is Lieutenant Larry James." James wore oversized shorts, and a beach shirt hung over his narrow shoulders. The shirt, buttoned to the collar, was more than adequate for his small long neck. Tiny stick-like arms protruded from the short sleeves. A crop of unruly black greasy hair topped his head. The small jaw hung beneath a long hooknose between round close-set eyes, giving him a mousy appearance.

Beau shook hands and noted the firmness lacking in his handshake. James's hands felt cold. Beau shook off his first impression telling himself a handshake did not make the man. After all, Marix had a firm handshake.

"Dismiss with the formalities. Away from the base just call me Beau."

Abruptly, Justin shoved two burnt marshmallows into his face. "Here Beau," the boy yelled triumphantly.

Gently he pulled one of the black balls from the metal hanger and acted like he was trying to see inside. "Any surprises?"

Justin started laughing then moved to Marix, offering him the last one. "Hey!" Marix snapped, pushing the shaft and the black object on the end away from him.

"Justin, don't shove that in his face," said his mother.

"Sorry," Justin said dejectedly. "Here, Mike, you want my last marshmallow?"

Marix's lips curled in disgust at the sight of the ashen object. "Are you kidding, you've ruined it."

Defiantly, he held the shaft behind him and stuck his head toward Marix saying, "I'll share with Beau. He'll eat it!"

Children were a nuisance, thought Marix. They always got under his skin. He tried to smile, but he had already decided if he and Krysti ever became serious, he would really have to discipline the little bastard. She would let him control the boy or else.

Backing away from Marix, Justin faced Beau. He slid the marshmallow from the blackened shaft. Then with his sandy fingers he handed him half of the burnt offering. Together they shared the last marshmallow.

Ruben shoved a handful of chips in his mouth, took a drink from his beer, and raised an eyebrow to Marix. "Hell, I was sure the Red Baron would eat one of those crispy critters," he said, mocking Marix and playing with Beau's words.

Mike tensed when the men laughed. He would not let Ruben's constant needling go uncontested, but the awkward situation prevented him from doing anything about it. He managed a feeble grin, trying to show he thought it to be funny. The anger went undetected.

The attitude of the two men toward her son was not lost on Krysti. Nor were the actions lost on Sunday, who decided the situation was getting too tense and moved to action.

"Ruben, tell us the story of Moon Shadow," she begged. She need not have pleaded because Ruben was always ready to tell the story—his grandfather Grandy's story.

Krysti tried to ease the situation but only made it worse when she turned to Michael and asked, "Do you have a story about the Red Baron?" The statement brought a few chuckles from the throng gathered closely to hear the tale of Moon Shadow. The question caught Marix unprepared and off guard. Things were swiftly going awry. "Uhhh, no, I really don't have one," he stammered.

Ruben smiled. "Ahhh, yes, Moon Shadow. Alright, I'll tell it."

Softly, Beau squeezed Krysti's knee. "You'll enjoy his story." Justin crossed his legs and sat next to Beau. Everyone moved closer to the fire. Then Ruben started telling the legend of Moon Shadow.

"A long time ago, right here, here on this very island, there were—," Ruben stopped, when he heard the noisy exhaust of dune buggies. Two vehicles roared past. One turned a half circle at the water's edge, raising a wall of water vertically in the air as it slid backwards down the beach.

"Wow! Cool," said Justin.

Sullivan grinned. "Beau, your brothers are here." The small group rose to watch the antics of the dune buggies. Only Beau moved toward the beach and his brothers. The second buggy did a complete circle, and then slid to a stop next to the black Corvette, spraying sand against the left side. The driver jumped from the buggy and spying Beau, moved toward him.

Beau and Jack clasped each other close so hard it almost knocked them to the ground.

His brother pushed Beau away and held him at arm's length; then he extended his hand, which was greeted with enthusiasm and a rugged shake. He followed with a hard slap on Beau's shoulder.

"Hey renegade," he said with a grin. "Hunting for another war?"

"I think not. I'm ready for Big Bend with ya'll." A beer tab popping made Beau turn. Brook offered him one with his free hand. "Should've known where the beer was, I'd find you," said Beau, taking the drink.

"Hey, you slimy scum bag," laughed Brook. "You sure as shit didn't write very much." He scanned the fireside and recognized some of Beau's friends. "Hey, Ruben how is it?" Ruben waved as did Brook. About the same time, he spotted Krysti and jabbed Jack in the ribs.

"Cut it out, Brook," said Jack.

"No. This is serious. Look at that gorgeous doll," Brook half whispered, motioning with his eyes without pointing.

"You're too young for her," popped Beau.

"She sure is a looker," said Jack. "Sure is a shame you don't like them short."

"In her case, I might change my mind," Beau said, wondering if he hadn't already.

A tall blond kid stood silently in the shadows. "Guess who that is?" said Jack, giving Beau a playful blow to the midsection.

"Danny?" Beau asked.

Chugging a beer, Brook stopped long enough to comment. "Sure as shit is. Hell, we should've fed him weed killer. Guess that makes me the dwarf of the family." Obviously Brook was the smallest of the four. Two inches shy of six feet, he was the leanest and probably in the best physical condition of them all. None of the brothers could match him in endurance. Not only was he the smallest, he was the only one with dark hair, although Jack's was light brown.

"Well, we can't all be dwarves," laughed Beau. Then he turned to Danny and extended his hand, and in return found a firm grip. He observed the boy from head to foot. "Damn, you're all grown-up."

Danny was a few inches taller than his brother Beau. "I always thought you were bigger," he said, looking down on the shorter man.

"I thought you were smaller," quipped Beau. "Y'all been staying out of trouble?" His brothers were better known for the trouble they found, than the trouble they avoided.

"Of course," Brook said as he drained the last drop from the can, then crushed it in his hand. "Hey, Ruben, where's the cerveza?"

"Over here," echoed the familiar Bostonian accent from the shadows.

"Hey BJ, I didn't know you were here," said Brook, shading his eyes from the light of the fire.

"I tend to blend into the background when it gets dark," BJ said, bringing a chuckle from some. Brook and Jack made their way to the beer BJ offered. After introductions, everyone settled down to hear Ruben's story of Moon Shadow.

"Now you guys mind your manners and let me tell the story," said Ruben, aiming his comments directly at Jack and Brook.

"No problem," quipped Jack. "You know us."

Ruben's shoulders sagged. "That's what worries me." He squinted his eyes at the wild trio. "Okay here goes again.

"A long time ago, on this very island," Ruben began.

The splashing surf, crackling fire and the full moon overhead only added to the mystique of the story.

"Yes, right on this very spot roamed one of the wildest bands of Indians ever—real Texas Indians. The Karankawas."

Ruben continued the story passed from generation to generation—a tale passed down to him from Grandy, his beloved grandfather. "South Texas was where the Karankawa Indians were found. They lived around Kingsville. Inland as far as Victoria and north to Matagorda, Padre Island was theirs.

"After a battle, legend has it that the Karankawa Indians would wrap and preserve their dead warriors. They would take the enemy they captured and feed them, keeping them alive until the full moon."

"Whyyy?" asked Justin.

Ruben held his hands in the air. "Patience. I'm getting to that. When the Moon was full." Then Ruben peered into the bright nighttime sky and pointed to the full moon. "Just like it is tonight. The Karankawas would wrap their dead, set them on litters and have their captured enemy pull the stretchers while they marched to this island."

"Why didn't they ride horses?" asked Justin. Krysti held her finger to her mouth. "Well?" asked Justin again.

"Good question," said Ruben nodding his head. "The Karankawa had no horses. There weren't any horses until the Spanish brought them over.

"Anyway, they marched to this island." Ruben looked straight at Justin and pointed to where he sat. "Maybe even the very spot where you're sitting." Justin's eyes opened wide; Krysti chuckled and squeezed Beau's arm, and Sunday giggled. Beau was hoping the story would last longer. Marix ignored the tale and pressed closer to Krysti. Kipp and Fitz found themselves engrossed in the legend. Although BJ, Sully, and Natasha had heard it before, they never grew tired of listening to Ruben tell the story of Moon Shadow.

Ruben continued. "The Karankawas would raise their dead warriors to overhead platforms constructed from old driftwood and tied with vines." From around his neck, Ruben took a small leather pouch and poured the contents into his hand. Inside was an even smaller leather pouch filled with sand, three hawk feathers, six pieces of flint, and a small aluminum piece of molten metal that resembled a face.

He took a step toward Justin to show him the contents. "The Karankawas would sprinkle a little sand over the dead body," he said showing the boy the sand in the small pouch, "and lay a feather and two pieces of flint on the body, so the spirit could travel with earth, wind, and fire." As Ruben spoke, he touched the sand, the feather, and the flint. He held the molten piece of metal up and kissed it. "They would kiss this, which they say was a piece of the Moon, to send the spirit on its way.

"With the Moon full, they set the wooden structures ablaze. All the time, they chanted and danced around the separate fires of each of their fallen comrades. The ritual was the legend of Moon Shadow. The Karankawa Indians believed a warrior's shadow had to be seen during the full moon, then disappear with the fire in order to set his spirit free. As the fires blazed, they would chant the words to the Legend of Moon Shadow:

*When Moon Shadows fall,*
*Come footsteps in the sand*
*Where no one follows.*
*From brave warriors far away.*

*In flames! The spirits recall,*
*Memories by the sea.*
*They dance the land of Moon Shadows,*
*Eternal rest from the warriors' earthly stay!*

"If the ritual was not performed, and the fallen Indian's shadow remained after the first full moon, his haunted spirit would roam the island forever never finding peace."

Ruben cocked his head and held his ear to the wind. His eyes opened wide and his mouth dropped. "What you hear is not the wind—" Ruben turned to Jack and Brook. Just behind them crept Sully, nodding to Ruben as he readied to scare the pair. "Those howling sounds are lost spirits that weren't sacrificed!"

As Ruben yelled, Sully grabbed the brothers. They let out a terrified scream and jumped straight in the air. Everyone laughed, except Fitz and Pick who were at first as startled as the two brothers, but they soon began to chuckle. Marix laughed, finding it funny since it did not happen to him.

Warren prodded Fitzhenry. "Ask him what happened to the ones they captured." Fitz failed to see the grin on BJ's face, spreading from ear to ear.

Fitzhenry waved his hand like a school kid. "What happened to the captured Indians? You never said anything about them."

Ruben held his right elbow with his left hand while he rubbed his chin. Then he threw his hands in the air. "The Karankawas ate them. You see, the Karankawas were cannibals."

Fitz's jaw hung open and the others chuckled.

"Ooohhh! They ate them?" Justin asked. Ruben nodded. "Is that really a piece of the Moon?"

Ruben shrugged his shoulders. "That's what the Karankawas believed. They say they saw a piece of the Moon break away and fall on the earth. That's what Grandy told me." He smiled.

Sunday frowned at her husband. "Justin, that piece of metal is probably from a meteor."

Justin kept staring at the molten piece of metal while Ruben held it out. "I like Ruben's story."

"We all do," said Beau.

Brook stood abruptly. "Hey Ruben, ya got your banjo?" Ruben nodded. "Get it." Then Brook trudged through the sand to one of the buggies while Ruben retrieved his instrument.

They both arrived at the fire simultaneously. "Here's your old guitar," said Brook, handing it to Beau. "I saved it for you."

Affectionately, Beau fondled his old guitar and struck a few strings. He turned to Ruben. "Did Grandy get his wish for Moon Shadow?"

Ruben smiled again when he thought of his grandfather. "Well it wasn't easy. You know what would happen if you tried to burn a body on this island. I had him cremated, and the first night of the full moon I came to the Island and did as he wished." Ruben squeezed the small pouch around his neck. "Earth, wind, and fire. I took one of the hawk feathers, two pieces of flint, and sprinkled a little sand on the fire. Then I took that piece of meteor and kissed it for the spirit."

"Good," said Beau, with a slight tightness in his jaw.

Ruben shrugged his shoulders. "Now maybe I'm the last of the Karankawas. Or at least one who knows it."

Beau nodded as he tuned his guitar. At first his efforts were awkward; then they picked up. Ruben started strumming his banjo, and when they got in rhythm they began strumming and humming to *Michael Row the Boat Ashore*. It wasn't long before Beau had the hang of his old guitar again. The two went into a series of soft melodies, singing as they played their songs. The women started to sing along.

"Any requests?" Ruben asked.

"Yes," said Sunday. "I want to hear *Where have all the Flowers Gone.*" Both men started the tune and immediately Sunday and Krysti joined in, then Natasha, Sully, and BJ. The rest started to hum or sing along with the rest. All too soon the music stopped, bringing the party to an end.

"I hate to stop," said Sunday.

"Me too," admitted Krysti.

Jack turned to Beau. "Hey, Beau we got something else for ya in the buggy." Justin tagged along behind the four brothers, while the others packed for the trip home.

Now was the time for Marix to talk to Krysti freely. He waited until he caught her alone. "Krysti, why don't we let the evening continue? I know a special place you and I can go."

"This evening has already been special," she replied with a smile.

"I know. Just being with you is special," he said pulling her near.

"No, Michael, not now, I'm helping load. Why don't you help?"

"What about later?" Marix asked angrily.

"I can't, I have Justin."

"Leave him with Ruben."

"I'm sorry, not tonight."

"It's Beau," Marix snapped. "I can tell. He's not your type. If you knew more about him you wouldn't even talk to him."

Then Krysti lit into him. "Mister, you could stand some more manners. First, I'll decide who is my type. You won't! Second, I think you are entirely too aggressive for your own good, so cool it. And whatever you have to say about Beau Gex, I think you should say it in his presence."

Marix regrouped swiftly and expertly. "Sorry, I was out of line. I hope you will accept my sincere apology."

Krysti dropped her defense. "Apology accepted. Now why don't you be a dear and help?"

Reluctantly, Marix helped. Except for military camp, servants did all other work. This was not a job for him. He was more interested in getting Krysti away from the others so they could be alone.

Krysti made a quick check for Justin, locating him near the dune buggies with Beau and his brothers. How kind and gentle Beau is, she thought. What could Michael know about him?

Jack pulled a rifle case from one of the buggies and opened it to reveal Beau's old firearm, a Winchester 30.30. The old lever action rifle was something his father had given to him when he was ten. His brothers had kept it with them while Beau was gone. The wood stock was polished and the gun freshly cleaned.

"Thought you might want it back," said Jack.

"Thanks guys," said Beau as he pulled the lever down and checked the chamber. Then he lifted the rifle to his shoulders and sighted it in, feeling its weight as he swung it toward the Moon.

Brook interrupted. "Got something else for you." Beau handed the rifle to Jack and took the new gift from Brook. It was a special high-powered crossbow equipped with a scope. The wooden stock was hollowed out to allow for a half dozen steel bolts.

"It's something you might use when you return to West Texas with us," Danny added.

Brook grinned and wriggled his eyebrows. "You know, something for target practice since it's illegal to hunt with them," said Brook, winking and poking Beau in the ribs. "'Course the game warden can't catch you if he can't hear you."

"Thanks guys, it's beautiful."

"Let me see, let me see," begged Justin. After Beau showed the ever-inquisitive boy the gift his brothers gave him, he placed the weapons in the back of his Corvette.

Watching Justin walk back to his mother, Jack turned to Beau. "Shit, man, that kid could pass for your own. Hell, he must be the same age as . . ."

"Shawn would be? Yeah he's about the same age," Beau said with a sigh. "Justin is twelve. The same age Shawn would have been."

"Sorry, Beau it's just—"

"Forget it," he said with a casual shrug.

Warren's bellowing suddenly interrupted the party. "Bullshit, kid. No one has ever beaten me and you sure as hell can't," BJ said defensively, aiming his words directly at Fitz.

"I think I can beat you in a hundred yards," Fitzhenry said with an air of confidence.

"Bullshit," BJ said again. "Hey Ruben, Beau, Sully. This kid says he can beat me in the hundred."

"Hey Fitz, you don't want to run against BJ. He was the state champ in high school," said Beau.

Fitzhenry was on one knee, calmly tying his tennis shoe, when he offered the challenge to BJ. "Hunerd bucks says I'll beat you."

Everyone gathered around the pair to listen to the taunts and the challenges.

"You got a bet," answered Warren. "Hey, we have a race."

A few friendly bets were wagered and Larry agreed to carry the money. The betting met with his approval. He knew BJ would win. Kipp, Pick, Marix, and Beau picked the kid, Fitz. Krysti somehow felt he could also win. Marix only picked Fitz because BJ was Beau's friend. BJ was disappointed Beau didn't pick him. The others went with BJ and what looked like a sure thing.

"How can you pick Fritz?" Warren asked dejectedly.

Beau told BJ, "The day is coming and this might just be that day."

Warren was quick to point out, "It's night so you are already wrong." Then flashing a big white grin in Ruben's direction, he said, "It's in the bag."

Deliberately taking longer than normal strides, Pickett stepped off one hundred paces to what he estimated was a hundred yards. Close behind him were Fitzhenry and Warren ready to race.

At the other end, with the others watching, Ruben took a piece of driftwood and with it in both hands marked a line in the wet sand to represent the finish line.

Pickett waved his hands to signal they were ready. Ruben acknowledged Pickett and waved back.

"Are you ready?" asked Pickett.

"Well kid, are you ready to taste a little defeat?" BJ asked.

"Sure," he said. Then smiling at Warren he added, "Why don't you tell me all about it when you get to the other end."

"Ready?" asked Pickett. They nodded. "One, two, three, go!" They took off side by side. A third of the way down, Warren decided to lose the kid. He put it in high gear, but Fritz was still matching him stride for stride. They could hear the yells as they neared the finish line. Thirty yards from the end, Fitz turned his head to BJ and smiled. BJ was already straining and couldn't believe it when Fitz exploded ahead and crossed the finish line nearly two yards ahead.

"Son-of-a-bitch, Fitz is fast," said Warren dejectedly as he tried to catch his breath.

"What happened?" asked Ruben. "I thought you could win."

"He's fast," Warren said shaking his head. "That white boy runs like lightning."

"White Lightning!" shouted Ruben. "Hey, White Lightning, congratulations. Even if I did lose some money on you." Now Fitzhenry had his own name just like the others.

Bending over BJ's dejected shoulders, Beau patted him on the back. "Changing of the guard, BJ, just a changing of the guard." While loading the vehicles, they all talked about the race and congratulated Fitz while the men teased BJ. Immediately, he asked for best two out of three.

Jack made a special point to say goodbye to Natasha and gave her a hug. A long hug. He hugged no one else. Then Beau's brothers left with a promise to visit him at the base in the morning.

Casually, Krysti approached Beau. "Would you like to stop and get something to eat before we go home?"

"It's kinda late. You think Justin will be able to handle it?"

"I'm sure he will do just fine."

"Then let's get him and go." They gathered their things and Justin, and were off before Ruben and the others.

Someone else made his way to a car, all the while cussing under his breath. Marix had overheard Krysti's invitation to Beau, and was talking to himself, "Wait until she finds out about him."

* * *

From the balcony of the Holiday Inn overlooking the bay of Corpus Christi, two men leaned over the railing of the hotel room and sipped on their drinks. A knock on the door diverted their attention from the refreshing view. Wearing baggy white pants and flowery short sleeve shirts, both men stepped from the balcony. One of them went directly to the door while the other stopped at the bar and poured another orange drink.

Dressed for the beach and appearing like any other tourist, the guest moved directly to the bar. He had a small moustache and a nose crooked from a previous accident. He dropped a bag to the floor from which fell painter's overalls. In clear English, Lieutenant Juan Ortega addressed the man pouring the drink. "Everything is in readiness, General Sharafan."

Rasht Sharafan handed Lieutenant Ortega a mixed drink while he sipped an orange beverage, since the Muslim religion forbid the consumption of alcoholic beverages. Both men sipped from their glasses.

"This is the last base for me to check. I will return tonight," said Sharafan. He gazed thoughtfully from the window out over the bay. "I think I shall return here when the city is under control. Now tell me of your preparations."

Ortega ticked off his list:

Men were at the public airports. One of the three decoy airliners would be grounded, so the reproduction could slip into the original's flight pattern unnoticed. The other two were in California and Florida. Civilian maintenance crews were inside the Naval Air Station. A half dozen sharpshooters were strategically placed outside the base. With the confusion over the new Persian Gulf conflict, over 500 reservists were called to active duty, with a dozen of their men already at the Naval Air Station. It had been easy to infiltrate the reservists' unit. Men were in place within the armory.

"The snipers?" Sharafan asked.

"The best, General."

"It is imperative that no planes take off for a counter strike against us."

"That will not happen here. In fact Juan Bravo will be leading the group."

Sharafan had heard of the man from Mexico, Juan Bravo, who was considered one of the best snipers in the world. "Good!" Sharafan smirked, knowing that the leaders of the eastern and western part of the invasion had made like preparations.

Ortega sipped his drink and snickered. "The Americans are so unsuspecting. Only four have discovered the attack, but my men intercepted and eliminated them. They will not be missed for a week."

"How many men do you have?"

"Five hundred armed and waiting, with 5,000 waiting along the border to come to my aid."

"They know their missions?"

"Yes. Destroy all legal records. Secure all areas vital to our cause. Exchange property and power to all workers who are sympathetic to our cause or who agree to maintain and run refineries and power plants and do other necessary jobs. A list of gun dealers and wholesalers has been compiled. We checked records of registered guns and have accumulated a list of people who own five or more rifles. We will confiscate all these arms immediately. Public officials, high ranking officers, their children, and those who offer resistance will be taken prisoner and confined in areas likely for possible counter attack."

"Excellent! Yours is one of ten bases in Texas prepared for the invasion. We will lead the spearhead through the center of the United States. Similar preparations have already been made for the East and the West."

"For ten years we have prepared. We are ready. And your part?" Ortega asked.

"Your men will have grounded the real passenger jet so it will be easy to have our duplicate appear to be making an emergency landing. When the airliner lands at the Naval Air Station your men are to move quickly. The jet will not be filled with passengers. Instead more than 150 expertly trained and armed fighting men will exit when it lands. There should be minimal resistance since the Americans will have already been alerted and sent after our three major decoys."

"I have been here for many years and one thing I have learned about the Americans is they will be more concerned about their Orange Bowl and Rose Bowl than anything else," said Ortega with a laugh. "But they will never see the Rose Bowl."

The thought of someone interfering with American football brought a sadistic chuckle from Sharafan. "Yes and may Allah watch over us so the Americans do not lose their precious cable television before our plans are finished. I want all Americans to see."

Sharafan could still remember when the raw plans for this mission first evolved more than thirteen years earlier. The war dead of more than 3,000 in New York and the Pentagon was to be the initial act of the ultimate invasion of the United States. Men from South America and the Middle East had met in Cuba under the pretense of vacations. They started to formulate a plan . At first it seemed almost a joke, but it soon became serious when their determination was shown to be sincere. Rasht Sharafan had attended those meetings. He had wanted to destroy the United States more than any man there. The obstacles seemed almost insurmountable. He tried to explain how the United States had shown a very dangerous pattern during the nineties and there was no reason to believe it would change. The assault on Panama and General Noriega. Then Saddam Hussein and Iraq were attacked for their aggression; while *Desert Storm* was proclaimed a world victory for freedom, but it also exposed the United States' weakness; then Somalia and Bosnia.

Somalia was interesting in showing the United States' inability to beat a backward country without modern weapons. But even after discussing the obvious pattern of danger, still the group hesitated. Disgruntled they broke off the meetings but continued their contact with each other, always keeping in mind Sharafan's explanations.

He and his many cells carried out terrorist attacks across America blowing up buildings, sporting events, and even using biological weapons sparingly. The terror in America continued. Red Eagle was an immense success.

Once again Sharafan and the others met with the knowledge that victory was now more than just a possibility. Taking a page out of history, Sharafan showed how the Coalition could beat the United States just like the Americans had beaten the British to win their independence. A trap that the United States would follow just as before was designed and set. The trail it pursued would lead to the country's own destruction.

As the plans evolved, the United States proved its interference throughout the world when it gave a show of force in Brazil and Zaire. Many more became angry. And it gave credence to the small group's plan against the United States. The Americans would also interfere with other countries' internal affairs, using the United Nations—an organization that in reality was only an extension of the United States military. The United States told the United Nations; they didn't ask. More discussions passed back and forth between the leaders. Patiently they waited and formulated a plan. Osama bin Laden made preparations, and when Sharafan orchestrated the successful bombing of the U.S.S. Cole, the plan gained force.

When the United States *Enduring Freedom* actions attacked Afghanistan after the American strikes, they almost telegraphed their moves. Both Sharafan and Osama bin Laden had waited out the attacks in Pakistan while watching CNN to hear about America's actions. Then the anthrax started. America turned chaotic and terrified. A few years later came the China-

Taiwan incident. Soon after *Operation Liberty* they realized a concentrated effort would succeed because the United States had done just as Sharafan had described.

One more time the United States made a show of force before China without taking the initiative and attacking. The United States paraded before the enemy like the British soldiers had done centuries before in their bright red uniforms—with bravado and arrogance, more like a street bully.

First the Coalition would rid themselves of the freedom fighters. With fierce intensity they lobbied both political parties using money to gain their objectives. Less than three years after the China-Taiwan incident, the Republican leaders who led the charge were soundly defeated by the lobby effort. Gone were the French president, British prime minister, and all the leaders in the Middle East. Only the leader of the United States, Obama, and the king of Saudi Arabia remained. And like the king it looked like Obama would run and win a third term.

Next they planted thousands of key military Special Forces operatives in the southern part of the United States. This was done with their numerous cells through another blanket amnesty program initiated in 2007 for illegal aliens. Ironically, the amnesty was accomplished through padded re-election campaigns and by heavy lobbying. What really helped was the money and lobbying for the American Civil Liberties Union. The ACLU made it possible for many terrorists to simply walk across from Mexico into Arizona where their Muslim friends picked them up. Everything was falling in place.

Under the pretense of free enterprise, they convinced the politicians to let the oil industry continue its own course. The Arab countries lowered and raised prices on oil so often, it brought an end to American exploration. Even the environmentalists unknowingly helped the Coalition when they unwittingly prevented American drilling in many parts of North America, especially Alaska. The Middle East controlled the oil industry. In 2010, Arab countries exported more than eighty percent of America's oil needs.

American reserves were non-existent after Obama refused to allow drilling, and gave away huge Alaskan oil reserves to Russian through a secret agreement that was finalized early in Obama's second term. All remaining oil reserves were in the southern part of the United States, where the invasion would initiate. Therefore, even if the United States were able to regroup and initiate a counter attack, they would have no fuel, similar to what happened to the great German forces in Africa during World War II. The invasion was well planned.

The Coalition, with Sharafan firmly established as one of the leaders, had discovered the United States' *Achilles Heel.*

Juan Ortega interrupted Sharafan's thoughts. "I have found a building downtown to serve our elite group. A helipad is on the roof and no counterstrike will be able to penetrate." Slowly Juan filled his glass. His brow knitted and he turned to Sharafan. "And the man Beau Gex?"

"Do they believe his story?"

Juan Ortega smiled slyly. "No. I listened to the pathetic Civilian Review Board as they examined him. They plan to inform the Obama after the New Year's football game."

Both men laughed. "New Year's Day will be too late," Sharafan said with a sadistic smile. "I hate to see Obama go. He has been our greatest asset in destroying America. We could not have done it without him."

"Should we kill Beau Gex?"

"No," Sharafan said calmly. "As long as he is alive our plans will continue unhindered. In two more days it will make no difference. Have you learned his plans?"

"Yes. He is assigned to a training group leaving for Laughlin Air Force Base on New Year's Day. His aircraft should arrive there before noon on Tuesday."

"Excellent, excellent! He will be there when I arrive," he said eagerly. "Then I will finish my business with him." Sharafan held his glass high toward Juan. Both glasses rang out as they touched, and Sharafan made a toast to their plan: "More than twelve years of work is about to be put into action.

"To the Coalition. To the new America—our America!"

## Chapter 6
# TO TOUCH A STAR

The sun rose slowly from the Gulf, burning away the thick clinging haze. An earlier front left a damp, crisp chill hanging in the air.

Krysti opened the curtains of her bungalow nestled in the security of the Naval Air Station. The rooms were comfortable and efficient, like those of a small apartment, and afforded a beautiful view of the bay. She sipped her coffee and gazed across the calm waters. Not far away a lone figure jogged along the bluff skirting the bay. As the man came into view she recognized Beau. Partially closing the curtains lest she be caught spying, she continued to watch and drink her morning's coffee.

For a moment she thought about inviting him in, but she didn't want him to see her in her bathrobe and with no make-up. Mechanically she glanced across the room into the tall narrow mirror attached to the inside of the open bathroom door. She moved her head side to side and ran her free hand through her auburn curls and then continued to watch Beau.

He had been such a gentleman the night before, taking her and Justin to dinner. After eating, he and Justin played video games. She laughed aloud then glanced at Justin to see if her laughter stirred him from his sleep. She reflected on how the two "boys" were playing the games. She had noticed that both were trying to lose to make the other feel good. Beau had driven them back to the base and carried Justin to the exact spot where he still lay. Only the week before, Justin had beaten Michael soundly on the same video game.

Krysti sighed when he jogged from her view. There were so many things she wanted to know about him. Then she thought about his upcoming physical, and she smiled and blushed at her thoughts. After his test flight he was scheduled for a routine physical to check the effects of the flight. For a doctor, she knew she was too eager to do the exam. Only the day before she had seen the jet he would fly, and she thought it appeared like something from an old *Star Wars* movie.

Instantly her thoughts returned to Beau. She shook her hair, and as she started the water for her shower hummed the tune from the song she had heard the night before. She sang, "*Imagine there's no Heaven . . . It's easy if you try . . .*"

* * *

The cavernous gym filled with men doing their various early morning exercises. Ruben and Sully were on the mat practicing throws, their bodies slapping onto the pads. Warren was showing Fitzhenry how to pump iron and was happy he found something in which he was superior over the young man. After Fitzhenry finished the bench press, Warren tripled the weight and effortlessly raised and lowered the heavy iron five times; the clanging of the barbell echoed through the gym.

"Don't pay any attention to him, Fitz. BJ is just showing off since you beat him last night." Beau laughed, cooling off from his workout.

A few minutes later, Marix entered the gym for his session. His body was sleek and powerfully muscled. His motions were quick and smooth. He stopped to watch Ruben and Sully as Sully managed a lock, pinning Ruben to the mat.

"How about a go," he challenged.

"Sure, Marix," said Sullivan, ready and anxious to take the measure of the man. They moved to the center of the mat, crouching cat-like, searching for a hold. With astounding speed, Marix flipped Sully and pinned him as though he had been no match at all. Momentarily stunned, Sullivan scrambled to his feet. They worked for a hold and again Marix got the advantage and threw Sullivan to the mat with unnecessary viciousness. Everyone stopped what they were doing to watch the match. The final fall drew the ire of all the men within the gym when they heard Sully groan from the pain Marix inflicted.

With a sneer on his lips, Marix glared straight at Beau. "Any challengers?" No one stepped forward as all eyes turned toward Beau. Marix continued to stare. "How about it, Gex?"

"Sorry, wish I could accommodate you but I have to fly in a few hours."

"You're a coward," Marix hissed in a low growl. An unusual silence cloaked the gym. All eyes turned to Beau and they waited for him to respond.

Slowly, he stood erect and holding the towel with both hands flipped it around his neck. "Maybe next time." He turned and walked to the showers. Behind him it sounded like someone had simultaneously let the air out of a half dozen tires.

To the displeasure of all the men present, Marix gloated at what he considered a victory. "Gex is afraid because he knows of my reputation as a Golden Gloves in the service. He wouldn't have a chance against me." The gym remained silent until Marix departed.

Sullivan continued rubbing his neck. "What the hell happened to Beau?"

"That's not like him," added Warren who was standing next to Sullivan. The others failed to see Ruben follow his old friend into the locker room. He would get the answer. He found Beau sitting in front of his locker.

"Why the hell didn't you beat the shit outa that asshole!" yelled Ruben.

"Because I'm flying Blackbird in two hours and I don't want anything to interfere with that. Besides, what would it have accomplished?" Beau asked.

"Sure as shit would've made me happier than hell. He's been asking for it and you go and pass up the golden opportunity," whined Ruben. "Hell, he's strutting around now like he's King of the Jungle."

"Ruben, you measure your opponent before you attack. Remember that even the lion must be cautious, because one day he may step into a steel trap from which there is no escape." And with those words of wisdom, he stepped into the showers and left Ruben standing there rubbing his chin and wondering what the hell that was all about.

Ruben mumbled, "You still should've beat the shit out of him."

* * *

"Hey guys," beamed Beau to his friends gathered around. His eyes went beyond them and to the sleek black craft he was about to guide on its mission—the SR-71 Blackbird. Dressed in a space suit for the journey to the edge of space, he lumbered slowly toward the gathering in his cumbersome outfit.

"Have fun," said Ruben.

Krysti held her hands against her cheeks. "My God! You look like a space man." As a civilian, Krysti had received special clearance, which was really unnecessary since she would be the attending physician. And the flight would be a public spectacle, with the media there.

"Rad!" said Justin. Beau had managed a last minute clearance for the boy after reasoning with Admiral Garrett that even if he was underage, his mother was after all the attending physician, and, added to that, the government was trying to go public.

"Beau, no clowning around. The SR-71 is an expensive machine. Hit 300 and come back," said Admiral Garrett as he and three flight personnel, including General Waddle, followed the pilot, leaving the others behind.

"You forget I've flown these before. I'm just glad I could get one more crack at this baby." Beau turned to Waddle and stopped; his eyes gradually brightened. "General, do you still have those photos?"

"Yes."

"Let me see them."

General Waddle rummaged in his briefcase. He pulled the photos out and handed them to Beau, who studied them intently. "There," he said, pointing with his fingers. "See the tire marks at the end of the runway? They're too close together to be anything but fighter jets. See, single tires, not the multiple as on airliners. If you look really close, you will notice the separation and see that most are singles," Beau yelled enthusiastically.

General Waddle nodded. "Yes, I see."

Again Beau pointed. "All of the hangars are closed. It's too hot for that; most airports leave the hangars open to keep the heat out. They're hiding something, General. Also, there are a number of starters outside." Beau's finger slid along the photo and stopped in three different areas. "These are special starters for the F-4 Phantom; there's no mistaking them."

"You're right," General Waddle confirmed. "After the takeoff I'm taking this to Washington, D.C. to show the Joint Chiefs of Staff. This could be what we needed to prove what you're saying. I will make sure the president sees them tomorrow."

General Waddle returned the photos to the briefcase and walked away from the area with the new information.

Garrett could only shake his head. "I guess you have what you needed for them to see the truth now."

"It's about time; I just hope it's not too late," said Beau, the relief evident in his eyes and the smile on his face. "Hey Ted, thanks for putting my name in for this test flight."

Garrett shook his head. "I didn't do anything. You are the only one here who is qualified."

Most of the group was present and in a bit of awe at the spectacular flying machine. The SR-71, known more affectionately as the Blackbird, appeared to have come from the future, when in reality it had been built very secretively in the early sixties. It was the last of the slide-rule designed aircraft, painted a dull colored black, and had a heat shield covering the wavy nose or chine. During flight the nose would reach a temperature over 1100 degrees Fahrenheit, the heat stretching the titanium nose and smoothing out the waves in the metallic skin.

The SR-71s had been used in the early seventies to map the Soviet Union and monitor their activities. The Blackbird had been shot at hundreds of times by Soviet rockets and outran them all. Unlike the U-2 spy plane, the SR-71 had never been shot down in any of over 500 attempts. It could literally travel faster than a speeding bullet at Mach-3. And now it could travel in excess of Mach-8. Upon leaving the thin atmosphere, the scramjets would kick in enabling the Blackbird to attain Mach-25, a speed with which it could leave earth's gravitational pull and enter space. All of those were reasons for the space suit.

The SR-71 Blackbird was an intricate part of the space station Starburst, aboard which was built a sophisticated laser system capable of knocking out any target within a thousand miles of the United States. In addition, a series of huge mirrors took the sun's energy and used it as a weapon, much like a giant magnifying glass. It was more than just a warning device. Starburst also controlled a series of satellites with their own laser capable of the same destructive powers. Even when Starburst was not in view it was in contact with the military laser satellites that protected the United States. When Starburst became operational, it could transport crews in a conventional method, and do it daily if needed. Crews would stay on Starburst six months to a year. Four Blackbirds were strategically placed in California, New Mexico, Cape Kennedy, and the one in Corpus Christi. One eight-man space plane, four modified SR-71s, and the space station Starburst were what made up the *Aurora Project.*

Near the modified space plane were the two pursuit craft, an F-14 Tomcat with a crew of two, and an F-16 Falcon. Both would pursue to an elevation of 70,000 feet. The F-14 could reach Mach-2.5 while the more sophisticated computer-designed Falcon would pass Mach-3.

The computer-operated wings of the Tomcat could adjust in flight, changing the width of the fighter from 64 feet at takeoff to a much narrower 38 feet in high-speed flight and combat. With a length of 61 feet it came closer to being more like a kite during takeoff to lift its 37 tons. The Falcon was a sleek picture with fixed wings and a total weight of 14 tons—28 tons loaded for combat. The wingspan was seven feet narrower than the Tomcat with drawn wings and five feet shorter.

Both were dwarfed next to the modified version of the SR-71 Blackbird, almost twice as long as the Tomcat, with a fixed wingspan of 55 feet. But the Blackbird also carried 55 tons aloft.

The closer Beau came to the Blackbird the more unreal it appeared. As he prepared to enter the cockpit of the sleek black aircraft, he noticed for the first time the recessed attachments in the aircraft's skin. They aligned along the edge of the canopy and would connect to the space station Starburst, allowing the Blackbird to dock. Two men helped him inside the cockpit. He attached all the lines, scanned the gauges, and then checked the radio.

"Commander, are you ready?" asked the tower.

"Roger," he said and then to himself, "I'm ready to go out of this world." The jets started to a thunderous roar and he rolled toward the runway. The tower gave him clearance and Beau accelerated. At 250 mph the SR-71 became airborne.

The tower cut in. "Climb to 300,000 feet, then start your descent."

"Roger," he answered mechanically. The official record was 85,000 feet, but unofficially he knew of men reaching 150,000. He had exceeded 130,000 once. Today, he would do it again—and much more!

He moved across the bay. In one motion he shoved the throttle forward, pulled the stick back, and began his almost vertical ascent. He was now at 450 mph. An invisible force crushed him back. The G-force was a thrill. Euphoria filled his body, the likes of which he experienced every time he flew. This flight would be an exception and a new thrill he had never known.

He reached Mach 1 and crossed the sound barrier for the first time. Traveling vertically, the shock waves or sonic booms created from crossing the barrier moved perpendicular to the Blackbird and parallel to the ground, instead of toward it. At sea level the speed of sound traveled 750 mph. At higher altitudes, in the thinner air, the speed of sound could be reached at 650 mph.

The first barrier was crossed at 20,000 feet. He pushed on. The Blackbird eagerly obeyed his touch cutting through the atmosphere a few degrees off a vertical position.

Chatter continued from the tower and the two pursuit aircraft. "40,000 feet, 1300 mph . . . looking good."

Mach-2, Beau reflected, and he smiled when he realized the flight had only just begun. "Roger," came his mechanical answer. He was nearing 60,000 and 1800 mph. The tower confirmed, and he pushed the nose over to a seventy-degree angle then hit the afterburners, leaving the Tomcat and the Falcon behind. It was as though he had been kicked in the butt. Swiftly he shot past 120,000 feet as he watched the needle twirl on the altimeter. The computers took over adjusting mechanical input on the controls, allowing smaller output on the guidance system.

"150,000 feet, 3250 mph, Mach-5. Looking good. Activate the scramjets," came the order from the tower.

At this speed, Beau was capable of catching and passing a bullet fired from a high-powered rifle. And there was still more to go! His gloved hand touched the switch. "Activated." Now he waited for the new engines to kick in. They did so with tremendous force. In an instant he reached Mach-6 and 200,000 feet. It took less than 20 seconds to reach 300,000 and Mach-8. So far the trip had lasted but a few minutes.

"Mission completed, you can return home," ordered the tower.

"Roger," he lied, keeping the Blackbird aimed for the heavens. There was no sound from the powerful jet engines of the Blackbird. The cockpit was silent. The aircraft was traveling at eight times the speed of sound and the thunderous roar of the jets was unable to reach forward into the confines of the SR-71 cockpit, where virtual silence prevailed. He was streaking toward the stars at more than 85 miles per minute, more than one mile every second. He had passed 300,000 feet and was still climbing. He pointed the nose over at a forty-five-degree angle.

At this altitude, the air was so thin the sun took on a different appearance than on Earth. Here, it could be seen in all its dynamic intensity. From here there was no day or night; instead he saw an abyss of grandeur and stars changing from blue to purple, finally blending to the black of space. Over 320,000 feet below, it was still daylight and just before noon. But here he shared his secrets with an infinite number of brilliant stars. He felt a sudden urge to push faster and higher!

"Commander, this is the tower; you've passed 330,000 feet and are exceeding Mach-8. Return to base!"

Smiling, he switched the radio on, then made static noises and answered, "Repeat over . . . You're . . . break . . . up. Problem wi . . . throt . . . Repeat I—," he said trying to garble his voice; then he flipped the switch on the radio.

In the thin air, the outside temperatures were minus sixty degrees Fahrenheit, yet the gauges of the Blackbird showed a nose skin temperature of 1125 degrees, while the sides approached 455. Everything was normal. He marveled at the gauges and the information being fed to him. The jet was 100 miles out to sea and had traveled 120 miles in less than three and a half minutes. Mach-9; 5900 mph. The altimeter passed 340,000 feet. He wanted more. A rush passed through Beau's frame. For a moment he felt immortal.

The words of a fighter pilot, dead long ago, registered on his brain: "Up, up the long delirious burning blue, I've topped the wind-swept heights . . ." How true, he thought.

Crossing over to another world, Beau thought of God. He had his own beliefs, his own doubts, but every time he came to this point, he believed. Truly God existed. If God heard prayers he would hear them here. Somebody or something was with him. He sensed it.

Those few thoughts took only milliseconds, during which time the SR-71 traveled an additional thirty miles. Instinctively, he leveled the Blackbird out and prepared for the descent. He was over 150 miles out and his air speed had dropped under Mach-8 to 5000 mph.

As the SR-71 leveled out he gazed to the heavens. "Sorry for what I've done. But do me a favor and watch after Becky and Shawn. I'll be seein' ya." With those few words, he began his earthly descent.

How small, how insignificant the earth seemed. He could see the Gulf of Mexico and the Texas coast. He put his ship into a gentle earth-bound dive. The strangest feeling prevailed over his senses, as though his ship was motionless while the earth spun continuously before him. Eight times the aircraft shuddered, caught in its own sound waves as it decelerated through the sound barrier.

Beau zeroed in on the approximate spot he had left and headed home. It seemed strange but at that very moment, his thoughts were of Krysti.

## Chapter 7
# PLAYING GAMES

All hell was about to break loose when he landed, and Beau was prepared. As he taxied down the runway he popped the old communications panel and pulled a couple of the fuses. Then from a pocket within his suit he extracted a battery with a wire attached to each end. When he touched the wires to the fuses, they burned out. He replaced the fuses and closed the panels. This was all completed in a matter of seconds just as he stopped in front of the hangar. The canopy lifted slowly. An insulated ladder had already rolled against the black, still hot skin of the SR-71. The angry commander of the mission stormed the rungs.

The first face Beau saw was not pleasant. "You stupid son-of-a-bitch, I'm gonna have your wings." The lieutenant in charge angrily reached across Beau and popped the same panel, extracting the same fuses, and then he quickly descended the ladder.

Beau smiled coyly to himself. After a few minutes of disengaging the attachments and cables holding him prisoner, he crawled from the Blackbird and was assisted once again to firm ground.

Garrett walked toward him and motioned the other men away. "I was afraid you would do something like that. You have the commander and lieutenant real pissed off." Garrett turned to see if anyone was watching, then held his hand out. "Give me the battery."

"What?" Beau was stunned. "I don't—"

"Cut the crap," he said smiling. "How do you think I know? They'll find the battery in the suit. Hand it over."

Sheepishly, he handed the battery to Garrett.

"Now go get your physical. Krysti is waiting."

"Thanks Ted."

In the distance, Beau spied Krysti waving. She wore white tennis shoes, tight jeans, and a red short-sleeved button shirt tied in a knot in front. Her auburn curls were pulled tight in a ponytail. Her left arm was wrapped around her son's shoulders. She looked more like a teenager instead of a mother with a twelve-year-old son.

"Git!" bellowed Ted. He held the battery in his hand, grinned, and stuffed it in his pants pocket.

Krysti, along with an angry commander, led Beau to the infirmary for the check-up. Justin tagged along.

"You weren't gone long. Where'd you go?" Krysti asked.

"Just to the stars and back again," Beau said nonchalantly.

"Come on, quit kidding."

For the next few minutes Beau explained the details of the flight as to how far and how fast he had gone. She listened to the story in amazement, unaware of the Blackbird's capabilities. The only things he left out were the fact he had gone beyond the limit and that his thoughts had been on her.

The commander followed the two into the small medical room and waited impatiently as Beau went behind a screen and changed into his Jockey shorts for the physical. The commander snatched the discarded suit and disappeared.

After the flight Beau described, she expected to see his vital signs elevated, but they weren't. She couldn't believe his physical conditioning: pulse rate 50 and his blood pressure was 118 over 65. It was as though he had been resting all day instead of traveling at five times the speed of a bullet.

Krysti checked his heartbeat three times, and found that the touch of his body excited her. For a moment she regretted the latex gloves. She could sense her own heart rate increasing. This was not supposed to happen during a check-up. It had never happened before, even when she checked Michael. This was supposed to be a job and she would conduct herself properly. She shook her head in anger.

"Problem?" Beau asked when he noticed her shaking her head.

"No," she came back, feeling the flush in her face. "You're fine."

Then Beau asked her the question she had been dreading all day. "You wanna go to the officers' party tonight?"

"Beau, I'd love to, but I promised to go with Michael," she said, while wondering if what she had with Michael might be a mistake. She had promised to go with him and she would not break a promise even though she felt badly but didn't know why.

"I understand. Well, I'll probably see you there," he said, with a shrug of his broad shoulders.

"Michael and I are going to dinner with Sunday and Ruben first, then—"

"That little shit!" interrupted Beau.

"What?"

"I'm sorry. Now I know why Ruben was laughing when he invited me to dinner with them tonight. He even said find a date if you can," said Beau apologetically. "I'll tell him I can't go."

"Nothing of the kind. I'm glad you're going with us," she said sincerely.

Krysti gazed at Beau dressed in only his shorts. A smile lit up her face and she could hardly suppress a chuckle. She held her hand up and made a point to wiggle her middle finger and started to bend over.

"Now when I tell you I want you to cough."

Beau jumped from the table to the floor, grabbed the towel, and held it in front of him. "Whoa, wait! A shot, anything you want, but not that." He continued to back away from her trying desperately to defend himself as she moved nearer. "This isn't part of the physical. You can't!" he pleaded.

It was Krysti who caught Beau off guard. She started to laugh and took her glove off. "I'm sorry, I was just kidding. I just couldn't help it when I saw you in your shorts." She continued to laugh. "You seemed so helpless."

With a sigh of relief, Beau relaxed and laughed at his own predicament. They were interrupted when Sullivan burst into the room breathless.

"Excuse me, Doctor Socorro. Have you finished with Beau?"

"Yes"

"Good," said Sully. He turned to Beau. "You know those Special Forces Marines visiting the base?"

"Yeah."

"Well Kipp challenged them to a game of football. Ruben's trying to explain to Kipp, they don't mean soccer. Those Marines are serious."

"Who do we have?"

"There's BJ, Ruben, Fitz, Pick, Marix, Cozmo, Dean, your brothers, me, and you. But we haven't got a prayer without you. Shit, those Marines are huge and they want to play with eleven."

His eyes turned to Krysti and for a moment he appeared to be more like a kid asking permission to play. "Well, doc? Do I clear waivers? Am I safe enough to play?"

She laughed and pushed him away. "Of course you are."

He turned to Sully. Like an eager boy he said, "I'll change. Tell Ruben, I'll be there. Krysti, why don't you come watch? We might need a doctor." He was already opening the door and aimed for the gym and his clothes.

"Sure," she shouted, as the door slammed shut. She turned and grabbed Sully who was returning to the game. "Why do you need Beau so bad?"

"With him, we won't lose," was all he said.

Krysti put her equipment away and made her way to the field. If she were going to bet money, she would have placed it on the Marines. They were bigger, younger, and appeared to be organized—thirty Marines ready to play.

In the middle of the field, Ruben shook his head at Mulholland in a negative manner. He was giving him a crash course in American Football. Krysti saw Sunday and made her way to where she and two other women watched. She recognized them both. One was Natasha, and the other was Ted Garrett's daughter, Tracy. Ruben had drafted Tracy's husband, Gene Demarr.

As Ruben walked from the field, he noticed Krysti and rolled his eyes. "Damn, these gorillas are gonna kill us."

Marix strolled over to the women. "Seems to me like those guys are a tough group. I'd say they have it in the bag, but we should have some fun. Kipp was a little premature in his challenge. Ruben!" he yelled. "I have the plays set. Everybody is on the field. Let's run a few."

"G'day ladies," said Mulholland.

Ruben shook his head in defeat. "Where's Beau?"

"He's coming," confirmed Krysti. "Ruben, the five of us should have a wonderful time tonight."

"It's okay, five will fit in my van." His eyes lit up. "Shit! Beau knows?"

"Yes."

"Damn, he's gonna kill me." Ruben grinned and shrugged his shoulders. "Oh, well, on to the slaughter."

Sunday yelled encouragement. "Good luck!"

With a bow to the women, Ruben waved his hand toward the team. "G'day mates, cheerio, and all that stuff. Hell, half our guys aren't even American. Where's Beau?" he mumbled as he ran onto the field.

Curiosity more than anything made Krysti ask Sunday what was so important about one man. Sunday explained the past about the high school rivalries—even the fact Beau's wife and son were dead, but she eluded details of how the deaths occurred. And she didn't tell about his exploits in Israel, which she felt wasn't her place to do, and besides, she wasn't sure how Krysti would handle the story.

"Did you and Beau have fun last night?" Sunday asked inquisitively.

"Sunday!"

"Well?"

"Okay. He's got magnificent shoulders, the most powerful legs I've seen on a man, and great buns. Does that make you happy?" She said the words in jest but who was she trying to kid? She had been attracted to him the instant she had seen him at Shanghai Pete's, so she passed it off to a physical attraction.

"Is that all?"

Krysti sighed. "He's not handsome like Michael but he is cute and sweet and I felt safe with him."

"Oh, no!" groaned Sunday. "The kiss of death—he's sweet and safe. And Michael isn't handsome. He's pretty."

Both women laughed and again they were little girls. "All right, he's a gentleman. Justin likes him and that's a big plus, because usually Justin doesn't like anyone I date."

"That should tell you something. He didn't kiss you, did he?"

Krysti was surprised. "No, he didn't."

"I knew he wouldn't. Beau's not the aggressive type. He did the same with his first wife. Becky had to make the first move on him, but did she ever get a response!"

The thought of the response piqued Krysti's curiosity. She wanted to know more, but she was too embarrassed to ask. Against the protest of Ruben and Sully the game started. The Marines kicked the ball and Ruben ran it back.

"Go Ruben!" yelled Sunday.

Krysti shook her head. "Sometimes I think I'm hunting for Prince Charming to take me away."

Sunday put two fingers in her mouth and let out a shrill whistle on the next play. She glanced at Krysti, who seemed somewhat startled at the unfeminine gesture. Sunday just shrugged her shoulders. "Sometimes you have to kiss a few frogs to find Prince Charming."

"I've kissed enough frogs for a lifetime," said Krysti. For a moment, she was quiet as she reflected on her husband, her high school sweetheart—a match made in Heaven, which turned into a violent frolic in Hell. She was a fool to have stayed, but she was always sure tomorrow would change things; it never did. He hit Justin when he was three years old and it was the last day they were ever together. She had decided if she didn't care for herself, she had an obligation to the son she loved.

The violence was not the only thing bothering her. Had she ever experienced real love? At first it was good, or so it seemed. A year into the marriage he would make love to her and when he was finished, he would look at her with eyes void of emotion, roll over, and go to sleep. He did not make love to her. He had sex. All she wanted was a kind word, for him to touch her, to have his eyes filled with love and tenderness, and know he thought only of her. There was nothing. It had become the same with Michael. Krysti wanted more, she needed more. She wanted to be touched. To be loved. Was she asking for too much?

"Maybe I expect too much from a relationship." Krysti sighed. "When a man makes love to me, I want him to touch me tenderly; caress me. I want to see the love, the sparkle in his eyes. I want to feel special. Shouldn't you have that in a relationship?"

Sunday let out with a scream of disgust as the Marines maneuvered in for a score. "Of course! Ruben is always affectionate. Sometimes he teases but I know I'm the only one for him. He always makes me happy."

"You make me believe in fairy tales."

"Is the problem Mike?"

"No," she lied, as her thoughts returned to the many sexual nights she had spent with him: nights that sometimes made her feel used and dirty. Twice she had confronted him for his lack of sensitivity, but always he used his charm to disarm her. "Oh, Mike's not perfect but he's trying."

Smiling, Sunday placed her hand on Krysti's arm. "You deserve the best. Don't settle for less." Then Sunday shook her head. "It's none of my business but you wouldn't have said those things if there weren't problems between you and Mike."

Krysti started to speak but Sunday held up her hand. "Let me finish. You must do what you must do. No one can tell you what that is, but it should feel right in your heart. Remember it's better to be alone than to be lonely with someone."

"But," Krysti smiled, "Que es la vida, sin el amor?"

Sunday laughed. "What is life without love? It is nothing."

Both women hugged each other and Krysti kissed Sunday on the cheek. Ruben intercepted the ball and the women screamed encouragement.

After the first four possessions, the Marines had scored on three. The fourth drive was stopped when Kipp intercepted. He was extremely excited about using his hands, something denied in his beloved soccer. Ruben asked to stop the game and awarded Mulholland the game ball.

Beau arrived, still tucking his shirt in, but Marix refused to relinquish his leadership as quarterback. The team fell no farther behind but could not cut the lead. They managed to hold their own. Unexpectedly, Kipp, Ruben, BJ, and Sully threatened Marix with mutiny unless Beau ran the team for the last part of the game. Marix grudgingly let him take control. The women continued yelling encouragement from the sidelines.

Promptly Beau evaluated the men and set their positions accordingly. Setting himself as a rover on defense, he watched each play develop and followed the direction, moving with his instincts, reacting to where he believed the ball would be. Each time they got the ball he moved them down for a score. The Marines never scored again.

To Ruben, it was like the high school glory days. It was homecoming without a marching band. This time, Ruben was on the right team. There were only five minutes remaining as the Marines moved down field. Beau's brother Brook intercepted on the five-yard line. Still down by four points, they huddled up for what would be the last play. They were all breathing hard, and their eyes appealed to Beau for the miracle play.

"Well, what are we going to do now, coach?" Marix asked smugly, confident Beau would fail.

Beau made a point to look at each one, and then with an almost childlike grin he said, "Well, guys . . . let's score!" Slowly and with control he set the play. "Kipp, BJ, up twenty. Kipp right and BJ left." Then he laughed. "The Marines will be expecting BJ, but the ball will go to White Lightning straight down the middle. I wanna see what I saw at the beach." Fitzhenry beamed confidently. The ball was snapped to Beau. He rolled left, pulled up, pumped once to BJ, and once to Kipp, which pulled in the defense. Then with a quick flick of his left wrist, the ball spiraled gracefully downfield. The play went just as diagramed in the huddle. When Fitz took the ball over his shoulder, the closest player was fifteen feet behind. He scored easily, taking them to a two-point victory over the Marines.

Everyone started shouting and hollering. Ruben and Sunday, Sully and Natasha, and Mike and Krysti were celebrating as were the rest of the team. The Marines belatedly congratulated the victors.

Krysti stopped long enough to search out Beau and congratulate him, but he hadn't paused to celebrate. Instead he had taken a bottle of Gatorade to Fitz who was still on his knees at the far end of the field and away from the celebration. The heat had gotten to most of the players and all were soaking wet with perspiration. Fitz was no exception, and after the long run, he was too tired to return to the group and the celebration.

She watched as Beau handed Fitz the drink and patted him on the shoulders. Fitz took a few moments for his breathing to become normal again. Beau waited so they could return to the group together.

Sunday walked over to Krysti after Mike moved his celebration to the players. "That's another thing about Beau. He always worries about his men. In combat, Ruben said he always went first and the rule was if he didn't make it, no one else was to try. He never lost a man on any combat missions." Then she pointed to the men. "I'll bet he has saved Ruben, Sully, and BJ each at least twice."

Beau walked up half-carrying Fitz. "Hey, Krysti what did you think of Fitz's catch?" He looked all around. "Where's Justin?"

She waved toward the celebrating group. "He's with Ruben."

Just then they heard, "Beau!" He turned just in time to catch the small boy and swing him to his shoulders.

"Whatcha think of the game, Champ?"

Justin tapped Beau on the head. "You're the Champ. You played great. I hope I can play that good."

Beau tried to turn his head up and back so he could see Justin. "One day you will be better than we ever were."

"You think so? Really?"

"Yep, really."

Krysti watched, wishing Justin's dad had done the same thing. Even so, watching Beau with Justin made her feel warm inside.

"Come on you guys. Let me get you some drinks," she said.

Soon they were with the rest of the team and the impromptu celebration. Marix strolled over to Krysti and put his arm around her shoulders. "Not a bad game."

"All of you played very well. Congratulations on your catch, Mark," she said to Fitz. She wanted to say what a beautiful pass it was that won the game . . . but she didn't. Marix would only get angry, but as every minute passed she regretted her decision.

"Yeah Fitz, it was a beaut," said Beau as he sipped his soft drink.

"Nice pass," Fitzhenry admitted.

"Yes, we played well," added Marix. "Krysti, you ready for tonight?"

"Yes."

"Good. What time, Ruben?" asked Marix.

Ruben coughed into his drink and Sunday frowned at him. "Oh, about 1900 hours."

"I have a quaint place picked out for dinner. I have to go now. See you at 1900 hours," said Marix, making sure to give Krysti a peck on the cheek in front of Beau before he made a hasty departure from the small group.

After Marix left, Beau called out, "Hey, Ruben."

"Yep?"

"What time?" he asked and both women snickered but Ruben again choked on his drink and didn't answer.

"In case you didn't know," said Beau with a sigh as he crushed the tin can in his hand, "I'm going to kill you." He jumped up and started running toward his friend. But for once, Ruben was faster as he tried to make his escape. The women broke into a fit of laughter.

* * *

The small executive jet made a perfect landing at the newly completed Mexican airport 200 miles south of the Texas border. Half a dozen commercial airliners rested quietly at the terminals, with no travelers and no tourists. The nearby roads were barricaded and guarded with military troops. Numerous large hangars surrounded the airport. Unobserved from the air, all the hangars were filled with jets and men working furiously to ready them. But they were not commercial jets. They were fighter jets, and nearly combat ready! Recently two new airports had been built in Mexico. One was located near the Gulf of Mexico while the other was near the Gulf of Baja on the Pacific side. The two large airports were more than fifty miles from the nearest city. Before construction had started, government officials were informed the distant location from nearby cities was due to the environment. The distance would alleviate pollution and noise problems from the surrounding towns, which would also allow room for growth.

But no officials questioned why neither airport was near a major highway. And no one asked why private foreign investors had purchased the land and started construction. American intelligence had readily accepted the explanations.

The executive jet taxied to the main terminal. Two men exited the plane and were hastily ushered in. Sharafan and his leading officer and trusted friend, Tahar Zahir, who had fought with Sharafan in Iraq and Afghanistan, were the last to arrive. Inside the large meeting area were gathered the military leaders of the Coalition prepared to overthrow the United States government. Five years of careful preparation had narrowed down to a single day. The final details were being carefully arranged and rechecked to assure no mistakes.

The most remarkable part of the whole plan had been the minimal leak of information about the invasion. The first five years had been spent hand-picking the warriors. Leaks had been most feared. There had been some, but those who leaked information and those who found out were all dead. Plus, and most important, no one believed and no one reacted to the leaked information anymore.

At the front of the room stood three men: a Cuban, a Syrian, and a Colombian. Each was the leader of one of the three separate points of attack. The Cuban would originate the attack from Cuba. The Syrian would lead the attack through the western part of the United States. The Colombian, General Navarro, was in charge of the attack through Texas. He was to secure all bases as far north as possible. General Navarro stood before the group in front of a large map of the United States, using a pointer to show and explain how the attack was to take place. "Our attack will consist of three fronts. We will attack the east, west, and central United States. Three groups of twenty men will control the attacks based from the two new airports in Mexico and one in Cuba. Once the bases in the United States are secure, they will relocate to strategic bases under their control."

So far the plan was working to perfection. Only two weeks earlier, war had apparently broken out between Israel and Egypt, leaving Iraq caught precariously in the middle. American troops returned determined once again to have their demands followed and obeyed. As in *Desert Storm* of 1991 and *Operation Iraqi Freedom* of 2003, the United States sent two-thirds of its million-man army and started to activate reserve units.

The United States sent 1500 of the more than 3500 fighting aircraft to the Persian Gulf, leaving less than 1500 aircraft in America. More than 500 were already placed in strategic areas around the world. Most of the destroyers and frigates were sent to protect the five nuclear aircraft carriers. American troops had arrived and preparations were being made. Half the troops were already placed on Saudi soil. The aircraft carriers were still fully loaded, and vulnerable.

The United States had acted just as predicted: exactly as they had in the preparations of *Desert Storm* and *Operation Iraqi Freedom*. President Obama found the apparent turmoil in the Middle East a chance to show the American people his true character. When he backed the sending of troops, he had done the predictable, the same as the previous presidents before him. Now, all the Coalition had to do was execute the plan. The American reaction was, day for day, exactly as the response to *Desert Storm* and *Operation Iraqi Freedom*.

For Sharafan and his men, the time for waiting was over. They were ready for action. His only regret was not being present to see the destruction of the American forces in the Persian Gulf. But he was assured of greater pleasure by being one of the first foreign invaders on American soil in 200 years.

Navarro looked into the faces of the men. "New Year's Day has been chosen for the invasion. The attack will occur at noon in the United States, while our forces in the Persian Gulf will initiate their part under cover of darkness. The initial attack on troops in the Persian Gulf will come from Yemen, Oman, Qatar, and Iraq."

What at first had appeared like a defensive build-up against Israel was, in reality, an offensive four prong attack against American troops.

Located at airstrips in these countries were 300 small single-engine planes similar to Cessnas. Only they were completely loaded with high explosives: enough explosives to blow a hole the size of a train through the thick steel plates of an American aircraft carrier. All the pilots were to fly a one-way mission to damage and destroy as many naval vessels as possible.

The only problem was there were too many volunteers for the mission who were willing to die for such a cause. They would willingly give their lives to be with Allah. At the same time, Libya, Egypt, Iran, parts of Pakistan and other secluded parts of the Middle East were to launch their nearly 800 aircraft in a concentrated effort against the American forces. Unlike the wars of 1991, 2001, and 2003, they would not sit back and let the enormous firepower pound away. The Coalition was willing to sacrifice all in the belief the Americans could not be victorious in the face of such an attack.

"A total of 500,000 ground troops are ready. An additional million civilians are currently in position—resembling fleeing refugees. Already the civilians armed with machetes, hammers, and shovels are moving toward the Americans in waves. Innocent-looking people prepared to give their lives for Allah. When in position, they will mob the unsuspecting Americans. It is estimated we will lose more than a million men in the assault—but we will defeat the estimated 500,000 American troops."

Navarro's words were electrifying to the men gathered before him. They started chattering to each other about the attack.

With a smile Navarro added, "American troops are overseas. Only a handful of untrained National Guard remain behind to defend the United States."

Even more clever was the plan for the United States. More than 2000 aircraft had been assembled and ingeniously planted below the American borders. Even more ironic was the fact some had been observed, but it had been explained they were to be used in a Mexican celebration to take place on New Year's Day. In a way it was the truth, because the attack was to be initiated on the first of January. Those observed would naturally be assumed to be taking part in the celebration.

Navarro continued, "Before we launch our attack, three passenger jets are to be sent as decoys toward the American cities of Washington D.C., New Orleans, and Los Angeles. The United States will respond and bring the remaining American aircraft to red alert. All armed and ready aircraft will become airborne and pursue our decoys."

The Coalition hoped the aircraft would be chased to a point of no return. The pilots of the three passenger jets would then bail out, but it would be too late.

"Those American jets airborne will have enough fuel to return to base or commit to air combat for only a short time. You could say we will be taking them to a point of no return." Again the group buzzed at Navarro's statement. "At that time the Coalition's air force, two-thousand strong, will be airborne along with thirty passenger liners to replace their intentionally disabled counterpart, while the others will to be shot down. The duplicate airliners will radio for emergency landings near strategic American air bases. All are filled with trained fighting troops. Supporting fighter aircraft will follow."

The United States had granted amnesty to more than 500,000 illegal aliens before 1990. Fourteen years after *Desert Storm* the United States again granted amnesty to over 700,000 aliens from El Salvador, Columbia and Nicaragua. Nearly 5,000 of those had been planted specifically to prepare for the invasion. Smiling to his men Navarro said, "The faithful will be rewarded. Fifty American bases are to be attacked, and for each base fifty or more men are ready and waiting for the attack to begin."

To prevent a leak about the invasion, the 5000 soldier volunteers had themselves recruited people. They were told they would live in the United States and not be contacted about the invasion until thirty days before it was to take place.

Secretly a lead man in each cell had been given the names of ten of the 5000 and told they were to monitor those persons to make sure they did not leak information about the invasion. They were not to mention they were a part of the Coalition, but actually act like new American citizens. Only 200 of the 5000 returned to their own countries. Another 200 either talked too much or, after a change of heart, decided to save their new adopted country rather than go through with their part of the invasion. Almost all were killed. Only five managed to get to authorities. The very people running the country they were trying to save scoffed at them and their silly accusations.

"More than 300,000 ground troops are already moving to the United States' southern border from thousands of different locations. They are in position and waiting for our first move." Even with all of this the leaks had been few. All those who gave out information and those who learned about the invasion were dead. Added to this were the intentional daily leaks of false reports that, when pursued, all led to dead ends.

According to the plan, California, Texas, Florida, and all states along the southern border of the United States were to be taken. If all went as calculated, Sharafan was to arrive at Laughlin the afternoon of New Year's Day. After he concluded his business, he would move to Corpus Christi where he would set up his permanent headquarters.

General Navarro finished the briefing and offered to answer questions. While Navarro spoke, Sharafan reflected on how plans had developed to get them where they were and on the success of *Red Eagle*.

Revenge had always been paramount with Rasht, and he could still see the day when he had come in contact with another man whose desire to destroy the United States was almost equal to his. The man was Osama bin Laden. When Rasht had described plans of the "Coalition," Bin, as Rasht called him, listened attentively. Soon bin Laden controlled the Coalition, much to the satisfaction of Sharafan, for bin Laden was much revered in the Middle East. He quickly masterminded the organization with a stress on secrecy. Quickly, Sharafan had gained the confidence of bin Laden's commanders, including Khalid Sheikh Mohammed, Hambali, Atef, and Rahim al Nashiri.

Bin Laden, with his power and wealth, began to attack the United States electronically using the Internet. One test virus used would destroy sector zero in the hard drive, destroying the dynamic link libraries or files with a ".dll" extension. A test was sent with "a virtual card for you" and the virus. The experiment showed great potential.

Electronic destruction was not enough for Rasht, and he explained to bin Laden how the United States exposed itself time and time again. In 1997 hundreds of devout Islamic fundamentalists were placed in the United States and funded by bin Laden with the intent of being used in the future. Ten cells consisting of five men each already resided in the country. To this, Bin Laden added twenty more cells—a hundred more dedicated Islamic fundamentalists that believed in revenge for Iraq and the innocent people the Americans had killed.

Rasht volunteered to give his life for Allah, but bin Laden saw in Sharafan a leader he needed for his plans in the future. Bin Laden called him Alef Rasad, after his close friend who had been killed by Israelis. This, he explained, was so Sharafan could hide by using the name to escape detection from the authorities tracing the cells. As long as those in the group of cells knew him as Alef, he could travel and do wherever he pleased as Rasht Sharafan without any worry. Many of those in the United States and Germany were also under assumed names.

For the United States, bin Laden was already a marked man, but he had slipped through the American's hands numerous times. Twice, President Clinton had let the opportunity to kill bin Laden slip from his grasp through inaction. After all, President Clinton had more important personal matters to contend with in his own country. Bin Laden escaped and became more of a danger to the United States. Only a few knew of his plans and the deadly visions he held for America in his future actions.

Khalid Sheikh Mohammed had talked with bin Laden about crashing passenger airliners, while bin Laden told of his dream to destroy the American Twin Towers in New York. It was Sharafan who had devised a plan capable of accomplishing the task both men wanted. When Rasht explained to Mohammed his idea of using passenger airliners like guided missiles loaded with more than 11,000 gallons of jet fuel, the idea so intrigued Mohammed he took the idea to bin Laden who agreed completely and gave them the task of organizing and carrying out such a mission.

With more than a dozen Muslims living in Germany and the United States, and some having already taken flying lessons, Sharafan put his plan into action. But bin Laden delayed.

Rasht grew impatient and begged for bin Laden to let him prove how he could defeat the United States. "All in good time," bin Laden had promised. While the plans were temporarily cast aside, Sharafan attended the wedding of bin Laden's son to the daughter of Mohamed, bin Laden's second in command. Sharafan had become like a son to bin Laden. In 1998 bin Laden declared war against the United States and told all Muslims, "Killing Americans and their allies, civilians and military is an individual duty for every Muslim who can do it in any country in which it is possible."

Not long after that announcement Americans began dying.

A year later, in 1999, Sharafan again pleaded with bin Laden to let him show how he could cripple the United States. Bin Laden finally agreed. Sharafan immediately enlisted the aid of Abu Mombassa, Khalid al Mihdhar, and Nawaf al Hamzi. They coordinated the plan as all three men traveled to Germany and the United States, while Khalid Mohammed controlled the financing for the project. Cautiously Sharafan, al Hamzi, and Mihdhar started recruiting in Saudi Arabia, England, and Germany.

Sharafan, Mombassa, and Mohammed discussed targets. Khalid Mohammed wanted to hijack ten planes and crash them into a variety of targets including the tallest buildings in California, Washington, and New York. He also wanted to target a nuclear power plant along with the CIA and FBI headquarters. Then he wanted to land another airliner at an American airport, kill all the men aboard, and then give a speech about the evil support the United States gave to Israel.

Bin Laden listened to the proposal, but finally decided it too grand and more than likely impossible. Eventually they decided on five passenger airliners and all would originate on the East Coast.

The recruiting began, and Mihdhar enlisted Ziad Samir Jarrah while he was in Germany. Jarrah was excited to serve in the *jihad* against America but he also had a girlfriend, Aysel Senguen, who posed a potential problem. Still Jarrah assured Mihdhar that she would not create difficulty.

Slowly, so as not to arouse suspicion, Sharafan had those he recruited for the operation move to the United States. They were given instructions to blend in, take jobs, learn English, and take flying lessons. Sharafan led the way to lay the groundwork for the project they all laughingly called "Red Eagle." The "Red" was for the blood of Americans to be spilled.

Mohammed found other sources to finance Red Eagle.

The first were Mihdhar and Nawaf Hamzi in January 2000. They arrived in Los Angeles and a few weeks later moved to San Diego. Unlike the others, they had not spent much time in the West and they spoke very little English. It became necessary for Sharafan to help and support them financially until the appointed time. After they gained assistance within the Muslim community in Culver City, Sharafan enrolled them in English classes. To cover his trail, both Hamzi and Mihdhar called him Khallam. Both men took flying classes but they failed miserably. When Mihdhar learned about the birth of his first child in Yemen, he returned in June 2000. Hamzi remained behind. Upon Mihdhar's return to his country, Khalid Sheikh Mohammed became enraged and concerned that their plans might be compromised. He tried to remove Mihdhar from the operation, but with Sharafan's insistence bin Laden decided against Mohammed's demands.

Hamzi continued to wait for a new member to be added to his cell. Knowing him to have once been a pilot, the al Qaeda noted Hani Hanjour as a prime selection for the operation. Sharafan set things in motion, and after money and paperwork were in place, Hanjour arrived in San Diego in early December and joined Hamzi. Within a few days they moved to Mesa, Arizona, where Hanjour took refresher courses in flying. After Jarrah received his license in August, he returned to Germany to be with his girlfriend, Aysel Senguen. While visiting England, Mombassa went to a restaurant where he found the disgruntled Muslim, Alli Maussan. Depressed with his life and the way he was treated as a waiter in the restaurant, he eagerly joined them for the five thousand cash advance.

Sharafan tried everything he could to get Ramzi Binalshibh to join the operation, but everything failed. A visa was denied because the United States was afraid Ramzi would stay to work in America and not return to Germany. If the United States had only known. The plans were going well and Sharafan continued to look for another potential candidate to train as a pilot.

During the summer of 2000, operatives from the other cells in Hamburg began arriving in the United States. At the end of May, Marwan al Shehhi flew from Brussels to Newark where he waited for the others. Mohamed Atta arrived from Prague the first week of June. They immediately tried to enter a flight training school. When Ziad Jarrah arrived in Newark at the end of June, he let the others know he had entered a flying program at the Florida Flight Training Center in Venice, Florida, and would be unable to join them. Looking for flight schools, Atta and Shehhi checked out the program at Airman Flight School in Norman, Oklahoma, before eventually enrolling at Huffman Aviation, another school in Venice where Jarrah lived.

Helping Sharafan with his plans, bin Laden personally recruited Zacarias Moussaoui. Sharafan agreed with the decision; they intended to use Moussaoui to replace Jarrah whom they feared would not return. At first Moussaoui trained in Malaysia, but Khalid Sheikh Mohammed demanded that Moussaoui train in the United States. From London, Moussaoui flew to Norman, Oklahoma, where, on the recommendation of Atta, he took up flying at the Airman Flight School.

A problem surfaced in 2000 when Alli Maussan had second thoughts about giving his life. After spending the money he had been given, he found a better job and even an American girlfriend. Death no longer seemed so wonderful. He turned himself into the FBI and recited his story. He told the government agents he believed there was a terrorist plot that would use passenger planes to fly into buildings.

Soon after that, Mombassa and Sharafan became aware of what Maussan had done, but they were at a crossroads. Tension and fear threatened to thwart Sharfan's well laid plans. Mohammed suggested they kill Maussan, but Sharafan feared such an action might alert authorities, thus revealing their plans. The decision was made to let Maussan live.

This worked to perfection as the FBI refused to believe a wild fabricated story such as Maussan recited. Even though Maussan passed a lie detector test, the FBI knew such a plot would be impossible to carry out.

No one believed his story and Maussan was returned to England. His new girlfriend refused to go with him.

The cells remained intact and the preparations continued as planned.

Still, Osama wanted to see something that would show him Sharafan could succeed. With bin Laden's blessings, Sharafan had sought out a place to show him an example of America's weakness and a solution for defeating the United States. Revenge was almost forgotten when in October of 2000, in a small port of Aden, Yemen, the warship USS Cole was almost blown out of the water. The incident was a great accomplishment and had moved Sharafan up in the ranks of terrorism. The deed also made him one of bin Laden's right-hand men. Most importantly, the USS Cole showed a weakness that better prepared the Coalition. The United States looked for a terrorist called Alef. Both bin Laden and Sharafan were pleased with this. The plan gained more strength when George W. Bush, the new American president, bombed Iraq. Iraq, being the whipping boy of the Middle East, was another weakness the United States revealed when it took the role of "policeman of the world." This was a weakness Sharafan was sure he could expose—if done properly—and with bin Laden's help there was almost no limit as to what he could accomplish. Bin Laden was not so sure, but Sharafan explained in detail how he could accomplish the goal of taking out the economic landmark of the Twin Towers in New York and make bin Laden's dream come true. This plan was of great interest to bin Laden, who, being an engineer, knew the plan could work. He agreed even though he knew it would probably mean his own life.

Bin Laden knew that destroying the Twin Towers in New York would ultimately become the symbol of America's downfall. Sharafan explained his plan in detail. With over a hundred strategically placed Muslim fundamentalists already in the United States, he would gather them together and activate eight cells—with none of the groups in contact with the others until the last day. Bin Laden had sent money for their training and nearly a dozen had already been trained to fly big commercial jets like the 747 and 757.For more than a year, Sharafan and Mombassa had worked with the five groups. All were prepared and excited to become martyrs for Islam. Five men were sent to each cell. Many looked like every-day Americans with the same goals and dreams, but they had very, very different goals. The oldest was thirty-three and had been in the United States for over eight years, but he never wavered in his ideas toward his faith. Most were twenty-two to twenty-five years of age and all were eager to serve Mohammed. They practiced diligently in July and August of 2001.

Everything was running smoothly until Atta and Shehhi returned from Germany in January of 2001 and both men were denied entry. They convinced the INS they needed to finish their flight training. Eventually their re-entry into the United States was cleared, and they both returned to Florida to continue their flight lessons.

In 2001 Hanjour started training at Pan Am International Flight Academy. The lessons were in a simulator for a Boeing 737. The pilots became the leaders for each group, with Atta exerting control over all while being instructed by Sharafan.

The money continued to flow and the men continued to train. With the pilots situated, Sharafan set about finding men to control the planes they would hijack. He wanted groups of five for each cell. Now Sharafan set out to find those who would complement his pilots. What he needed were muscle men that could carry off the hijackings and protect his men.

Ahmed al Ghamdi and Majed Moqed arrived at Dulles airport in May and joined up with Hanjour and Hazmi. Together they rented an apartment in Paterson, New Jersey.

Soon others joined them including Ahmed al Ghamdi, Abdul Aziz al Omari, and Nawaf's brother Salem Hazmi. The last to arrive was Khalid al Mihdhar who returned in July 2001.

Slowly and patiently, Sharafan assembled the five cells: Satam al Suqami, Wail al Shehri, Waleed al Shehri, Abdul Aziz al Omari, Ahmed al Ghamdi, Hamza al Ghamdi, Mohand al Shehri, Majed Moqed, Salem al Hazmi, Saeed al Ghamdi, Ahmad al Haznawi and Ahmed al Nami, Ihab Ali, and Fayez Banihammad. Also to join with the group were three of Sharafan's close associates: Yazeed Aziz, Satam al Majid, and Abu Mombassa.

The original date was to be May but they weren't ready. Then a problem surfaced in June when bin Laden sent another hundred terrorists to set themselves in positions to take action against the United States at a later date. Somehow the Israeli Massad discovered the Coalition's actions and notified the American FBI and CIA. They warned them something was about to happen, but they did not know what the terrorists had planned. Neither American intelligence agency responded to the information even though the Massad pressed that their intelligence was accurate and time was critical. President Obama waved off Israel one more time and all his men dismissed the reports. This was an action they would regret for the rest of their lives, which was short to say the least.

Now Sharafan and bin Laden knew their plan would work. The date changed to July but internal problems continued to plague them. Most were devout Muslims but not Suqami and Salem Hazmi. The two would drink in bars and harass topless dancers, even bragging about things they wanted to do to America. Sharafan had Salem's brother Nawaf rein both the men in with threats. The intimidation was mildly effective.

Bin Laden had delayed the original target date of September fifth. He needed two days to transfer his wealth, which was now near a billion dollars. He sold his airline stocks and the stocks in the companies that insured the Twin Towers. He explained to Sharafan he would sell short in the insurance and airlines, causing his fortune to triple. They would then have nearly three billion dollars to invest in their plans to destroy the United States.

Sharafan thought it ironic and sadistically humorous that they might actually get wealthy after they had killed thousands of unsuspecting Americans. He also noted how close he and bin Laden were to striking a real blow for their promised *jihad* and *fatwa.*

The final date was September 11, which Sharafan thought to be ironic as the date, since 911, was what Americans used on their phone for panic situations or an emergency. Sharafan snickered to himself when he realized how many 911 numbers would be dialed on that day.

The weapons for the hijackings were simple and would be knives and box cutters, with threats of bombs to deter any overzealous passengers. After a few test flights between New York and Los Angeles, they found these items could be easily concealed in their toiletry bags. They would also carry mace as an added deterrent to any would-be heroes. They were to attack the first ten to fifteen minutes after takeoff when the cockpit doors were still open. Their targets were the Twin Towers of New York, the Pentagon, the White House, and the Capital Building. All were excited to strike the first blow against America.

Late in July of 2001, Sharafan contacted the groups and announced everything was ready for the new mission. Some were sent tickets, some bought their own. Sharafan reminded them all to buy round trip tickets even though it was a one-way campaign. Four even bought tickets for October so there would be no suspicion. Who would suspect someone of dying as a martyr when they had tickets for the future? Everything went as planned. A little more than a month later they were ready to put their plan into action and strike the first blow.

They were also told which targets they would hit. Atta would be first, hitting one of the World Trade Center's Twin Towers in New York. Next Shehhi would crash into the other Tower. The Pentagon was Hanjour's target. The Washington Capitol Building would be Jarrah's mission, while Moussaoui was given the privilege of crashing into the White House.

With only weeks before the mission, many of the men wanted to say goodbye to their families, but Sharafan expressly forbid them doing so. On August 4 the last hijacker, Mohamed al Kahtani, arrived but was denied entry.

Over time, another problem had been simmering between Atta and Jarrah. They argued constantly. Jarrah did not like being controlled and ordered around by Atta. He expressed his concerns to Sharafan who reluctantly allowed Jarrah to see Senguen one more time with the promise to fulfill his obligation for the *jihad.* It was well Jarrah followed through with his promise, because the INS arrested Moussaoui on August 16. Sharafan did not learn about the arrest until after Red Eagle had been completed. If they had known Moussaoui had been arrested, Sharafan would most likely have decided to cancel their plans. But later the arrest would create a major problem for him.

He stressed no contact with family members, but what Sharafan did not know might have also caused him to call off the mission. Atta refused to let anyone get in touch with their families while he made contacts back in his country. Jarrah communicated with Senguen, and a few days before the attack he left a letter to her stating what he was about to do and how honored she should be. Khalid Hamzi began to brag to his American friends about what was going to happen. Sharafan knew none of this and the mission continued.

Two days remained and the men were already moving into position. Only one problem confronted Sharafan. No one had heard from Moussaoui. With time running out, Sharafan purchased a ticket with the intention of being the fifth pilot. The time had come for operation Red Eagle.

On September 11, 2001, the day dawned clear and beautiful on the eastern coast of the United States. It was anything but a day for death. But death was coming.

In Portland, Maine, Atta and Omari began Red Eagle, boarding a plane for Boston at 6:00 a.m. When they arrived, Atta called Sharafan and Shehhi to firm up plans. Everything was going as scheduled. Sharafan had already contacted Hanjour who was at Dulles and Jarrah who was at Newark, waiting.

Atta would control American Airlines 11, Shehhi would take over United Airlines 175, while Moussaoui would command American Airlines 181.

In Newark, United Airlines 93 would be commandeered by Jarrah. Not far away at Dulles, Hanjour was ready for American Airlines 77.

All was in readiness except for one thing. Sharafan had still heard nothing from Moussaoui. He was fully prepared to take the position as the pilot. If everything went as planned, Atta would be the first to strike a blow against America when he hit New York's North Tower of the World Trade Center.

Slowly, and one at a time, the men arrived for each flight. Everything appeared normal when Atta, Omari, Suqami, and Wail and Waleed Shehri boarded American Airlines 11. Wail and Waleed took their seats in first class, ready for their mission. Six rows back the other three waited. The aircraft pushed away from the gate at 7:40 a.m. Nineteen minutes later the plane was in the air.

United Airlines 175 rolled away at 8:00 a.m. with all five terrorists in place. Banihammad, Shehri, and Shehhi were secure in first class with Hamza and Ahmed Ghamdi only a few rows back. The aircraft was rolling down the runway and into the air at 8:14 a.m.

Casually Sharafan strolled toward his gate and the flight on American Airlines 181. Already he had spotted Ihab Ali. Soon Yazeed Aziz, Satam al Majid, and Abu Mombassa would arrive for the flight. Still he waited for Moussaoui, but if he didn't arrive it didn't matter because Sharafan now had a date with history. In the Dulles airport, five individuals made their way to their gate. Nothing appeared to be unusual as they entered American Airlines 77, bound for Los Angeles. Moqed and Mihdhar boarded the plane first, and were seated in row 12. A few minutes later Hanjour followed them and made his way to first class. Then the Hazmi brothers, Nawaf and Salem, arrived and took their first class seats four rows behind Hanjour. Like it did every morning, American Airlines 77 pushed away from the gate unaware of any danger, prepared for their normal 8:10 a.m. departure. The plane lifted from the runway at 8:20 a.m.

When United Airlines 93 pushed away from the gate, they were already behind schedule but all the men were in position. Jarrah, Nami, and Ghamdi were comfortably accommodated in the first three rows. Only three rows behind them sat Haznawi ready for action. The unsuspecting passenger airliner entered into the air at 8:42 a.m.

All nineteen men had managed to defeat all of the sophisticated security steps the FAA's aviation security system had in place and which all truly believed would prevent any hijacking. How wrong they were.

Fifteen minutes after takeoff and after climbing to an altitude of 26,000 feet, the terrorists moved swiftly to take the plane. Wail and Waleed moved quickly, stabbing both of the first class flight attendants and pushing their way into the cockpit where Atta took the controls. A passenger tried to stop Omari, but Suqami stabbed him from behind.

They immediately filled the first-class with mace, making the passengers retreat to the back of the plane. They warned the travelers that they had a bomb and told them not to do anything. The passengers were under control, with no intention of doing anything. And why should they take action? All hijackers made demands, released passengers after their demands were met, and then would fly to a safe country.

At 8:21 Atta turned off the transponder and American Airlines 11 disappeared from radar, causing much confusion. Atta changed course. They had been in the air a little over twenty minutes.

Less than thirty minutes after being airborne, Banihammad and Shehhi moved into action to take United Airlines 175. They were followed closely by Shehri, with the others spraying mace. In a fit of rage, Banihammad and Shehri killed the protesting captain and co-pilot as Shehhi took over the controls. Ahmed Ghamdi stabbed one of the flight attendants then threatened the other passengers telling them there was a bomb. Again the passengers bent back in submission. This time the transponder was not turned off, but at 9:41 Shehhi managed to change the codes on the aircrafts' device with the same devastating results. He quickly changed course for New York not far behind Atta.

American Airlines 77 had been in the air only thirty minutes when the attack commenced. They used knives, mace, and box cutters to move everyone out of first-class so Hanjour could take over the aircraft. Threats of a bomb quickly subdued the crew and passengers. At 8:56 Hanjour turned off the transponder and changed directions setting a course for Washington, D.C. and the Pentagon.

Timing had fallen off. First United Airlines 93 delayed on the ground and now the group hesitated, moving slowly before taking action. More than forty-five minutes into the flight they moved into play. The captain of the flight managed to radio in a "Mayday" before the aircraft was taken over. Things went rather smoothly and a few minutes later Jarrah was at the controls. After the transponder was turned off at 9:41, Jarrah also set a course for Washington, D.C. and his target: the Capitol building.

Skimming across the tops of the buildings in New York, American Airlines 11 crashed into the North Tower of the World Trade Center at 8:46 a.m. History had changed and the initial crash began a new type of war no one had ever experienced before.

People on the ground gathered around to watch, as did spectators in the South Tower. Sixteen minutes later United Airlines 175 screamed across the skies, crashing into the South Tower with the same devastating results.

In Washington D.C., American Airlines 77 aimed initially toward the White House veered away and headed toward the Pentagon, dropping altitude quickly. With the Pentagon in view and at an altitude of 2000 feet, Hanjour aimed at the target like a huge missile the world had never seen before. With an air speed of 534 miles per hour, Hanjour crashed the aircraft into the Pentagon at 9:37 a.m.

Twenty-two minutes later the World Trade Center South Tower collapsed.

Cellular phones sabotaged Jarrah's mission. Information was rolling in after the first three crashes. The passengers on United Airlines were using their phones and they all received the same message. They were sitting on a missile that was not going to land safely.

When the passengers attacked, Jarrah and Nami were forced into a defensive posture within the cabin. Jarrah tried vainly to stop the attack. He tipped to the left then the right and when that didn't work he dove and then climbed. Still the passengers maintained their onslaught of the cabin.

Jarrah knew he wouldn't make his target. He asked Nami, "Shall we put it down?"

Nami said, "Yes, pull it down." With a jerk of the control wheel, Jarrah turned the aircraft on its back and sent it into a deadly plunge all the while he and Nami screamed, "Allahu Akbar!"

With a speed in excess of 580 miles per hour, United Airlines 93 crashed into a field in Shanksville, Pennsylvania, at 10:03 a.m. They were more than 100 miles short of their target.

At 10:28 a.m. the World Trade Center North Tower collapsed.

Confusion was success and America was confused. The events were almost impossible to believe and came with a staggering nightmarish intensity—a nightmare that filled the American landscape, only this nightmare played out in real life.

No one associated with Red Eagle had any way of knowing how successful their attack had been until much later. Information about the crashes was agonizingly slow in reaching the authorities in control. All four airliners had crashed before anyone took any affinitive actions. The President and his czars had little knowledge of the events that transpired.

Ironically many federal agencies knew nothing about the crash until the news media broadcast video of the North Tower smoldering. Ever alert, CNN was on the spot transmitting the horrifying video when minutes later they caught the second airliner crashing into the South Tower.

It was after 10:30 a.m. before any action to stop air traffic occurred. Flight 181 was delayed and still connected to the gate. Information of the tragic incidents had forced the airport to shut down flights temporarily.

The American Airlines flight was still on hold at the gate when the pilot made an announcement over the intercom. "Ladies and Gentlemen, we have disturbing news that a plane just hit one of the Twin Towers in the World Trade Center."

People laughed. One passenger snidely said, "I don't see why they let those small planes buzz those buildings." A few laughed; some like Sharafan shook their heads in agreement.

A moment later the pilot made another disturbing announcement. "I'm sad to announce that a second passenger airliner just crashed into the other Twin Tower. I'll have more information in a minute."

A few cried, some showed fear and confusion. Everyone started talking at once. A few tossed out wild guesses and a few gave their personal theories as to what had happened and who had done it. Sharafan tried to act as surprised as the others.

An older woman behind Sharafan ventured, "Do you think it was China attacking?"

In perfect English Sharafan assured her, "I'm sure it wasn't China." Who should know better that he?

Someone said, "We arrested those drug runners from Colombia. Do you suppose they did it?"

"What about Russia?" guessed another.

A middle-aged man stood up. "It's none of those. Think about it. Russia and China need our business. Whoever did this committed suicide. No drug runner is willing to commit suicide." Sharafan tried to hide his smile. The man continued. "The last time something happened like this we all pointed our fingers at the Middle East, but it turned out to be an American. Still if I had to venture a wild guess, I would say it was some group from a Middle Eastern country. I'm sure you remember the 1993 bombing of the Twin Towers?" He paused to get their attention, which he had, including Sharafan's. "The man behind that attack was a man called Osama bin Laden. Again, I'm probably wrong, but if I could pick someone who might have been responsible for this thing, he would be my choice."

Very astute, you will find out very soon, thought Sharafan with a slight smile. He decided that when they took off he would tell this man just how correct he was—before he killed him.

The pilot made another announcement. "Ladies and Gentlemen, we have more bad news. A passenger airliner has crashed into the Pentagon." There were gasps and cries as he continued. "The president has ordered all planes grounded. I'm sorry but this flight has been cancelled. You will need to go inside and make arrangements for an alternate flight."

Sharafan made himself appear as upset as all the other passengers. President Bush had grounded all airlines after the crashes. But it was too late, the damage had been done.

The airport was in bedlam. Sharafan and the others exited the planes unmolested and unnoticed. All five of the terrorists made their separate ways to a safe haven, all the while taking time to catch the video broadcast throughout the terminals. Everyone watched in horror, unable to turn away from the ghastly sight.

None noticed the smirks and even smiles on the five men as they made their way away from the airport. Red Eagle had been a success and had made its mark on American history and the world.

Sharafan shook himself from his thoughts, and smiled as General Navarro finished with the questions from the briefing, demanding everyone's attention.

With confidence the general added his own personal comments. "The bleeding heart Americans have helped our cause when they refused to make English the national language. Remember, hundreds of thousands of Americans do not speak English. Since all of you are versed in Spanish and English, it will be easy to sway them to our side. If they do not understand English, you will be able to convert them under the pretense they are helping America." Navarro laughed. "In the end they will join us anyway.

That is also why you will be wearing uniforms similar to American forces. All the markings on your uniforms will be in English."

In mock seriousness Sharafan said, "There will be only one thing that could possibly prevent us from completing our invasion."

Concerned, all the men turned to him to find the reason they surely expected Sharafan to know. He grinned wide and continued. "We will no longer have CNN to warn us of the Americans' actions. Everyone present burst out laughing.

General Navarro raised his glass and tried to quiet his men. He smiled sadistically and knowingly, and then toasted. "Millions are poised and waiting at the border to take their new lands."

## Chapter 8

# NEW YEAR'S EVE

The atmosphere was tense at best, but the women eased the situation, and Marix reluctantly agreed Ruben was justified in inviting his friend. After dinner they were to continue their celebration at the officers' party, bringing in the New Year, 2017. The women had secretly decided if the night went poorly, they were going to hang Ruben. Luckily for him, he had no knowledge of the agreement and felt everything was going perfectly.

Marix had made reservations at an elegant nightspot in the downtown portion of Corpus Christi, resting atop one of the many buildings with a view overlooking the bay. The definitive features of the popular docks were very distinguishable in the bright lights surrounding the man-made piers. Because of their shapes two were called the T-heads and one the L-head. All three piers were lined with pleasure boats, sailboats, and shrimp boats. Two floating restaurants were busily taking patrons around the bay. In the distance, the 200-foot harbor bridge sparkled in the night sky.

They rode a glass elevator to the thirtieth floor. The view was spectacular. The three men were dressed in their military best.

Sunday wore white chiffon trimmed in black. The dress hung loosely about her waist to afford room and comfort for the baby. A sparkling pearl necklace, accented with a piece of black coral between each pearl, hung elegantly around her slender neck against her naturally brown skin. Her dark hair was pulled tight and rolled into a bun atop her head.

In complete contrast, Krysti's outfit was a fine skintight black satin dress trimmed in gold with a gold waistband that made her long auburn hair stunning. The dress gathered toward her right side showing her leg far above her knee. Cut wide and open in the back, it formed a V in the front making the gold and diamond cross stand out boldly.

Ruben and Beau were bringing up the rear as they exited the glass elevator. "Psssttt, hey Beau," whispered Ruben. "Which fork do I eat the salad with? The big one or the small one?"

From between clenched teeth came the reply, "Just because I didn't kill ya this afternoon, doesn't mean I won't tonight."

"Shit, look at this place. Now I know how a black man feels when he stumbles across a KKK cross burning party alone."

"You're not alone. I'm afraid we're gonna fry together. But don't worry Ruben, I promise to take you with me," Beau snickered.

"With all that etiquette Marix has, you haven't got a chance tonight. He'll—," Ruben stopped when Beau abruptly turned down a side hallway. "Hey, where do you think you're going?" Ruben almost yelled, at the same time reaching for Beau as though he were a security blanket.

Beau stopped long enough to say, "Tell them I went to the bathroom. I'll be back in a minute." Then he disappeared around the corner of the short hall.

"Shit!"

"What did you say?" asked Sunday.

"Oh nothing."

"Where's Beau?" Krysti asked.

"Maybe he decided to leave," Marix said, hoping.

"I don't think he would," Krysti replied.

"He said he'd be back in a minute. He had to . . . you know." They all laughed at Ruben's awkwardness.

The waiter took a few minutes before seating them, and not long afterward Beau reappeared. He sat at the end of the table with Ruben on his left and Krysti seated to his right. The table was a thick piece of glass covering a detailed wrought iron stand. Suspended over the table was a glass chandelier with three burning candles. In the center of the table was a hand-embroidered piece of yellow Japanese silk on top of which rested spices and bread, all laid out in fine-cut crystal. The inlaid silverware and linen were all in matching colors.

The waiter, wearing a black tux with tails and white gloves, passed around the menus. When he returned he asked if they would like to order drinks. Marix wore a cold calculating smile and asked for wine. When the waiter returned with the bottle, Marix motioned him toward Beau so he could do the honors. Ruben squirmed in his seat when he realized it was Marix's intention to embarrass Beau.

The waiter brought the cork to Beau and Ruben froze in terror. He wondered if his friend knew what to do. All he could do was watch, but Ruben was shocked when Beau accepted. He sniffed the cork and nodded his head to the waiter. Then he turned to Marix and with a sly grin quoted the type of wine and the year. Marix was deprived of what he assumed would be a small victory over his rival.

The rest of the dinner was uneventful as they discussed the trip to South Texas on New Year's Day and the Bowl games they would miss. From their table, they watched as sailboats and party boats made excursions from the docks out into the bay. When dinner was finished, they started for the Officers' party. Ruben made sure he brought up the rear of the group and eventually pulled Beau aside.

"Hey, where the hell did you learn about wine?" Ruben asked. "You don't know any more about wine tastin' than I do."

"To the contrary, my good man. A little etiquette would do you no harm," Beau said. He held his nose haughtily in the air, but only for a second, then he started to chuckle but immediately covered his mouth to keep the others from hearing him.

Ruben frowned. "Come on, spill it."

Finally, with a sly grin he said, "I didn't go to the bathroom. I asked the waiter about the wine. How it would be served, what I was supposed to do. Then he showed me the three wines chosen the most often and how I could recognize them. And, as you see, I have become an expert."

* * *

General Navarro called Sharafan and Zahir into his room to coordinate their plan of attack with his. He had an elegant suite at the new airport. Everyone who worked on the facility had been well taken care of. Over a two-year period, the construction crews were replaced with men sympathetic to their cause. A little money in the right hands had accomplished much, and most of the money had come from the United States.

Sharafan found it hard to believe no one had exposed the invasion. Most of the aircraft had been dismantled, moved in trucks to avoid suspicion, and then reassembled in the large hangars. So many jets in such a small area. Removing them from the hangars would be more difficult than the invasion.

Navarro offered brandy to the men. Sharafan declined but Zahir accepted. Again, they went over the plan of attack. All was in readiness.

Tahar Zahir seemed to fidget as his hands squeezed the thick arms of the plush velvet seat within which he sat. "I think I will take some more brandy, Sir," he said addressing General Navarro. The general waved his arm and Zahir poured himself another drink.

Relaxed and with a half-smile on his face, Sharafan watched his friend's nervous efforts. Sharafan had also been nervous in the beginning, but with the success of Red Eagle that had changed. So many things had happened just as bin Laden had predicted. Americans had been creatures of habit.

He still remembered returning after the attack on New York. It was like yesterday. He had made a hasty retreat from the airport. From there he'd found a hotel where he waited and watched the non-stop news broadcast replaying the attack on television.

Again and again the World Trade Center North Tower smoldered as United Airlines 175 crashed into the South Tower. Mohamed Atta had been the first to succeed followed by Shehhi. CNN and other news broadcasters devoted airtime exclusively to the disaster as teams of experts tried to give their personal analyses to the situation: how it could have happened and who might have done the evil deed. All stations continued to replay the collapse of both towers from every possible angle. Sharafan was surprised at the devastation.

Even the sacred Pentagon, a symbol of America's might, had been violated with disastrous effects. Hanjour had succeeded. But cellular phones defeated the fourth plane when, through their phones, Americans on the jet learned of the events taking place and discovered what had happened to the others. The brave Americans had stormed the terrorists. All lives had been lost when the plane crashed in a remote part of Pennsylvania. The Capitol Building was spared and Jarrah had failed to realize his dream. The cancellation of all flights saved the White House.

In secret meetings Bush and his cabinet understood that the warnings they had overlooked were accurate and true. Only then did President Bush go into action. His response, though slow, had prevented American Airlines Flight 181 from becoming airborne when he grounded all aircraft. The White House had been spared, but the damage had been done. America would never be the same.

The United States screamed revenge on Afghanistan but the leaders of the attack were from every Middle Eastern county including Saudi Arabia, Egypt, Morocco, Somalia, India, and Pakistan. Some were even from the United States of America.

It took almost a month for Sharafan to return to Afghanistan where bin Laden waited for him with a warm welcome. All had great rejoicing and celebration. Allah had been good to them, for they had succeeded beyond their wildest expectations. Sharafan found the more the United States pushed and threatened to get bin Laden, the more united and determined the devout followers of Islam became. Palestinians became more brazen as suicide bombers attacked Israel, showing no mercy.

Sharafan learned the United States was looking for Alef Rasad. Bin Laden told him how a little more than a week after the bombings he had divested himself of all his stocks and the monies. They now had over three billion dollars to fight the United States, and that money was spread to places and names the United States could never locate.

The United States bombed Afghanistan but neither Sharafan nor bin Laden were near when the attacks occurred. Exactly as Sharafan expected, the United States bombed the locations given when rumors leaked to the FBI and CIA told of bin Laden's location. Only innocent people were found in the targeted areas. Sharafan could not understand how the American people believed the president and Congress when they said their "intelligence" knew exactly what and where to bomb in a country they knew nothing about. Yet that same intelligence had no idea about the Twin Towers of New York or the Pentagon in their own country.

Bin Laden and Sharafan had accomplished something most of the world would never have thought possible. Both men watched again and again as their friends crashed into the Twin Towers and the towers crumbled to earth. The Twin Towers' collapse symbolized the financial crumbling of the United States that would take place over the next twelve years. Less than two weeks following the terrorists' attack, Muslims from around the world swarmed the Al Qaeda to join the *jihad* against America.

Bin Laden, Sharafan, and the other leaders of Al Qaeda leaked information to American Intelligence through the Afghanistan Northern Alliance stating that they were still hidden in the mountains of Afghanistan. Just as Sharafan had predicted, the United States assembled their military forces in the Middle East. This brought conflicts in every Middle East nation. More Muslims joined Al Qaeda. When America bombed Afghanistan they had done just as Sharafan had predicted.

Bin Laden and Sharafan had watched the bombings on cable and CNN from the security of a farm nestled in a remote valley of northern Pakistan. Over the next few weeks more volunteers came to the Al Qaeda. Money continued to flow in, and the Americans were only able to halt the flow of about fifteen percent of their funds. Red Eagle was a smashing success. One by one the Muslim nations turned against the United States.

With heightened passion at the success of their plot, Sharafan and bin Laden had discussed the future. Sharafan described in great detail his ideas to destroy the United States. Bin Laden liked many of Sharafan's plans.

Over the next ten years the terrorist acts continued and leaders on both sides died. Sharafan survived and the Coalition grew in leaps and bounds. The secret cells in the United States doubled every year.

Many of the cells placed in the United States after the terrorist attacks simply flew to Mexico, found transportation to a town called Agua Pierta on the Arizona border, and then walked across and into the United States. From that point other cell members would pick them up and casually drive them to their new destinations: secure homes in the United States. Heavy contributions made to the ACLU in the middle nineties paid dividends when the ACLU argued the issue of discrimination and that the United States could not suppress the rights of illegal immigrants walking across the border from Mexico. This had enabled many of his men to walk into America unmolested.

More Al-Qaeda contributions to environmentalist groups helped prevent the United States from oil exploration and becoming energy self-sufficient. A year after the New York Twin Towers triumph, bin Laden and Sharafan saw what they had believed all along. Enron, Dynegy, Aldelphia, WorldCom, Xerox, Arthur Anderson, and the CEOs of many large American companies now had no honor or integrity. Politicians became blatant in giving lucrative contracts to those who donated money to their re-election campaign as shown by the wealthy Collier family. They made huge donations, and in return had received more than 120 million dollars not to drill in the Everglades of Florida, when the actual value of the leases had been estimated to be from five to twenty million.

All were motivated by greed, and that American greed helped bin Laden and the Coalition destroy America without firing a single shot. It was only a matter of time. Bin Laden and Sharafan found it easy to contribute funds to CEOs in return for reports of huge contracts. Major accountants were no different, even in the light of all the current scandals. Actually the accountants were the easiest to manipulate with small offers of monetary rewards. For as little as a few hundred thousand dollars, accountants could be trusted to show huge profits for any company they desired.

The real windfall came when members of the Coalition were able to buy members of the board for companies in America's Fortune 500. After all, who couldn't be convinced to give hundreds of millions in interest-free money if a million could be passed on to that same board member. Greed had destroyed America's honor and integrity.

The final piece of the puzzle came into place in 2003 when the United States attacked Iraq against world approval. *Operation Iraqi Freedom* and *Shock and Awe* worked against the United States when the American president proved he would do what he wanted, even if it meant avoiding the truth or making the world angry.

Rasht Sharafan, bin Laden, and others dedicated to the Muslim cause had watched with great satisfaction while the United States charged into Iraq and the unity of the world against terrorism crumbled, while the Muslim nations united and became stronger. In a way Saddam Hussein was victorious in defeat. Suspicion and distrust of the United States spread throughout the United Nations. Even when the United States attacked with what it called its Coalition Forces, all knew that it was only Great Britain, the United States, and in a small capacity Australia who were involved. And these countries were promised large contracts in the reconstruction of Iraq.

President Bush told the world they would side with him after he defeated Iraq and rid the world of the Weapons of Mass Destruction, while secretly giving broad lucrative contracts to American construction and oil companies like Halliburton. They all wanted black gold. Strangely, no one remembered that Saddam Hussein had murdered his son-in-laws because they had told the world Iraq had no such weapons. They had told the truth and paid for it with their lives.

Two weeks after the invasion something happened that should have alerted the world, but sadly it went unnoticed in the frenzy for a blood war and revenge. The American people believed it to be a war to avenge the attack of 9/11. Secretary of Defense Rumsfeld addressed the media at this time. He told how well the invasion was going and that American troops had secured more than 200 oil wells. While he spoke in his arrogant controlling manner, the news media showed video of Iraqi people looting and stealing from a nuclear power plant.

No one asked why the American troops had failed to secure a location with obvious Weapons of Mass Destruction. What the world failed to notice was there were two reasons the plant was never secure. The nuclear power plant did not hold the financial rewards oil wells held, and the worst and more obvious reason was because American leadership secretly knew there were no Weapons of Mass Destruction to be found.

The rest of the world saw the truth. Even so, France and many other nation members of the United Nations jumped in on Iraq like it was a piñata that had been cracked open by the United States, and like little kids they all scrambled for pieces of the candy.

The unity was gone; allies were now hard to find. Even in the United States, *Operation Iraqi Freedom* became a catalyst as Americans bitterly turned violent against each other for their stand on the war.

In Pakistan, bin Laden relaxed and watched CNN, MSNBC, and Headline News with great interest. The Americans complained about Iraq not adhering to the Rules of War while marching ahead triumphantly and literally slaughtering the Iraqi army with their technologically advanced weapons.

Both bin Laden and Sharafan found it to be a little amusing that Bush called the handful of countries that attacked Iraqi the *Coalition*—the same term they used for their organization to defeat America: a group they had originated years earlier.

With the bravado and swagger of a bully, President Bush had landed on the aircraft carrier Abraham Lincoln. Behind him hung a large sign: "Mission Accomplished." It was almost as if the media frenzy had been staged. From Pakistan, bin Laden and Sharafan watched all that transpired on CNN.

Sharafan was angry but bin Laden snickered at Bush's image saying, "You have never accomplished any mission."

To shouts and cheers the president swaggered up. Smiling out of the side of his mouth he addressed the media and said, "Major combat in Iraq is over. The war has ended."

Again bin Laden smiled. "The war has only just begun."

Days later President Bush again was seen on CNN. "The world will see that we are rid of an evil dictator and the people of Iraq are better off. We have given them freedom. Because of our actions, Saddam Hussein's torture chambers are closed."

Even though President Bush had tried to convince the world Iraq had Weapons of Mass Destruction, he failed to show proof to back up his accusations. The American president tried to change his stories, and immediately threatened Iran, Syria, and Korea. He called those countries evil in an effort to take the heat off his unwarranted actions. While never doing anything to Israel, he demanded sanctions against the countries he called the *Axis of Evil.* Rumsfeld also continued his arrogant, condescending ways toward the Iraqi people. While he said Iraq had been given a democracy, they had instead been given chaos. While American troops held all the black gold, they allowed the destruction of ancient artifacts of antiquity. Banks were stripped and laid barren. The economy collapsed and it became impossible for the Iraqi people to rebuild on a foundation of a new democracy when all they had been given was chaos.

When Rumsfeld was asked how America planned to help Iraq, he came back with the snide response, "This is a war. Iraq will have to deal with chaos." And with those words and inaction the tide turned and the Iraqi people slowly began to despise and hate Americans. To the immense satisfaction of Sharafan and bin Laden, the world also started to fear and loathe the United States.

Sharafan laughed and said to bin Laden, "The Americans repeat history."

"How so?" bin Laden asked.

"Memories are short," he said. "When the United States won its independence from England in 1776, the British cried foul because when they marched in with their bright red uniforms, the Americans would not come out to meet them and be killed. Instead the Americans fought like guerrillas and shot them from the cover of the forest. The British complained the Americans did not wear uniforms and they could not tell the enemy from those true to the crown. The British complained that the Americans did not fight war with the code of ethics and honor that all countries used to fight war. Now the Americans make the same complaints."

"So what is the point?"

"That war marked the beginning of the end for the British Empire. So too America's *Operation Iraqi Freedom* marks the beginning of the end for the United States."

Bin Laden smiled and nodded his head. "If only Hussein had listened to us."

"Yes, just a little military planning would have dealt a harsh blow to the Americans," Sharafan noted. He smiled broadly and looked bin Laden in the eye. "Now his defeat will mean our victory. While the United States and its former allies bicker over the spoils of war, we become more united." Suddenly, Sharafan's face reflected a deep concern even bin Laden noticed.

"Something troubles you?" bin Laden asked.

"While we plan to destroy America, your agents make lucrative contracts with American companies. I don't understand."

For one of the few times those near bin Laden could remember, he not only smiled, but he also laughed. "Not all things are as they appear. Yes I make contracts with American engineering and computer companies. Greedy executives line their pockets with American dollars that one day will be worthless. Each time Fluor, Halliburton, Brown and Root, and Kellogg send us jobs to engineer, we put another nail in their coffin. Even as the president gives the military contracts to Halliburton, the same company is sending jobs to India and the Philippines, taking jobs away from Americans. And those companies we control indirectly. Each time they take away an American job, we put to work at least ten men with ties to us."

Now, Sharafan understood bin Laden's plans even better. He smiled. "The American companies have laid off thousands."

"And that means tens of thousands of our people are working and planning for the future. A future that will bring an end to America." This time bin Laden laughed silently. "Even as President Bush and other infidels like Rumsfeld condemn Iran for harboring Al Qaeda, their own American companies hire us by the thousands and feed us as we prepare to destroy them. Only recently Bill Dudley, the CEO of Bechtel, said he was moving work from London and Houston to a New Delhi office in India."

"Ahhh," smiled Sharafan. "More for us."

"Correct. We could never accomplish what we have without the aid of America's politicians and CEOs. What they cannot see is that in ten to twenty years there will be no more Americans that can do engineering or program computers, and then they will need us like they need our oil."

Sharafan nodded then asked, "But why help computer companies like Microsoft with programming? You only line the pockets of their billionaires with even more money."

Again, bin Laden managed a smile. "Already, American software companies like Microsoft and Texas Instruments spend more than ten billion dollars making software in India. We have a hand in more than half of that." Bin Laden rubbed his chin and smiled. "If you have watched the technical side of America, you would see greed is also there. IBM, Silicon Laboratories, and Intel have their chips made in India where we can control what we send them. They too have become arrogant and passive and do not check their software and chips because it would be too expensive.

Even Microsoft's Bill Gates had his picture in the newspapers with India's Narayana Moorthy as he gave billions of dollars of work to Infosys in Bangalore, India." Bin Laden laughed out loud. "Hence the problems they currently have, and the ones they will have."

"I must say I do not understand."

"We do programming for many of the computer companies because we are so cheap. But at the same time we are doing something else."

"What?"

Waving his hand in the air confidently, bin Laden said, "You might say we are decorating these programs."

"That makes no sense."

"Oh, but it does. You see, we add a few marks of our own that go undetected. A virus, so to speak. One that will sleep until we tell it to awake. And when we wake it the systems will collapse and become totally inoperable."

"Ahhh," mumbled Sharafan with a deep understanding.

Bin Laden grunted. "We have already tested it on Microsoft and were able to shut them down for a few days. Now we design others. Already our *sleeping virus* has been planted in ten major computer companies that have sold those programs to thousands of other American companies that depend on the software for their daily operation. The power systems of America will collapse. Anyone who has a Windows program on their computer will no longer be able to use their computers or access the Internet." Bin Laden actually laughed. "What good is a gun without bullets? When America's computers crash they will be unable to continue. You will find that without their computers, Americans are helpless."

"But you also make money building more American weapons."

"Yes but you do not see the whole picture."

"I understand the computer programs, but this."

"We play the Washington lobbying game. We pay their politicians and military leaders like all lobbyists and now the Pentagon's chief weapons buyer is not only listening to us but giving us the jobs we bid on. The American military already buys a Brazilian made spy plane. The largest U.S. military contractor, Lockheed Martin has foreign offices. We no longer need spies to access secrets. All we need is a contract to supply parts for their secret weapons. Our lobbyists are capable of virtually buying those contracts."

"Ahhh."

"Even now we are working on a three-hundred billion dollar job for a Strike Fighter jet to replace the F-16."

"But if you help with these weapons how can we hope to destroy them?"

With a wicked smile bin Laden continued, "Let me finish. Seventy-three foreign suppliers provide parts for 12 of America's most important weapons. Through India we provide most of the electronics and chips thanks to American computer companies. We make and sell the critical chips and electronics for their aircraft and ground vehicles, including the Strike Fighter jet, Predator drones and Tomahawk missiles. When they attack us we will be capable of controlling or even shutting down most of those weapons because we will actually understand their military weapons better than they do. What better way to understand the weapon of your enemy than to be the one who makes those weapons. And when you make a weapon and understand its flaws, think how easy it shall be to make the same weapon for you but even better than your enemy! And when we shut down their foreign parts suppliers—"

Sharafan interrupted as the words brought a thorough understanding, "They will not be able to maintain their weapons."

A smile of victory beamed from bin Laden, "Correct Rasht. Absolutely correct, and when we attack we will be able to control American's mighty weapons. America has made the wolf the shepherd of their flocks."

Again, Sharafan nodded his understanding.

When the United States accidentally captured Saddam Hussein it was another victory for Osama bin Laden and his people. Although President Bush again claimed triumph over the villainous Hussein, the people of Iraq were bitterly divided. While half of the people of Iraq were relieved and happy the terrible reign of Saddam Hussein was finished, the other half vented their hatred and anger on the United States for destroying the countless centuries of tradition, whether it was bad or not. The people of Iraq did not want another nation occupying and controlling their country.

It is said that when three percent of a country rises up against the powers that be, then that country can be taken over or overthrown. More than five percent of the whole population of Iraq was determined to find a solution to remove the United States. All they could rely on to satisfy their deadly desires were Osama bin Laden, his men, and his promise to rid the Middle East of the American infidels forever.

The United States military let chaos reign in Iraq over the next few years. The economy lacked stability. The Iraqi people lacked all the simple necessities of life while the American military became more brutal than the Hussein regime. America set up puppet leaders who would agree with American business. When America started to shut down newspapers and deny freedom of speech and press, a little known cleric, al-Sadr, stepped up and brought on a battle against the American military no one expected. The Iraqi people were not behind him until photos leaked out that detailed the abuse at Abu Ghraib prison—ironically, a location where Saddam Hussein had also tortured those against him.

The Iraqi people had become disillusioned and infuriated with the American occupation, and it was reflected in the popularity of al-Sadr as more than half the people now backed him. Now American troops had to fight the people of Iraqi. It was Vietnam all over again. While the popularity of al-Sadr soared, President Bush's plummeted.

From the safety of an exquisite bungalow hidden in the mountains of Pakistan, Sharafan and bin Laden watched all that transpired on cable. CNN gave them more information than their own agents.

Sharafan noted the sadistic humor of the situation in the prison and laughed as he told bin Laden, "Abu Ghraib is under new management."

Another important thing also happened in Iraq that pleased and assisted bin Laden with his plans. "President Bush has accomplished something in less than a year that Muslims and the peoples of the Middle East have not been able to do for a thousand years."

Curious Sharafan asked, "What is that?"

With a grin of evil satisfaction, bin Laden said, "The Sunni and Shiites. Bitter enemies for centuries, now, side-by-side they are loyal comrades fighting a common enemy: America."

Even Sharafan understood the significance of bin Laden's words. "With what the American president has accomplished in less than four years, think what he will be able to do for us if he is elected again."

Bin Laden also said, "While they say an invasion and occupation of Iraq will rid the world of terrorism, they have let our strength magnify while showing the world they are the true terrorists. America's allies are pulling away. Even the media notes the evil done by America. The Americans give Iraq a democracy but they pick Iraq's leader."

And it was true. The Americans had installed former Iraqis like Izzadine Saleem and Aquila al-Hashimi. All were handpicked leaders of the Bush Administration, assassinated one-by-one.

The administration also picked Ahmed Chalabi to lead Iraq. He had been exiled for embezzlement in 1989. The United States put him in power in exchange for his promise to cooperate with American "big business." But he proved his greed was not much different than that of his American counterparts. The American military broke into his house because they had information he was corrupt and in contact with Iran giving vital information to Iran about U.S. movements.

When bin Laden heard of this he smiled to Sharafan and the others telling them, "It has always been this way. The U.S. ousted the dictator of

Cuba and replaced him with Fidel Castro. They made Noriega their choice in Panama, only to find he did what the U.S. was trying to stop.

"It's ironic they can destroy Iraq but not stop the drug trade. You would think the American people would realize the reason there is still a drug trade in America is because that is what their corrupt leaders want. The only difference here is that the American puppets in Iraq will be executed."

As they talked, CNN showed President Bush again under the sign broadcasting "Mission Accomplished" but this time it showed eighty Americans dead. Then it noted that after almost a year more than 800 Americans had died and there was less control in Iraq than in the first month of the victory. As pictures of the Abu Ghraib tortures filled the screen, a commentary echoed from the monitor.

"Has the president falsely led us into war only to satisfy his personal ego? His incompetence led us into a world that is more unsafe than ever before. Is our nation safe? Now the world is against us. And who is leading America? Is it Bush? Or is it Cheney, Rumsfeld, or Israel? Let us pray this was not a war for oil. If there is a road map to peace in the Middle East then let us also pray Israel will follow it. This administration has tarnished the beacon of freedom and hope America once offered the world."

Sharafan and bin Laden gloated at what was happening around the world. Instead of being a group of renegade Muslim militants, bin Laden, with the help of President Bush, had turned it into a popular movement, fueled daily by America's actions.

Within weeks the torture at Abu Ghraib prison pointed to Rumsfeld. Again President Bush came to his defense, praising him for his superb job and courageous leadership in Iraq. To defend his stand, Bush made the military move quickly to court-martial a few common soldiers, while Rumsfeld and the generals in "control" never had charges brought against them.

President Bush also stressed that the tortures were the acts of only a "few soldiers" while Congress viewed thousands of photos and hours of video the Pentagon offered. No one asked the obvious questions: How could only a few make so many videos and photos? And the more disturbing question was what else had happened to the prisoners that the soldiers and generals were smart enough not to record? What else was the Pentagon hiding?

This was not lost on bin Laden, Sharafan, or any of the others that followed him. He said, "Now the Americans prosecute their own to cover up their crimes. They will do it so fast to appease us that their own soldiers will never trust them again."

Then an American was beheaded and Bush quickly sent Powell to do damage control. On the news, including CNN, Powell said, "Torture of any kind is unacceptable, and Arab leaders need to look at what's happening to their own societies. They need to reform their societies."

The Arab countries became angry. Powell continued. "When you are outraged at what happened at Abu Gharib, you should be equally, no, doubly outraged at what happened to Mr. Berg."

Many Middle Easterners were silent. Again Sharafan noted this and wondered why the obvious question on all of their minds hadn't been asked. Why should they be doubly outraged at an American being murdered over an Arab being murdered?

Bin Laden waved it off and pointed to Powell. "He is but a puppet to the American regime. They are on a witch hunt but there are no witches."

Over the next few years, strong and dependable companies had crumbled, while the stocks tumbled. And the president never stopped passing out the money in huge chunks. Just like bin Laden told Sharafan, the president made dynamic speeches and granted tax cuts while at the same time increased expenditures for war that were more than ten times the amount of the cuts. The deficit grew in leaps and bounds. America was going broke and didn't know it or didn't care. More lives were destroyed and money lost in this fashion than Al-Qaeda was able to accomplish through terrorists acts. And the terror never stopped. Still the United States was strong, and the only way the United States could be defeated would be if it were crippled. As Sharafan had said to bin Laden, "I could never beat a World Champion Boxer, and no one could ever beat the United States in battle. But—let me break the boxer's arm before I enter the ring and I will win."

"And how do you break America's arm?" Bin Laden asked.

"We will bring the United States to its knees financially. In less than ten years we can make the United States a financial cripple."

"They destroy themselves; how can you add to that?"

"Terror," laughed Sharafan. "Every time a letter has white powder or someone threatens a game or a holiday or a national shrine, the Americans will spend millions to protect themselves out of fear. If we never do another thing except make them think something is about to happen, their president and politicians will spend money defensively out of fear and will eventually spend all they have. America's president spreads more terror to his own people in one month than we could do in a year."

Then Sharafan laughed and added, "But we will also continue to kill Americans in their own country. They will be afraid to go to the store to buy milk. The fear in America will become an uncontrolled epidemic, and thus hasten America's demise." Knowingly, bin Laden nodded his approval. Terrorist acts around the world continued and like that of his father's, President Bush's popularity waned. Only months before the Presidential election, and with his reelection in jeopardy, President Bush relayed a message to the people of the United States that his intelligence forces had learned terrorist acts in America were about to begin again.

The president also noted that Syria was harboring terrorists and making Weapons of Mass Destruction so he levied sanctions against them. In a desperate move to seize the Latin American vote, he tried to rally the people of Florida when he issued sanctions against Cuba.

In May of 2004, President Bush warned of imminent al-Qaeda-sponsored terrorist attacks that would be carried out on American soil. In a desperate effort to get re-elected he used the age-old ploy of country, and managed to get more than a majority of Americans to rally around the flag again. Middle Eastern countries became angry as American military continued to hit innocent targets, and Israel used missiles, tanks, and aircraft to kill Palestinians and destroy their homes.

Although Kerry tried to mount a charge against the money machine of President Bush and his wealthy supporters, he might have had a chance if not for what happened in the latter part of the summer before the election. A war hero, Kerry was branded a coward and immoral.

Osama bin Laden was prepared for attacks on the United States but stopped Sharafan. He explained that President Bush was spreading his own personal terror across America and making a dangerously high deficit beyond a point of recovery. Bin Laden understood that at the rate Bush increased the deficit, another term under Bush's regime could quit possibly bankrupt the United States. Sharafan understood and delayed attacks in the United States until after Bush was re-elected.

With the world against the American people, U.S. citizens did just as bin Laden suspected. The president's popularity soared and there was much flag waving. Almost all American homes brandished an American flag on the exterior of their houses. Another thousand American soldiers died in Iraq.

With a platform of ethics and morality, Bush was reelected. Defense spending accelerated. Promises were broken and more troops were sent to the Middle East. Declared an imminent danger, Iran and Syria were threatened and accused, but again no Weapons of Mass Destruction were found and all the accusations proved to be false.

Then something happened in America to aid Sharafan in his quest at the same time change American opinion of their government. Katrina. A tropical storm, Katrina hit New Orleans and showed the true ability and power of the United States. For the first time Americans saw their government unprepared for any emergency, contrary to the 9/11 promises of President Bush. Americans became angry and bitter. Slowly the flags began to disappear from the fronts of American homes. The next four years found the National Debt soaring to over eleven trillion dollars.

Terror continued. Republicans and Democrats blamed each other for the ineptitude at finding the terrorists. While both sides pointed fingers and tossed accusations at each other, the terrorist network quietly shipped Russian-made SA-7 surface-to-air missiles and U.S. made Stinger anti-aircraft missiles obtained from former American allies. While ships were checked when they landed in American, this was not true in Mexico where the missiles were sent. When the deadly cargos landed in Mexico and were simply driven across the border in large trucks. The NAFTA treaty prevented a thorough inspection of the freight when it crossed the border. The missiles were distributed across the United States.

When a truck load of the missiles were accidentally discovered the truth shocked America. It was too late but just knowing they had been shipped created fear. However, fear of what might happen ended for all Americans when the missiles were used during heavily traveled holidays on July 4th and Christmas. The American government spent billions trying to find the missiles. They did find some, but not all. Terror spread quickly and the financial collapse accelerated.

With the help of Sharafan and many others like him the Coalition had survived. Over the next few years, when bin Laden's Coalition received opposition from local groups or leaders, the solution was easy. Leak their location to American intelligence and make sure the word "terrorist," "Al Qaeda," or "biological warfare" was linked to the group. Within weeks the area would be destroyed by American attacks. This worked as a double-edged sword for bin Laden. First, Americans eliminated the opposition and, second, those that remained would most times join the Coalition just to kill an American. Financially the United States began to crumble. Within eight years of the New York disaster, the United States Government was spending or giving away nearly a trillion dollars a year for defense or to help allies fight terrorism. Many times those same countries given assistance or money turned on the United States.

Foreign investors divested themselves of American bonds. In an effort to save his wealthy friends, President Bush forgot about the people. He put Secretary of Treasury Paulson in command thinking it would move America forward, but it was too late. Bush and Paulson gave away more than a trillion dollars to the wealthy and corrupt. The end of President Bush's second term found inflation running high, and the debt had reached nearly eleven trillion dollars. A large port of the American budget was marked to pay just the interest on the debt. Even the new president, Barack Obama, was unable to stop the increasing financial burden. During Obama's first year he also gave away more than a one and a half trillion in welfare for the wealthy matching Bush's last year in doling out to worthless bankrupt companies to keep those that had donated to their elections happy.

Bin Laden and Sharafan had almost accomplished the impossible without firing a shot. The Americans had almost destroyed themselves.

Sharafan could still remember bin Laden saying, "Americans have dug their own graves. Now it is time for us to bury them." Bin Laden did something seldom seen by others. He laughed. "The Twin Towers worked better than suspected. Single handedly Bush has almost destroyed America for us. Each year he over spent to fight a war against a word--terror! Something he can never defeat. He has doubled his countries debt and added another trillion to the debt in his last year just to help his wealthy friends on Wall Street, just as I suspected he would. Americans are angry that he is giving welfare to the wealthy and that is good for us. Obama will be no different and will be unable to slow the financial slide. In less than four years the United States will be bankrupt and nothing will save them. I predict that at the end of 2016 the great American Empire will come to an end and will be ours for the taking."

There were bombings at professional sporting events and vacation resorts, and bio-terrorism in the mail. Rockets shot down commercial airliners. Cyanide was used in Los Angeles where thousands more died. A small briefcase-type nuclear device bought from Pakistan was used in downtown New York. Although not very powerful, it had devastating results. Over a period of time the radiation slowly killed thousands of people. This completely demoralized the American people. Thousands moved away from New York each day. Property values in New York plummeted to that of desert property outside of Phoenix, Arizona. Eventually people moved back to New York but it was too few and too late. The United States was crippled.

With each terrorist act the United States would bomb some Middle Eastern country and spend billions more on defense and give billions more to buy countries that had no intention of becoming an American ally. Fear controlled Americans, and the politicians' rhetoric only compounded that fear. America issued sanctions against Middle Eastern countries while pampering Israel. World hatred for the U.S. continued to grow. While the United States demanded the Middle East stop the movement of arms and terrorists across their borders, they failed to see Coalition forces simply walking across her southern borders daily. Al-Qaeda had a standing joke that it was easier to bring weapons and hide in America than it was to do the same in Syria.

Terrorist attacks against the United States had continued unabated until 2010. The United States was on the verge of bankruptcy. During this time a few changes were made to the secret cells strategically placed in the United States. They now consisted of ten dedicated men per cell with one leader. Every other cell had a sleeper, whose job it was to act like he wanted out and to weed out any traitors to the cause. Although it was a risk that some might begin to like America, every member of a cell was expected to find a job and pay for all his expenses. They would be notified when their cell was activated. All were expected to buy high-powered rifles, join gun clubs, practice with them, and become proficient enough to be rated marksmen.

Of the original eight cells activated, four cells perished on aircraft, and ten of the remaining men were caught and held for trial. Of the original 150 only 122 remained: twelve cells with ten each. But the next year that number tripled to thirty-six cells. In 2003 it had grown to sixty cells. The Coalition of the Al Qaeda was growing in leaps and bounds and helped tremendously when groups of South Americans tried to join. This number nearly doubled each year until 2010, assisted by many new members from South American countries. There were now almost 6,000 cells with a total of 60,000 men waiting to be activated.

Then in 2010 all terrorist attacks stopped. Rumor was Alef Rasad had been killed. The new American president claimed victory and blatantly proclaimed terrorism in the world had been brought to an end through the United States' dogged determination. This was all part of the plan. Now rumors of terrorism surfaced monthly in all parts of the United States. The cry of "wolf" took all that financially remained from the United States.

America began to implode under President Obama. He was no different that Bush had been. In fact in less than two years in office President Obama became the Muslim Brotherhoods greatest asset. Billions, literally trillions were doled out to the wealthy with nothing going to the American people. Obama touted change but hired those that served under President Clinton. The same financial mistakes were repeated only on a grander scale. The home loan debacle, or "toxic loans" as many called it, brought America to its knees. In response to the corruption of Fannie Mae and A.I.G., billions in bonuses were passed out with the bailout money they received. Obama hired financial gurus from Fanny Mae where the "toxic loans" began. Those responsible for America's financial collapse were put in a position to finish what they had started. And finish it they did. Greed overcame their dedication to America, just as Osama bin Laden had predicted. The end was near.

Americans had been taxed to death the previous eight years, but what all Americans learned in 2011 was worse than a nightmare or terror. Congress and President Obama were determined to keep the large companies of America and their accounting practices in check, only to have their own accounting practices, or lack there-of, become the most scandalous and shocking event in American history. Ironically, an outside accounting firm brought to the attention of the news media, and the American people, that the interest on the government debt exceeded the taxes collected. This was worse than any terrorist act. The United States was bankrupt.

This information had only aided Sharafan's plans. He survived, and the Coalition prepared for the final steps of their plot. He never forgot his *fatwa*, but something else had become more important, and that plan was already in motion. With the financial collapse of the United States, they would literally be able to walk across the border to take America. Rasht Sharafan was about to bring a final and lasting defeat upon the United States of America!

Everything Osama bin Laden had set in motion had worked like a finely tuned watch almost to the minute. Sharafan could still remember his last meeting with Osama bin Laden. Less than two years before, he had been sent an urgent message to meet with bin Laden. Upon the request he had rushed to the expensive hideaway in Pakistan.

Sharafan hurried into the Pakistan mansion and into the presence of Osama bin Laden. The Muslim leader looked sickly. Rumors among the faithful was that their leader was gravely ill. When Sharafan saw his great leader, he instantly knew the rumors were true. Even so he refused to believe Allah would let this happen.

Rasht bowed low to Osama, "Allah Akbar. You called for me?"

"Yes." He turned his head and coughed. "I am sick. In fact I don't have much time."

"Allah will take care of you."

Osama smiled, "I think Allah calls." He took a deep breath, "Listen to me. The time is near. The American president is doing exactly as we expected. I have intentionally leaked my location. In a few days or a few weeks they will arrive and they will kill me."

"No, that will not happen."

Again Osama smiled, "It will happen, and in death I will be more powerful than in life. Our people will rally around and we will be able to destroy America in less than two years. The American president, Obama will succeed for us and destroy America."

"How?"

"Religion. He claims to be Christian but doesn't respect them. He has even sided with Muslims but when he kills me, the Muslims will rise up against him." He coughed a few more times, then said, "He will bring America to its knees financially. America will not survive."

Moving to aid his friend, Rasht propped a pillow behind Obama to make him more comfortable. The great leader poured a few pills from a bottle, picked up his bottle of water and washed the medication down.

"I am concerned," said Rasht.

With a slight smile Osama said, "Why?"

"How do we deal with the American's superior aircraft, especially the F22 Raptor."

Navarro nodded his head and smiled. His eyes sparkled with delight, "It will be taken care of."

"Our pilots cannot battle with the Raptor." In thought Sharafan added, "Excellent pilots cannot defeat the Raptor."

"Remember the animal the Raptor was named after?"

"Yes, a quick deadly animal not easily dispatched by others."

"And where is that dinosaur now?"

"The Raptor is extinct."

Navarro knew something but he kept the secret, "Don't worry Sharafan. Soon the American Raptor will also be extinct."

Rasht nodded but Osama could see he was still concerned. He gave Rasht a reassuring smile, "You can thank the American leaders of Microsoft for the soon to be extinction of the Raptor. Not far over the border in India our friends have finished programming modules that are already in the Raptors. We must always be grateful to Bill Gates and Microsoft for bringing all their programs here so we could create them so they would work for us. It is good they brought the American jobs and programming here so great ease we could not only destroy America but also get paid to do it by their American leaders."

Both men chuckled for a moment and Osama was able to put Rasht's concerns aside.

Bin Laden looked at Rasht and smiled, "Soon you will get your revenge for Allah. Did you bring the list of those that betrayed us?"

"Yes, but why do you show the traitors as great leaders and spies for our cause? We should kill them, not glorify them"

A seldom seen smile creased his face, "Precisely. When the Americans kill me they will take my files and do our work for us. And it will serve a double purpose. Since the men on the list secretly help the Americans it will make others think the Americans have betrayed them."

The revelation brought a smile to Rasht, "Ahh!"

The conversation continued for a while and then, with a heavy heart, Rasht departed. Less than a month later Osama bin Laden was murdered in the mansion exactly as he had predicted. The American president, Barrack Obama, claimed his own cleverness and stealth in the death of the Muslim leader.

And in death, Osama bin Laden united the Muslim world.

Sharafan sighed at the memories. So much had happened and they were so close to realizing their dreams. He smiled at Zahir, who continued to fumble nervously with his brandy. He had known Zahir for only a year but he had proven to be trustworthy and an excellent fighter pilot. Zahir would be the one leading the charge on Corpus Christi. With him in the air, and Ortega on the ground, Sharafan was sure the Naval Air Base would fall. But now he watched his friend pace nervously.

"What is troubling you?" Sharafan asked.

Zahir fumbled with his drink then chugged half of it. He wiped his lips and peered at Sharafan. "What of the American Allies? China, Russia, Europe, Canada?"

General Navarro laughed. "Russia? They are broke. China isn't an ally and doesn't care. In fact they will probably be happy. With America out, China can take Taiwan and the United States won't be able to stop them like they have in the past. Europe is neither militarily prepared nor willing. And Canada has nothing we should be afraid of."

A nod from Sharafan confirmed Navarro's statement. Then Sharafan added, "The United States has no South American allies. As for Europe, especially Great Britain, the Middle East countries will simply cut-off their oil supply if they try to help." Then he turned his hand up and made a fist as though he held something. "We have them by, how do they say in America, *the balls?*"

"And Japan?" asked Zahir with a shrug of his shoulders, more relaxed than when he first asked the question. Already he expected an answer to put him at ease.

"Maybe, but remember they have had no military power for over sixty years." Sharafan laughed. "And that is thanks to the United States. To convert their industry over would take many, many months, maybe years. In two weeks, it will be too late. And," he added with a smirk, "they will also need oil. When the Americans quit buying Sony and Toyota, they will find themselves in a very vulnerable position."

Navarro asked Sharafan, "The Internet and the computers?"

"Already taken care of. Our little *sleeping virus* will awake on New Year's morning."

"What do you mean?" asked Zahir.

With a smile to Navarro, Sharafan said, "Why don't you tell him."

"The chips and programs the Americans have been importing from us for the last decade will crash all of their systems just before we invade." Navarro smiled. "They will have no more Internet."

Sharafan laughed. "We have some nasty surprises for the United States that four of my cells started more than two weeks ago. You might remember that more than ten years ago we mailed anthrax to some of the American politicians, but in our haste and zeal we told them the truth in the letters. Three weeks ago we mailed out contributions to everyone in Congress and the president and his cabinet. Some were typed and some hand written, but this time we complimented their actions and asked them to use the money for re-election."

"Why give them money now?" Zahir asked.

Navarro snickered and Sharafan laughed out loud. Sharafan added, "The checks will bounce but all of the letters were laced with more anthrax." Zahir nodded his understanding.

Sharafan went on to say, "And tonight we have another big jolt for America that will knock them to their knees. The celebrations in New York, Chicago, Detroit, Boston, and Los Angeles will be the last for many. Two cells of ten each in Los Angeles and New York contracted smallpox. They are very sick. In fact, my information says four of the twenty are on their deathbeds now. The others are to go through the crowd coughing and spreading as much as they can. We also have another two cells that will be spreading anthrax among the crowd and subways. The anthrax virus will be put on cars and trucks so it will spread when they drive off. At midnight anthrax will be thrown from the top of buildings and will mix with the confetti. We should infect well over a million people."

"What about us?" asked Zahir.

"You were vaccinated like the rest of us. You might get a mild case of flu but you will be immune from the disease," said Navarro.

Again, Sharafan laughed. "If the invasion doesn't destroy America, the diseases will do the rest."

General Navarro stood and held his glass high. "To a new year that will bring us the American's power and wealth! To victory!"

* * *

The Officers' Club, located between downtown Corpus Christi and the Naval Air Station, sat on a bluff with a fantastic view of Corpus Christi Bay. Inside the club, fifteen-foot walls were covered with a thick mahogany and maple wainscot. Textured rose-flowered wallpaper covered the panels between the wood columns lining the walls. On one side was a continuous ornate beveled glass panel from floor to ceiling, broken only with an occasional maple column. Fine cut glass chandeliers, suspended from the high ceiling, added glamour to the room. One massive detailed chandelier hung over the center of the dance floor. Lush luxurious champagne-colored carpet covered the floors except for the large dance area made of inlaid champagne-colored marble. On one side of the dance floor was a stage, from which hung lighting equipment, and a sound system a local disc jockey operated. Tables covered with fine satin lined with lace and set to accommodate eight, filled the room. A single candle burned in the center of each table along with a bottle of wine and eight crystalline wineglasses.

A waltz started to play and Marix rushed Krysti to the dance floor.

"Hell, the guy can dance too," said Ruben sipping his drink.

"Any more encouragement you can offer?" asked Beau.

Sunday nudged Ruben and whispered, "He's jealous."

"Really?"

"Yes."

This was Ruben's chance to goad his friend. "Well, Marix is rich and handsome too. Looks like he's just gonna sweep her off her feet."

"Ruben," snapped Sunday, swinging a hand he easily eluded.

"Thanks, I needed that," said Beau with a touch of dejection. "I guess if I'm gonna sweep her off her feet, I better get a broom."

Ruben laughed. "No way. They don't make a broom big enough for you." Both Ruben and Sunday laughed.

"I'm sorry," Sunday said with a chuckle.

Beau held his drink in the air. "A toast. To my best friend and his wife. I wish you the best. I'm glad to be home and happy I can be with you again," he said with all sincerity. They accepted the toast graciously; then Ruben took Sunday onto the dance floor while Beau watched them move to the music.

The formal setting was like home for Marix. He was light on his feet as he stepped to the tune. "Krysti, you are the most dazzling woman here." The compliments flowed effortlessly. "You are ravishing, my dear."

She was embarrassed. His accent was so charming and stripped her of her defenses. "Thank you," she whispered.

"Krysti, will you marry me?" he asked while moving her about the floor with the precision of a professional.

Yes, how wonderful, how romantic, she thought. The wine made her head spin. Michael was so wonderful, but in her mind danced a vision of Beau. She hesitated. Was Michael the one she wanted? Why had she thought of Beau?

"I don't know. I must think about it," Krysti replied.

Marix was aghast she had not said yes. No woman had ever told him no. "I can give you everything. I have property and power in England and a title to go with that. There's nothing I can't give you."

Krysti had regained part of her senses and knew the only thing she would have wished from a marriage, he had not mentioned or offered. Not a word of love, no touch, no caress and no sparkle in his eyes. The strange detached look in his eyes when they made love still haunted her. The question was mechanical and not coming from the soul. She was confused. What was in her heart?

Slowly, the band switched to rock and roll. Marix stopped dancing and they walked from the floor. Mike tried to pull Krysti away from the direction in which she headed. She moved toward Beau, Sunday, and Ruben.

As she approached, Beau spoke. "You were very good out there. You two were probably the best dancers I saw."

Marix sneered. "I wish they would play the classics. This rock and roll is out."

Krysti rolled her green eyes and laughed. "It's a shame you don't like rock and roll. It's some of the most inspiring music. Did you know the song we danced to was an old Beatles tune?" Even in the dim light, it was obvious the color of Marix's face had changed a shade.

"Right on, rock and roll forever," said Sullivan, who had just walked in and joined the conversation. With him were Natasha, Fitzhenry, and Warren.

"Soon it will be a new year," Natasha said.

The DJ started playing the song Beau and Krysti listened to the previous night after Shanghai Pete's. She walked over and stood directly in front of Beau, touched his arm with her fingers, and gazed cheerfully into his eyes. "What if there were no Heaven?" she asked, the dimples showing when she smiled.

For a moment he devoured her with his eyes. Without looking, he held his glass in Ruben's direction, which Ruben took but fumbled for a moment. "How could there be no Heaven? You just brought me a little," Beau answered. He held his arm to Krysti. "May I?"

"I'd be honored," she said taking his arm.

"Hey Beau?" popped Ruben, still holding both drinks. Beau and Krysti turned at the call of his name. All they saw was a grin on Ruben's face as he asked, "Ya want me to bring that broom?"

It was one of the few times Beau had ever been caught off guard and he blushed and had no retort for the question.

"Broom?" asked Krysti.

Beau tried to evade the question as they continued to the dance floor. "Ruben's just clowning around."

"Ruben, that was mean," said Sunday, tugging at her husband's sleeve. "Uh oh, we're in trouble. Mike's obviously mad," she whispered.

"Who cares about Marix," he said, oblivious to Mike. "Just look at Beau. That's the way he used to be."

When they reached the center of the dance floor, Beau smiled and said, "Watch your feet."

Krysti laughed. When the dance was over, the band went into another slow song. Without saying a word he pulled Krysti near and they danced close. He bent over and put his face against her cheek. Her hair smelled sweet like wild flowers, and felt soft and pleasing. He pulled away enough so he could gaze into her eyes. "I'm not too good at this stuff. All night I've been thinkin' it, but I just didn't know how to tell ya."

"Thinking what?"

"I think you're just about the prettiest woman here. No, I take that back," he said as he got lost in those large green eyes. "You are the prettiest." Embarrassed at what he had said, he pulled her close again. She was so small, so pretty, so soft he thought. Was he beginning to—?

"I'm not tall," she whispered up into his ear, breaking through his thoughts.

"I didn't mean . . . you see, I," he said, stumbling over his own words.

"Hush. Just hold me close and dance."

Beau did as she asked. The next song was also a slow one and they continued to dance. To Krysti it felt so right to be encircled in his embrace. He was strong and not just in a physical way. There was an inner strength about him that couldn't be touched or defined with words. Krysti felt safe and content in his arms. So unlike Michael, she thought. And Beau was so gentle. He danced better than she thought he would. Or was it because she wanted to dance with him? But Michael was everything a woman could ever want in a man. As she continued to dance, her thoughts only confused her more.

The music finally ended and Beau stood on the floor holding both her hands. "I really enjoy being with you."

Slowly, they walked across the dance floor to where the others had congregated. Ruben handed Beau his drink. Marix had gone to refill his glass.

Lieutenant Barry Pickett and Major Fred 'Cozmo' Deberg arrived at the small gathering. Cozmo escorted two young women, with one on each arm. When Beau saw the two women, with one on each of Deberg's arms, he thought what Ruben had said about him seemed to be true.

Beau shook Cozmo's hand and whispered in his ear, "Major, don't you think two women is a little risky?"

Deberg grinned and raised his thick black eyebrows; he stuck his tongue out and up, almost touching his nose, and laughed. "What can I say, they love me."

With both women in tow, Deberg escorted them in the direction of the bar. The only person Beau had not met was the Choctaw Indian, Dean Blackman.

Beau turned to Ruben. "Where's Lieutenant Blackman?"

Ruben shrugged his shoulders. "Blackman is a quiet guy. He's not much into these kinds of affairs. He stays pretty much to himself. You won't see him until tomorrow when we leave."

Across the dance floor, Mulholland was having success of his own. He was teaching two resident women about the land down under and how they played football. Robert Schmitt stood to the side nursing a drink.

Beau held his drink aloft: "To my friends and to America. May the coming year bring good fortune to all of us. It's good to be home."

Sunday noticed when he spoke, he only had eyes for Krysti. "Ruben, do you think he knows she isn't tall?"

Unnoticed by the others, Marix and James entered into an agreement at the far end of the dance floor. "I want you to tell Krysti about Beau's past. But wait until the proper time."

"Why don't you?" asked James.

"Because she will think I'm doing it to get even with him for interfering with her."

"Well, aren't you?"

Marix smiled smugly. "Of course I am. I'm going to get even with him and get Krysti back, and you can do it for me."

"What's in it for me?"

"I will make it well worth your while."

Always ready to do something for financial reward, James said, "Okay, you've got a deal." Besides, this would be no trouble at all, he thought. He might have even done it accidentally, but now he was to be rewarded.

Marix returned to the party and promptly took Krysti to the dance floor. After the song, the small group became engaged in a discussion with a senator over the protests for welfare and people's rights movements. A friendly argument erupted between the senator and Marix. The politician, Senator Richard Selmon, argued it was the people's responsibility to house and feed the poor and homeless. Marix felt they should be fed but housing was beyond the responsibilities of the government. All listened as the two debated their points and a few ventured their own opinions. Krysti listened intently.

At one point, Selmon asked Beau's views of the issue. "You were in the Middle East. You've seen poverty. What is your stand?"

Abruptly all eyes turned to Beau. "I'd rather keep my opinions to myself."

"Uh oh," Ruben whispered to BJ and Sully. "I hope this Selmon guy doesn't push."

The politician waved his arm. "Surely, you have an opinion. Tell me how you feel."

Beau stood erect and seemed to tower above the others. "Survival of the fittest. No work, no eat." At first the candid statement seemed to shock all but those who knew Beau.

Senator Selmon was staggered. "Surely, we must take care of the helpless."

"Men like you create the helpless. Housing them, feeding them. Why should they work? Their children are learning to be lazy and live on welfare. Their numbers continue to grow larger. Why not take abandoned Army bases and force the people to stay there? Make them rise with the sun and work till sunset, no matter how small the tasks. Force them to be useful people."

"Right on," said Sullivan.

"They shouldn't be forced to do work against their wishes. They have rights," said Senator Selmon.

"You force us to take care of them," snipped Ruben. "I don't want to be forced to do that anymore."

"They do have rights. So do we," said Beau. "If they don't like the life on the barracks then they can get a job and work for their money. But if they're going to live off this country, give them initiative and desire to do better. Teach them respect. Teach them personal dignity. You've taken those things away from them."

"It is our duty to help the people," said Marix, feigning sympathy for the underprivileged.

"We are obligated to take care of the homeless," Selmon added.

"And I'm saying they should be expected to get off their dead asses," snapped Beau.

"Well, the people won't listen to you," Selmon said haughtily.

"The sad thing is . . . you're right. Your kind is helping our government breed a cesspool of waste and neglect. The burden you have created has been put on the working class. A group that is growing smaller and smaller. People with your mentality will bring this country to its knees."

"We are the strongest country in the world. We must be concerned with the minorities and their suffering," offered the stuffy politician.

The cold steel eyes came to life, anger in his voice. "Minorities! You've made everybody minorities. You've even made the gays a minority! My God, man, sexual preference is a choice. If a Democrat wins the election, are you gonna give special minority status to Republicans? God, I hope not—but I wouldn't be surprised! No one should receive special treatment. All you do is cater to the voters. If minorities are so hung up on their roots, why are they here? If they don't like it here, then why not return to their roots! What minority are you, Mr. Selmon?"

Ruben and Sully were a little miffed at the politician and they began to show it as Sully said to Ruben, "He appears to be yellow. What minority is that?"

With a nod Ruben finished Sully's thoughts. "That would make him either a Democrat or a Republican."

Surprised at their comments, Selmon failed to respond as he tried to collect his thoughts.

"There are three words I'm afraid I shall never hear again. Words I haven't heard since I was a small boy. Words I don't think you've ever heard, Mr. Selmon. Words spoken with pride by my father and his father. Words I speak with pride: I'm an American." Beau shook his head and his lips squeezed to two thin lines. "Guess that makes me a minority."

"All right! American!" snapped Warren raising a clenched black fist.

"Yeah, you've given those minorities so much of my paycheck, I can almost afford to quit and go on welfare," quipped Ruben.

"Given? You mean more like taken," snapped Sullivan. "We're so damn strapped with taxes no wonder our companies can't compete against foreign products. If the government isn't taking half, the state and the city are taking the rest. How much do you want from us, Mr. Selmon?"

Even Ruben was angry. "I can't pay my bills but you keep approving raises for yourself and the other politicians. You don't even pay Social Security."

"We deserve what we get like any other business executive. We are responsible for this country," Selmon added smugly. He wielded an arm of enormous power as a senator in Congress. Although he justified his words, he had become wealthy as a senator. His insider trading with many business executives had gone undetected. His fortune was diversified and he had hidden his money in other countries.

He maintained a staunch stand against Americans taking their money out of the country, and his high profile on the issue had made him a hero to the people. In reality he had learned all the loopholes, which had enabled him to hide a vast fortune overseas—a fortune that would be impossible to find. Hypocritically, he stood before them and defended his stand for the people, all the while feeling justified in his actions because of the good he had done for his country, making him deserving of the fortune he felt he had earned.

"What we had it seems the CEOs of America have been stealing. And nothing has been done to them. Creative accounting, I think they call it. Why hasn't Congress done something to them? You just let them steal more from us without suffering any consequences. When are you going to help the people you represent?" said BJ, adding his beliefs. The thought of the government waste and inaction burned at him. With his parents sick and unable to retire, he had been sending his sister half of his government pay to take care of them.

The small group grew larger and more boisterous and antagonistic in their opinions. "We are doing everything we can," Selmon puffed.

"It's been going on for ten years and I haven't seen anything but some wrist slapping," said Sullivan.

Ruben smirked. "Longer than that, Sully. I remember all those Savings and Loans problems my parents were always crying about. All that killed my father and drove my mother to an early grave." This was one of the few things that seemed to anger Ruben. He was still resentful of his father dying right after he'd entered the service, and he still felt the Savings and Loan scandals were responsible for his death.

Surprised at Beau's views on the subjects, Krysti listened intently to his stand on the varied issues. "Beau's points are well taken," she whispered to Sunday and Michael.

Marix was stunned. "You cannot end government programs like that."

Krysti shook her head. "You can't continue to give everything away and never get anything back."

"Well, you sure as hell can cut some of the fat off," Ruben added. "Those politicians are always going on fact-finding missions, when the fact is they're wasting our money."

"I just hate to see them make him angry," sighed Sunday.

Ruben continued instigating his friend. "Way to go Beau. Burn him."

Others were angry at such an outspoken stand that was not politically correct. "What makes him think his ideas will work?" said Larry James.

"None of the other plans have worked. Beau's right about the minorities," said Warren. "We need to give them respect for who they are. It's something they don't have. My family has been here for ten generations. My roots are the United States of America. I'm an American."

Unlike Beau, and those who knew him, most were hesitant to voice their true opinions. Instead, they listened to the argument move toward its heated conclusion.

"The Republican Party is making a comeback and uniting once again," said Selmon.

"You don't understand. Damn it, can't you see? It's not your party. It's not the Republicans or Democrats, or the Liberals or Conservatives. All you politicians are so hung up on your party. When you win an election you are still supposed to represent the people, even if they are not in your party. You've forgotten the main issue—no, the only issue! You've forgotten the people."

"So what are you, Liberal or Conservative?" Selmon asked.

"Neither."

Ruben mumbled, "At times he tends to be radical."

Sully added, "Especially when pushed."

BJ nodded. "No joke."

Selmon grunted at their comments and aimed his question to Beau. "How do you feel about the resurgence of the Democrats?"

Beau sipped his drink. "They should be taken to the nearest tree and hung."

Aghast at the comment, Selmon said, "That's murder!"

Beau threw back, "That's justice."

"We've done so much for this country," Selmon almost spit out.

Ruben said, "I haven't seen anything you've done."

"Neither have I," BJ added.

Almost pleading, Beau said, "Senator, look in your heart. What have you really done for the American people or our country?"

Trying to skirt the question like a professional politician, Selmon asked, "So you think the Republicans can solve our problems?"

The others, except for BJ, Sunday, Ruben, and Sully, listened in shock and awe to the banter between Beau and Selmon.

Almost laughing Beau said, "Oh no, absolutely not. I think the Republicans should be hung next to the Democrats."

Selmon blurted, "You're a radical."

Behind him Ruben shrugged. "I told you."

"You and the others are the problem, Senator," said Beau.

Before the bewildered senator could respond, Beau continued. "America will never be destroyed from the outside. If we falter and lose our freedoms, it will be because we destroyed ourselves."

Recovering quickly, Selmon responded with, "That is the most un-American thing I have ever heard."

Beau smirked. "I was quoting someone else."

"Then he is a despicable person for saying that," Senator Selmon added

Slowly a smile filled Beau's face. "The person who said those words was Abraham Lincoln."

Regaining his composure, Senator Selmon asked, "So, pray tell, what is your solution?"

Even Marix was curious. "Yes, what do you suggest?"

Sully smiled, Ruben shook his head, and BJ gritted his teeth. All three knew their friend's feelings and how he would answer.

Beau said, "You don't want to know."

Selmon nodded. "Yes, I do. Tell me."

His lips became two thin lines and his temples pulsed; then from between gritted teeth Beau responded. "A total violent overthrow of the system as it exists today."

Shocked at the revelation, Selmon gasped. "That's treason."

"No Sir. What you have done is treason," said Beau. No one was able to respond as Beau took a swig of his drink. "If Jefferson and Washington were alive today, they would overthrow this government."

While the others failed to respond, Ruben held his drink high in a toast, and jumped to a mock attention, then blurted, "To the revolution!"

Immediately, Sully and BJ chimed in as they clinked their glasses to Ruben's. "To the revolution!"

Always the good politician, Selmon tried to control the runaway rhetoric. "We're doing everything for the people we can."

"I don't mean giving it away." Beau shook his head. "Don't you see that you're destroying our country?"

Smugly, Selmon said, "Nothing will happen to our country."

The disgust was evident in Beau's eyes. "I'll bet the leaders of the Roman Empire said the same thing as you." There was a slight pause and then Beau finished. "Where are the Romans now, Mr. Selmon?"

"Our country is different," Selmon retorted.

"No it's not," said Beau. "This is worse because we have the opportunity to learn from history but we're making the same mistakes."

"You're a soldier and must serve God and your government," Selmon threw at Beau.

With a heavy heart Beau shook his head. "God has nothing to do with this, but I do serve the people of my country, not the government."

The men rallied to Beau's defense. Ruben moved in front of Mr. Selmon and rolled his eyes. "Mr. Selmon, you said God. In a war, which side ya think God will pick?"

"The righteous side, of course."

"I assume it's us," interrupted Warren in his best Bostonian accent. "I'm sure both sides pray to God before they go into battle. Indeed it has to be a difficult decision for God to choose which side lives and which side dies."

Beau shook his head. "Personally, I think God's pissed at both sides."

The words stunned Selmon, and his small entourage gasped. Trying to direct attention away from the issues, Mr. Selmon predictably found an out when an assistant whispered to Selmon who Beau was. "I know who you are," Selmon said.

"Forget me, why don't you worry about the system you've created. Fear the system you've taken part in making."

"How can you be so righteous when you have killed people on your missions?" snapped the politician.

"That's right. I've killed so many I can't count," he said, the blue eyes slashing out at Selmon.

The politician laughed. "You are crazy?"

"Maybe." Beau tilted his head and finished the last of his drink. "Mr. Selmon, you solve the world's problems. I'm sure you know what's best for the people. You don't need me." Beau eyed the bar, and alone moved away from the large crowd gathered to listen to the arguments and opinions.

Krysti watched Beau walk away and pulled at Sunday. "What did they mean about killing people?"

Angry, Natasha quickly pursued Beau.

Unsure what to say, Sunday mumbled, "The Middle East wars they fought in. Some people died in the bombings. Beau was involved in some of those and people feel he was wrong. But how do you control and run a war on paper?"

A little confused, Krysti nodded but continued to listen to Selmon. The politician promptly moved his conversation to Marix and others who would listen to his ideas. The group divided into separate factions, mumbling and discussing their own diverse opinions.

When Natasha caught up to Beau she forced him to stop. She spat words filled with anger. "Beau, your attitude is horrible. You should show more respect for those that run this country."

With a shrug Beau responded. "I showed him the respect he deserved."

"Our politicians do the best they can."

"They can do better."

"You didn't get enough revenge and killing in Israel," she snorted. "Now you want to bring death here?"

"That's not what I'm doing," said Beau. "I'd like the killing to stop, but—"

Natasha interrupted. "I don't want to hear excuses." Suddenly she calmed and fear filled her eyes. "I'm afraid you're going to get Sully killed."

The hurt showed in Beau's eyes. "I'd never do that Natasha."

Anger and sadness filled her words. "I hope not." She spun about and returned to the others, leaving Beau alone. When Natasha arrived back at the small group she took Sully's arm and smiled at him.

Slowly the conversation drew away from the more volatile subjects and more toward the coming year and the upcoming New Year's Bowl games. The main critical issues were ignored and once again swept aside. The soldiers issued challenges as to who would win the Rose Bowl: UCLA or Michigan State. Others were interested in the LSU Nebraska Orange Bowl where the president would be in attendance.

Even with the changing discussion, the debate between Beau and Selmon had not been lost on Krysti, and she wondered where all the hostility had gathered to bring such a reaction from him. She passed it off to a normal dislike of men in politics. She did not agree with his view of welfare and thought "survival of the fittest" was archaic and harsh in the civilized world and the New World Order former President Bush had created. Still his views had merit—a little stronger than most—with distinct and clear convictions. She cast her beliefs and ideas aside like the others, and concentrated more on the party at hand and keeping Michael's amorous advances at arm's length.

For all but one it was New Year's Eve. It was America. There were no problems. And if there were any problems, they would be solved tomorrow or the next day or the next. The party prepared for the countdown to the midnight celebration. Beau disappeared from the crowd just before the stroke of midnight and the New Year. The minutes disappeared as the appointed time approached. Then it dwindled to seconds . . . ten, nine, eight

. . . three, two, one! Horns blasted and streamers flew through the air. The old year was gone, taking its rightful place in history. Champagne was held aloft to celebrate the beginning of a new and better year. The New Year arrived and with it new dreams and hopes.

Mike made a toast with Krysti to the New Year, and then he grabbed her roughly, seeking the deserved New Year's kiss. For some reason the kiss made her feel uncomfortable. When she found the opportunity she stole away from him so she could wish one certain person a happy new year. She searched in vain, but could not find Beau. Then she did the next best thing and sought out Ruben in the midst of the mad celebration. When she located him, he was embracing and kissing Sunday. She asked, "Where can I find Beau?"

Ruben pulled away from Sunday long enough to tell her. "You'll find him outside. He always brings in the new year watching the stars." She started to walk away when Ruben stopped her. "Hey Krysti, you'll have to give him the New Year's kiss."

"Why?" she asked, feeling warmth in her cheeks.

"Because he's shy," laughed Ruben. "He wouldn't make a move on ya. Now me, I'd just grab ya and plant a big one on ya."

"Ruben!" said Sunday. She grabbed her husband and kissed him hard and long on the lips.

Krysti continued to the seclusion and quiet of the balcony outside. True to Ruben's words, she found Beau absorbed in the beauty of the heavens and the sparkling gulf waters. She was taken back with the spectacle. "It's beautiful!"

Beau turned his head toward her and smiled contentedly. "Yes it is. One day I would like to go to the stars." He took a deep breath and sighed as Krysti walked near and laid her hand on his arm. "A very peaceful feeling. I prefer to bring in the New Year out here. Gives me time to think about the old and plan for the new. Something I haven't done in a few years."

"Ruben told me you'd be here," she said, admiring the stars and enjoying the tranquil night. The air was brisk and cool. Her head still danced from the champagne and she wondered why he had made no effort to give her a New Year's kiss. "Thank you again for last night. I must say, you were wonderful with Justin."

"I enjoyed it more than you know." For a moment his face became serious. "As you get to know me, you may find I'm not as wonderful as you may have thought me to be."

"I doubt it," she said, feeling the full effects of the liquor she had drunk. She moved enticingly closer.

"I hope what you learn, you won't hold against me." His words were more of a plea than a statement. The past would haunt him forever and it was better she knew now, so he decided to tell her the truth about himself. The whole truth.

"Krysti, you need to know I served with—"Krysti put a finger to Beau's lips and halted his words so they could listen. Music could be heard from the balcony. Again John Lennon's *Imagine* played. Squeezing between the railing and Beau, his final statement ignored, Krysti touched her fingers to his chest and asked, "Aren't you going to give me a New Year's kiss?"

A gentle smile creased Beau's face. With his left hand he touched the cross hanging from her neck. A strong gentle arm slid firmly around her waist, the other behind her head as he pulled her near. He felt the warmth of her body and the beating of her heart. His left hand rubbed her neck gently, then he slid his fingers upward into the thick, soft auburn hair. She moved closer and closer until her lips found his. He responded to her kiss. For a few brief moments, they melted into each other's embrace and the past was forgotten.

Standing in the doorway unnoticed, Marix watched silently as the two celebrated the New Year. Mentally he made plans. Plans to get Krysti back and plans to discredit his hated new rival.

## Chapter 9
# INVASION

Plans to leave early New Year's Day changed when they encountered problems with the installation of new electronics in Ruben's F-16. Ruben and Beau waited patiently for the aircraft's final checks. The caravan of cars and vans was to travel to San Antonio, pick-up a small arms expert, then continue to Del Rio and Laughlin Air Force Base and arrive before lunch. At the base, they were to conduct a seminar for those hopeful of entering the advanced flying program.

In the cold morning air, the group appeared to be in total disarray, and anything but ready. Some were nursing headaches or hangovers from the celebration the night before. Overnight, a dry front had moved across and sent a chill throughout the state. Their breath could be seen in the unusually dry air.

The only one ready for the planned 6 a.m. departure was Lieutenant Dean Blackman. The Indian from Oklahoma impressed Beau. A large man of spectacular proportions, Blackman was as quiet as he was big. He was a man of few words who spoke only when spoken to. The firmness of his handshake and the unrelenting gaze of his piercing black eyes gave one the feeling of a dove about to be pounced upon by a hawk. His rugged fine features gave no indication of an Indian heredity. Instantly Beau took a liking to the loner. Blackman would be a tremendous ally or a deadly enemy—nothing in between. Beau identified with the lieutenant.

They were two hours behind schedule even before they departed. The caravan would take three hours to San Antonio, an hour there, and another three to Del Rio. Last minute plans had also changed for Beau and Ruben. They would not arrive in Del Rio before noon. Instead they would leave a few hours after lunch but still arrive in Del Rio before the others.

During the two-hour wait, Robby Schmitt installed radios in all the cars. In Robby's van was a radio that would enable him to communicate with Ruben and Beau during their fly-by. All of them thought it would be amusing and fun to listen in as the jets approached and passed. Although it was illegal, Robby had the capability of communicating with the jets. The flight pattern would take them to San Antonio where they would turn directly west for Del Rio.

The caravan pulled away from the Naval Air Station at 8:30 a.m. Robert Schmitt drove one van accompanied by Admiral Garrett, Mulholland, and Fitz. Mulholland and Schmitt seemed to hit it off at the New Year's party. But now Mulholland hoped he could sleep off the remainder of his hangover in the back of the van.

Sunday drove her van and took Krysti, Justin, and Sully. Earlier Sully bid farewell to his wife, Natasha, who was to take a noon flight to El Paso to visit her sister. Deberg drove another van with Marix, Pickett, James, and Blackman. Deberg still had a grin on his face from the night before.

Tagging along for convenience were Brook and Danny in the pick-up, pulling the two bright red rail dune buggies. Jack, along with BJ, tagged along in Beau's Corvette. At Del Rio they would leave the Corvette with Beau, then continue to their property near Big Bend where they would wait for their brother to arrive after he was discharged.

The only problems they encountered before leaving came from Robert Schmitt and Krysti. Neither had been able to access the Internet to retrieve their e-mail. Schmitt was really concerned and voiced his opinion. "It's not like anything I've ever seen. Something strange is happening."

Garrett laughed at them and said, "Hopefully you can survive for a few hours without the Internet?"

The trip went without a hitch to San Antonio. At Lackland they picked up the small arms expert, Lieutenant Chen Tang, who would ride with Garrett's group to Del Rio. Chen Tang's parents had escaped from China with him, and had gained their citizenship after they arrived. It had been Chen's desire to serve in the American armed forces since he was a small child, something he never swayed from. Weapons had been his specialty. He still spoke with a heavy accent and was never able to rid himself of addressing men as "Mister" followed with their first name, except when addressing officers. For some reason his speech when in the presence of higher-ranking officers was perfect.

Schmitt noted that the problems with the Internet were worse.

They departed San Antonio just before noon, which would still put them in Del Rio well behind the original schedule.

* * *

Both men were in their flight suits. The scream of the jets forced them to shout to be heard. Lieutenant Tahar Zahir yelled to Sharafan. "It has been confirmed, Sir," he screamed. "The American Air Force has been alerted and are on their way to intercept the decoys."

"We are ready!"

"Yes . . . but we were unable to ground some of the passenger airliners."

"Then shoot them down and replace them with their duplicates!"

"Yes sir," said Zahir with a starched salute. He ran to the radio room to give final instructions. Sharafan waited until Zahir returned.

"Sir, everyone is ready. You will need to take care of one passenger jet that will be leaving from Corpus Christi and is headed for El Paso. We were unable to ground it. You will be on a direct intercept course. It must be taken out."

Sharafan nodded. "Consider it done." As an afterthought he asked, "Any reports on the American's Internet?"

Zahir nodded. "The systems are crashing everywhere. The Internet should be down permanently in a matter of hours."

"Good." Both men went to their aircraft to make final preparations.

All around the airport, jets poured from the massive hangars like hornets from a damaged hive angry and ready to attack. Before the Americans could collect and distribute surveillance photos, the attack would be over. The passenger jets, filled with trained military, were already airborne matching predetermined commercial airline schedules and paths for those already sabotaged.

Sharafan climbed to the cockpit of his F-14 and glanced all around, making sure everything was ready before he strapped in.

They had very few of the modern jets, so the ones they had were given to the men with more experience. Most of the attacking forces were older jets from wars past. A few Korean F-86 Sabres dotted the field. Having barely missed the Korean War, but arriving in time for Vietnam, were many discarded F-4 Phantoms and A-4 Skyhawks.

The Skyhawk, an excellent aircraft, had been used to train American pilots at jet training schools because of its versatility and ability to duplicate enemy aircraft maneuvers. The jet had proven a handful for American pilots to shoot down in their own war games. As it was discarded for the more modern aircraft, Sharafan and his men found themselves in possession of hundreds of the deadly jets. He mused to himself, wondering what they would think about fighting an aircraft previously used only for war games, but which would now be in deadly pursuit of their adversary, the Americans. All aircraft were equipped with bombs and cannons.

There were many others like the ground-hugging A-6 Intruder attack jets. Leading the first wave were the more sophisticated aircraft of French Mirages, Russian Migs of various types, American swept wing aircraft F-

111s and F-14 Tomcats, and only a few dozen of the F-15 Eagles and F-16 Falcons.

They were an inferior group, but they outnumbered the American air forces whose majority of aircraft was spread around the world. As inferior as they might be, they were about to strike with nearly 1300 fighter aircraft from an assorted number of strategic points south of the American borders. Nearly 500 would take flight from Cuba, a portion of which would help Sharafan in his efforts in Texas. Three hundred assault aircraft surrounded Sharafan with nearly 400 located in the matching airport south of California and 300 more waiting in predetermined places.

The total attack force was more than five times what the Americans managed in any one full day in the *Operation Iraqi Freedom* attack against Iraq. Much had been learned in that short war, and now it was all being used against the Americans—Americans that had proven to be creatures of habit.

The invaders relied on overwhelming surprise, like they had in New York, and with the letters containing anthrax. If the well-placed ground forces performed as expected, their job would be easier. Hopefully the attack would come as such a stunning blow, they could capture many American jets not flight-ready. Preset snipers were to kill any American pilots trying to enter the battle.

Sharafan smiled to himself. The attack was like a boxing match, letting the opponent swing and show his weakness. Then, when he is weary and unsuspecting, launch a quick deadly attack and dispatch your opponent. America was about to be knocked out.

With his belts secure, Sharafan made a radio check and lowered the canopy. Then like he had done countless times before, he stuck the old faded and yellowed picture of his mother on the instruments before him. He could still remember the cameras from twenty years before.

Only a child then, Rasht Sharafan had never forgotten the horror of that moment. Cameras zoomed in on the mourners' chorus of torment. Only a momentary pause was given to the Syrian father and son, their heads bowed over the smoldering debris. Although hardly noticed against the cries of the other mourners, the anonymous father and son sifted through the rubble, the smoke, and the bodies. With his father, Sadi, beside him, Rasht Sharafan could find nothing of his mother, his brothers, sisters, and aunts.

Sari Sharafan had been a beautiful woman, even by the world's standards. The clothes she was required to wear could not hide her figure, and when she covered her face her eyes were enough to make men die for. In a world of chaos she brought love, unity, and peace to the Sharafans. Sadi could look upon the beauty of his wife all night—but no more. For

Rasht his mother would become only a cherished memory, as would the rest of his family.

The young boy had watched as his father knelt in the hot smoking debris, picked up a handful, and squeezed with such an abnormal strength that stones broke in his grip. Luck, fate, destiny, or whatever terrible thing it might be called—that a father and son should endure such a horrific final memory of their loved ones—was dealt to Sadi and Rasht that day. Before the bombing started they had raced through the streets content their family had reached the safety of the underground bomb shelters before the terror started. They had found shelter in buildings that were in harm's way, but it had not been the first time and they had survived before. Thank Allah their family was safe underground.

The boy had seen the jets come in and the rockets fired. In a hypnotic trance they had watched helplessly as the technologically-advanced rocket streaked for the shelter like a slow motion movie. In an instant, all they loved and cherished was gone.

Tormented at the sight before them, Sadi and his son Rasht screamed to Allah. The agony and despair were more than they could bear. Sadi swore a *fatwa*—an oath of death to the American pilots who had committed this act and an oath of death for their families—so that none of their seed would continue. Also, he swore a *jihad* on the United States of America, and to that end he promised to do everything in his power to bring down that great country. And fifteen-year-old Rasht grew into manhood quicker than the rocket that had taken his beautiful mother. He took a picture of her from his pocket and held it to his heart. Through his tears the boy became a man and swore the same oath as had his father: death to families of those who had killed his own.

In the cockpit of his jet, Rasht wiped the tearful memories from his eyes and looked lovingly at the picture of his mother. He would not be finished until Beau Gex was dead. "Today Mother I will take many American lives for you," he said. He kissed his fingers and touched the photo.

Prepared and ready for the attack, he shoved the throttle forward and the jet responded, lifting effortlessly from the ground. Soon hundreds more followed, ready to strike.

The first aircraft Sharafan encountered was the passenger jet Zahir had described that would be coming from Corpus Christi, bound for El Paso. He made a quick check. The jet was to have been grounded and a Coalition clone was to have taken its place, but the passenger jet had managed to get flight ready and take off. This would create problems for the Coalition should it continue on unless Sharafan reacted immediately. Swiftly, he went up to meet the jet. A moment later it was in a deadly smoking plunge. Soon he was back with his group and in the lead for the attack on Del Rio.

Then Sharafan's thoughts returned to Beau Gex. He couldn't wait to see the horror on the man's face when he confronted him again.

* * *

The arms expert, Chen, talked incessantly to Schmitt and Garrett. The trip was going well until about noon, when they were only a few miles out of San Antonio. Then something strange occurred.

Robby had the radio tuned to a familiar Corpus Christi station listening to the Orange Bowl game when a Boeing 727 passenger airliner roared overhead less than a thousand feet above the ground. Stranger still was what came minutes behind the airliner. A string of thirty or more fighter jets of older vintage and varying types followed at the same altitude. The close proximity to the ground made it impossible to determine their numbers as they flew over.

The strange happenings were also noticed in the trailing vehicles as all eyes strained skyward. In Deberg's van, Marix snapped. "Is this the way they do maneuvers in Texas?" But when he observed the shaken and concerned appearance upon the other men's faces, he knew they were as alarmed as he. Pickett and Blackman watched as more planes flew overhead.

"What happened?" Tang asked Robby.

Robby could only watch and wonder, as did Admiral Garrett. Robby said, "Must be that crazy Texas Confederate Air Force. I didn't know they had so many planes." Everyone agreed only because not to would mean some frightening ramifications none of them wanted to consider or admit.

Unexpectedly, the football game Robby listened to was interrupted. The disc jockey became frantic with his broadcast:

"This is KEYS in beautiful Corpus Christi. Coming up is another of your—" For a moment the radio was quiet. "You may not believe this, but it appears that the Naval Air Station is putting on an air show of its own this New Year's Day. Hey, any of you listeners know what it is, give us a call."

The disc jockey seemed confused at what he saw. The questions he asked those within his studio confirmed his puzzlement. The obvious impromptu questions carried across the airwaves.

"My God!" he blurted over the radio. "Two of those planes crashed. No . . . they, they were shot down. What the hell is happening? Have they lost their minds?" All of a sudden fear was clear in his voice. "No! No—"

Those were his last words.

Admiral Garrett and Schmitt looked at each other.

"Check the other stations," Garrett ordered with a frantic wave of his hand.

Schmitt scanned the radio. Only two stations remained active. Something was happening, but the broadcasters seemed confused and unable to get any information. One station thought it was a colossal aerial accident, while the other laughed, saying it was more like a movie where war had been declared. Soon both broadcasts were interrupted. Two other stations previously off the air now played uninterrupted music.

Garrett ordered Schmitt and the other four to remain silent. At the top of the hill, Admiral Garrett spotted a rest area with a breathtaking view of a small valley where the narrow, rock-strewn Hondo River flowed. He ordered Schmitt to pull off the road and into the rest area.

Outside, the cold clear waters of the spring-fed river rushed along. Thorny mesquite trees dotted the rolling terrain. An occasional jackrabbit could be caught scurrying in and around the brush. High above, two buzzards circled in curious anticipation.

They all gathered together in the roadside park; Garrett told Krysti, Sunday, and Justin this was a chance to rest and stretch their legs. He had Schmitt and Chin break out the drinks and sandwiches. Then he gathered the pilots and tried to explain the situation.

Sunday, Krysti, and Justin—with food and drink in hand— walked to the river's edge unaware of anything wrong and proceeded to explore the stone-filled river and the tranquil surroundings at their leisure.

Near the vans, the men talked to each other, curious about what happened and startled with the revelation of facts Garrett spilled forth and Schmitt verified. Mulholland, Tang, and Fitz discussed what they had heard on the radio.

Garrett raised his hands trying to maintain order. "Calm down. I'm sure we will make contact or learn something soon."

"Robby!" Garrett barked. Instantly Schmitt was at Garrett's side. "Use your cellular phone. Try to call Laughlin. Let me know what you find." Schmitt nodded affirmative. "Are those radios you set for Beau and Ruben working?"

"Yes, sir."

"Then let someone else operate the phone. I want you to stay on the radios until the batteries die or you reach Beau and Ruben." Ted stared long and hard in the direction of San Antonio. "If they are coming, it won't be long."

* * *

The empty cafeteria enabled Ruben Alonzo, Beau Gex, and a pilot friend Ron Bohannon to fill their plates to capacity and grab two large ice teas just before the noon rush. They found an empty table and seated themselves.

While they were eating, two enlisted men walked past. Both were angry.

"I couldn't get the tickets; the Internet is haywire," said one who was extremely irritated.

The other man commented, "I had the same problem. Can't even retrieve my e-mails."

Beau turned to Ruben. "Is the Internet down?"

His mouth full, Ruben nodded and mumbled, "Yeah. I couldn't get my e-mail." He noticed the concern on Beau's face. "Forget it. Some computer geek managed to screw up the system again. It'll be back on line before we finish eating."

Shrugging his shoulders Beau said, "You're probably right. I guess Microsoft never has solved Windows' crashing."

Bohannon roared, "That's a big ten-four."

Swallowing his food Ruben said, "That's what Gates gets for spending billions of dollars on programming in India."

"Hey, all those companies sent the work over there," snapped Bohannon. All three laughed and continued to eat.

Ruben questioned Beau about the food in Israel, but soon Beau was asking questions about Krysti Socorro. He told Ruben about his plans to go with his brothers to Big Bend and their home Big Rock. He hoped to purchase an old Cessna and take tourists for flights over Big Bend. For some reason he could not explain, the desire to go to Big Bend was slightly less than his desire to know more about Krysti. At high noon, the cafeteria was three-quarters full.

A radio operator and another enlisted man walked up to the table and sat next to Ruben and Beau. They started to eat. The radio operator laughed and said to his friend next to him, "Some stupid ass commercial airliner is trying to make an emergency landing here. Can you imagine?"

Ruben interrupted. "Civilian aircraft aren't allowed to land here or at any military installation."

The radio operator shrugged his shoulders and with his mouth full managed, "Yeah, but if we don't let them land and something happens there'll be all kinds of hell. My CO checked it out with the airline schedule and it's all A-Okay." He stuffed his mouth again, laughed, and added, "Besides, what kind of trouble can a commercial airliner be? Probably have a few good-looking hides anyway."

Memories from a burned out building in Lebanon filled Beau's mind. He lowered his fork, and instead of hearing the radio operator he could see and hear Sharafan—the Cobra—as though he were standing in front of him laughing and saying, "When you least expect it. Commercial airliners!" The hair on Beau's neck stood out and a chill made his body shudder. They were going to use commercial airliners to hit American military bases. The whole picture was clear to Beau: Sharafan's warning, the Mexican airports unfinished, and the commercial airliners. The commercial planes about to land had to have military personnel on board and Beau knew it. He turned to Ruben.

For the first time ever Ruben saw fear in his friend's eyes.

"Ruben, this is it. We need to warn everybody now!" He stood to yell a warning. It was too late. A thunderous explosion suddenly broke the peaceful lunchtime. Those in the cafeteria momentarily froze. "What the hell was that?" Ruben squealed, dropping a spoonful of mashed potatoes in his lap.

"A bomb," Beau mumbled almost disbelieving. "They're here!" As if in answer to his words, two more explosions came in rapid succession, surrounded with machine gun fire. Then came another blast, blowing open a corner of the cafeteria farthest from the two, killing a half dozen men and burying a dozen more. The percussion knocked Ruben, Beau, and almost everyone else in the cafeteria to the floor. They were showered with debris and dust.

Chaos reigned supreme. Men ran in all directions. All around the cafeteria they screamed in pain or pleaded for help.

Springing to his feet, Ruben grabbed Beau, and turning to Bohannon screamed, "The jets!"

The three men broke into a run for the flight ready area where their flight suits and equipment were stored. Outside, fighter jets came from all directions, strafing and bombing as they went. Smoke and flames poured from buildings. Sporadic explosions dotted the base. On a distant runway men poured from an airliner firing automatic weapons, cutting down American Marines in their tracks.

Beau, Ruben, and Bohannon were a hundred yards away from the flight ready building when a bomb blew it apart. They were knocked to the ground. In prone positions they raised their heads staring in disbelief. No words were spoken, but both understood when Beau pointed beyond a nearby hangar to a group of parked fighter jets. Any available aircraft would do. They must get airborne now and fight back!

They ran for the jets, dodging gunfire and explosions as they went. When they started to charge past the last hangar before reaching the aircraft, four Marines and an engineering sergeant jumped out.

The sergeant yelled, "Stop!"

"No," Ruben instantly responded, making an effort to pull away from the men blocking his way. "We have to fight back."

When they tried to continue, the four Marines threw the three men to the ground. The sergeant dove between the three angry men. Before Beau and Ruben could say anything, he pointed to the jets.

"Those boys felt the same way," said the sergeant.

Near each jet lay a dead pilot. One man hung from the side of the cockpit. An F-15, aflame, was still rolling down the runway, the pilot killed with a sniper's bullet like the others.

"Snipers," said the sergeant. "Can't see them, but they can see us."

"We have to do something!" Beau yelled over the guns and explosions. A series of bombs hit less than fifty yards away, and for a few moments all the men buried their faces in the dirt as debris cascaded down and all around.

The sergeant raised his face first and grinned at Beau. "I'd hoped you'd say that. C'mon." Instantly, the sergeant and his Marines were on their feet with Ruben, Beau, and Bohannon close behind. A few strides and they were inside the hangar.

The Marines stopped just inside to guard the door. Inside the hangar were three F-15s. "They're not totally fueled or completely armed, but they got enough. You can give those bastards a little shit," said the sergeant.

"Suits?" Ruben asked.

"Nope, but a helmet's in each. Maybe the snipers won't get ya if ya get a running start from the hangar."

The three pilots looked at each other. Without hesitation Beau responded, "Let's do it."

* * *

Three snipers and a spotter lay hidden behind a fence a little less than half a mile from where Bohannon, Beau, and Ruben were preparing to take off in the F-15s. The spotter, Pepe, tapped one sniper on the shoulder and pointed to the hangar where the three men and five Marines had disappeared.

In English Pepe said, "Hey, Johnny," at the same time he pointed to the hangar. He always called his best friend, Juan Bravo, Johnny. "Eight men went in the hangar."

Bravo motioned to the other two snipers. He pointed to one saying, "I will take the lead. You take the second." He pointed to the other and said, "You take the third. If there are more I will take them. There will be three, maybe four at the most. Be ready."

* * *

Ruben and Bohannon nodded. "Go!" yelled Beau, running to the far jet. Ruben did likewise and soon both men were strapped in.

"Moon Shadow, radio check," Beau managed to say in a calm controlled voice. He was in his world: a world he knew and knew well.

An equally controlled voice answered, "Roger, Mongoose. Let's see if we can return the favor."

"Roger."

Using his call sign, Beau asked Bohannon, "Cannon?"

"Roger. Let's take it to them," he answered.

"Follow me, I'll take the lead," said Beau. The three men gave the thumbs up sign to the sergeant as the jet engines started to whine. He smiled and returned the sign. The sergeant yelled to the Marines; they rolled the hangar doors open.

The roar became deafening. Swiftly, the three jets seemed to leap from the hangar and roll along the tarmac, rapidly accelerating and ready to jump into the sky. With his fingers still stuck in his ears, and over the roar of the jets, the sergeant yelled, "Kick some ass, boys!" Then he and the four Marines ran for cover.

* * *

The first jet rolled from the hangar with two more following swiftly behind. Bravo sighted on the lead jet. "Here they come." Never had he missed a shot. Pepe kept watch. The other snipers prepared for the kill.

Bravo aimed for the cockpit of the lead F-15 and fired his rifle where he knew the head of the pilot would be located. Then in rapid succession the other two snipers fired. They watched as the middle jet veered from its path and plunged into a hangar, creating an explosion and a ball of flame.

* * *

When Beau rolled from the hangar he made a turn for the nearest runway. As he did, a spare helmet rolled out and bounced across his feet.

"Damn," he muttered. He tried to lock it behind his feet but failed. He loosened his shoulder strap and bent forward to try and shove the helmet back. The bullet from Bravo's rifle ripped through the cockpit and grazed his back. He groaned when he felt the pain; still he managed to lock the helmet back with his feet, tighten his shoulder harness and then charge ahead.

Bohannon was not so lucky, as another bullet pierced the cockpit and found his heart. His jet veered from its path and crashed through a hangar, bursting into flames.

When Ruben turned his head all the way to his left to see what happened to Bohannon, a bullet intended for him crashed through the canopy and only grazed his helmet in what would have been a perfect head shot.

Beau screamed, "Moon Shadow, start weaving, snipers are trying to pick us off."

* * *

The middle jet crashed through the hangar but the other two continued.

Pepe was stunned. "You missed!"

"No," said Bravo. "Something else happened. But he is a dead man now."

Bravo prepared to fire on the lead jet again when bullets zinged all around their area. Pepe alerted all three snipers and pointed to a half dozen Marines charging their position and firing their rifles as they came.

Calmly, Bravo glanced quickly to the other two snipers. "Get the jets; I will take care of this."

The snipers prepared to fire on the two weaving jets while Bravo turned around to take care of the charging Marines. Pepe watched.

Slowly Bravo took aim on the farthest Marine, and in rapid succession fired from back to front until his sixth shot took out the last man who led the charge. When he turned back to the jets the other two snipers were still firing, and the jets were lifting from the runway almost vertically. For the first time ever Bravo had failed. But even in failure he had been a success. More than two dozen pilots had been killed across the base as they had made futile efforts to become airborne. Still it was two jets more in the air than he had anticipated.

* * *

Once airborne, Beau started barking instructions.

"Watch your ass, Moon Shadow."

"Mongoose, be careful," Ruben answered. "We have no suits or parachutes. What we're doing is stupid. I mean, like this is dumb as shit." He moaned, abruptly realizing the death situation they were both thrown into.

"Roger, Moon Shadow, watch your six o'clock, here they come," Beau warned. He checked the fuel. Only half remained.

Both incoming jets were F-4 Phantoms. Ruben immediately peeled left, while Beau did a loop. Just that quickly they were on the tails of the enemy's American aircraft and just as fast the phantoms were earthbound in flames. Beau took out an A-4D Skyhawk, while Ruben easily handled an unsuspecting F-14. They climbed higher. Far below, they could see the base fall completely to the invaders; however, they made one strafing run to free the sergeant and his four Marines, then watched the five escape, which brought a smile to each pilot. The sky was full of aircraft and it was apparent Beau and Ruben were the only ones on their side.

"Mongoose, running out of fuel and firepower. We gotta get outa here."

Ruben was right, and Beau knew the sheer numbers of the invaders would mean their eventual death.

"Moon Shadow, set a course for San Antonio. Let's see if we can find the others. Maybe we can land there, refuel, and rearm," said Beau. He was afraid it was a false hope but it was their only alternative.

"Roger."

"Let's hope Robby is listening or San Antonio picks us up; otherwise, we're outa luck."

"Roger."

* * *

The time had come to explain the situation to everyone. For the safety of the group, Admiral Garrett needed to tell them all, in detail, what he knew about the current events and of the possible takeover of the Corpus Christi Naval Air Station. Shock could clearly be seen in all of their faces. Krysti listened earnestly, trying to find a shred of hope in the devastating words.

Admiral Garrett told them he had no knowledge of the attack's extent or severity. Robby had learned of other attacks on San Antonio and Del Rio, but Garrett was keeping this quiet, not lying and not telling the whole truth until he learned more. Instead, he explained that Robby was trying to make contact with San Antonio and Del Rio. He gave specific orders for Robby to continue with his attempt to contact Ruben and Beau on the radios. Of one thing Garrett was sure: those two men would have first line information.

"I want everyone to relax," Garrett ordered. "There's no sense in worrying about something we know nothing about. This could be some kind of protest. Maybe a few nuts creating a little chaos, or even people playing with the airwaves. Maybe it's a small terrorist action again. Right now I just don't know what is really happening."

Garrett doubted his own words but felt it necessary to give encouragement to the others until they knew for sure. Beau's warning of an invasion continued to haunt him.

"Mom, what's happening?" Justin was insisting on an answer and continued pulling at Krysti's arm.

"I don't know, Honey," Krysti said, somehow managing a smile.

Marix confronted Admiral Garrett. "Sir, I think we should proceed—"

"Sorry, Marix. My decision is final," said Garrett. "Until we learn more, or know the extent of this thing, we're staying put. We will not continue until then."

"You don't really believe Commander Gex's story?"

"That's all, Marix."

Sullivan and Warren cornered the admiral.

"There's trouble, isn't there?" Sullivan asked.

Garrett watched the two men and then let out with a heavy sigh. "We'll know soon. For now I need your help keeping this group together."

"Yes, Sir."

The unsettling calm was broken when Robby yelled. Near the van he was jumping up and down and yelling at Admiral Garrett. "Sir, I have them! I have them on the radio!"

* * *

The two planes flew cautiously, protecting each other as they neared San Antonio and the Lackland Air Force Base. Caution was their main concern as they tried to raise the tower on their radios but failed to receive any response. Back and forth Beau and Ruben discussed their alternatives. Low on fuel and with virtually no more firepower, they would be helpless in a fight against the enemy should Lackland also be overrun like Corpus Christi. An empty feeling gripped the two men when they realized they had nowhere to turn, with no safe avenue of escape. With only speculation for hope, the radio came alive.

Instantly Ruben responded. "Read you loud and clear; this is Moon Shadow requesting your location for a fly by."

The radio clicked on as Robby unknowingly squeezed it in his excitement. Both Ruben and Beau could hear as he yelled to the others.

Robby steadied himself and responded. "We're about thirty miles west of San Antonio on Highway 90 where it crosses the Hondo River."

"We're less than ten minutes away," Ruben said.

The two pilots were twenty-five miles south of San Antonio when Ruben answered Robby. Immediately both men set a course northwest to a point where they would rendezvous with their team.

Time passed quickly, as did their fuel, and it was with a bit of relief they spotted the waiting caravan along the seemingly deserted highway. The rolling hills posed a tricky problem for the well-trained pilots, but with no parachutes bailing was out of the question. The years of training and experience paid off in their landing as it had in their escape from the invasion. The stretch of highway was relatively flat and both jets came to a safe stop less than a hundred yards from the caravan.

Everyone raced forward to greet Beau and Ruben, and to learn the truth. The severity of their current situation was undeniable. After all, how often did two F-15s land on a state highway? Never. Instinctively they already knew the truth. Still, they would not let their last bit of hope die.

With tears in her eyes, Sunday ran to Ruben and pulled him to her.

The others congregated around the two men hoping something would happen—hoping things would change and return to the way they had been. It all seemed unreal but it wasn't.

Beau threw his helmet aside and walked straight toward Ted, at the same time pointing and yelling to his brothers. "Jack, take the buggies down."

The three men responded immediately and moved to unload the cars. Beau stopped in front of Garrett. "Ted, I'm taking the buggies and my brothers to San Antonio to see what's happened to Lackland. Find the next side road and pull off the highway. If we're not back tonight, break out the gear and spend the night there; we'll return by morning. Crank up the radios and see what you can find out."

"What about Corpus?" Garrett asked.

Beau grimaced and shook his head no. "Ruben will give you the details."

Garrett clasped Beau's shoulders. "You and the boys be careful."

As Beau started to leave, Garrett pulled Ruben, Sullivan, BJ, Schmitt, and Mulholland aside to discuss plans. The others stood in shocked disbelief, unable to comprehend the concept of war. War on American soil!

Jack and Danny unloaded the dune buggies while Beau and Brook took their guns and rifles from the truck and car. With the task finished, they loaded the buggies with their rifles and were ready to go.

Krysti stopped Beau, not believing, but wanting to know, and asked, "What's happened? How bad is this?"

Beau responded with a reassuring smile. "You're safe here. I'll find out exactly what has happened and be back soon."

His calm words afforded some comfort to Krysti and eased her mind somewhat, but when he turned around to walk away she saw his shirt was torn and soaked in blood. She reached forward and grabbed his shirt.

"You're hurt," Krysti exclaimed.

Turning to her, Beau reached back and felt with his hand. "It's just a little more than a scratch. Don't worry." Then anxiously he said, "I have to go but I'll be back." He turned and continued to the dune buggies and had gone only a short distance when Ruben, who had pulled away from Garrett, stopped him.

"My buddy," smiled Ruben. "You want all the fun."

"I thought you'd had enough fun for one day," Beau said. "Hold down the fort while we play a little *hide and seek*."

"Good luck. Don't let them catch you with your pants down."

With a silent prayer for Beau's safe return, Ruben watched his friend drive away.

Schmitt made an attempt on the portable phone, but the effort to contact Laughlin accomplished nothing. Next, he tried Lackland Air Base in San Antonio, but again no response. He managed to reach the Naval Air Station but the line was unexpectedly disconnected.

As everyone prepared to leave, Schmitt and Garrett opened the back of Schmitt's van where he kept his powerful combination radio/short wave. If they could contact no one with the phone, maybe they could rouse some of the short wave radio operators.

The year 2016 was a cycle year when sunspots were high, which meant radio waves would bounce all around the atmosphere and all around the country. With this knowledge, Robby thought he would pick up something on the radio.

Although everyone was obviously shaken by the strange events, they were trying desperately to maintain their composure. Garrett readied everyone for their departure to find a safe place to hide and wait for Beau and his brothers to return.

A few miles down the road they turned off and went over a rise. The highway behind them disappeared from view. After traveling but a few miles, they parked the cars and vans in a little circle much like the old wagon masters did with the Western wagon trains. Within view of their camp a large spring-fed creek trickled along on its way to the nearest river. Everyone was lethargic except Justin. He enjoyed his surroundings like a small boy would. The rest made sandwiches and took drinks from the iced-down coolers. They tried to make themselves comfortable in the backs of the truck and van and in the seats of the cars. Ruben, Garrett, Kipp, and Blackman remained awake well into the night discussing the problems they faced and the options before them. Their final decisions would rest on the information Beau and his brothers would bring back.

## Chapter 10
# HIDE AND SEEK

Sharafan's force arrived against little opposition. He intercepted a lone American F-15 fighter jet in flight, and after he engaged the Eagle, it took only a few moments before he realized it was unarmed. Hurriedly he dispatched the jet before it could escape. Already on the ground at Laughlin was the false passenger jet. The Coalition had the base under control. Dead Americans sat in the cockpits of their jets or lay on the runways nearby. This attested to the accuracy of the well-placed snipers, who were once aliens granted blanket amnesty from the bleeding heart Americans.

On the ground, Sharafan promptly searched out Captain Reynaga who controlled the offensive for the attack on Laughlin. Soon he was in Reynaga's presence.

"Well done, Captain! Better than I expected," said Sharafan, extending his hand. "What of the caravan and Commander Gex?"

Reynaga shook his head. "I have questioned the officers. We have checked at the gate. They never arrived."

"What?" he screamed in disbelief. "Send a search party. Have your best men find them. Bring Beau Gex back alive. Kill the rest if you must, but I want him."

"Sir," Reynaga interrupted. "We do not know if they arrived in San Antonio. Texas is a big place. Where do we start?"

The Captain's question suddenly caused memories from the past to swirl through Sharafan's head. He remembered how he and his father, Sadi, had hunted for the pilots that killed his wonderful family and beautiful mother.

They had continued to look for the men who murdered their families, but the military was good at keeping the names from the public and the media. Yet they never gave up hope that they would someday extract revenge for their loved ones.

On April 19, 1995, something happened that helped them find the men that had flown that deadly mission. When Timothy McVeigh blew up the building in Oklahoma City and Middle Eastern terrorists were blamed, it came as a shock that a former member of America's military had become so disgruntled with his country's leaders he had committed the cowardly act. But tongues loosened and people in the military talked.

Discrimination was supposed to be a thing of the past, but in reality it was just something that had been shoved under the table. The women in the military endured sexual attacks and even rape. Blacks were still discriminated against even though it wasn't supposed to happen in America. And even though America stated a belief in religious freedom, one religious group had been targeted, taunted, teased, and ridiculed. The victims of this abuse were people of the Muslim faith.

A disgruntled officer who had worked on the aircraft that flew the mission killing the Sharafans was also of the Muslim faith, and he had endured continual humiliation during his prayers. People pointed at him and said "his kind" were the ones who had done the dirty deed in Oklahoma. When it turned out to be just another American, none of the people that had ridiculed him offered up apologies. So it happened one night while the Muslim officer was with some of his other Muslim friends that his tongue loosened and they heard the story about the pilots that had bombed Baghdad. One of those that heard the tale told a friend of his, and the story continued. Sadi and Rasht had learned that the officer was still stationed in Saudi Arabia, and it took no great effort for them to find him and make friends. Unhappy with his position, the disgruntled officer unwittingly told them his story. Soon the father and son who were bent on revenge learned the identity of the two men who had flown the mission that had killed their family. With the information they obtained, Sadi and Rasht set upon their quest, their *fatwa*, to kill the pilots Jonathan Bryce and Robert Gex, and all of their families. They began their search in the hopes of exacting revenge and fulfilling their oath.

One of the most important and vital things they learned in their quest was that Muslims in the American military could be counted on to help their cause when needed.

With the passing years the father and son had developed and discovered something far greater than their original plan for revenge. An idea evolved for the downfall of the United States of America. They formulated a massive plan from the United States' attacks of *Desert Storm* and similar operations conducted after that strategy. They noticed that the United States repeated a pattern, much like a boxer telegraphing his blow to the opposing fighter, and thus revealed its Achilles' heel. The lowly Sharafans enlisted the aid of insurgents from all the Middle East countries and a few from South America. Toward this end, the secret organization of the Coalition, as it eventually became known, raced toward a much greater and united goal: the downfall of the United States of America. Revenge had been the original motivating factor, but the destruction of the United States was now seen as a much grander prize. Still, problems with the plan to destroy the United States continued to plague them.

During this time Rasht Sharafan had developed into one of Iraq's youngest and best jet fighter pilots. With revenge as his companion, he had become a cold, calculating killer. He was called "Cobra." No one knew if it was because of his cold personality or his deadly skills.

Five years after *Desert Storm*, revenge became much more prominent for the Sharafans when news came to them telling of Bryce and Gex visiting in Spain with their families. For the father and son, revenge would be sweet and immediate.

The explosion was blamed on Middle East tensions between Israel, America, and the Palestinians. The only flaw to the plan had been that Gex's family was not to be present. Regardless of this, the Sharafans stalked the two men and Bryce's family. At the opportune time they had put their plan into action. If not for the police stumbling upon the scene after the explosion, the plan would have worked to perfection, because Bryce, his family, and Gex were dead. Even with the appearance of the police, if Sadi had remained calm and calculating instead of running and shooting, he would never have been caught, much less killed.

With a heavy heart after his father's death, Rasht Sharafan had returned home alone and doubled his efforts with the Coalition while keeping a watchful eye on Beau Gex and his remaining family. Patiently, Captain Reynaga waited for an answer to his question, but Sharafan was still consumed with memories of revenge.

Too much time had passed. Sharafan had killed the father and now he would kill the son. Beau Gex must be found! Sharafan was too close; he could not let it happen again. Livid with rage he barked his demand to Reynaga. "I don't care how you do it but find them!"

* * *

In the distance, sporadic columns of smoke rose high in the sky. As Beau and his brothers neared Lackland, flames became visible. The base was in trouble. They pulled the buggies off the main road and advanced as cautiously as possible. From far away came the sound of explosions and gunfire.

Suddenly, men from two Jeeps and a personnel transporter ambushed the four brothers. Men jumped from the truck and started firing, pinning all four down. Guns at the ready, they prepared to return the fire when they heard an American's voice.

"Okay, you cocksuckers! Give us your vehicles and maybe we'll let ya live."

Beau responded. "Hey, ya'll from Lackland?"

Silence reigned for a moment. "Yeah! Ya speak good English. How do we know you're Americans? Who's the president?"

"Some Muslim terrorist. Who gives a shit," retorted Beau.

A couple of the men laughed. The same man spoke. "Where ya from?"

"Texas."

"Who'd we beat at the Alamo?"

Beau laughed. "Didn't, but we gave them thirteen days of hell they never forgot. How do we know you're not some of them? Tell me about Goliad."

The same man spoke. "Fannin surrendered. But we kicked ass at San Jacinto. If you're telling the truth, we better hurry and get the shit outa here. You step out and I'll step out."

With those final words, the officer stood erect with a rifle held overhead and moved toward Beau, who also stood and did likewise with his rifle. Both men walked slowly and cautiously toward each other, holding their weapons above their heads. They met between both groups and exchanged greetings. The officer called his men out and Beau beckoned to his brothers.

The officer explained how the invaders called in, saying their commercial jet was attempting an emergency landing. A quick check verified the flight. Nothing seemed suspicious until it landed, and before anyone was aware, more than a hundred armed men were running across the runway firing automatic weapons. A few pilots attempted to reach their aircraft but most failed. Those who succeeded were killed in their planes or shot from the sky. Swarms of enemy aircraft, flying low to elude American radar, successfully filled the air around Lackland. The officer and his men managed to commandeer the vehicles and a few weapons and escape. The attack was executed swiftly and surely, completely surprising the Americans. Enemy aircraft landed virtually unopposed.

Beau nodded his understanding, knowing the attack had been excellently synchronized, since the story was exactly what he and Ruben experienced. Beau went on to tell the officer a similar tale of his own personal account in Corpus Christi.

The officer shook his head in disbelief. "If they hit all the bases, where do we go?"

Beau had no answer. "I don't know."

The soldiers told of their intentions to move into the hills. At night they would start northward where they believed they would eventually reach America's remaining forces, or die trying. They invited Beau and his brothers but they declined, explaining their situation and the importance of their return to warn the others.

The men departed under the safety of darkness. Beau and his brothers found cover and bedded down for the night.

* * *

The previous night had been rough for the group. They caught sporadic accounts of the attack on the short wave radio. Speculation did more for their fear than what they heard. Sleep was slow in coming and for some it failed to come at all.

When Ruben took his shift watching, he found it hard to fathom the United States had actually been invaded. Mulholland and Blackman protected them through the night because they understood this type of war.

For the others, it was different. It was more like watching a movie. All they knew was what they heard on the radio. They had not experienced war for themselves or seen it yet.

The new morning brought an uneasy tension within the small group. Garrett tried to maintain control over the nervous and impatient men. Schmitt didn't help, pacing nervously about the temporary campsite. The only relief for Garrett came from the two women who were busily preparing breakfast. Luckily for the small group, Sunday had packed groceries for their arrival in Del Rio. She knew they would be too tired to shop, so she had bought supplies the day before. The food and coffee seemed to keep the group's spirits high along with the dwindling drinks from the two large ice chests.

Early morning coffee made all eager to resume their journey. The makeshift camp was along the Hondo. The peaceful creek and crisp cool air helped buoy the spirits of all in the little camp.

The new day made the previous day's events seem unreal and so far away. The fact they had not continued on their trip was not the only reminder that something was terribly wrong. The sight of two jets resting on the side of the highway not far from where they camped was still fresh in everyone's mind. Everything had happened and it was real.

Ruben brought a cup of coffee to Ted, and again Ted asked him to detail the attack in Corpus Christi. BJ and Sully approached as Ruben finished telling him about the attack.

Warren spoke. "Ted, we're not stupid. It's evident things are really bad. We know what Beau has been saying is true. I think it's time to tell us everything. We're not camping here for our health."

Warren knew they were in trouble when Beau and Ruben had landed. He clung to a remote hope that what he saw and felt might be wrong. In reality they already knew the answers to their questions—all but Justin who had no concept of war and death.

Garrett frowned and heavy lines formed in his forehead. "The truth is, they hit Corpus Christi, but I don't know any more than you do. Hopefully, Beau will return with information as to the extent of this thing so we can move on. Until then we stay put."

As though in answer to his words, the sound of the two buggies could be heard approaching. They roared into camp and stopped. Everyone gathered around, but the sullen faces of all the brothers boded ill. Beau recanted his story while they listened in stunned silence. He finished with, "This is it." The words were simple and clear, and he uttered them with contempt for the men who had been warned and failed to listen.

"You're bloody crazy," snapped Marix. "You and your bloody delusions. It must be something else."

Garrett interrupted the two. "Right now there is no reason for alarm. Robby will continue to monitor with the short wave radio. Hopefully this attack will be squelched and we can get back to normal. Right now, it would be foolish to charge forward without knowing what might lie ahead for us. We need to know what has happened and who is in control."

Schmitt sat on the ground, his whole body shaking. "We've been invaded! Those bastards actually did it."

"Get up, soldier. Get control of yourself," ordered Garrett. "I want you to set up some type of communications with the short wave. Understand?"

Schmitt jumped smartly to his feet. "Yes sir. Pardon me, Ted, but we're in some bad shit, aren't we?"

"Maybe. It's up to you to verify the extent of the invasion. We need to find a base still under our control," said Garrett.

Beau suggested hiding in the hills until they could learn the extent of the invasion. Just because Corpus Christi and San Antonio were overrun it didn't mean the others had been taken. All surmised the United States had countered with a powerful offensive of their own and even now moved against the invaders. How big and how successful the offensive was still unknown. Patience and caution would be their approach to the situation. To charge helplessly into the unknown would be foolish.

Some wanted to return to Corpus Christi until Garrett reminded them of the futility and danger. The two bases in their path of escape were confirmed hits. To advance to the south was foolish since that was the direction of the attack. After all, they had failed in their attempt to contact Laughlin. Wait and see would be their approach until they could contact a base in American control.

Marix thought it cowardly to hide but the others agreed with the cautious approach.

Barking instructions to his brothers, Beau helped prepare the buggies for yet another trip.

"What are you doing?" asked Garrett.

"I'm gonna get Tracy and her husband. We can use John."

"You can't—"

"I have no choice. She's in danger and you know it. She can't handle something like this. Besides, it will give us a chance to see how bad things are in Corpus. Maybe we pushed them back. If so, I'll be back for everyone. If the invaders are there, we need to get Tracy while they're disorganized. We won't have long before the city is cut off."

As he spoke, most of the others gathered near. Both women listened intently.

"You and your brothers have been out here all your lives," Garrett said. "What do you suggest?"

For a moment, Beau paused in thought. "I've read the men's service reports. Kipp and Blackman are best qualified to make the decision as to what should be done. Head to Hondo and get what you need. You need rifles, guns, and knives. Non-perishable food, water, and containers for water. Find some four-wheel drive vehicles, and leave the others behind; they will be useless. Set up a camp on one of the bigger rivers, Frio or Sabinal, and close to spring water if possible—then hide! I'll find you."

"I'm a pilot," Marix said with a belittling tone. "We need to return to the base."

The reception he got from the cold blue stare quieted even Marix as Beau spoke between clenched teeth. His muscles quivered on the sides of his face. "Fine, then come with me and I'll drop ya off at the nearest airport. If ya don't like that, find one yourself. You won't last an hour once you're gone." With a bit of disgust he stared at Marix's uniform. "I also suggest you discard your uniform as soon as possible."

"I'm a soldier and I will not bring shame on my uniform."

"Shame has nothing to do with comfort—and common sense, which you seem to be sadly lacking. When ya get in the foothills and those dress shoes rub blisters on your feet, and ya can't walk around or bend over in that uniform, just remember I warned you," Beau said sarcastically.

For once the normally boisterous Mike Marix had no answer. He was so taken back at the bluntness of the attack on him he simply didn't know what to say.

With the buggies readied, Garrett led the rest of the group to the vans to organize their plans and make preparations.

Krysti walked to the dune buggy and stood beside Beau as he dressed for the trip. She watched in awe as he stripped to his shorts in the chilled winter air and replaced his uniform with loose fitting fatigues. Then he buckled a series of thin belts over his shoulders, and in a sheath behind his neck inserted a long, slim, and wicked looking knife. Over this, he slipped a heavy shirt lined with pockets. The knife disappeared from sight. Another knife, like the one under his shirt, was inserted in his left boot. Next, he unrolled a belt, revealing a deadly revolver: a 357 magnum with an extended barrel locked in a holster. Hastily he wrapped it about his waist, slipping the gun into the holster. The flap was snapped securely, locking the gun within. He threw his hat to the side, revealing thick blond locks. After tying the heavy boots, he took the crossbow and the quiver filled with deadly steel shafts and placed them in the dune buggy. He stuffed the pockets of his jacket with ammo, and then grabbed his rifle.

The change was swift and complete. In mere seconds, his appearance transformed from an everyday person to that of a war-hardened fighter.

Krysti watched in astonishment and horror at the truth of the situation as the transition took place before her eyes. "I'm afraid," she said to the man standing before her. She no longer recognized him.

He turned toward her with a smile, and the soft blue eyes let her know the gentle man she knew still lay beneath this new, deadly facade.

"You'll be fine." Then he took her face gently in his powerful hands and kissed her softly on the lips. "I'll be back."

Justin, who had remained quiet, ran swiftly to the side of the buggy. "I wanna go."

Beau turned to Justin and smiled.

"Not this time," he said. Then, like it depended on Justin, he added, "I need you to help Ruben and take care of your mother for me till I get back. Promise?"

"Yes sir," said Justin, snapping to attention and giving a mock salute.

Beau returned the salute then jumped in the dune buggy and buckled in. With his left hand he grabbed the overhead bar to the buggy's pipe frame and with his right hand held the side rail. The two dune buggies roared off on their mission: destination Corpus Christi.

Krysti watched in silence.

Larry James moved in to take advantage of the situation. He walked behind her and acted almost apologetic. "You'll be better off now. We won't be seeing him again. Sometimes, it's hard to believe Beau is the renegade he is, having killed all those children."

Krysti spun at the horror the words generated. Defensively she said, "You're a liar!"

"Don't you know who he is? Haven't you heard about the mercenary for Israel? Beau Gex is that man. Hell, he's probably gone so he could save his own skin."

"You're wrong!" she yelled at James's revelation. Her thoughts returned to Beau. How could he be the same man? Yet the pieces were beginning to fall together. In the newspaper and on CNN she had read and heard about the Israeli mercenary that had been described as a murderer and killer of children. After his transformation before her only moments before and now with the doubts James had created, she wondered how Beau could just leave them alone as he did. "It doesn't matter!" she snapped in a controlled voice.

"I really am sorry; I thought you knew," said Larry his voice sounding sincere.

"Go away!" she demanded. "Leave me alone."

As he walked away, she failed to see the sadistic grin of success on his face. He accomplished what Marix had requested with no great effort on his part. He had succeeded regardless of what she said, and he knew it.

The words staggered Krysti. Although she showed no outward signs, the pain of James's admission tormented her in both mind and body. She leaned against a large rock, locked in her own reflections of the current events, as a tear rolled down her cheek. But she refused to cry.

Justin came to her side and put his arm around her. "It's okay, Mom," he said. "Everything will be all right when Beau gets back."

* * *

The F-14 landed unhindered at the Corpus Christi Naval Air Station. Everything seemed as it was, only the military base was no longer under control of American troops. Invaders had total and complete control of the base. Their new leader, Rasht Sharafan, landed uncontested at his new conquest.

Zahir and Ortega met him. Both men briefed Sharafan on the situation. Ortega told him how he was making offers of power and security in exchange for help. The most enticing offer was for life. When Ortega finished, he departed to continue his work.

"Do you think Ortega will succeed?" Zahir asked.

"The Americans prey on each other like a terminal cancer on its host. As the Americans say, 'a house united, we stand, a house divided, we fall.' Within their houses are black, white, and brown: all divided, each fighting the others just as fiercely within as without. Even now they fight with themselves while we continue to move and conquer uncontested. Their house is divided. Yes, they will fall," said Sharafan reassuringly.

"Can we count on the Americans for help?"

"Yes. The common workers will turn to our side. After all, where else will they go? What will they do? Do not detain those who leave. They will return. We can give the working American more than his own country leaves him. The rich, the executives, and the leaders will be removed. They are non-producers and can either work or be killed. For the men who will dedicate themselves to our cause, give them a taste of the better things life can offer. Let them live in the finest places." Sharafan smirked. "After you have picked the finest for yourself and your officers."

Sharafan continued. "Now brief me on how our attacks have gone."

They entered one of the finer offices. It belonged to Admiral Garrett. They poured a drink, and Zahir detailed the progress of the attack. Sharafan settled into Garrett's old and comfortable leather chair.

"We lost more than we expected. The Americans retaliated faster than we had anticipated. But we captured more aircraft than we first estimated. Our advance has stalled, but we control a line from Los Angeles through southern Oklahoma to South Carolina. We control the southern part of the United States.

"The American president is dead," Zahir laughed. "Killed while watching football."

The information about the president only confirmed what Sharafan had heard. The American president was attending the Orange Bowl when a commercial airliner made a suicide dive and crashed into the stadium during the game. The same thing happened in the Sugar Bowl. Their intention was to make an impression on the Americans. The football games and military bases were hit simultaneously. National coverage of the invasion only aided their cause and showed the feeble efforts of the Americans to defend their own country. Sharafan snickered. "America is as defenseless as the Pentagon was in 2001."

Zahir noted, "The American forces in the Persian Gulf are almost totally destroyed. We have taken Saudi Arabia without resistance. Once they knew the Americans were defeated, they wanted to negotiate."

Sharafan derived sadistic pleasure from the revelation.

"Europe mounted a protest, but when they learned they would not be invaded and the oil would continue to flow, they issued an official reprimand."

Sharafan let out with a laugh. "You mean they slapped our wrist?"

"Yes sir."

With his hands behind his back, Sharafan stood and paced the room. "You have information on the family of Beau Gex?"

"Yes Sir. Men have gone to check on his brothers. Also we learned a woman, Tracy Demarr, is related in some way."

"Find her and bring her to me!"

* * *

A war zone surrounded the city of Corpus Christi. Even more than that, it was a war where they had lived, and the spectacle stunned the four returning brothers. What they saw was dreadful. Uncontrolled terror directed the people fleeing Corpus Christi. In the distance, they could see large columns of smoke from the vicinity of the Naval Air Station. As they entered the city, they found an empty service station and wisely filled the tanks before they continued on their way. The road into Corpus Christi was empty, but the one leaving was jammed. In an effort to escape, some dared to go the wrong way on the other side of the highway. People abandoned their cars and were on foot, taking whatever they could carry.

Above the roar of the engines, Jack yelled to Beau, "We're gonna have to take the back roads if we expect to make it out."

Beau knew his brother was right but for now his concern was Tracy.

Hours later they arrived at her wood frame house, only to find the front door open and the house empty. Her car was in the driveway and still running. She had not been gone long!

Beau ran from the house looking in all directions for clues to her location. Two blocks away came the sound of an explosion surrounded by sporadic gunfire followed with a column of smoke rising from a house on fire. In the distance came sounds of occasional gunfire. Across the street, he spied an old man rocking gently on his front porch, seemingly oblivious to the events or his current situation.

After a moment, Beau recalled the old man's name. "Mr. Griffon! Mr. Griffon!" Beau screamed as he began to run toward the old man trying to attract his attention. He bolted across the street until he was in front of him. "Have you seen Tracy?"

At the sound of his name, Mr. Griffon stood. The baggy overalls sagged like the deeply furrowed cheeks on his face, but the large suspenders held up the pants. He squinted as if to see more clearly, taking the unlit pipe from his mouth. Casually, he glanced down at Beau from his concrete porch, which was about three feet above his yard.

"Beau?" Mr. Griffon's face brightened, when he associated the face with the name. "Beau Gex! I declare."

Mr. Griffon leaned against one of the two columns on the porch, bent his left leg, and tapped the pipe on the heel of his shoe to remove the tobacco from the already empty bowl.

Perfectly manicured azaleas and nandina lined with crepe myrtles surrounded the porch, and this was trimmed with oleanders. In the five years since his retirement, his yard had become everything.

With one stride Beau cleared the three concrete steps and stood on the porch facing Mr. Griffon. "Have you seen Tracy?"

The old man returned to his rocker, waving at the matching chair for Beau to seat himself. Patiently Beau waited for Mr. Griffon's response, as did his brothers standing at the edge of the porch.

"Tracy?" mused Mr. Griffon, pondering the elusive answer as he squeezed his white whiskered face and closed one eye as though in deep thought. "Pretty little lady, Tracy," he said, as he struck a match and tried to light his still empty pipe. Satisfied he had done so, he shook the match and placed it carefully in the ashtray on the old white wicker table next to his rocker. "Other men in uniforms just left. They spoke strange English.

Thought they were Mexicans, but they weren't. They wanted Tracy. I told them I hadn't seen her."

"You haven't seen her?" Beau asked.

Mr. Griffon made a feeble smile and continued to rock slowly. "Yes, I saw her."

"Where'd she go?"

"Well—," but he was interrupted when his wife, Martha, swung the screen door open.

"Bobby!" Martha beamed, staring straight at Beau. She turned to her husband and frowned. "Poppa, why didn't you get me when Bobby came home?" Martha beamed with a toothy laugh aimed at Beau. "Bobby, you wait here. I'll go fix some of your favorite strawberry soda. You still like a dip of vanilla ice cream?"

Not waiting for an answer she danced merrily into the house to prepare drinks for Bobby and his friends.

"Mr. Griffon, your son, Bobby . . . I thought he was—"

"Dead? Yes, he died ten years ago."

"But—"

"Martha? Oh, maybe it's a blessing in disguise for the old girl. Sometimes I wish I was like her. I miss Bobby too; for her, he is still alive. But the old girl still loves me and that's what counts." He scratched his bald head in thought. "Oh, Tracy. She left just a little while ago with Scott Walker's wife. About five minutes before those Mexicans showed up."

"Scott Walker?" Beau quizzed

"It's okay," interjected Jack. "We know the Walkers." Then he turned to Brook. "Get over to Scott's and get Tracy. Beau and I will be right behind ya."

Brook and Danny nodded, ran for the dune buggy, and were gone.

Again, Beau turned his attention to Mr. Griffon. His heart was heavy when he looked upon the old man. "You need to come with us. Do you know what's happening?"

He managed a small smile and stopped rocking. "Yeah, I know. But I reckon I can't go, I'd just slow ya down. Besides, if Martha and I didn't get ourselves killed, we'd most likely get you killed. Everything I have is here. Tell me, where would I go? What would I do? My time is almost up."

"I can't leave you."

"You must. Go. Go on, go now!" Mr. Griffon said. "And good luck."

To leave Mr. Griffon was wrong and Beau knew it, but he had no choice. He turned and headed for the remaining buggy. No sooner did they reach it than Tracy's next-door neighbor came running and screaming in their direction.

"Help! Please help me!" she pleaded. She grabbed Jack and pulled him toward her back yard, while Beau trailed behind. "My husband."

Once in the back yard, they found the woman's husband sitting in a gazebo. He appeared to be fine.

"Tell him we must leave!" she begged.

"Sir?"

"Name's Terry Hines. I know why they sent you. You think I believe this shit is really happening? You want my commissions. Tomorrow I'll be rich, you'll see. The markets will open again and I will make a fortune selling short. They did this so they wouldn't have to pay me."

"You need to leave," said Jack.

Unexpectedly, the man pulled a pistol hidden in the back of his shirt. His hand shook nervously.

"Leave now, or I'll kill you. No one is taking my money!" he yelled hysterically. The shaking gun pointed in all directions.

"Hey, no problem," said Jack, slowly backing away.

The two brothers moved away from the crazed man with their hands in the air. When they reached the buggy the woman was hysterical.

"You can come with us," said Jack.

She hesitated, nodded her head, and accepted his invitation. Then, glancing to the back yard, she cried out, "No I can't." She burst into tears and ran for her house.

The hand gripping his shoulder kept Jack from racing after the woman. He turned to face his brother.

Beau shook his head. "There's nothing we can do, Jack. We need to get Tracy and get the hell outa here. We can't save everyone."

With a sigh Jack shook his head in a somewhat reluctant agreement. He knew the wisdom of his brother's words, and a moment later they were on their way to the Walker's.

The dune buggy roared down the street.

Jack took a shortcut to reach Scott Walker's house—a shortcut that took them through a very expensive neighborhood and one in which Representatives Lipton and Washington lived in high fashion.

They came upon Washington's property first. The house was a display home, well-manicured, and nicely decorated. But what they saw in the finely trimmed front yard startled both men. Jack brought the dune buggy to a screeching halt. In the yard was Washington. He was obviously dead. His wife and two children knelt over his body, and all three shrieked out in horror.

When Jack and Beau ran up to the woman, she again screamed and covered her face with one hand while trying to crawl away from the two men. She had been beaten. There was a bullet hole in the back of Washington's head, and it appeared he had been executed.

"Please no more!" she screamed.

Jack tried to soothe her as Beau kept a watchful eye out for whoever might have done the cowardly act. "Mrs. Washington, we want to help. What happened?"

Washington's wife buried her face in her hands. "They dragged him out of the house. It was horrible," she screamed.

Beau put his arm around her and she wilted against him.

"I tried to stop them but they beat me. Then they. . . they. . . shot him!" Again she screamed in a voice filled with terror.

"It doesn't make any sense," said Beau.

Jack was confused. "Why would the invaders do this?"

Mrs. Washington pushed away from Beau and glared up into his face with a strange horror in her eyes. "They were Americans. Americans killed my husband. At least a dozen men and four pickups. They all had rifles and guns. They said they were going to clean up the mess the politicians had made."

Horrified Beau turned to Jack. He hated Sarah Lipton but she was in danger. He mumbled, "Lipton."

"I heard them say Lipton needed to die," interjected Mrs. Washington.

The brothers jumped into the dune buggy and immediately the smoking tires tore at the concrete roadway as they made every effort they could to reach Sarah Lipton's house before it was too late.

They were less than a hundred yards away. Four pickups were parked in front and still running. Men with high-powered rifles stood in the bed of all but one truck. Eight men dragged Lipton out into her front yard. Almost all of them wore jeans, boots, and cowboy hats or baseball caps. They were a savage-looking group of redneck cowboys out for something. But what?

The most striking thing about them was their jackets. They all wore the same type of military green jacket with an American flag patch on the left arm and a logo that was a throwback to the American Colonial days of 1776. It looked like a freedom fighter kneeling and firing a musket. In an ark above the logo were the words, "The Minute Men."

Hurriedly, Lipton's husband ran from the front door of the house, his white shirt stained red with blood. He had already been beaten. Mr. Lipton came running to save his wife. He held a gun in his hand and fired as he ran at the two men. A bullet knocked one of the eight men to the ground but the rest responded with a barrage of their own gunfire. Sarah's husband was dead before he hit the ground.

Beau and Jack started running. They were less than twenty yards from her. Things seemed to happen in slow motion, and it would be something so atrocious the two brothers would never forget what they were about to see.

On her knees, Lipton faced Jack and Beau as they raced forward. A man held each arm while a third had wrapped his hand in her long beautiful hair. With pleading terrified puppy dog eyes, she stared at the two brothers trying to rescue her. Her face showed hopeless desperation and terror. Tears flowed from her eyes.

"Please don't do this," she cried. "I'll do anything you want. I'm a member of Congress; you can't do this!"

The one holding her hair, Rourke, was a powerful man bigger than Beau or Jack. He wore a revolver at his side like a throwback to old Western days and appeared capable of using his firearm. He pulled the weapon from the holster and put it to her right temple.

Both brothers yelled, "Stop!"

All the men gave the two brothers only a cursory glance as though they had come to help them. A dazed recognition filled Lipton's pleading eyes when she saw Beau, and the words, "Please help me," formed on her lips but the words never came out. The man continued the execution and pulled the trigger. The sound of the gun discharging halted the brothers. Disbelieving, Jack and Beau watched as the men laughed, and the one holding Lipton let her body fall unceremoniously to the well-trimmed grass of her front yard. A few yards away lay her husband.

Rourke laughed at the two brothers. "You're too late. We already got her."

In shocked disbelief Beau mumbled, "This is murder."

With the gun still in his hand the renegade killer pointed at Lipton with the barrel of his gun and said, "That is not murder. We executed a traitor to the United States of America."

Another cowboy, Baker, said, "We're in this mess because of all the politicians like her."

One of the Minute Men, who had held Lipton's arm, shoved her with his foot until her body rolled over and soulless eyes stared into the clear blue sky. "She'll never be able to take our things away again."

"Or destroy our country," said another.

"You can't do this," said Jack.

Another laughed, "We already have."

"Who are you that you think you can do something like this?" Beau asked.

Rourke broke in, "We're called the Minute Men. We organized in 2003 after ninety-three members of the United States Senate refused to vote on the Iraq war appropriations because they knew it would lose them the next election no matter which way they voted. A war to make the rich wealthier. A war that bankrupted us."

This time Frost, another rough looking character interjected, "All they cared about was what they could get out of it." He thumped his chest with his fist, "We created an organization dedicated to their execution should our country go bankrupt. Now they will pay for what they've done." He pointed to Lipton. "This is justice for the treason she committed."

Shaking his head in disbelief, Beau said, "You can't kill them all."

Laughing out loud Baker said, "You haven't been listening. This was organized ten years ago. Right now in EVERY STATE, units of the Minute Men are serving out justice to all members of Congress for the treason they have committed to our country."

With a smile Frost shook a sheet of paper in the air. The list was filled with names. He said, "We can give you a copy. It's a list of the CEOs and businessmen who sent American jobs to other countries. For the American lives they destroyed we will take their lives today."

In stunned silence Jack and Beau could only stare at the list.

Beau mumbled, "You can't do this." Frost snickered, and then stuffed the list back in his pocket. A few of the men picked up their wounded friend. Finished, they all returned to their trucks.

The brothers had charged in unprepared. Jack and Beau knew things like this didn't happen in a civilized land. But it had just happened and they had seen it and they had been unable to do anything about it. The United States of America had become like the streets of Bosnia more than a decade before, with chaos like Iraq or any other country with civil unrest and strife. Now it had come to America. The Gex brothers were so stunned they couldn't even respond. Beau was the first to react and reached for his gun.

When he did one of the Minute Men reacted with lightning reflexes and moved upon the two brothers. He was a mountain of a man and when he clenched his fists they looked more like huge sledge hammers than a human fist.

But Rourke called out, "No Kilkenny." He looked at the others, "Hold back the Mucker."

Kilkenny stopped, and turned to look at Rourke, who shook his head no to the large man.

"Not today Mucker," said Rourke.

Kilkenny turned back toward Beau with a death look in his eyes. Kilkenny or the "Mucker" as Rourke referred to the big man, was more than intimidating as the muscles rolled and tightened to steel beneath his shirt. All he lacked from being the *Incredible Hulk* was green.

"Doom," said Rourke.

From the bed of the empty truck, two wicked eyes slowly rose into view like a submarine periscope and those eyes were ready to kill. The head emerged slowly, revealing a large pit bull chained to the bed. This was no normal pit bull. Larger than most pit bulls and with massive scars, the dog, Doom, was more than a fighter, it was a killer. The animal had tan fur almost matching the skin color, giving it a hairless almost grotesque monster quality. Huge muscles bulged from beneath the skin of the animal. Doom was a monster.

Luckily for Beau his brother had reacted just a little faster and he stopped Beau's hand from taking the weapon out. Beau's angry eyes shot through Jack, but he just nodded to the trucks. Three men still had rifles trained on them.

Jack showed a grim face to his brother as he said from between gritted teeth, "You said we couldn't save everybody. What's done is done. It's too late, we can't help now."

Rourke moved to the truck where Doom waited eagerly, "Down." The pit bull collapsed to the bed of the truck. Pulling the door closed on his truck, Rourke laughed again and yelled to the brothers, "Only a few traitors left. You can still get your own. We're headed to for the main traitor now. He's hunkered down, well reinforced and trying to make a stand. It won't help him though.

Rourke grunted, "We gave him a chance to save his family if he surrendered."

"Who?" Beau asked.

Rourke continued, "A coward as president, and a coward now. In the end he will be ours." Rourke pointed to Sarah Lipton's body lying lifeless on the ground. "Just like Lipton and the others. Death is too good for him."

With a wicked smile, Rourke finished, "We're headed to Crawford."

All of the Minute Men started laughing. Rourke motioned to Beau and Jack, "There is still time to join us if you want."

Neither Beau nor Jack responded. Hanging his arm out the window Rourke waited but a moment, nodded his head and smiled, "Have it your way but you're going to be missing out on a lot of fun."

As they drove away Beau pulled at Jack. "Come on, we've got to stop them."

With a jerk, Jack freed himself from Beau's grasp. "No."

"What?"

"If this is what is going on it is all the more reason we need to get Tracy and get her now."

Staring at the bodies of the Lipton's, then at their exquisite house, and then back at his brother, Beau understood fully. He ran both his hands through his blond hair and his body shuddered. "This is a living nightmare. What has happened to everyone?"

"I wish I could tell you, but I don't understand it any more than you do," said Jack.

With one more disbelieving glance at the dead bodies—something that would be branded in his memory forever—Beau shrugged his shoulders, and then he and Jack returned to the dune buggy.

* * *

A mile from Hondo, the small group came upon an earthen berm recently built across the road. Behind it were half a dozen men with assault rifles. Beyond them two bulldozers worked furiously, cutting a wide path across the road. On the other side of the trench were three 4-wheel drive trucks, ready for retreat.

In the lead, Admiral Garrett stopped his van and approached the men with his arms in the air. Ruben, Sullivan, Blackman, and Warren came alongside the admiral. Not too far behind them were Marix and James.

"Halt!" yelled a man from behind the barricade. "What do you want?"

"I'm Admiral Garrett from Corpus Christi. We need to get through."

"You don't look like military," snapped the same man. "How do we know you're not civilians trying to take what we got? Or maybe you're those damned invaders."

Ruben yelled, "We're pilots. We want to find our command so we can fight back for you and for us."

The man behind the earthen mound lowered his rifle and stood. "We knew this would happen one day. The people from the cities won't be able to just come and take what we got. Those that try to force their way into Hondo will die. You don't have much time before the road will be cut. Take your people into town and get what you need, if you can. Good luck on finding your command."

Garrett paused and asked the man holding the rifle, "Why are you cutting the road?"

The man showed no humor and placed the butt of his weapon on his hip. "To protect against city folks. In a few days they'll become like cornered wild animals, huntin' and killin' anything they can find. With the road cut, it will take special vehicles to get through. Those with the proper vehicles already know what to do. The *crazies* will turn back."

Garrett nodded, and then shook his head in disbelief at the truth of the man's words. So much had happened and all in less than a day.

Garrett, Ruben, and the others returned to the vans and proceeded around the barricade. Soon they were in Hondo. At the entrance to the town, they passed four trucks and two police vehicles. In the bed of each truck stood at least four heavily armed men like sentinels. They waited to warn the town should the invaders arrive.

People moved quickly along the main street. They didn't appear terrified or even aware of present events. They hurried about collecting items from the various stores like a herd of squirrels preparing for the winter. An unusually large crowd gathered in front of the general store and the hardware store. Everyone was stocking up on food and goods. The only difference in their appearance from those in a city was they all carried rifles or guns.

Sunday, Krysti, and Justin rode with Ruben in the van. Sully drove Beau's Corvette and BJ drove Jack's black truck with the empty trailer in tow.

During the short drive Krysti said nothing, which most attributed to some sort of shock due to the catastrophic events. Krysti was a strong independent woman and would be a critical asset to the group. They all needed her, especially now. No one had any way of knowing her reactions were related to what she had learned about Beau.

A rustic town frozen in time, Hondo appeared to be a throwback to the 1950s with a touch of Western flair. Quaint stores lined the main drag of the town and the green street sign with white letters quite aptly called it "Main Street." The two-story city hall was made from cut stone taken from a local quarry. The small park area in front of city hall was lined with enormous oak trees, many over a hundred years old. Most of the stores that lined both sides of Main Street were shops for souvenirs and items of interest. And there were necessary stores for drugs and food and a few small hotels.

The stores that lined Main Street were all two stories or more and occasionally broken up by small alleys that led to the back. A few boasted electric neon signs, especially all of the hotels and two of the more elaborate restaurants. The rest of the businesses had hand painted or rustic wooden signs with their names carved out in large bold letters. At any other time it would have been a wonderful place to visit and spend the day. But this wasn't any other time.

Garrett led them through town. On the outside of Hondo, where the stores stopped, he found what he wanted. A small car dealership lined with used cars, most of which were pickups, SUVs and four-wheel drive vehicles, beckoned to the small group's very needs.

Garrett turned into the dealership, and the short line of cars followed. They all gathered around him. He barked instructions. Mulholland, Blackman, Pickett, and Chin Tang were to find and collect weapons for defense. Admiral Garrett sent Pickett and Sullivan to find camping supplies. Schmitt, Fitzhenry, Deberg, and Warren were to negotiate and pick out the transportation they would need: specifically four-wheel drive vehicles or trucks. Ruben, Sunday, and James went in search of food and non-perishable items.

Having spotted a pharmacy, Krysti took her son to find the medical supplies they would need. Marix argued he should go with her and after much persistence prevailed under the pretense he could provide protection. Garrett remained behind to watch the vehicles and prepare to load their few belongings into whatever Fitz, Deberg, Schmitt, and Warren could wrangle from the owner of the dealership, while the others started down Main Street to acquire the items they would need for a prolonged stay.

Warren talked to the owner who was about to leave. He showed Warren the wall with the keys to all of the cars and told him, "Leave your cars here and put the keys on the wall. Take what you want." He pointed to the copying machine and said, "Print out your driver's license and a credit card. If this thing isn't as bad as I think it is, I'll get back with you in a few weeks."

He shook his head. "I'm afraid it's not good so take what you need and good luck." He jumped into his loaded out four-wheel drive crewcab and drove away. For Warren, who was a car buff, this was a dream come true, but at the wrong time as he looked across the acre of used cars.

A large wooden sign with the words "Guns and Ammo" hung over a store and drew Mulholland, Tang, and Blackman. They entered the store and inside found a small armory. After learning they were with the military, the owner gladly provided them with rifles, ammunition, guns, knives, and assorted dressing gear appropriate for long periods of exposure to the elements.

As the group made up the only people in the store, Mulholland asked, "Why aren't the people stocking up on weapons?"

The old man laughed. "Son, this is Texas. If you don't already have guns and know how to use them . . . well, you're plum worthless. The people of Hondo have their guns."

When Mulholland offered payment, the old man said he would be interested in trading for their uniforms. He refused the money saying, "You take these here guns and promise to kill some of them there commie bastards."

Mulholland and Blackman willingly obliged the old man as did Tang and Pickett. They went to the cars, retrieved their uniforms, returned to the store and turned them over in exchange for the hunting garments. They took extra coats, boots, and jackets just as a precaution and a supply of tents so there would be enough to put two people in each . One tent opened on four sides so it would provide shelter away from the sun. They took knives and guns for each person and then began to stockpile ammunition for the weapons they had selected.

Ruben, Larry, and Sunday collected a large quantity of food in three pushcarts. Sunday made the men load up four large plastic ice chests a little more than four feet in length. While she continued to collect food, Ruben and James took two ice chests outside per Sunday's orders and crammed them full of ice bags. When the three carts were full, Ruben handed the checker his American Express card. He noticed the unwelcome glare from the storeowner as he stared at the card and frowned.

"Sonny, that piece of plastic is worth about as much as a Confederate dollar. In fact, I'll take Confederate dollars," he said with a touch of anger, his arms folded before him.

Sunday pushed her way to the front and pulled out cash. "Here, let me take care of this."

Managing to find humor in the obviously ludicrous situation, Ruben turned to Larry. "Gee, I don't think I exceeded my limit. I'll have to check on this when I get home. And to think I'm a gold card member."

"Ruben," snapped Sunday, not finding the situation humorous.

Larry said nothing. He stared ahead in silence, the reality of the situation finally began to register in his brain. Using the same three carts, they pushed the food from the store.

Ruben hesitated at the counter and held his card in the face of the old man. "And they told me, don't leave home without it." He laughed at the teller then flipped his American Express card to the counter.

The old man picked the card up, flipped it over so he could see both sides, and then threw it in the trash where its real value could be realized. Once outside, Larry waited with the food and ice while Sunday and Ruben got one of the four-wheel drive Ford Expeditions Warren had waiting. They returned to James and loaded the SUV full of supplies.

Searching through the drug store, Krysti pulled down aspirin, antibiotic cream, special items she knew the women would need, creams, handfuls of toothpaste, tooth brushes, deodorant, toilet paper, and all of the other items necessary for a long duration. She talked to the pharmacist and showed him her credentials; he willingly loaded her with antibiotics, pain pills, and assorted drugs. Also he supplied her with equipment and materials for small operations that might be required.

They had finally selected all of the vehicles they would need. While they were collecting the supplies, a family approached Warren and Fitz.

Stephan Gray introduced himself, his wife Joan, and their daughter, Lindy. He was dressed like someone well-to-do. The loaded out Cadillac SUV was the first indicator, and the designer clothes they wore told him the rest. They were terrified and asked for help. Someone in town had identified Warren and the others as being American military.

Warren didn't know what to do and took them to Garrett. All the while he could hardly take his eyes off their beautiful daughter. He was sure the girl was a model of some kind. He guessed her to be between nineteen or twenty. And Warren was good at guessing a person's age.

After the Grays were introduced to Garrett, Stephan said, "Please let us go with you. We are afraid to return to Houston. At least let us stay with you until we know it is safe to return home."

The time was not to watch out for others. The group's first reaction was to deny the Gray's help; after all, they were military and this was a war.

But Garrett paused to reflect on his job and decades of military service to his country. The primary objective of anyone in the military was to protect his country, and in reality, wasn't someone's country made up of all of the people? He was required to protect the people as much as his country.

In the end Garrett said to Stephan, "Bring your family with us. When it is safe you can return home."

The Grays were very gracious.

After everyone returned to the vans, Garrett introduced the new members of their party.

When he finished, Garrett gathered the group around. "About twenty miles west of here, we're going to set up a camp on the Frio River. Robby, Fitz, and BJ have found transportation. We have four Jeeps and two 4-wheel drive trucks. Also, Jack's truck." Garrett paused to let his statement sink in. "Okay gentlemen, I suggest we get a move on. Pack them up. Let's go!"

They scavenged what belongings they could use, and loaded them into the off-road vehicles Warren and Fitz had acquired.

James, Marix, Deberg, and Warren were almost embarrassingly helpful to the Grays, especially Lindy, who, with all the help, needed only point to what she wanted moved. Talking to each other the men guessed at the young woman's age. James guessed her to be near nineteen or twenty, Deberg thought nineteen and Marix assured them all she was at least twenty. Pickett watched from a distance

Unable to stand it any longer Deberg waited until a time when Lindy's parents were occupied and at a distance. Then he asked Lindy, "How old are you?" The other three men listened intently.

With a quick glance to her parents and assured they wouldn't hear, Lindy turned to Deberg, glanced to each of the other three men, fluttered her eyes and with a mischievous sexy smile said, "Going on twenty."

"You should be a model," James blurted.

Again she smiled, turned and sashayed away, enjoying the eyes she knew followed her every move.

Snidely, Deberg turned to the other three men. "Told you she was nineteen." The four then continued about their unfinished business of loading the trucks.

In the process of loading things, Krysti grabbed Beau's duffel bag, accidentally spilling the contents in the Corvette. A small leather case popped open revealing many medallions. One was a five-point star with a ribbon to be worn around the neck, another was an ornate star, and the third a round medallion with a wreath surrounding an eagle. The Medal of Honor, the Distinguished Flying Cross and the Distinguished Service Medal, none of which Krysti recognized. Nor did she recognize the medal with the Hebrew engravings: The Hero of Israel. She knew they were medals of some kind and might be important so she returned them to the case. Due to her short time with the military she had no way of knowing they were his and that they were the medals awarded for bravery, while fighting for what he believed in.

Krysti tried to ask Garrett a question, but seemed hesitant. Finally she spoke. "Is Beau the one from Israel?"

"Yes," he said firmly, watching her reaction. It was as though he had dealt her a crushing blow as she momentarily staggered from the single word. "Girl, let me tell you something. War is hell and you can forget the Geneva Conference, because there are no rules in war. As much as we try to follow rules, it can't be done. You may not understand it, but we're in real trouble, the likes of which this country has never seen. Honey, we need you now more than ever. Don't fall apart on us. Enemy forces are all around us, and the straight truth is an invasion has been launched against the United States and we don't know its magnitude."

"He doesn't know where we are. How will he know where to find us?" Krysti pleaded.

Garrett could see Krysti cared a great deal for Beau. She seemed oblivious to what he told her. He tried to comfort her when he said, "Beau has the uncanny ability to do what is required when it is needed. Like a magician, he always has one more rabbit to pull from his hat."

Bewildered at the strange events occurring with deadly speed, Krysti shook her head in confusion. "Yes . . . but will he return?"

He could tell she was worried and concerned. Garrett smiled and assured her. "He'll return. Tough times go away. Tough men don't."

* * *

A man in civilian clothes, with a military rifle at the ready, stood guard outside Walker's house. Already alerted they were coming, he let them pass.

Inside they found three officers hastily changing to civilian clothes. Tracy sat on the couch crying, while two of the officer's wives tried to comfort her. Walker's wife, Katy, recognized Beau and pulled him to the side.

Katy said, "Tracy's husband is dead. He was killed yesterday trying to take off and fight. Snipers shot him while he sat in the cockpit of his plane. He never had a chance. She's in no condition to stay here, so we were going to take her with us."

"That won't be necessary. We'll take her," Beau interjected.

"You're lucky you found us. We've been hiding since they landed. This was our first chance to gather a few things and leave. It's awful. Those men have control of the base."

"Who were they?"

"I don't know. My husband said some were speaking Spanish. They all spoke English and a few had a Middle Eastern accent. I know I've heard that accent when we were in Saudi. We barely managed to escape from the base. I still can't believe it," Katy said, in shaken disbelief.

Beau heard the same story from her husband, Scott Walker. He had decided with two other officers to head to East Texas, in the hopes they could find the four Harriers they tested only two days earlier. Scott invited Beau to go back with him and fight but Beau declined.

Most of the people in the neighborhood were afraid to leave and afraid to stay. The people had no idea as to the vastness of the situation. Scott told Beau people were waiting for the banks to open. Others were trying to cash in insurance policies. Some had left town but most had returned to their homes already. They had nowhere to go and were unable to do anything for themselves but wait. The people lacked the knowledge and/or the ability to survive on their own. Most wandered about aimlessly or hid inside their houses, terrified to venture out.

Scott warned Beau and his brothers of a danger worse than the enemy—other Americans.

Then Beau described what he had seen happen to Lipton and Washington. After what Scott had seen, Beau's story was not hard to believe.

"This might be a bigger problem than the invaders," said Scott. "There are a lot of people already looting, burning, killing, and raping. Even worse, those people are beginning to band together and have become extremely dangerous and deadly." Scott added, "I think it might be safer to have the enemy catch us than the marauding gangs of deadly Americans."

"That bad already?" said Beau.

Scott nodded. "Only our rifles have kept a few groups away, but those groups are banding together and getting larger and more dangerous every day."

Beau wished them luck and regretted not going with them. Maybe he could extract a measure of revenge if he found the Harriers, but his obligation to Tracy and the others forced him to remain behind.

He knew Cobra was probably near, but where and with what part of the invasion? Why were enemy soldiers hunting for Tracy? Only Cobra would order the soldiers to find her, but he discarded the possibility that those pursuing her could be doing so in some kind of retaliation against him. Quickly he collected Admiral Garrett's emotionally distraught daughter. With Tracy safely strapped in the back seat of the four-seater buggy, the brothers prepared for the return trip.

Less than five minutes from Tracy's house they met with resistance where an enemy barricade blocked the street they traversed. Bullets started to fly and they spun their vehicles around, crashed through two fences in a residential area, and eluded their pursuers. Only their familiarity with the area saved their lives.

Suddenly, Tracy started to scream hysterically. “Stop! God will take care of us! God will take care of everything!”

Beau grabbed the woman and shook her, but still she continued to scream. He slapped her and yelled, “God isn’t going to do shit!” She was so stunned, she quit screaming and he squeezed her arms with his hands and pulled her near. “God gave you a brain, Tracy. Use it! There will be no miracles today. If we survive it will only be through our own actions.”

She started gibbering incoherently, slipping into self-induced shock. Beau knew they would need to hurry, if only to save her. What problems had confronted the others? Hopefully they had not run into trouble.

Night was drawing near. Only a few more hours remained before it became too dark to travel. Still trapped in the city, they would need headlights to continue their escape in the nighttime hours, but the lights would make them easy targets. Night travel would be too dangerous and probably deadly for all.

When they reached the highway they came abruptly on a larger and more ominous barricade that the invaders had hastily but effectively erected. Trained soldiers with tremendous firepower blocked their escape. Quickly, they turned from the road, and created their own path.

***

For the small group west of San Antonio near Concan things were quieter and peaceful yet the imminent danger was concern but not immediate. The group led by General Garrett had taken refuge from the invasion. Kipp and Blackman with their survival experience made the situation better than tolerable. The others looked to them for guidance and well they should for none of the others knew much about basic survival and already depended too much on their talents. Even basic things like water and food were difficult for the others and it made many feel like survival might just be impossible. Their danger was not as immediate but it was of intense concern. Unlike their present situation and current events, the sunset was beautiful. They prepared to sleep best they could. While some spread blankets on the ground, others tried to sleep in the back of the vehicles or the beds of the truck. The night was cool and dry which helped. Some lingered around the campfire talking about what had happened, distraught and confused. They had heard about what had happened but they had not seen the death and destruction and without validation, many denied to themselves what had happened.

Krysti felt like she was on a camping trip. She loved camping, but this night was dark and ominous and added to the day’s events it was terrifying. She understood what had happened but it was still difficult to grasp and understand. She knew life would never be the same. The words James had spoken to her continued to work on her like a knife in a wound. Beau was the traitor and killer she had read and heard about in the news. The pieces had been there but she had been unable to put them together until now. The words and his sudden change in front of her tormented her. But she had seen him with Justin. It was impossible he could be the same man. This man, the invasion and even Marix continued to grind back and forth in her thoughts. But in the end her thoughts continued to be interrupted with visions of the man she had met at Shanghai Pete's. Was he okay? Were his brothers safe? Had they found Tracy was she okay? She wondered if any of them were still alive. Would Beau be able to find them? She shook her head in dismay and sorrow when she realized it would be impossible for him to find her.

***

The four brothers managed to elude the invading forces. There was no doubt America had been invaded and the invasion had been a resounding success. They traveled swiftly away from the main roads and soon found a secluded spot along a stream and stopped to rest for the night. Jack and Beau took the first watch, guarding the site while Danny and Brook readied themselves for a little sleep. Later that night Danny and Brook relieved their brothers.

As Beau rolled up a blanket so he could use it as a pillow he reflected on the invasion and how fast it has transpired. He placed his weapons on the ground next to his formed pillow. Before he turned in he took time to reflect on the events that had transpired so quickly like a non-stop marathon with no time to rest. Less than twenty-four hours had passed and the invasion as he saw it was a resounding success. The United States had started to implode before 2008 but the year Obama had been elected, marked a day of demise not only of America but also Christianity. The American politicians had destroyed America with the help of Muslims and atheists. The last few years Christians had been considered treasonous. No longer was America the "protectors or defenders of freedom" because Congress, the President and all of his men had taken away Americans freedoms under the guise of protecting those very freedoms. Self-satisfying greed had destroyed America. Ironically it wasn't Congress who was at fault but rather the self-satisfying people who had elected the politicians to give them more and more until there was nothing that remained. Even if there had been no invasion America was already finished. America had been destroyed from within through elected traitors who had succumbed to greed. If America survived it would no longer be the same and Beau knew it. And what could he do? He was only one man.

With a heart rending sigh he tucked the blanket under his head and peered up into the starlit sky. The stars reflected a serene peace from an eternity of no change; the opposite of America. He thought about the others. Were they okay? Were they safe? Would he be able to find them? His thoughts continued to be interrupted with visions of the woman he had met at Shanghai Pete's. Could he find Krysti? He had to find them—he had to find her. He would find her! He took a deep breath and let it out. He raised his face to the stars and held his hands before him as he tried to clear his mind but it was to no avail. Finally he uttered a silent prayer for the others and for Moon Shadow.

# GLOSSARY

**Ace** - Fighter pilot with five or more victories
**ACM** - Air Combat Maneuvering, or dog fighting.
**Bag** - Flight suit
**Bat Turn** - A tight, high-G change of heading. A reference to the rapid 180-degree Batmobile maneuver in the old "Batman" television series.
**Bogey** - Unidentified and potentially hostile aircraft.
**Bandits** - Identified hostile craft.
**Barrel Roll** - Medium-speed roll, course remaining constant.
**Bounce, Tap** - Unexpected attack on another aircraft.
**Check Six** - Visual observation to the rear of an aircraft from which most air-to-air attacks can be expected. This is in reference to the clock system of scanning the circular area around the aircraft: 12 o'clock is straight ahead, 6 o'clock is dead aft. Also a common salutation and greeting among tactical pilots.
**Chandelle** - Reversal of course by climbing turn.
**CIA** – Central Intelligence Agency
**Double Ugly** - Nickname for the enormous but less than beautiful F-4 Phantom. Also called Rhino.
**Electric Jet** - The F-16 Fighting Falcon, nicknamed because of its fly-by-wire controls.
**Fox One, Two, Three** - Radio calls indicating the firing of a Sparrow, Sidewinder, or Phoenix air-to-air missile, respectively.
**Furball** - A confused aerial engagement with many combatants.
**G-suit** - Nylon trousers that wrap around the legs and abdomen. Filled automatically with compressed air in high-G maneuvers, the G-suit helps prevent the pooling of blood in the lower extremities, thus retarding the tendency to lose consciousness.
**Gomer** - Slang for a dogfight adversary, the usage presumably stemming from the old Gomer Pyle television show.
**Gouge, the poop, the skinny** - The latest inside information.
**Hummer, puppy or bad boy** - Any ingenious machine-plane, car, weapon

whose actual name can't be recalled.
**HVAR** – High Velocity Aircraft Rocket
**Immelman** - A reversal of course by half loop and roll out.
**Jock, Driver** - Pilot.
**Knife Fight** - Close-in low-speed aerial dogfight.
**Mach** - The speed of sound is relative to the altitude and temperature. At sea level the speed of sound is approximately 750 mph. At 40,000 feet it is 650 mph.
**MP** – Military Police
**Mud-mover or Ground-pounder** - Low-level attack aircraft.
**Rhino** - Nickname for the F-4
**SAM** - Surface-to-air missile.
**Scooter** - Nickname for the A-4 Skyhawk.
**Speed Jeans** - G-suit
**Speed of Heat, Warp One** - Very, very fast.
**Split-S** - To half-roll and dive vertically.
**Three-Nine Line** - Imaginary line across the aircraft's wings. The adversary is to be kept in front of the three-nine-line.
**Tits Machine** - A good airplane. A favorite. Nostalgic term referring to great aircraft.
**Tits-up** - Broken, non-functioning.
**Tomcat** - F-14
**Trim** - to adjust control tabs for proper flying attitude.
**Turkey** - Nickname for the F-14 Tomcat.
**Viper Jet** - Nickname for the F-16.
**Whiskey Delta** - "Weak dick," a pilot who can't cut it.

# REASONS FOR THE COLLAPSE OF THE ROMAN EMPIRE

**Military** – the military was spread so thin around the known world that the Empire could not defend its own borders. Military forces expanded and so did the pay. The Empire conquered distant but wealthy provinces but were unable to continue holding the territories. The burden to support the military became so great that the financial collapse from within began. Slowly the Empire pulled the military away from conquered and controlled territories. Gradually other countries took over these territories.

**Taxes** - the emperors were forced to raise taxes to pay for the huge military spending.

**Health and the Environment** – these declined as the wealthy kept the money and the government lacked the money to help the people. Alcohol was abused.

**Corruption** – the corruption of political and business leaders became rampant as they rewarded themselves and their followers.

**Unemployment** - increased as the small farmer virtually vanished when they were bought up and run by a few of the wealthy who lowered pay and expected more.

**Inflation** – lack of work hurt the poor as the wealthy horded most of the gold coins forcing the people to barter or steal for their needs.

**Language** – numerous dialects and languages were allowed. Communications became increasingly difficult. Eventually the various languages prevailed, ending communications with the Empire.

**Urban Decay** – became more prevalent as the poor were unable to afford rent, forcing many to crime for survival.

**Technology** – arrogant about their own abilities leaders let the technology lag behind other countries.

**Chemicals** – lead in pipes made the Romans sick and many died.

***Values and Morals** – declined as leaders wasted money on lavish extravagances to please themselves and the people.

**Islam** - some even point to the rise of Islam as a reason.

**Where does the United States stand today?**

*During the reign of the Roman Empire, the leaders would give things to the people to keep them happy. The Coliseum with gladiators was created just for that purpose to keep peace among the people and make them happy. Today we have the gladiators perform in something called the Super Bowl. Now our politicians deem it necessary to give away high tech receivers so the poor will still be able to watch the Super Bowl on their antiquated television sets. Even now Congress is quickly approving an additional billion dollars so all the poor will be equipped with the new television receivers so they can be entertained at government expense or in reality the taxpayers' dollars.

## NATIONAL DEBT, THE DEFICIT AND SPENDING

***"The budget should be balanced; the treasury should be refilled; public debt should be reduced; and the arrogance of public officials should be controlled."*** **-Cicero. 106-43 B.C.**

For my novel *Moon Shadow* to be credible, I had to come up with a reasonable way the United States could be invaded. I looked at Russia, Mexico, and other countries that had collapsed previously. All had gone bankrupt. I wondered if the same thing could happen to the United States.

Let me clarify the National Debt and the deficit. The National Debt is the total amount of money owed by the government. The federal budget deficit is the yearly amount by which spending exceeds revenue. When you add up all the deficits and surpluses (of which there are very few) for the past 200 years, you will come up with the current National Debt. Our politicians love to brag about how "The deficit is down!" like it's a great accomplishment. Don't let them fool you. Here is an example: Let's say the amount of taxes collected is 2.3 trillion but the budget is 2.8 trillion, which will give us a 500 billion deficit already figured into the budget for the year. Suppose they only spend 2.7 trillion. Now they can brag about how they cut the deficit by 100 billion dollars when in reality they still added 400 billion to the debt. All smoking guns. Surely you will remember how under Clinton they continually bragged about the large surplus. Not true. Every year the National Debt increased under Clinton, but by using the example above they tell us we had a surplus. At the bottom of this article are the yearly increases in National Debt since 1978. Not since 1960 did the government spend less than the money it took in, which is something it should try to do every year.

The National Debt is huge and climbing at the rate of around $75 million an hour, but as long as the economy is strong there is no fear. The government and almost all politicians assume it will stay strong, hence the

National Debt continues to rise—at an alarming rate. The best comparison is you as an individual. You make enough money to pay all of your debts and there is really no problem. In thirty years the house is paid and most of your bills are gone. But suppose you were laid off or injured and out of work for six months without any other source of income. What happens? You go bankrupt. Here is another scenario that is happening to our own government. Currently our government is spending thirty percent more than it takes in each year. Suppose you did the same. As an example if you made $100,000 per year and added thirty percent to your debt each year along with interest it would take fifteen years to reach a point where you owed one million dollars. At this point the interest you owed would exceed what you make. You would be bankrupt.

Our government is not immune to the same problem. In 2003 the interest on the National Debt exceeded $322 billion. Only two departments in the government exceed that spending: the military is one of them.

During 2004 the Federal Government took in 2.5 trillion dollars but spent approximately 3.1 trillion for a 600 billion dollar deficit.

Here are some other interesting figures. Currently the National Debt stands at $8,003,104,666,539.23. To pay this amount off, each and every American would need to come up with $25,000 today. From 1980, when Reagan took office, until 1992 when Bush left office, the debt went from less than one trillion dollars to over four trillion dollars. From 2000 to 2004 the National Debt under our current President Bush has increased more than two trillion dollars to its current level. At this rate when President Bush's second term is finished we will have a debt of nearly ten trillion dollars. The interest on that debt at five percent interest will be $500 billion. But suppose inflation hits. At ten percent the interest is one trillion dollars. At fifteen percent the interest would be a staggering 1.5 trillion dollars. Think of those numbers. The interest alone would be more than the money required to run the government.

I know that sounds like heavy inflation and more like a depression, which surely won't happen. They probably thought the same thing in 1929. Still, interest did hit double digits as recently as the 1990s. It can and will happen again. But when? How safe are we?

Another sad note is that Social Security is treated like any other tax and has already been spent. Social Security is part of the deficit and really doesn't exist anymore. Social Security is not part of the Federal Budget Fund. It is supposed to be a separate account with its own source of income and its own separate trust fund. Social Security payments do not go into the general fund, and should NOT be counted as general revenue. The trust fund is supposed to be used to pay benefits. But Congress ordered the Treasury Department to use the money in the Social Security Trust Fund as though it were general revenue, promising to pay it back. Now that promise is part of the National Debt. In reality Social Security is just another very large tax collection tool.

The Social Security Trust Fund is simply a meaningless record of taxes that have been collected for future needs, spent for current desires, and then recorded and counted as an asset. Fraud is a better description.

If something severe ever occurred in the next eight years like a combination of double digit inflation along with double digit unemployment, then the United States of America could possibly reach its darkest hour. The possibility exists for the United States to be bankrupt before the year 2017.

What you will see in the next few years is loss of government benefits to the people, not government employees, and a severe rise in the taxes.

That is exactly what happens in my novel *Moon Shadow.*

If you are interested in the National Debt go to these websites:

www.brillig.com/debt_clock/www.toptips.com/debtclock.html
www.treasurydirect.gov/NP/debt/current

I went to the "toptips" site and found the National Debt increased approximately $20,000 a second. In four seconds the National Debt increases enough to pay my salary for a year. Only four seconds! On November 19, 2004 our Congress had to pass a last minute bill that enabled our government to borrow 8.18 trillion dollars. On average the National Debt is increasing more than 1.6 billion dollars a day.

Sometime on October 18, 2005, our National Debt surpassed $8,000,000,000,000.00 (that is eight trillion). Go to the websites above and see how much the National Debt has increased since this was written.

I'm neither for nor against our presidents. I'm against the debt and the potential problems such a huge debt will bring our country. Did you ever wonder if our representatives have ever told us the truth? They never actually told us a lie but what they said could be classified as lies by omission. Note the years under Clinton and the supposed "surplus." There never was a surplus. The last year Clinton was in office the National Debt only increased 18 billion dollars. Not bad, but definitely no surplus. Under Bush's administration the National Debt has accelerated at an alarming rate. From November, 2004 to November, 2005 the National Debt increased in eleven of those months. Of particular interest are nine of those months. The debt in "each" of those nine months exceeded the total added to the National Debt during Clinton's last year as President. Even more shocking is that on October 5, 2005, the next 24 hours found the National Debt increasing almost as much as the last year of Clinton's administration.

During the month of October, 2005 the National Debt increased almost 100 billion dollars.

On Sunday, October 16, 2005 at approximately 7:58:03 PM, Central Standard Time, the National Debt exceeded 8 trillion dollars for the first time ever.

Below are the years and the National Debt back to 1959.

10/17/2005 $8,003,897,406,911.24
09/30/2005 $7,932,709,661,723.50
09/30/2004 $7,379,052,696,330.32
09/30/2003 $6,783,231,062,743.62
09/30/2002 $6,228,235,965,597.16
09/28/2001 $5,807,463,412,200.06
09/29/2000 $5,674,178,209,886.86
09/30/1999 $5,656,270,901,615.43
09/30/1998 $5,526,193,008,897.62
09/30/1997 $5,413,146,011,397.34
09/30/1996 $5,224,810,939,135.73
09/29/1995 $4,973,982,900,709.39
09/30/1994 $4,692,749,910,013.32
09/30/1993 $4,411,488,883,139.38
09/30/1992 $4,064,620,655,521.66
09/30/1991 $3,665,303,351,697.03
09/28/1990 $3,233,313,451,777.25
09/29/1989 $2,857,430,960,187.32
09/30/1988 $2,602,337,712,041.16
09/30/1987 $2,350,276,890,953.00
09/30/1986 $2,125,302,616,658.42
09/30/1985 $1,945,941,616,459.88
09/30/1984 $1,662,966,000,000.00
09/30/1983 $1,410,702,000,000.00
09/30/1982 $1,197,073,000,000.00
09/30/1981 $1,028,729,000,000.00
09/30/1980 $ 930,210,000,000.00
09/30/1979 $ 845,116,000,000.00
09/30/1978 $ 789,207,000,000.00
09/30/1977 $ 718,943,000,000.00
09/30/1976 $ 653,544,000,000.00
09/30/1975 $ 576,649,000,000.00
09/30/1974 $ 492,665,000,000.00
09/30/1973 $ 469,898,039,554.70

09/30/1972 $ 449,298,066,119.00
09/30/1971 $ 424,130,961,959.95
09/30/1970 $ 389,158,403,690.26
09/30/1969 $ 368,225,581,254.41
09/30/1968 $ 358,028,625,002.91
09/30/1967 $ 344,663,009,745.18
09/30/1966 $ 329,319,249,366.68
09/30/1965 $ 320,904,110,042.04
09/30/1964 $ 317,940,472,718.38
09/30/1963 $ 309,346,845,059.17
09/30/1962 $ 303,470,080,489.27
09/30/1961 $ 296,168,761,214.92
09/30/1960 $ 290,216,815,241.68 * (The last surplus)
09/30/1959 $ 290,797,771,717.63

If the debt continues at this rate the United States of America will be bankrupt before the election in 2016.

One final thought. Could the National Debt reach ten trillion dollars by 2008? If so, what will happen to the economy? Remember I said earlier that our government collects about 2.1 trillion dollars but needs 2.7 trillion to run the government? Let's say we reach a 10 trillion dollar debt in three more years and suppose interest is say ten percent, then the interest on the National Debt will be one trillion dollars leaving only 1.3 trillion to run a government that is spending close to 2.8 trillion per years. This simply won't work.

Unless they do something very soon our government will be unable to pay off the National Debt. Financially our government is rapidly reaching a "point of no return." At the rate the debt is increasing we could reach a debt of $20 trillion by the end of 2016. The same time the Mayan calendar predicts the end of the world. A $20 trillion debt with ten percent interest would mean that in 2016 the interest on the debt would equal the taxes collected. In other words the end of the world for America.

April 1, 2009:

The above was added to in 2005 and has played out almost precisely as I predicted. This is no April fool's joke.

National Debt
04/01/2009$11,208,076,192,300.55

When Bush left office the debt was 10.5 trillion. Currently, China, Japan and Saudi Arabia owns about four trillion of our debt in bonds they purchase each year. I want to give you some new numbers to think about. President Obama has been in office a hundred days and I'm ready to predict his outcome in less than four years. Obama and Congress have established a budget of 3.9 trillion or about 1.8 trillion more than our government brings in. I truly believe more than this will be spent; closer to two trillion over budget the next four years. If Congress and the president continue to spend like this we will owe nearly twenty trillion at the end of Obama's first term in 2012. At that time China, Japan and Saudi Arabia will probably own close to ten trillion of that debt. Suppose the interest rate in ten percent. After all selling bonds on a debt ridden country is very difficult unless you raise the interest and make it more appealing. Remember we collect 2.1 trillion in taxes. In 2012 the interest on the debt will be two trillion. Do you see where this is going? Now just suppose the three countries that buy the majority of our bonds refuse to buy them any longer. Do you know what happens? The United States of America will be bankrupt and become a third world country. You might say our dollar won't be worth a peso.

September 11, 2013

I understand why Boston has so many problems. Seems a teacher decided to replace the "Pledge of Allegiance" with a Muslim prayer. We've come a long way since Obama took over as President of the United States of America. We are now able dismiss the word "united."

How much has Obama cost us? Under Obama the debt increases almost 150 billion per month. For 120 days the debt has not increased from 16.8 trillion, but it is going up more than 150 billion per month. This is called a Ponzi scheme, where you steal from Peter to pay Paul. Madoff went to prison for doing the same thing; so too should Congress and the President. Ironically those who u loudest are government employees or those on welfare. Detroit is bankrupt and will soon stop paying retirement for government employees. The same thing will soon happen to the federal government. They are spending 4 trillion per year but only collection 2.5 trillion in taxes. Same thing happened to Russia in 1988. Obama has added 6 trillion to the debt in his first four years. Most of the money has gone to banks and programs to satisfy his desire. To put this in perspective, Obama could have given 30 million of the poorest Americans fifty thousand dollars a year for each of his first four years. That would have spurred the economy. Instead the Nobel Peace Prize winner spent in on incompetence, gun running, killer drones and war after war.

But America has more problems. Christians are now classified as terrorists. You can't say anything against gays but they can say bad things about Christians. But the scary thing is what Obama has done for Muslims. They cannot be criticized or even watched as terrorists but 95 percent of the terror comes from six percent of our population. For the gays and lesbians I would like to say that Christians bear you no ill will; no thoughts of death or reprisal. On the other hand Obama calls America a Muslim nation. He has even said if he must he will side with Muslims. It is known that Muslims will force Christians to convert or be beheaded. Do you know how Muslims feel about gays and lesbians? If you don't you should. Now what do you suppose Muslims do to gays and lesbians? You might want to brush up on these religions. I don't think Obama and Liberals have your best interests at heart. Speaking of heart Obama wants to give a billion dollars to the Syrian rebel who cut the heart and liver out of his enemy and ate it. If you don't believe me just check it out:
https://www.youtube.com/watch?v=GfHSPLW63Gg

Who did 911? Who did Boston? Who murdered 13 people at Fort Hood? The Muslim Brotherhood offers them all of their support. Obama offers the Muslim Brotherhood all of his support; Libya, Egypt and Syria. Obama refuses to help Christians in any of those countries. To be honest you can count on one hand all of people in Congress and the Supreme Court who support Christians or Americans. I don't want to slay the Democrats because it appears the Republicans are no better. There are no Christian Conservatives that I see. They all want a socialist communist government and the way to attain that is to destroy Christian values. The American way of life as we know it may be gone forever.

If Obama has his way we may soon be greeting people with, "Allahu Akbar."

# COMMENTS FROM THE AUTHOR

*Moon Shadow* was intended to be a piece of fiction for enjoyment, but after I finished, I realized it had become much more. The original idea behind *Moon Shadow* was to grapple with the collapse of the United States and a following invasion. For a long time I worked over and over in my mind how such a scenario could actually happen and play out. I began *Moon* Shadow in 1987 and had been working on the manuscript for three years when President George H. W. Bush invaded Iraq. At the same time, American companies were going bankrupt while the corporate officers were being arrested and put in jail. Many wealthy political contributors managed to elude prosecution while the national debt skyrocketed by more than a trillion dollars.

I first completed *Moon Shadow* in 1990, but I've since updated the story to reveal a repeat performance by many of the same misguided and greedy people involved in the first fiasco. I asked myself, "How could a fictional scenario such as the collapse of the United States and a following invasion actually happen and play out?" Greed and corruption were my answers.

Much like raising a child, I have reworked *Moon Shadow* by pouring my life into the story. For this I have watched *Moon Shadow* grow, and at times I have been surprised by what it has given me in return.

Nostradamus I'm not, but many strange things described in my novel have come to pass. The first version of *Moon Shadow*—written from 1987 to 1990—opened with the United States sending forces to the Middle East to protect our interests. This slice of fiction ended up being very similar to Desert Storm; in fact, I had described Desert Storm in alarmingly accurate detail. But my fictional account was completed in 1990, a year before Desert Storm actually happened.

Another piece of history foreshadowed in *Moon Shadow* was the *Aurora Project*, a top-secret government project to make a plane that could fly directly into space. I wrote in detail about this project—by name—years before it was made public in 1996.

My novel also describes torture and the use of chemical and biological weapons. Most disturbingly, in 1995 I added a section to the original manuscript that detailed how invaders hijacked passenger airliners and killed the president. In my 1995 revision, the man behind the hijacking was Osama bin Laden.

Originally, *Moon Shadow* focused on the actions of the first President Bush. With each passing year up until the present time and the George W. Bush presidency, I molded the novel and added sections to keep up with current events. The events described in *Moon Shadow* have played out with shocking accuracy and similarities that are terrifying.

On September 11, 2001, I was on a flight from Seattle to Houston when word reached us about the World Trade Center and the Pentagon. Less than thirty minutes out, the captain made an announcement saying a plane had hit one of the World Trade Center towers. At first people laughed—including me—as we all wondered how a small plane might have hit one of the towers. Then, a few minutes later the captain made another announcement.

"We have terrible news," he said. "Another commercial airliner has hit the other Twin Tower in New York. We're sorry but when we land in Houston this flight will not continue and you will need to reschedule your flight."

I can still remember the shock, horror and terror on the faces of many of the passengers on that flight. Speculation ran rampant on the plane as to who had done this terrible thing. We still knew nothing. One of the passengers thought China had attacked us, another thought it might be Russia, while a few guessed it to be drug dealers from Colombia since we had just arrested the leader from one of their major cartels.

I assured them it wasn't Russia or China since they depended on our business to help their countries. There was also no way it could have been Colombia because whoever had done such a thing committed suicide and no drug dealer was willing to sacrifice his life.

"Then who could have done this?" someone asked me.

I responded with my own thoughts. "Whoever did this was someone who was willing to die for what he wanted. I'm probably wrong because the last time something like this happened it was Oklahoma City and many thought it was someone from the Middle East when it actually turned out to be an American. But I think I know who might have been involved. I've been reading and writing about a man, Osama bin Laden. His dream has been to destroy the World Trade Center. It is said he was associated with the Twin Towers bombing a few years ago. I'm probably wrong, but if I were to pick someone who was responsible for what has happened, Osama bin Laden would be my first choice."

Most of those listening looked at me like I was crazy.

Again the captain made an announcement that sent fear and chills through everyone. "Ladies and Gentlemen, another airliner has crashed into the Pentagon. President Bush has ordered all aircraft to return to their points of origin. We are to return to Seattle immediately. You will need to make arrangements for your connecting flights."

Everyone was talking, all were scared, and each time the plane hit a bump in the sky, some of the passengers would scream.

To me it was obvious there would be no more flights. I spoke loudly to those around me, "Think about this. The president has ordered us to return. Whatever has happened, it's very serious. Before there can be any more flights they must first figure out who did it, how they did it and how do we stop it? There won't be any flights today, tomorrow or for days. When I get back to Seattle I'm driving back to Houston. Who wants to go with me?"

Again they looked at me like I was some kind of nut, but many were lost in their own chaotic thoughts and fears. Something tragic and terrible had happened and we only knew what we had heard from the captain.

I added, "And when the flights do start again do you really want to be the first to test the airways? I don't. I'm driving back to Houston."

The flight returned to Seattle and when we disembarked it looked like the people were running from a fire. Fear and terror showed in all their faces. Everyone was deserting the airport. I went to the closest phone and started dialing. Two people, Rich and Maggie Pyle, approached me and asked if I was really driving back to Houston. I assured them I was. They also started calling for a car. In less than thirty minutes we were getting into one of the last rentals. It was so strange to see the rental garage void of all but two cars. It was empty. Never in my life have I ever seen an airport so deserted. We started our journey to Houston.

Upon arriving in Houston I contacted the FBI and told them what I had written and that I believed there were plans to do even more hideous things to America. They never returned my call. The reason I contacted them was simple. For more than fourteen years I had been putting together my novel *Moon Shadow*, studying the minds of terrorists and what they might do. In my book I had detailed numerous terrorist acts against our country.

There are things described in *Moon Shadow* that have not yet occurred. Will some of these events be like Desert Storm, the *Aurora Project* and the September 11, 2001, attacks? Will they too come to pass?

Our American military marches to victory not much differently than did the British troops in their bright red uniforms more than two hundred years ago. At that time the British were unbeatable, but they lost. Now

America is unbeatable but has exposed its Achilles' heel. There is still time to correct it before it's too late. Not unlike the British Empire, George W. Bush and his American Empire are headed for the same fate.

You say, "Impossible! You are wrong!" I hope so. After all, *Moon Shadow* is only a work of fiction, but it is said truth is stranger than fiction. And don't forget what we were taught when we were in school: History repeats itself.

I have always believed history repeats. Man is an intelligent animal but he refuses to learn from his mistakes. What truly terrifies me are not the terrorists but the political and business leaders of our country. They have lost their honor and integrity.

Two and two is four, always has been and always will be. But that is not true for the politicians that run our country. You can pay them to make two and two equal something else. Our congressmen can look us in the face and swear two and two is five and we'll believe them, while at the same time another congressman will tell us two and two is three, and we'll believe him. Because of this, unless our leaders change their ways, our country is doomed. I believe we are now looking at a president that is capable of destroying our country.

Abraham Lincoln could see this and summed it up best when he said, "America will never be destroyed from the outside. If we falter and lose our freedoms, it will be because we destroyed ourselves."

I finished the original version of *Moon Shadow* in 1990 and continued to update the manuscript to stay true to current events. As the years passed, I watched with amazement as many of the fictional scenarios I'd created became true events. Today, my old novel *Moon Shadow* is as fresh and true as if it had been written only yesterday. In a terrifying way this only reinforces the old adage, "History repeats itself." Today we see our leaders at a point in time where they can learn from their mistakes and change history, but instead they continue to repeat the same mistakes. Has anything really changed?

From the beginning of time every empire has collapsed. There have been no exceptions.

# THE MOON SHADOW SERIES:

An excerpt from Book 2:

## MOON SHADOW

## The Abduction and the Fury

An unusual chill filled the May air as five men, including Marix and James, worked their way through thorny mesquite, scrub oak, and thick brush and across the solid stone path toward the Frio River. They reached an impasse where the spring joined the solid rock base river. A thorough search revealed nothing of Krysti's abductors.

"Blimey bastards took to the center of the river," said Mulholland.

They searched in vain for signs. Finally, Mulholland pointed down the river. "There's a few roads. Musta gone this way, mates."

Beau shook his head. "I don't know. If you're wrong she'll be dead when we find her. I have a feeling. Ruben, you go with Kipp. I'll go upstream. Fire your rifle if you find anything." Beau never acknowledged Marix or James's presence.

"We'll go with you," Marix said to Beau. He despised and envied and hated Beau for his calm control. Marix was the senior officer and still felt he should be giving the orders. If Beau were dead, he would be the leader and Krysti would be his.

"I don't need you two to nursemaid," Beau said rudely. Then added, "Keep up. I won't wait!"

Immediately, Beau bolted upstream through the rushing, frigid, knee-deep waters of the Frio. He crisscrossed the crystal clear river trying to find signs of Krysti or her abductors. Marix and James trailed behind, but neither knew how to track, and both were having their problems just keeping pace with Beau's fleet, graceful, deer-like moves. Footing in the stony riverbed was precarious at best and moving fast only worsened the situation for Marix and James.

Beau continued over and around the sun-bleached rocks and boulders filling the river. With their feet wet and cold, Marix and James soon opted to use the worn stone bank and from there see where Beau went. Beau continued his quest ranging back and forth across the river, oblivious to fatigue or the icy water filling his boots.

A sparkling object beneath the water caught his eye bringing him to a sudden halt. Wedged between two rocks was a chain dangling in the current. He reached beneath the water and pulled free a cross with diamonds. Krysti's necklace! His rifle pointed skyward and a shot rang out. The unanticipated sound so stunned Marix, he stumbled into James who tripped and fell into the river.

In the distance Beau took note of a storm moving closer and gambled Haun and his men could not differentiate between thunder and the rifle. A gamble he had to take, knowing Kipp would hear and not be long in coming.

Momentarily turning about to check his support group, Beau leered at the helpless pair in the river. Before he resumed his urgent search for the woman he loved, he stuffed the cross in his pocket.

Both sides of the river rose sharply, creating a canyon through which the now waist-deep river flowed. The rushing waters deepened, forcing the three men to the narrow trail skirting the river at the base of the still rising cliffs. Farther into the canyon, the flowing waters appeared to stop as the river widened, creating a large, clear, deep pool, full of living creatures. Perch and minnows darted about the calm waters. A small perch, in search of food, broke the surface.

Shards of stone, the size of automobiles, broken from the sheer walls of rock above, filled the calm river. A portion of the cliff, fallen into the water thousands of years before, formed a natural arch. The three men continued beneath it. Still no signs, and yet this was the only possible direction Krysti's captors could go. Beau continued along the path with the other two men trying desperately to keep up the pace.

Large cypress trees lined both sides of the river providing abundant shade. The massive root systems wrapped like tentacles about the stone, and snaked into the river for additional support and nourishment. From the safety of a thick-leafed cypress, the inquisitive face of an owl turned around. The yellow trance-like eyes of the owl watched the intruders pass. A half-mile farther, the cliffs dropped away and the river again raced wildly among the rocks, forcing Beau into the water to continue his relentless search back and forth on both sides of the Frio River.

A small catfish darted between two rocks as the men neared. Surprised at the intruders passing, two doe and a buck, soon to start his new growth of antlers, stopped drinking. The three deer turned on their hooves, and silently melted into the rocky terrain.

Marix and James were exhausted from the desperate pace even though they had traveled only a small portion of the distance Beau covered, and with none of his intensity. They had observed none of the abundant life surrounding them during their painful attempt to maintain the frantic tempo. Beau had seen and heard everything.

Abruptly he came to a stop. He found what he sought: a sign where the men moved from the river! At the water's edge, something large and clumsy had disturbed an area of pebbles. Animals weren't clumsy. As though possessed by a demon, never uttering a sound, Beau continued his methodical search of every crack, every rock, and every bush along the path leading up and away from the river. Squatting, crawling, he searched, letting nothing escape his eyes. He seemed to glide across the rocks like a lizard.

Not far from the river along the sparse trail, Beau found a piece of Krysti's tattered and bloodied white blouse hanging from a thorny mesquite branch. His heart sank when he saw that her abductors had escaped in a vehicle, which he assumed was the truck he had seen when Haun passed through Hondo. In his mind he saw the image of the torn and twisted body of his murdered wife. He would not let Krysti die!

His controlled anger stirred him to still greater efforts, while two totally exhausted men barely managed to stay with the desperate hunter ahead of them. Fresh tire tracks, spotted with dripping oil, continued intermittently in the dirt filling the spaces between the large flat surfaces of stone. The tread marks came to an abrupt end on an asphalt road. The trail was lost.

Thunder from the north echoed Beau's anger. In the distance, dark clouds rolled ever closer as rain threatened to remove every sign of Haun and his men. Beau must hurry or Krysti would be lost to him forever. But which way should he go?

Bent halfway, holding his side and gasping for air, James whispered to Marix. "We can't go on. Tell him to stop."

"He won't stop!" said Marix, trying to catch his breath.

"He will stop!" said James with a sinister smile, tapping his rifle. Both men nodded, knowing they could force Beau to wait.

Unaware of their intention, Beau assessed the situation. He had seen Haun and his cohorts two weeks earlier. If they remained in the area, water would be their primary concern, so they would surely be camped on the river. The road west continued for fifteen miles before it crossed any river, while the road east wound to the southeast, crossing the Frio four times in a matter of miles. The sound of two rifles being cocked immediately diverted his attention.

Marix and James yelled in unison. "Stop! We have to rest."

Beau turned to confront his assailants and saw their rifles drawn on him.

"Krysti may be dying! I must go!" Beau pleaded.

"You'll wait for us," said James, assured he had finally gotten the best of Beau. "If you try to leave, we'll shoot you."

The response they unleashed was like coming suddenly upon a wild animal that was cornered. Beau's reaction to their threat was nothing like Marix or James expected. No longer could Beau restrain his rage, and with a quick motion of his wrist he cocked the lever action of his old 30.30 as it hung at his side. Simultaneously he flipped the cover from the deadly revolver.

Horrified, Marix and James watched Beau's eyes change to cold, steel gray. Marix felt the hair on his neck rise and James's knees quivered, almost buckling. They weren't looking upon Beau anymore but rather an animal bent on death and destruction. Death filled Beau's eyes. "People are gonna die today! Let it start here!" Beau snarled from between clenched teeth.

"You can't expect to get us both," said Marix, confused and now terrified the possessed man before him was serious.

"Maybe, maybe not. But guess who gets it first."

An excerpt from Book 3 (Coming in July 2015:

## Moon Shadow's Revenge

## BETRAYAL

Darkness shielded the intruder crouching at the foot of the bed. He clutched a steel pipe firmly in his hand. Before him lay a man and a woman sleeping peacefully.

Determined to carry out his wanton act of treachery, Mike Marix was no longer the English gentleman or the pilot who had risked his life unsuccessfully to drive the invaders from the United States. Instead, he had become instrumental in killing Beau Gex's best friend, Ruben Alonzo. Beau had been suspicious and threatened Marix. He had also taken Krysti Socorro from him.

Sleeping in the security of their room, neither Beau nor Krysti were aware of the deadly act about to be enacted.

Now Marix saw an opportunity to take Krysti back and rid himself of Beau forever. Quietly, he crept to the side of the bed where Beau lay unsuspecting. The desire to smash him with all his strength consumed him. As he stood with trembling hands, his desire to kill Beau and be rid of him forever was tempered with the fear it might wake Krysti before he could seize her. When Marix brought the pipe down against Beau's head, he held back ever so slightly. Confident when he saw no movement come from his hated adversary, he moved to the other side of the bed where Krysti lay undisturbed. A surreal peace surrounded her.

Quickly and tightly, his hand clasped about Krysti's mouth rousing her with terrifying effect from her peaceful sleep. The more she tried to struggle, the more she became entwined in the sheets wrapped snugly about her lithe frame. So tight was his hand, she was unable to scream for help.

Only now was Krysti able to catch a glimpse of Beau through her auburn curls. He appeared to lay peacefully beside her, oblivious to Marix's actions. Blood trickled through his blond hair and onto the bed from a wound at the back of his head. This time he was unable to come to her aid.

A familiar voice, crazed with revenge, whispered his demands into her ear. "If you want him to live, come with me and don't make a sound." The cold harsh words came with a calculating confidence. Marix added, "If you struggle he will die."

Gone was the British officer and gentleman Krysti thought she knew. Michael Marix had become a mad man bent on possessing her.

"You know I love you. I will prove it to you." With disgust he pointed to the motionless body of Beau Gex. "I'm going to save you from him." Marix added, "I'm taking you home."

Panic consumed Krysti when she understood Marix's intentions. He intended to take her across hostile country. The invading forces of the Coalition still occupied and controlled all of Texas and the area stretching from the hill country near San Antonio where they were to El Paso, where her parents lived. To attempt crossing this part of controlled America would be suicidal, or most assuredly lead to capture.

Marix dragged her from the room, out of Cliff Palace, their cliff hideaway, to the ledge overlooking the Frio River. Once on the ledge, Marix paused and told her something that sent a cold chill up her spine.

"You have nothing to worry about. I brought Justin along. He's in the back of the Jeep waiting for us now."

Krysti couldn't move stricken not only with the sobering thought Marix would try to take her across Texas, but now the frightening revelation her son was also a hostage. As long as her son remained in Cliff Palace with the others, he had a chance to survive.

"No, please leave Justin!" Krysti begged. Her pleas fell on deaf ears as Marix swung her over his shoulders and started down the trail leading to the hidden Jeeps.

To add to her horror, Marix laughed. "Justin thinks you want this." Suddenly, his eyes changed and it frightened Krysti. "If you say otherwise, I can't even describe what will happen to him."

# OTHER BOOKS BY JOE BARFIELD AVAILABLE AS EBOOKS AND IN PRINT

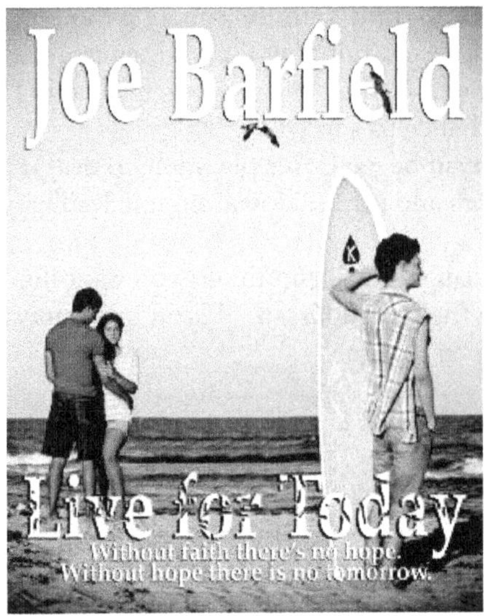


**LIVE FOR TODAY –** (YA coming of age – based on a true story) by Joe Barfield

Available in **print** at CreateSpace.com : https://createspace.com/4261312

A broken promise, takes a gifted teenager down a path of self-destruction. Will the persistence of a coach and the love of a girl be enough to save him? When someone asks him about his future he says, "I live for today, there are no tomorrows for me." Will the love of a girl and the persistence of his coach be enough to save him?

"Live For Today" is based on my high school days. It sends a message to let everyone know suicide is not the answer. There is always hope for tomorrow. One of the characters is Marilyn. I dated her when I was eighteen. Beautiful girl. She committed suicide. There was no reason. Just this week, People magazine, had an article about three students who committed suicide after being teased and tormented by classmates. This story has a time and it's now. The message is hope.

## A Note About *Live For Today*

The Movie

The story of *Live For Today* has been made into a heart tugging, anti-bullying, faith based movie.

It was filmed with Katy, Texas, locals and high school students using a $2,000 Cannon 7D camera. YouTube, Facebook, and our production company website are set up for viewing current news, trailers, movie posters, photos, cast members, author biographies, and fundraising information. Browse through our website and see how you can become part of this cause. The story is based in part on what happened to me in high school. The pictures in *Live For Today* are from the movie and accompanied by authentic photos from my 1967 Robert E. Lee yearbook. The production team still has more to do before we can completely finish the film and through financial help, such goals are achievable. For every book sold, a percentage will go towards efforts for finishing the movie. Help us prove that students can not only make a professional film, but that a big effort from a small town can make a huge impact on world-wide social media.

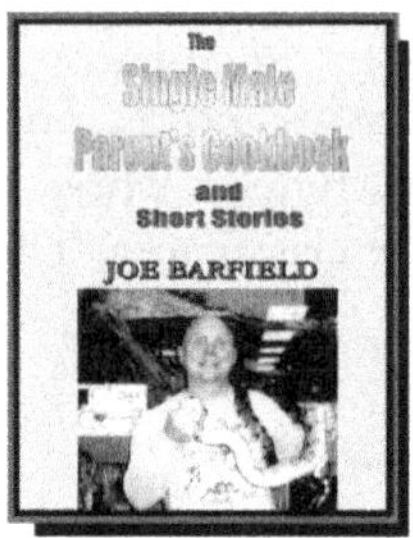


***The Single Male Parent's Cookbook and Short Stories***
by Joe Barfield

Available in **print** at CreateSpace.com : https://createspace.com/4354201

*The Single Male Parents' Cookbook*, is a delightful combination of food and humor, two subjects everyone will enjoy. As a single parent the author raised his children from the time they were four and six, and soon became an expert in the kitchen. As he said, "My cooking must have been good because both are adults now and still alive, which only attests to culinary skills . . . or luck!"

*The Single Male Parents' Cookbook* combines recipes with humorous anecdotes of things that did and didn't work in the kitchen (and in my life!). Joe includes lots of fun cooking ideas along with some that were not so good, and even a few you don't ever want to try at home! Everything from his Friday Night Special to his Motel Doggy (the electric hotdog). And let's not forget the ROC (Roaches on Chocolate). Each recipe is followed by a short story about his childhood antics or raising his children. Not everything always ran smoothly. There was that time his boiled eggs blew up all over the ceiling. Oh, and that grease fire. Don't ever pour water on a grease fire! But they say experience is the best teacher, and they are right. It wasn't always easy in those years, but he managed to retain his sense of humor. Joe said he once heard George Carlin say that although he's over sixty, he never stopped being ten. That describes the author perfectly. In fact, he said, "I've been ten six times over, and my life is as fun as ever." His final comments were, "Are you curious about my recipes for rattlesnake, rabbit, squirrel, and armadillo? I think you'd enjoy the rattlesnake. Can you picture me cooking the Roaches on Chocolate (ROC) on Rachel Ray's show?"

Don't let the cookbook confuse you. Joe is just a normal type of guy. Well, maybe except for the time he got married at midnight in a jail in Mexico. But that has nothing to do with cooking. Neither does the time he almost got kidnapped in the mountains of Colombia when he met his second wife. He's just a wild and crazy guy from Texas.

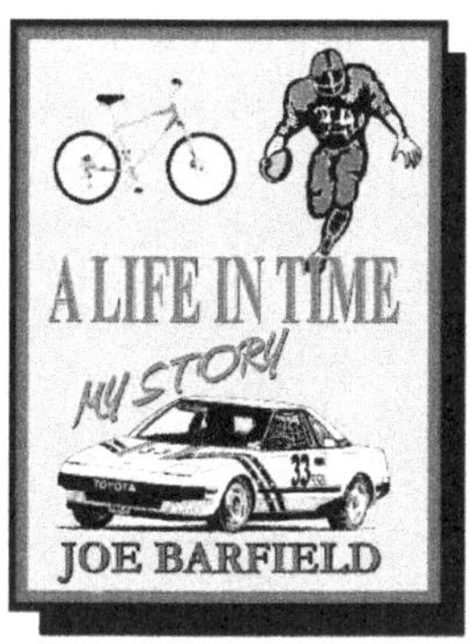


***A Life in Time, My Story*** – non-fiction
by Joe Barfield

Available in **print** at CreateSpace.com :
https://createspace.com/4354226

Remember lying on the grass in your front yard and watching the stars? Your best friend was beside you and neither one of you uttered a word. Then a meteor flashed across the sky and both of you got excited and pointed to the sky. Our lives are like a flashing meteorite. Often the moments go unnoticed, but we do manage to brighten and touch the lives of those around us. Although we are not all famous or well-known, our stories are important. Each of us has a life in time. These are a series of short stories about my life. In the past I have heard a comparison I'm sure you have heard before, so let me ask you again. Who won the Super Bowl last year? Who won the Indy 500? Who won the last game of the World Series? Who were the Best Actor and Actress at the last Academy Awards? You might remember one but you probably don't know the others. Now ask yourself these questions. Do you remember the names of some of your teachers? What teacher helped you in high school? What valuable lessons did your mother and father teach you? And who was your best friend? They may not be famous but they brightened your life the same as that flashing meteorite. I believe life has been an adventure and that we learn from all the things that have happened to us. The one thing I try to do is look at things in a humorous way. As a child I was called Tiger because I was always into things. I thought I was just curious. As a teenager the death of my father weighed heavy on me. We began to move around. I became angry; a "Rebel," as some of my close friends called me. I had conflicts with religion. When my children were four and six I became a single parent. I learned a lot from them. .Most of the stories, I hope, will keep you laughing. There are some that are sad, but that is life. And that is what *A Life in Time* is all about.

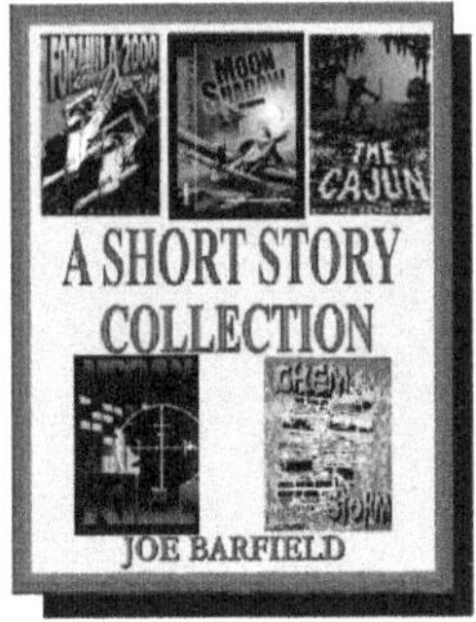


***A Short Story Collection*** – fiction
by Joe Barfield

Available in **print** at CreateSpace.com :
https://createspace.com/4354238

These short stories are based on actual events, and parts from some of my novels, and children's stories. *Sebring, the Rainman* is based on a race my son, Beaux, actually competed. What a race it was!

Some of the dialog from *Flight 223* actually occurred. You see I was on flight 223 from Seattle to Houston during the 911 attack. A very strange and chaotic event I will never forget.

I hope you enjoy these as much as I did bringing them to you.

***THE CAJUN* – (**action-adventure)
by Joe Barfield

A little Crocodile Dundee and a little Rambo. With a million dollar reward on her head, Kelli Parsons hides in the treacherous Atchafalaya Swamp where living or dying depends on one man--the Cajun!

*Meandering Scribbles of an* **OLF FART** – political essays by Joe Barfield

Available in **print** at CreateSpace.com: https://www.createspace.com/4220986

What has happened to America? People need to look at their government. I have written articles for over 20 years from the first Bush to Obama. We have problems we need to face and quit sticking our head in the sand. It's okay to be a liberal or a conservative, but neither exists in our government today. Our politicians do everything but what they were elected to do; represent the People.

If you are open minded you will enjoy this. If you only voted one party all of your life then don't read this book. Stop to look at what our politicians are doing today. If you are an open minded Christian you might enjoy this. And if you are you must admit God is probably not too happy. Atheists are offended. Everyone should be offended that they are offended.

When talking about being Christian in the military becomes an act of "treason" then we have bigger problems

America has spent so much time protecting each individual's rights that no one has any rights. Throughout history every great empire has collapsed; there have been no exceptions.

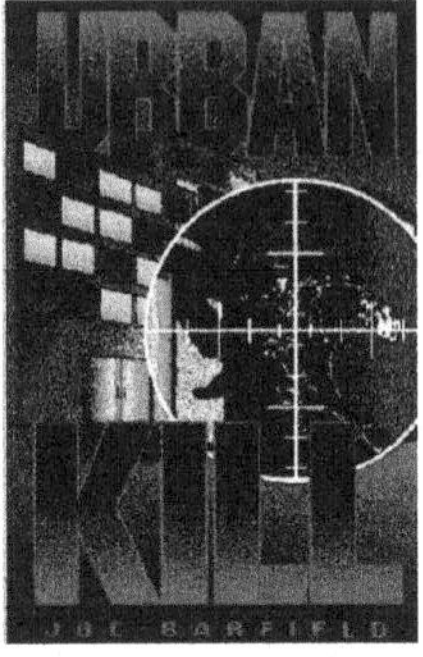


**URBAN KILL –** (detective thriller)
by Joe Barfield
Available in **print** at CreateSpace.com:
https://createspace.com/4038605

Ex-policemen are taking wealthy men on the hunt of their lives--human prey! The only two witnesses have already been murdered. To solve the case the lead detective must find a pimp called The Rat and the drug addict Pinky, because they have the answers. But the Rat and Pinky are trying to kill each other. The only ones that can help him are a gay bar owner, a hyper, absent-minded forensics expert from India, and his one-eyed, three-legged dog, Lucky.

**FORMULA 2000, *the DREAM* –** (action – based on a true story)
by Joe Barfield

Hoosiers on Wheels.

Keeping a promise, a father enters his son, Shannon Kelly, in the Formula 2000 race series with only a dream and a prayer. When things go from bad to worse it takes a crusty old mechanic, Charlie Pepper, to show them how to win. They soon learn that with Pepper almost anything is possible.

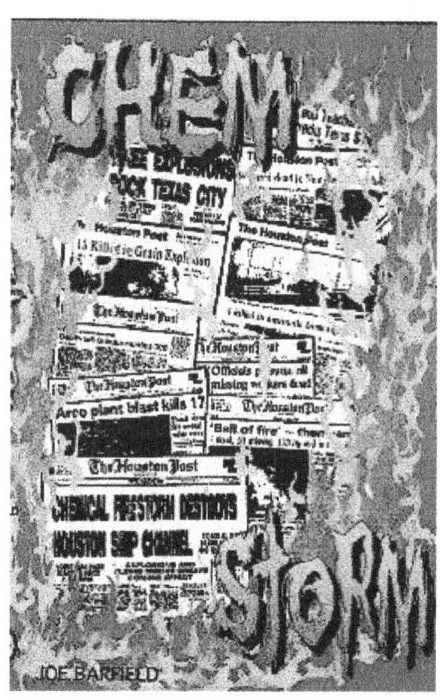


**CHEM STORM –** (action – chemical disaster)
by Joe Barfield

Available in **print** at CreateSpace.com:
https://createspace.com/4325910

A reporter and an engineer race to save Houston from a disaster worse than a nuclear explosion—a chemical storm!

Jean Alexander, a reporter for The Houston Post, is young and inquisitive and has gained unauthorized access to an area, where she finds five dead bodies. She wants to know why but a spectator alerts the guards to her presence and she is removed.

The following day a Civil/Chemical Engineer, Travis Selkirk, approaches Jean. She learns he is the spectator from the day before that alerted the guards. He points out the foolishness of her adventure and how the chemicals could have killed her. Jean baits Travis and gets him to agree to show her the dangers that exist on the Houston Ship Channel.

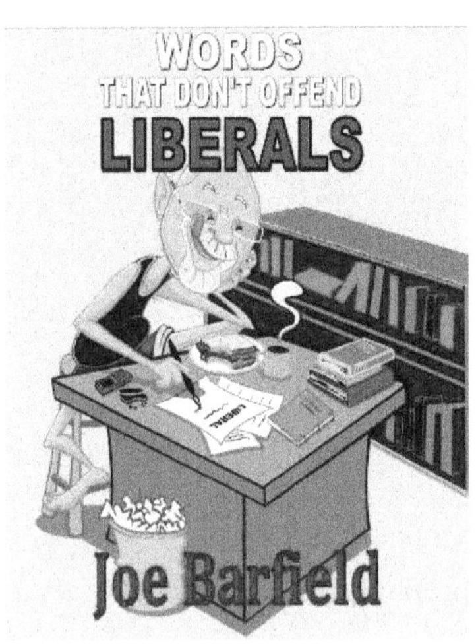


**WORDS THAT DON'T OFFEND LIBERALS –** (Satirical humor)
by Joe Barfield

Available in **print** at CreateSpace.com: https://www.createspace.com/4221000

A humorous look at words that don't offend Liberals. The book will probably offend Liberals. This is meant for the entertainment of open minded people. This is a book to keep notes. For a printed copy you can find the book here: https://www.createspace.com/4221000 Check it out before you purchase your printed copy. Fun gift for your Liberal friends. They may never forgive you.

**PALABRAS QUE NO OFENDEN LIBERALES** - (humor satírico)

Joe Barfield

Available in **print** at CreateSpace.com: https://www.createspace.com/4287573

Una mirada chistosa en palabras que no ofendan liberales. El libro probablemente ofender a los liberales. Esto es para el entretenimiento de personas de mente abierta. Este es un libro para guardar notas. Para obtener una copia, usted puede encontrar el libro aquí: https://www.createspace.com/4287573 Compruébelo usted mismo antes de comprar su copia impresa. Regalo de la diversión para sus amigos liberales. Es posible que nunca perdonará.

## ABOUT THE AUTHOR

The author, Joe Barfield, has led an interesting life, scuba diving, racing cars with his son Beaux Barfield, lifting weights and playing a variety of sports. He met his wife Lucia in Cali, Colombia while on a trip. One time she took him on a trip in the mountains of Colombia and at one point they thought they had entered a guerrilla camp and he would be kidnapped. It turned out to be a group of the Colombian military looking for kidnappers. He spent a few days with them and even has a picture of him holding a 50 caliber machine gun with one of the Colombian soldiers. Showing his tenacity, once he was determined to win a Halloween contest and went as far as making an eight-foot monster with moving fingers. He won the contest. For him racing has always been an exciting endeavor, winning his very first race and two years later winning his first professional race at Sebring. His son went on to be Race Director for IndyCar. Barfield said there were as many adventures off the track as there were on. A quote from Jim Fitzgerald sums it all up, "When you do it and do it right it is the greatest turn on in the world. A collage of pictures shows some of his adventures and cars he and his son have raced.

You might say I have led an adventurous life. I was married at midnight in a jail in Mexico when I was eighteen. Raising my children has proved helpful in my writing. My other activities include scuba diving, weightlifting, building houses, and even racing cars professionally; winning the 6-Hours of Sebring. On a wild adventure to Cali, Colombia, twelve years ago, I met my wife Lucia. She is one of the best things that ever happened in my life. While in the mountains of Colombia, I thought guerrillas had captured me but it was the military. I still remember my first thoughts when I saw their 50 caliber machine guns, "Oh my God I'm going to be kidnapped." To reassure my thoughts, Lucia turned to me and said, "Don't say anything I don't want them to hear your accent." Do you know what my next thought was? "OH Boy! I'm going to become a bestseller!"

For me writing has solved all the problems I couldn't in real life.

## Connect With Me Online

**My Webpage**
www.jbarfield.com

**SMASHWORDS**
www.smashwords.com/profile/view/thecajun

**AMAZON**
www:amazon.com/author/joebarfield

**See the Live For Today Trailer**
http://goo.gl/Oesoxd

**See the Moon Shadow Trailer**
http://goo.gl/NSN4Ho

Made in the USA
Columbia, SC
06 January 2018